THE
WHITE DRAGON

D1526217

THE
WHITE DRAGON

A SEAN O'BRIEN NOVEL

BY

TOM LOWE

K

Kingsbridge Entertainment

ALSO BY TOM LOWE

THE WHITE DRAGON is published in the United States of America by Kingsbridge Entertainment, Orlando, FL.

Library of Congress Cataloging in—Publication Data - Lowe, Tom.

ISBN: 9798847753135

THE WHITE DRAGON (A Sean O'Brien Novel) by Tom Lowe – First edition, August, 2022

THE WHITE DRAGON is published and distributed worldwide in ebook, paperback, hardcover, and audiobook editions. Cover design by Damonza.

Formatting and conversion services by Ebook Launch.

ACKNOWLEDGMENTS

This page is always my favorite. It's here where I can thank those people who helped me bring the novel to you, the reader. Publishing a book takes a team, and I have one of the best in the business. I salute their talents.

To my insightful and marvelous wife, Keri, who is my very first reader and editor. Thank you for your vision, inspiration, and support. You're the best. To Helen Ristuccia-Christensen and Darcy Yarosh. As beta readers, you far exceed the scope of that term. It's amazing how you can pour over a manuscript, looking for issues, and still retain a sense of story. But you do, and you do it so well. My thanks for your time and marvelous skills.

One of the reasons I enjoy writing fiction is because I can weave storylines through contemporary issues that often, to some degree, affect everyone. A special thanks to Derek Maltz who served 28 years as an agent with the Drug Enforcement Administration. Derek shared his knowledge and experience into some of what DEA agents face every day in the field. Also, for ten years, Derek was the Special Agent in Charge of the Special Operations Division within the U.S. Department of Justice (DOJ). Thank you, Derek, for your service and insight.

I tip my hat to the talented people at Ebook Launch. Your team is the best of the best.

To the artists and the graphic designers with Damonza. You turn book covers into art.

And finally, to you, the reader. Thank you for reading and supporting my work. I hope you enjoy *THE WHITE DRAGON*.

    -Tom

"If you're losing your soul and you know it ...
then you still have a soul left to lose."

- Charles Bukowski

For Abigail Hermance Slattery

ONE

Andy Ward didn't have a security camera near his apartment door, which meant he had no visual record of the person who left the package wrapped in brown paper. The important thing was that the parcel had been shipped and delivered as promised. *Excellent customer service*, Andy thought as he walked from the kitchen to the front door. He'd ordered the package yesterday afternoon and couldn't wait to open it. He had a slight guilty feeling, but it was his curiosity that won out in the long run.

He was dressed in cut-off jean shorts and a T-shirt with the words *Ron Jon Surf Shop* across the front. Barefoot, tall, and lanky, Andy wore his black hair short. His hazel eyes sparkled with compassion and vigor. At twenty-one, he was ending his senior year in college, hoping to play major league baseball. Andy opened the front door and looked at the package on the doorstep, morning sunlight streaming through the tall live oaks in the yard. It was Sunday, and he could hear church bells in the distance.

Andy glanced around the outside of the apartment building, the rustling of dried palm fronds in the breeze, the parking lot more than half full of cars. Most were owned by students attending the University of Florida. He saw a woman walking a beagle down the sidewalk, the thick Saint Augustine grass streaked in dark shadows from the tall palm trees, a glistening wet shine still on the grass from the morning sprinklers. Andy picked up the package, closed and locked the door.

"What's that?" asked his girlfriend, Brittany Harmon, stepping from the bathroom in a white terrycloth robe. She had long, honey-blonde hair, wide blue eyes, and the golden-bronzed, sun-drenched skin of a young woman who spent a lot of time at the beach. She was a competitive surfer—athletic, yet she moved with the rhythm of a young woman unaware of her own beauty.

Andy looked from the package in his hand to Brittany. "It's a magic potion." He grinned, walking over to the couch in the family room. A widescreen TV on one wall, a bookcase, two chairs, and a coffee table filled the rest of the room. A framed picture of his family—mother, father, himself, and two younger sisters, Leslie and Abbey, standing in front of a rustic fishing resort in the Florida Keys, boats in the background, sat on the corner of the table. Andy set the package on the couch and flopped down beside it.

Brittany crossed her arms, breasts just visible through the partially open robe. "Magic potion, huh? Is it a love potion?" She smiled, her blue eyes catching the soft sunlight coming though the sheer curtains.

Andy laughed. "I don't need a potion to make me fall in love with you. But I do believe you put a spell on me. Every time I see you coming, I feel a rush in my heart."

"Aren't you sweet. Okay, now tell me, what's in the box. It looks too big for an engagement ring."

He smiled. "You never know." He reached for the package, looking at his name on the printed address label.

Brittany sat down beside him. "Andy, there's no return address."

"Yeah, I know."

"Do you know who sent it to you?"

"Yeah. A guy sent it."

"Did you speak with him?"

"No. I ordered it online. You'd be surprised what you can order from social media sites, like Snapchat, Instagram, Tik Tok, and even Facebook."

"What'd you order?"

He looked across at her. "You know how much my shoulder hurts, and for so long, ever since I tore my rotator cuff during the school's tennis championship tournament. And now it's affecting my pitching. The scouts will be done soon. I gotta get picked up. I can't play through the pain."

"But you went to the doctor twice for the pain. Didn't you feel better afterwards? You said you did."

"The last time I got a cortisone shot. Doc stuck me with what looked like a hypodermic needle a vet would use to inoculate a horse. The needle was longer than my finger. Everything was fine for about three weeks, and then the pain came back. It has put the brakes on my game. I'm having a hard time even doing a few pushups."

She smiled. "I haven't noticed that."

He ripped open the package and removed what resembled a prescription bottle of pills.

Brittany studied the bottle. "What is that?"

"Something that should numb the pain. Oxy."

"OxyContin? I didn't know you could order things like that online."

He opened the bottle and counted twelve pills. They were light blue with the marking *M* on one area, the number *30* on the opposite side. He reached for a half-filled water bottle on the coffee table. "Wait a sec, Andy. Did these come from a reputable online pharmacy? Are they safe to use?"

He smiled. "Of course. My buddy, Jason, recommended this guy."

"Guy? What guy? A guy or a real pharmacy?"

"He's a retired pharmacist. Says his name is Doctor Pitt."

"Does he spell his name like Brad Pitt?"

"Yep."

"Is this Pitt guy a drug dealer?"

"He sells lots of medicines. Mostly those used to fight pain."

"Does he have reviews online?"

"I didn't see any."

Brittany looked at the pill in Andy's palm. "If you're going to take that, maybe you should cut it in half. Just take one half to see if your shoulder feels better."

He smiled. "I'm not gonna overdose on one little pill."

"It doesn't hurt to be cautious, at least until you know those pills are safe to use. That's what my mom always said, and she grew up in the eighties."

"Speaking of moms … my mother is coming over this afternoon. Dad's birthday is next Thursday. She wants to drag me shopping with her to get him some gifts."

"That's sweet."

"I hope you can come to their house for the birthday party. We'll have a big dinner. Probably lasagna." He got up from the couch, entered the kitchen, and returned with a small paring knife. He set the pill on the glass top of the coffee table and placed the blade across the M on the pill to cut it in half. "Here goes." Andy tossed one half in his mouth and sipped from the bottle of water to swallow it. "Maybe, in about twenty minutes, my shoulder will feel fine."

"I should get dressed and head back to my apartment before your mom comes over here. Even though she grew up in the time of free love and all, she seems conservative to me. What would your mom say if she knew I was at her son's place at least three times a week?"

"She wouldn't say a word. She likes you. So does Dad. He's just slow to show it. Mom's all about expressing her feelings … good or bad."

After Brittany got dressed and left, Andy used his left hand to touch his right shoulder, mumbling, "Jeez, it still hurts." He picked up the second half of the pill from the table, tossed it in his mouth, and took a long swallow of water.

TWO

Something had to be wrong, Andy thought. He sat on the couch, staring at his open laptop computer, unable to remember his password. He began to feel a range of emotions. First, a sense of contentment, happiness he hadn't felt in a long time. A few minutes later, he started feeling scared as he became more lightheaded, hands clammy, breathing growing shallower. He stared at the computer, the screen seeming far away, losing focus.

Andy tried to stand up from the couch, his legs weak, hands shaking. "This isn't good," he whispered. "Where's my phone?" He managed to stand, dizzy, sweat on his forehead, a drop tricking down the center of his back. The automatic messages from the brain, those signaling the lungs to breathe, were slowing. He forced himself to take breaths, staggering from the room, holding the walls in the hallway to the bathroom.

Andy stood in front of the sink, looking into the mirror. White foam was oozing at the side on his mouth. He ran cold water from the faucet, splashing it in his face. The foam disappeared, but the feeling of desperation grew worse. He stumbled into his bedroom, where his phone was on the nightstand. He fell onto the bed, trying to reach for the phone.

"Gotta call 911." Andy was too weak to crawl across the bed to his phone. He curled into the fetal position, nauseous, heart slowing down. He looked through the bedroom window at the puffy white clouds against the blue sky. His mind felt like it was leaving his body, separating, and traveling towards those clouds where he could look down and see the whole world below him.

***

Five hours later, Lauren Ward parked her car in the apartment complex lot and walked up the steps to the second floor, knocking on her son's door. Her brown hair framed her oval face, which was flushed and filled with anxiety. She waited a few seconds, looking at the time on her wristwatch, and knocked again. She listened for sounds in the apartment. All she could hear was the chortling song from a mockingbird at the top of a live oak tree.

She reached out, touching the dull brass doorknob. Something moved through her body. Maybe it was a mother's intuition. But she felt strange touching the cool door handle as if it caused a foreboding, physical reaction from her fingertips up to her elbow.

"Andy, are you home?"

No answer. She glanced over the wrought iron balcony railing behind her. Andy's blue Honda was in the parking lot. "Andy!" She tried the doorknob again and used the palm of her hand to pound on the door. She pulled a phone from her purse, calling her son's number.

It went to voicemail. "This is Andy. Leave a message, and I'll get back to you."

She disconnected and called her husband. "Hi, I'm at Andy's apartment. His car is in the lot, but he's not coming to the front door."

"Did you call him?" Clint Ward stood in his kitchen, a cup of coffee in one hand. Tall, wide chest, quick eyes. He looked through the sliding glass door to a weeping willow tree in the backyard, the trees gangly arms moving like a hula dancer in the breeze.

"Yes. I called him before I left the house and a few minutes ago, standing here at his door. Clint, I feel like something's very wrong. It's a weird feeling. When I touched the handle to his door, it was as if there was no energy at all in his apartment. I'm scared. Should I call the police?"

"Do you have the key to his apartment?"

"No. I rarely take it. The key is hanging on the key rack near our garage door. Can you bring it here?"

"Okay. He's probably just in his back bedroom, sleeping late. Maybe his music is on, earbuds or whatnot and—"

"No, he's not sleeping. He knew I was coming at three o' clock. Please hurry. You can't get here fast enough."

THREE

Clint Ward could barely catch his breath. He ran up the outside steps to the second-floor balcony of his son's apartment. Ward's wife, Lauren, stood next to the locked front door, purse strap over one shoulder, face filled with anxiety. "Where's the key?" she asked.

Clint reached in his pocket, pulling out a single brass key on a round ring. "Here it is." He stepped in front of the door, inserted the key, and opened it. He entered, Lauren following right behind him. "Andy!" Clint called out.

No answer.

"Andy!" shouted his mother.

No answer.

"Look," Clint pointed to something on the coffee table. He approached it, picked up the open bottle of pills, shaking one into the palm of his hand. "What the hell is this? Is it a prescription drug?"

Lauren took the bottle, examining the label. "There is nothing printed here. No prescription instructions. Nothing."

"That's because it isn't a real prescription. Let's check the rest of his apartment."

Lauren nodded, walking past the open kitchen, down the hall. There were two bedrooms. The doors were closed to each bedroom. Lauren started to open one door, paused, and knocked. "Andy, it's Mom and Dad. Are you asleep?"

No answer.

"Open it," said Ward.

Lauren opened the door and almost dropped to her knees. "Oh, dear God in heaven. Please, no!" She ran to the bed where Andy lay, his eyes wide open, as if he was staring at the ceiling, the look of fear locked in his bloodshot eyes.

"Andy!" shouted Clint. He stood next to his son's body, hands trembling, eyes welling. "Andy ... what ...." He touched the cold face, lips blue. No breathing. Clint pushed on his son's chest. Rapid CPR thrusts. "Andy! Breathe!"

"Please breathe," Lauren said, tears streaming down her cheeks. "Just take a breath, baby."

Clint made more pushes with his hands over the heart area before leaning down, cupping his lips on his dead son's open mouth and exhaling. He did this a dozen times before slowly standing straight, tears flowing, a stream of saliva dripping from one edge of his mouth.

"I'm calling 911!" shouted Lauren, her hands shaking as she tried to press the buttons.

He looked over at his wife. "He's gone ... our son is gone."

Lauren's phone slipped from her hand as she doubled over, making a long and painful wail. Something primordial, the sound that only a grieving mother could make, a woman who'd nursed her son at her breasts twenty-one years ago, and now looked down at his lifeless body.

Clint took his phone from a back pocket and made the call.

"911, what's your emergency?"

"Please get paramedics to my son's apartment. I think he had a drug overdose."

"Is he breathing now, sir?"

"No, but they might be able to revive him."

"What is the address?"

"It's 917 Sycamore Drive, apartment 59. Gainesville. Please hurry!"

***

A half hour later, after trying hard to revive Andy Ward, paramedics from the fire department and ambulance service ended their resuscitation efforts. Lauren and Clint Ward stayed in the small living room as EMTs and police came and left the back bedroom. One uniformed officer, a woman, dark hair worn up, late twenties, approached them. "I'm sorry for your loss. I'm officer Debra Cooper."

Clint nodded, his eyes red and watery. Lauren said, "Thank you, and thanks for getting here so fast."

"Yes, ma'am. The medical examiner will be here soon." She pulled out a small notebook. "I just need to ask y'all a couple of questions. "Did your son have a history of drug abuse?"

"Absolutely not," snapped Clint. "Andy was an athlete. He lettered on the university's tennis team and was pitching on the baseball team. He was so good that he earned a full scholarship."

The officer nodded, jotting down the information. "Those pills that you pointed out to us on the coffee table, did you touch the bottle?"

Clint looked from the bottle to the officer. "Yes, it was the first thing we saw when we walked into our son's apartment. If I got my fingerprints on them, I'm sorry. But, at that time, we didn't know our son was lying dead in his bedroom."

"Yes, sir. I understand. Do you know where he got that bottle of pills?"

"No," Lauren said. "That was the first time we saw them."

"Does he have a girlfriend or any close friends who might have been here when he opened that bottle?"

"He does have a girlfriend. Her name is Brittany Harmon. She's over here occasionally. We have no idea whether she was here when Andy opened this. We don't even know if the pills were his. Maybe a friend brought them to his apartment."

The officer said nothing, jotting in her notepad.

The last person to arrive was a man in his late fifties, cotton white hair, ruddy face, bifocals. He was the coroner. After examining the body and speaking with officers, he came back out of the room and approached Andy's parents. "This is tragic. I'm so sorry for your loss. I'm Dr. Jack Gardner, county medical examiner." He nodded at the officer.

She gestured to the open bottle of pills. "Dr. Gardner, the pills in that bottle might have something to do with the death."

"What are they?"

"We don't know until the lab can run test. They look like Oxy. Could be anything or a mixture that might contain fentanyl. We're seeing a lot of it now."

"Thanks." The ME looked at the Ward's and motioned to the open front door. "Maybe we can talk outside. Let all these folks work the scene. If these are illegal drugs, you can call it a crime scene."

The Ward's followed the ME onto the balcony, the air filled with the overlapping staccato noise of police and fire department radios. A few residents were in the parking lot, looking up at the apartment where all the action was centered. The ME glanced above the rim of his bifocals. "In any situation like this, I'll need to do an autopsy to determine the exact cause of death."

"What do you mean in any situation like this?" asked Lauren.

"Suspicious in nature. A healthy, twenty-one-year-old man never lies down on his bed and doesn't wake up again unless he was killed, had a drug overdose, or wasn't as healthy as he was perceived to be. Since your son was an athlete at the university, I'd assume he was in good physical condition, or he may have had some underlying heart problem that no one suspected."

"His heart was fine," Clint said. "He's been tested. No heart problems."

"Do you know if he had a Covid vaccine recently? Some young men, fellas his age, have experienced severe myocarditis as an adverse reaction to the vaccine."

"He didn't get the shot, and he's never had Covid. Because the vaccine wasn't required in Florida for students to attend college or participate in college sports, Andy chose not to get it."

The ME nodded and pursed his dry lips as two officers left the apartment. A middle-aged detective in a sportscoat arrived, nodding, and entering the premises. Clint eyed the ME. "Doctor Garner, what do you think caused our son's death?"

"In my preliminary review, I'd suspect a drug overdose. The body has every outward sign of that. Because rigor mortis has set in, it happened a few hours ago. Those pills on the coffee table could have come from anywhere."

A few seconds later, two members of the ME's team pushed a metal gurney through the open door, a white sheet over the body. The Ward's held each other up as they watched the body of their only son being wheeled toward an elevator to the awaiting dark blue van with the word *CORONER* on the side.

Clint leaned up against the outside brick wall, his face pale, perspiring. Pupils in his eyes at pinpoints.

"Sir," said the ME. "You need to sit down. It looks like you're about to faint."

Clint stared at the ME. "I feel unsteady ... so tired. My heart is racing, and I think I might vomit if everything doesn't stop spinning. I never faint, but this is too much."

"Did you try to resuscitate your son? Did you give him mouth-to-mouth?"

"Yes, I tried but ...."

"Maybe some of whatever was in his body could be in yours. It's apparently a very powerful drug. We need to have paramedics take a look at you."

Clint slid down the wall, his back to the bricks, into a sitting position on the balcony. Looking through the wrought iron railing, he watched as his son's body was wheeled across the parking lot. "Andy," he whispered, his eyes filled with tears and sorrow.

Dr. Gardner signaled for two paramedics. "We need medical help!"

FOUR

Two months later – Florida wilderness

Max surveyed the shoreline for alligators. At ten pounds, she took it upon herself to be the watchdog, barking when she spotted a gator slide from the muddy riverbank into the dark waters of the St. Johns River in Florida. Max, our feisty female dachshund, sat near the bow of my sixteen-foot Boston Whaler. Although she was getting a little gray in the snout, her vigor and energy level was like that of a much younger dog. She was and always would be a puppy at heart.

I used an electric motor to quietly enter some of my favorite backwater coves for fishing. The St. Johns was one of the few rivers in the world that ran north. It meandered for miles, traveling through moss-draped cypress trees in the wilderness on through towns and cities, from Vero Beach to the Atlantic Ocean, east of Jacksonville. Our cabin home was near the halfway point, overlooking an oxbow in the river.

Sitting next to Max was Wynona, the breeze moving like invisible fingers through her dark hair. In the dappled sunlight coming through the cypress trees lined along the shore, Wynona's skin had a warm olive cast to it. Her eyes were light brown and expressive. Wynona's mother is a full-blooded Seminole. Her Irish father came to America from Dublin as a sailor on a freighter. He decided to stay, finding a job as a boat salesman at a marina on Marco Island, eventually gaining his U.S. citizenship.

The warm air was soft and filled with the musty smells of damp moss and blooming honeysuckles. A large osprey alighted at the top of a bald cypress tree. Max barked. Wynona laughed and pointed in the direction that Max stared. "It's okay, Maxine. The bird is an osprey. Be glad it's only a fish eater because, with its claws and a large wingspan, that bird could snatch you off our dock if it wanted."

12

"No, Mama. That might make Max scared," said our daughter, Angela.

Wynona turned around, her smile as radiant as the golden sunlight reflecting off the river's surface. "I'm just teasing Max. Ospreys won't bother her. They much prefer fish."

Angela, age six, brown hair and dimples, eyed Max and then looked at the osprey at the top of the tree. "Max has teeth. So, birds really would be scared of her."

"That's right. Max is fearless. Just like you, sweetheart."

Angela beamed a toothy smile.

A year ago, she wasn't sitting in a boat on a fishing excursion with her family. She had been locked away in a steel container on a cargo ship with a dozen other children, being shipped like cattle in a human trafficking ring to buyers in the Middle East. It was a criminal ring that I'd tracked for three months. As a PI, I had been working as a consultant with the FBI.

Angela's biological parents died in a car accident. She had no other relatives and fell into the foster care system where she was exploited and sold to human traffickers with pedophiles as customers. I got lucky and managed to blow a deep hole into the engine that trafficked children. The day I rescued them, aboard the container ship that left the port of Tampa, Angela frightened and crying, clung to my leg like a baby koala hugging a tree as poachers came closer.

They were stopped.

My name is Sean O'Brien, at six-three and two hundred pounds, I served as a team leader in the Army's Delta Force. My deployment included Syria and Afghanistan. After military service, I worked as a detective with Miami-Dade PD. To track evil, I had to enter the criminal mind. The transition, back and forth, wasn't easy. My wife at the time, Sherri, before dying from ovarian cancer, asked me to promise her that I'd leave a profession she said had a grip on my heart and head.

Max was Sherri's final physical gift to me. It was just the two of us, Max and me, for a couple of years until I met and worked with Wynona. She'd spent eight years as a special agent with the FBI before coming back to Florida and accepting a job as a detective for the Seminole Tribe. Today, she owns and operates an antique shop in the heart of DeLand, Florida, about twenty-five miles from where we were in our boat on the river.

As our adopted daughter, Angela is the little girl I thought I'd never be fortunate enough to have. With her dark hair and complexion, she looked like she was our biological child. After spending time with her when she was freed from the traffickers, and after talking at length with Angela, Wynona and I decided to petition the court to adopt her. The process was a smooth one, and within a few months, Angela O'Brien had a new life and her own bedroom in our riverfront cabin. And she now occupied a forever place in our hearts.

"Daddy," she said sitting on the middle seat in the boat and looking up at me. "When are we going to fish?"

"How about right now?"

"Yippie! Are you going to teach me how?"

"Yes. And I have a feeling that you'll catch on quick."

She turned around to Wynona. "Mom, are you fishing, too?"

"I'm going to watch you and Dad do all the work. Max and I will be your cheerleaders. Between you two catching fish, and when the action slows down a bit, I hope to read a chapter or two from the book I brought."

"Okay."

Angela watched me bait her hook, eyes wide, face curious as I clasped a black artificial worm to her line. "Is that what fish like to eat … yucky worms?"

"Worms, minnows, bugs … fish like them all. I'm going to show you how to cast your rod. We'll aim for a spot near those cypress roots sticking out of the water. I have a feeling there is a bass just waiting for us in there." I picked up her Zebco, a child's rod with a purple reel and a smiling bullfrog decal on it. "Okay, watch me. I'm going to cast it, and as I make the throw, I will press this button right here to allow the line to come out of the reel."

"Can I do it?"

"Yes. But first, I need to show you how. The next cast will be all yours."

She grinned. I cast the lure about forty feet, just shy of the gnarled cypress roots, which grew like wooden stalagmites from the river bottom. I turned the reel's hand-crank a couple of times before handing the rod to Angela. Max tilted her head, watching us, tail wagging. I cast my lure, the plastic worm splashing ten feet from the largest cypress root. I waited a few seconds for the ripples to fade before turning the handle to work the lure near the river bottom.

Angela watched me and began doing the same thing, turning the handle, stopping, and looking at the spot where the line disappeared under the water. She was a natural. Patient and methodical in her approach to fishing. But I knew she'd grow impatient if she didn't catch a fish. I looked over at Wynona, who beamed with pride, watching Angela hold the small rod.

Then I noticed the tip of Angela's rod quiver slightly. A fish wasn't on, but something below the surface had its eyes on her lure.

***

Clint Ward didn't want to enter the building. But he had no choice. Not if he was going to find the person or persons responsible for the death of his son, Andy. He parked on the street across from the Gainesville Police Department, went inside, and asked the receptionist to speak with Detective Winston Porter.

The receptionist, a middle-aged woman, white roots beginning to show in her shoe polish-colored, dyed black hair. She sat behind the desk and made the call. "Detective Porter, Mr. Ward is in the lobby. He wants to speak with you. He said he doesn't have an appointment."

Porter, dark skin, puffy round face, wore an open sports coat. No tie. He sat at his desk in the homicide division, a dozen detectives working the phones or behind the glow of computer screens. "I have nothing to offer him since he called last week."

"Do you want me to tell him that?"

"No. He's a grieving father. None of this is his fault. Tell him to come on back."

"Okay." She clicked off and looked over her purple-framed glasses to Clint. "Detective Porter will see you. The homicide division is down the hall and—"

"I know where it is. Thank you, ma'am."

***

A minute later, Ward was sitting in a metal folding chair next to Porter's desk. "Mr. Ward, I wish I had some news—good or bad—something I can tell you. But I don't. As I told you on the phone last week, our investigation continues. The final toxicology reports indicate that Andy died from an overdose of fentanyl. We have no eyewitnesses to your son's death. There is very little evidence and, so far, nothing to tie it to. His girlfriend, Brittany Harmon, said he took one pill against her suggestion not to do so. She said the pills arrived in a sealed parcel. She didn't know who sent them."

"Did you find fingerprints?"

"The only fingerprints we could find on the box, or the pill bottle were Andy's and yours. Those pills were mixed with deadly portions of fentanyl. The exposure you had to the drug while trying to resuscitate your son made you sick. You could have gone to the ER." This is deadly junk that's flooding America. From the DEA on down to local police departments like ours, we've never seen anything like it."

"Then do something to stop it."

"Sir, I wish it were that easy. Fentanyl is often a hundred times more powerful than heroin. Andy, like other young people, apparently ordered the drugs online. I'm sure he had no idea that something sold as Oxy was laced with fentanyl. Trying to find these dealers or traffickers online is like whack-a-mole. They pop up, do some deals, and are gone. Some deals are done on the dark web, other sales are in the open with fake IP addresses and on social media sites like TikTok, Instagram, and Facebook Marketplace. These companies have strict policies against this. But even they have a hard time policing their own sites."

"Somebody must do something. My son can't be poisoned, and the killers just walk away to do it again and again."

"Mr. Ward, my heart aches for what you and your wife are going through. I have a son about Andy's age. Please know that we're doing all we can. It's just very slow going."

"I've tried to work within the system. But if you can't find my son's killer, I will. I served my country well in the Army to protect the borders of other countries. This poison is coming across our borders and killing people like my son. Somebody must stop it."

"Please, don't go out and do anything that may get you hurt or killed. We don't know who's behind this."

"When I find out, I'll let you know." Clint Ward got up and left.

FIVE

On Angela's first cast, she caught a tree. The black plastic worm hung like an ornament from the low-hanging limb on a cypress tree near our boat. She looked up at me, her face turned into a frown. Embarrassed and anxious at the same time. She held her rod in one little hand and brought the other hand to her mouth. "Uh-oh." She eyed the dangling worm. "Daddy, can you get it down?"

I looked at her and smiled. "I think so." I glanced at Wynona who was doing her best to keep from laughing hard so that she wouldn't fall out of the boat. Max tilted her head and looked up into the tree as if to say, *Oh boy.*

I stood on the bench seat in the stern and reached for the lure, its hook embedded in the cypress branch. A curlew called out from across the river. At that moment in time, the bird's chortles sounded like primal laughter. Wynona held Max in her lap, laughing so much she was tearing up. Angela followed suit, giggling.

I pulled the cypress branch closer to my chest, looking down through the needlelike leaves at my snickering family. "Okay girls, and I'm talking to all three of you. I could use a little empathy while trying to steady the boat with my feet, using this limb as an anchor rope, and attempting to pull a hook out of the branch."

I worked the entrenched hook, pulling it out while keeping the Boston Whaler under my boat shoes. "There. It's done. No problem, and the hook is still in good shape." I sat back down and looked across at Angela, who was amazed that her dad could do such a heroic feat. "Okay, let's try again. This time press the button on the reel when the rod is pointed toward the river. Get the bait close to the cypress knees in the water."

"Okay. Why do you call them knees? They don't look like my knees?"

"That's a good question. They're really roots. Most of the cypress roots are in the mud. Occasionally, some will grow straight out of the water. And the fish love hanging around them. Let's try that cast again."

Angela took a deep breath, nodding. She stood in the boat, using her arms and shoulders to cast the lure, pressing the button with perfect timing. The lure sailed in the air about twenty feet before splashing through the river's surface. "I did it! Mom, did you see that? I did it."

Wynona clapped her hands. "You certainly did. Way to go!"

I gestured toward Angela's reel. "Now you can turn the crank handle a few times. What you want to do is make it seem like the worm is slowly crawling just above the bottom of the river. You want to let a hungry fish see it swimming."

She listened, following instructions well, one hand on the rod, the other slowly winding the handle. Her rod bent, almost pulling out of her hands. "Daddy!" she squealed.

I lowered my rod, reaching over to help her. "You got one! Keep turning the handle."

Max barked twice. Wynona picked her up, pointing to where the line zigzagged across the dark surface. "Way to go, Angela! You caught one!"

Angela grinned as she held the rod, trying to turn the handle. I used one hand to steady it for her as the tip of the rod bent down, about to go into the river. "You wind the fish in, and I'll help you hold the rod. I think you have a big one on the line."

"Me, too!"

I readied the dip net. Seconds later, a largemouth bass broke the surface, shaking its head and trying to spit out the lure. Angela giggled, fighting, winding the reel. I held her rod with my right hand, using my left hand with the net to come up under the bass, lifting it out of the water. The fish slung river water over both of us. Angela stood, still holding the rod, her face and life jacket dripping with water.

"Look, Mama! It's a giant fish!"

"It sure is. Hold on tight." Max was about to lose herself, barking, her long ears cocked, eyes bright, pink tongue just showing.

I reached into the net, lifting the bass out, carefully removing the hook from the inside of its mouth. Angela's eyes were wide, filled with wonderment.

Wynona picked up her phone. "Let's take a picture."

I held the bass to one side as Angela stood next to me. Wynona snapped the photo. I looked down at Angela. "What do you say we let this big fella go back to his home in the river? You want to release him or have him for dinner?"

Angela shook her head. "No, we can't eat the fish. He has to take care of his family. Please let him go, Dad."

"Okay." I lowered the bass back into the river, holding its mouth and jaw as water circulated through its gills. Seconds later, I released it. With one flap of its wide tail, the bass was gone. But the fun it brought to our little boat would last a lifetime in memories and stories.

***

Three hours later, we were back at our dock, gear unloaded, and the boat tied to the posts. We'd caught and released four fish. The time on the river further cemented Angela's love for being on and around the water, experiencing nature in some of its most primitive form. We walked up the stone path through the three-acre backyard of our home, a sprawling cabin built from heart-of-pine, cypress, and cedar, with a tin roof, a fireplace, and a large, screened-in back porch overlooking the river. The sweet scent of orange blossoms floated in the soft air.

The adjacent property was the remnant of an ancient mound left behind by the Timucuan Indians a thousand years ago. Across the river was the Ocala National Forest, the largest in Florida. My nearest neighbor was two miles away.

Wynona and I sat on the back porch in wicker chairs, sipping sweet tea as Angela and Max played in the yard, yellow and blue butterflies flittering like confetti in the warm air, a mourning dove crooning. Wynona looked at her left hand, the diamond engagement ring sparkling in the speckled sunlight coming through the screen. She glanced at Angela in the yard and then eyed me. "You're a great father. I knew you would be a natural."

I smiled. "Really? How'd you know?"

"Just because of the man that you are, putting others first. Angela has a mom and a dad now. Two people who love her. She has a little girl's bedroom filled with toys and stuffed animals. She has your last name, but I don't. Since we're engaged, maybe it's time we picked a date for our wedding. This beautiful diamond ring reminds me of that every day."

I raised an eyebrow. "Does it? I guess the power of a diamond goes beyond its beauty, whispering in my woman's ear. What does it say?"

"That Sean O'Brien is the man for me. God knows that I *know* the difference." She watched Angela and Max play. "Since you aren't working a case for a client right now, your schedule is light. Why don't we go on and set a wedding date? Something small. Just close friends and family attending."

"Where would you like to get married? On a beach somewhere or someplace else?"

"I haven't thought about the location, but now that you asked, how about that little church at Ponce Inlet near the lighthouse. It's a white chapel. Looks very old. Sits back off the road. I can check on it."

"Sounds good. You're right about my calendar. There is nothing pending or scheduled in terms of PI work."

Wynona smiled. "Great. You can take a break from danger."

"The danger has never really bothered me. It comes with the territory. I'd like to think the service I provide, if I'm successful, brings people closer together and helps them heal."

Wynona reached for my hand. "I'm sure it does. I know you don't take every case. You can't. But the cases you do take, when you solve them, make a positive difference for families."

"I must walk toward evil, not away from it. Maybe that's why I volunteered for dangerous or special assignments in the military. Maybe that's why I wanted to work the homicide cases as a cop. I feel an obligation to right wrongs, to help when I can … if I can."

"I know. That's one of the many things I admire and love about you."

I said nothing, watching Angela and Max chasing butterflies.

"Sean, what's on your mind? Whatever it is, I can handle it." She looked down at the diamond ring and then up at me. "If you're having second thoughts about getting married, please tell me now. And tell me why? If I'm being a neurotic, engaged woman whose emotions are off the chart, tell me that, too." She held my hand.

"I'm not having second thoughts. I just don't want the danger of my work to bleed into my family. Not after what Angela's gone through. And not after what you experienced of being shot, almost dying, amd losing our unborn child. But I can't change who I am."

Wynona squeezed my hand. "I'm not asking you to change. It would be like me demanding that you change your DNA. I understand the risks and the potential danger, and I accept the stakes because I love you. Our marriage comes with no conditions attached, except that you love our family … and you consider the risks. Okay?"

"Okay."

"Good. And now that you're not working a case, let's pick a date for a simple wedding."

Angela and Max stopped playing, Max tilting her head, staring at something to the left of the cabin, in the long driveway. She snorted and barked. Angela looked at us, her face frightened. She pointed. "Daddy, a man is standing over there." She ran from the yard, up the wooden steps to the safety of the screened porch, her lower lip trembling.

I stood, reaching behind one of the ceiling timbers, palming my Sig Sauer P-238, placing it under my shirt before Angela could see it. I stepped from the porch, watching Max vanish around the cabin.

SIX

Durango, Mexico

Tony Salazar was six months into the most dangerous assignment of his life. At the ten-year mark in his career with the DEA, Salazar volunteered to leave his comfortable office in San Diego to enter Mexico as an undercover drug agent. Because he was the husband of a loving wife and the father of a teenage son and an eight-year-old daughter, Salazar had deep reservations concerning the transfer.

In those moments of trepidation, he remembered what his Mexican grandmother would tell him as a boy growing up in Nogales. Madre Rosa sometimes took him by the hand to harvest ripe tomatoes and corn and collect hen's eggs. She insisted that Tony accompany her as she delivered the food to a few neighbors who were poorer than his family. Her deep Catholic faith directed everything she did.

"Come with me, Antonio!" she'd say in Spanish on Sundays after mass. *"Ven conmigo Antonio!"* He remembered Madre Rosa wearing a faded scarf over her silver hair, brown face rutted from sun and age, hands knotted by arthritis. Most of all, he remembered her wide smile. It was a smile his mother said he had inherited from Madre Rosa. He'd thought about what she would tell him on the way back home after making the deliveries, after seeing the neighbors' appreciative faces. *"Try to help others with their burdens. That way you don't carry the weight of the world on your shoulders ... and you do what we are called to do. Can you remember that always, Antonio?"*

"Yes, I will remember."

Now, all these years later, after legally entering the U.S., learning English at night school, earning citizenship, finishing college, joining the

Army, starting a family, and working a job he loved with the DEA, Madre Rosa's voice called him back to his childhood home from the grave. He thought it was probably from heaven. A whisper.

Salazar, late thirties, swarthy complexion, bright smile, had to leave his wife and children for two months at a time, making covert and secure phone calls back home when he could. He worked deep undercover in the bowels of the most threatening drug trafficking operations anywhere in the world—the notorious and deadly Mexican cartels. He was one of fifty DEA agents working out of the major cities—Mexico City, Guadalajara, Durango, and others.

In a field of international covert work, the most important tool an agent has is his or her talent to find and recruit human assets—people the agent can trust with information and to help facilitate spying. It's how the CIA and FBI operate. The DEA is no exception with one exception—Mexico. Salazar trusted very few people. He couldn't afford to do so. That made his job, and that of the other DEA field agents working inside Mexico, much harder.

In his small rental house, he slept with a Glock under his pillow, a sawed off 12-gauge shotgun hidden in his closet, deadbolts on the doors, locks, and burglar bars on the three windows. His sleep was sporadic at best, unable to turn off the defense mechanisms at nightfall. His mind often replayed conversations he had with informants and people within the Mexican government, military, and police whom he was working with on a reciprocal arrangement with Mexican agents sent to the U.S. in an extended, often weak, effort to stop drug and human trafficking.

But the mutual agreement was becoming unraveled, starting to look like a one-way arrangement as more corruption was discovered among some of the top people in Mexico's government, military, and police. After the retired Minister of Defense was arrested by DEA agents in the U.S. for working with the H-2 Cartel, at Mexico's request, he was extradited back to Mexico to face charges and a trial.

Six months later, charges were dropped, and the Minister of Defense was staying at his lavish mansion overlooking the Pacific Ocean in Puerto Vallarta. Tony Salazar thought about that as he parked his blue Honda Civic in the driveway of his rental house. He parked in an area where the motion-detection camera near the door could monitor the car. Before getting back in the car and cranking the engine, he always used his remote-control ignition key, starting the Honda from fifty feet away.

Salazar approached the front door to the small brick house, black shutters faded from age and neglect, Bermuda grass the color of October hay. He entered the house, taking a moment to unarm the alarm system, the beeps coming to a stop. Salazar walked into the small kitchen, the linoleum floor yellowed, the finish on the particle-board cabinets worn. He got a Corona from the refrigerator, popped the top, and took a sip. Then he sat down at his computer, which sat atop a strawberry-colored table, the paint flaked and chipped.

In less than a minute, Salazar established a secure connection through the DEA's use of the dark web, the multiple servers encrypted and hidden in bunkers across the nation and sections of the world. He logged into the DEA's headquarters southwest of Washington, D.C., in Springville, Virginia. Salazar reported directly to Brian Bergman, Deputy Chief of Intelligence. Bergman was at his office desk, an American flag a few feet behind him, a half dozen neat stacks of paper and files on his desk. He was nearing fifty, gray at the temples, black-framed glasses perched on his long nose. "Good to see you, Tony. Sorry I missed you earlier today. I wanted to talk with you because I'm meeting with Administrator Bowman in the morning. What's the latest with the Durango cartel?"

"Our asset is in their ranks. He's doing foot soldier work, trying to cultivate closer ties to the Navarro family. We meet on his days off. He told me that Diego Navarro, in his quest to manufacture the purest fentanyl coming out of Mexico, has brought in a renowned chemist from China, paying the guy a lot of money to train Navarro's cooks. Navarro is doing everything in his power to take on and beat the others, including the Sinaloa cartel. Since his father was sent to prison, Navarro is working the system to its fullest levels of corruption."

"Any idea who he's bought off in the Ministry of Defense?"

"Probably a more accurate question would be this … is there anyone left in that department with enough moral fiber not to take the bribes? Brian, we need more agents down here. The challenge, the territory, is so vast, we can't do what we're in Mexico to do. It's now a no-win situation."

"It used to be a win-win for us and Mexico. After the arrest of Manuel Rodríguez, Mexican legislators passed a measure sharply restricting what the

DEA can do inside of Mexico, regardless of whether it's mutually beneficial for both countries. We can't get Mexican visas for our new agents"

"If they rewrite the laws … maybe we rewrite the rules of engagement. Either that or pull the hell out of there before the cartels start beheading our DEA agents."

SEVEN

The stranger was in silhouette. Backlit by the sun. I watched his hands. Watched every subtle movement that he made. I could see a car fifty yards away just beyond the closed and locked gate to my driveway. I couldn't see if someone was in the car. Even though his face was in shadow, there was something about the man that I recognized. It was in his body posture—the way he stood, the way he walked and paused, stopping as if I was going to pull my gun on him.

But my gun was hidden under my shirt and wedged in my belt. He couldn't see it. Didn't know if I was armed. But I knew he somehow *felt* it. He stopped, slowly raising both hands. "Don't shoot. I come in peace. I'm hoping that killer dog you have won't damage my ankle."

He was still thirty yards away, but I recognized the voice. It was one I hadn't heard in a couple of years. However, the give-away was his southern accent. Mississippi. Oxford, to be exact. His name was Clint Ward. We served in Delta Force together in Afghanistan. He'd been a good soldier. Fearless. A patriot. He left his ego aside and took orders well. He was a team player.

"How are you, Clint? It's been too long. You didn't have to park back there."

"I tried calling you, Sean. As I recall, you weren't much for cell phones."

"I was on a boat fishing in the river. Didn't take my phone with me."

"I'm the first to understand." He looked at the blooming yellow roses, and the red and white impatiens along both sides of the gravel and crushed oyster shell driveway. It was partially covered in shade from a live oak sodden with moss that hung like long whiskers of gray iron.

He smiled. "I never pictured Sean O'Brien as much of a flower kind of guy. Last time I was out here, I don't recall so many flowers. Hell, for that matter, I don't remember any flowers. You must have found your green thumb."

"I found something else. These come from the talents of my fiancée, Wynona."

Clint came closer, a wide grin on his face filled with stubble and worry despite his outward appearance. I could tell that something was weighing heavily on his mind. As he got closer, Max gave him the official perfunctory sniff test. "Hello, Miss Max. You remember me? It's been a while."

Max angled her head, studying his face for a moment before trotting off in the front yard after a squirrel that scampered up a sycamore tree.

Clint opened his arms as he came up to me. "How 'bout a brother hug for old times' sake."

We hugged, and I could feel damp sweat through the back of his T-shirt. "Good to see you, Clint. Come inside. I want you to meet Wynona and our daughter."

"Whoa … you have a fiancée and a daughter? When you decide, you move fast."

"We adopted her. It's a long story that I'll share with you."

"A lot has happened in a couple of years. And now you're engaged. Better invite Lauren and I to the wedding."

"Will do. Are you okay? I detect something heavy behind those bloodshot eyes of yours."

"You always were perceptive in that regard. No, I'm not okay. Not in the least bit. Andy is dead. It's been more than two months now. I'm about to blow up inside. As you know, he was our only son, and he was about to graduate from the University of Florida. He was being scouted by the majors."

"Clint, I'm so sorry. I remember Andy well. What happened to him?"

"He never used drugs. He was dealing with a lot of pain from a pulled rotator cuff in his right shoulder. Went to the doctor a few times. Got a couple of cortisone shots. After rest and moderate exercise, every time he tried to swing a tennis racquet or throw a fastball, he reinjured the shoulder. But he was the kind of young man who tried to power through the pain."

"Did he overdose on something?"

"Fentanyl. Police believe he bought it online. Ordered in like you'd order a damn pizza. But with a pizza, it's only peperoni. With the pills Andy got, it was fentanyl disguised as oxy."

We stood under the shade of the old oak as Clint told me the story, the hammering sound of a woodpecker drilling into a dead pine tree near the Indian mound. When he finished, his eyes welled with water. He used the back of one big hand to wipe away the tears. I'd been through combat with Clint, saw our Army brothers fall around us, helped to patch his shattered left leg, and never in the heat of war or after did he cry. Not until the death of his son did the pent-up emotions finally flow like a cracked dam.

I wasn't sure what to say beyond expressing how sorry I felt for his horrific loss. I touched his big shoulder. "Come on inside. I want you to meet Wynona and Angela. Wynona had a career with the FBI as a field agent before coming back home to the Seminole tribe where she worked as a detective. She's good and might offer a perspective into the police investigation of Andy's death."

We headed back to the screened porch, Max leading the way, ignoring the fleeing lizards, and returning to the backyard like the conquering hero—the watchdog that she embodied. I introduced Clint to Wynona and Angela. He looked at Angela. "I heard that you caught a fish."

"It was a big one. A bass." she grinned. One front tooth and a lower tooth missing. "I caught it after Daddy got my hook out of a tree."

"Were you fishing for squirrels?"

She wrinkled her little nose. "No. Never. Max chases squirrels, but she can't catch them. Her legs are too short."

"Well, that's a good thing."

I nodded. "Angela, why don't you take Max into the backyard with some of her toys and play catch, okay?"

She smiled. "Okay." She stepped over to Max's "toy box" in one corner of the porch, taking a mini tennis ball and a red rubber bone. "Come on, Max. Last one to the oak tree is a rotten egg." They flew down the steps. Buddies forever.

We sat in the wicker chairs, Clint watching Angela and Max race to a rope swing I had tied to the limb of a massive oak tree. His eyes were misty, reflecting some concealed and distant memory. He looked at us. "It'll be just a blink of an eye, and your daughter will be a teenager. I remember when Andy was her age. So innocent and trusting." He cut his eyes from me to Wynona. "Before I go into detail as to why I showed up in your driveway, I'd love to hear how you two adopted that precious little girl."

Wynona leaned forward. "You mentioned when Andy was Angela's age, he was so innocent and trusting. She was as well … until she was abducted and sold into a human sex trafficking ring."

Clint made a dry swallow, clearing his throat. "I'm so sorry to hear that. I hope they got the thugs that did it."

I said nothing.

Clint, a friend and an eternal optimist, a man who faced life head on with a sword and a sense of humor, appeared somewhat awkward, his emotions now on his broad shoulders. "Maybe I shouldn't have come here."

I shook my head. "This is what friends are for … good times and in bad times. If you're dealt a lucky hand, you'll get more good times than bad."

"We're glad that you're here," said Wynona. "Can I get you something to eat or drink?"

"No, thanks. My appetite is way down. After I tell you more about why I'm here, I might share a drink with you two before leaving. Without going into explicit detail, can you tell me what happened to Angela, and how you found and rescued her?"

I heard a jarring sound: engine noise from a boat on the river. I stood, picking up a pair of binoculars hanging from a hook on one of the roughhewed cypress timbers. I used the binoculars to watch a small boat coming upriver. It was less than one hundred feet south of my dock. I spotted one man in the boat, moving slow, fishing rods near the bow. I studied him as he slowed, coming adjacent to my dock. He glanced at my Boston Whaler, looking up from the river to the cabin. He watched Angela and Max for a moment before passing by the dock, heading toward the wide oxbow, soon vanishing around the bend.

Clint watched me hang the binoculars back on the hook. "Sean, your stance there for a few seconds, it reminded me of the many patrols we did in Afghanistan. Always on guard. Always searching the horizon for the enemy. Whatever happened to Angela, I take it that everyone is a potential new threat."

EIGHT

It was the kind of conversation that Wynona didn't want to have. Nor did I. But because of Clint's suffering from the loss of his son, a brief synopsis about what happened to Angela seemed to fit the gloomy tone. Wynona gave Clint a shortened version of Angela's history and how we adopted her, adding, "Yes, her innocence was stolen. Her trust is something that doesn't come easy. Nor should it, not after what she's experienced."

Clint shook his head. "I am so sorry. I hope there's a special place in hell reserved for human traffickers and pedophiles."

"At her young age, she suffers from a form of childhood PTSD. Sean and I do everything we can to fill her with the exact opposite of what she faced. Angela's surrounded by love and friends of ours who care deeply about her. Angela's bedroom, with all of the stuffed animals and toys, is her sanctuary—a safe place where she can be who she is—a little girl. For the time being, we're homeschooling her. But we don't want to isolate her from life, just from the evil that's part of it."

"I admire you both." He eyed me. "Did they catch the people who did this to Angela?"

I nodded. "It wasn't only Angela. She was one of the youngest. There were dozens and dozens of kids and teens, shipped like cattle across the country and the world. To answer your question, yes, they caught the perps … the ones who were still alive."

Clint stared at me. "I've seen that look in your eye, Sean. More so when we faced the enemy overseas. I take it that you had something to do with the investigation, right?"

"That's how I found Angela. I was searching for another girl, this one thirteen. In the end, they were both rescued and brought out of the dark to safety. Angela was the only one who didn't have a home to return to after her ordeal."

Clint was quiet. He watched Angela and Max playing, his large chest swelling with air. "You, too, are facing a lot of personal challenges. That child is your top priority, of course. I don't want to burden you with my problems. I'm sorry for coming." He rubbed his left palm on his pants.

I shook my head. "No. We're glad you're here." I gave Wynona a brief rundown of the history I shared with Clint, mostly through our days in the military service. I told her some of what he revealed to me about his son and added, "Andy was an athlete. Had a good head on his shoulders, and a bright future. What occurred could have happened to a lot of people, especially young people who are perhaps a little more trusting."

Clint nodded, giving Wynona more details. "In the case of my son, I think that Andy was very naïve. He did trust people until they gave him a reason not to do so. It was in his nature. An innocent, open young man who'd give you the shirt off his back if you needed it."

Wynona leaned forward in her chair. "Clint, you said it has been more than two months since Andy passed away. What's the status of the police investigation? Do they have a suspect?"

"No. To be frank with you, I think the police have put Andy's death on the backburner and moved on to easier crimes to solve."

"Why?"

"I don't know for sure, but it's the feeling I get every time I talk with them. Maybe they chalk up drug overdose cases as simply poor choices made by the victims, particularly addicts who can't break the cycle. That wasn't the situation in Andy's death. I'm going to call it what it is … a homicide. When a drug dealer knowingly sells a drug as one thing but, in fact, it's mixed with other drugs like fentanyl, and someone dies from that, in my book, it's murder."

I said, "Maybe they'll get a break in the case and find a suspect. Andy's death probably isn't this dealer's first fatality."

Clint blew out a breath, moistened his lips, and eyed me. "That's why I came down here to see you. The investigation into my son's murder is flat. Every day it gets colder. In Delta Force, you found the Taliban in places nobody else thought to look. When you worked criminal cases as a detective in Miami, you had one of the best, if not the best, closure records in the history of the department. I was hoping that you'd look into what happened to Andy. Maybe find the evil bastard who put the poison in those pills. I don't know where else to turn. I'm sorry."

I said nothing. I watched Angela and Max run around one of the orange trees in our backyard. I looked over at Wynona. She was silent, but in my thoughts, I could hear what she said earlier before Clint Ward walked down our driveway.

And now that you're not working a case, let's pick a date for a simple wedding.

NINE

Northwestern Durango, Mexico

From the valley, he gazed at the mountain range, looking at the leaves on the branches before reaching down to pick up a fistful of dry dirt. In Spanish, they called the old man *curandero*. He was known as a medicine man—a shaman. The Mexicans said he knew how to use herbs to heal the mind, body, and even the human soul. But he wasn't Mexican. He was Chinese.

His name was Hu Cheng. He'd come to Mexico for a month as part of a unique trade agreement. Cheng was really a chemist with forty-five years of experience in organic chemistry. Today, he stood in the center of a cow pasture, more than two hundred acres fenced with barbed wire. The camp was deep in the mountains of Northwest Durango, Mexico.

The highlands ran through the Mexican states of Senora, Durango, and Sinaloa. Some of the craggy mountains were more than nine-thousand feet in elevation. Dozens of cattle grazed in the lush grass of the valleys. The warm air, tinted with the banana-like scent of blooming yucca flowers, was mixed with the smell of cow dung.

Cheng, face leathery and lined with furrows around his eyes, looked at the seven hand-picked men who formed a semicircle around him. They would be the new generation of "cooks." Some were former farmers, men who'd raised vegetables, mostly avocados, before growing marijuana and poppy plants. They adapted to seasons of change driven by economic conditions and easy money. Under their breaths, they sometimes called it a harvest of shame because of what drug crops, especially poppies, did to the users.

But the men didn't dwell too much on that. Not if they wanted to put food in their bellies. So, they put aside any thoughts of creating addictions to thinking their work fed an insatiable need, a growing demand in America for drugs. Planting and cultivating acres of marijuana and poppies was labor intensive, often exposing their drug operations to the authorities. When that happened, greedy hands came out, police demanding a cut. Bribery and payoff money would eat into their profits.

Now the vast fields of poppies and marijuana were gone. Something replaced them. It was not a crop at all. It was synthetic—a manmade opioid. Fentanyl. Most of the chemicals, the ingredients needed to process and cook fentanyl, were produced in China. Although there were laws that prohibited the distribution of fentanyl, the ingredients to make the drug, all shipped separately, could be moved around the globe legally on cargo ships.

Cheng held out his hand. He looked at the men. His Spanish was excellent. "Watch what I do. When you cook outside, this is the most important step. If you forget this first step, you could be lying dead in a matter of a few minutes."

Some of the men shifted their weight from one foot to the other, standing and watching what the old man was about to do. All the men wore faded jeans and T-shirts. Some wore sweat-stained Stetsons and sombreros to keep the hot sun off their faces. A cow was mooing by a creek bed, other cattle moving around the mesquite trees, grazing, tails twitching as flies followed them. The animals were at least one hundred feet from the men.

Cheng looked up at the foliage on branches, slowly opening his palm, the dirt and bits of dead leaves scattering in the wind, blowing in a southwest direction. He nodded. "That is where the smoke from the fentanyl will travel. You, as cooks and assistants, always must be on the opposite side of the pot when that happens. Why? Sometimes your respirators could be old and not functioning as well as they should. Your eye goggles may have a cracked or missing bit of rubber. You do not want to risk blindness or death. Both are real possibilities—no, they are probabilities if you do not take every precaution available to you. Safety first."

Some of the men exchanged glances. Cheng wiped his right hand on his pants. "It is time to learn to cook. Last week, I taught some men in warehouses in Durango and Torreon. Cooking inside is different from working outside. Hazmat suits are required, and the buildings must have large exhaust fans to remove the smoke. I prefer the mobile labs like this in the open countryside. Let us unload the trucks."

Three men began unloading plastic bags of white chemicals from the bed of two pickup trucks. The others unpacked large metal pots and galvanized tubs, a tank of propane fuel, various rubber hoses, and steel grates to support the pots under the fire. They carried a half dozen ten-gallon plastic jugs of water from one truck to the cooking areas. Cheng gave the men instructions, and within a half hour, the propane burners were glowing red hot, with water in one of the large, galvanized tubs beginning to boil.

Cheng nodded. "Very good. You must follow these steps carefully to achieve the best results. Too much of one chemical over the others or too much water will result in an inferior product. Our goal is to create the very best fentanyl in the world. In China, we've had a lot of experience with opioids from the days of the poppies to today's synthetic opioids. Fentanyl is the result of years of trial and error. Man has made something the poppy could never do. Those plants gave the world morphine and heroin. When man stepped in and discovered synthetics, we created the world's most powerful drug. Fentanyl. In China, it is called the white dragon. Your goal today is to learn to cook while avoiding the fiery breath of the dragon. Any questions?"

A man in his mid-twenties, thick neck, and skin the color of roasted coffee beans, raised his hand. In Spanish, he asked, "Out here in the open, can we wear bandanas over our faces rather than respirators?"

"I always advise respirators and eye protection. As you become better at cooking outdoors, you may choose to wear cloth bandanas. But, when the wind changes directions, you must turn your back, hold your breath, and move to the opposite direction from where the wind is blowing. If not, you could be dead within five minutes. Any more questions?"

Some of the men shook their heads. No one spoke up. Cheng nodded. "Here is how you will make the best fentanyl in the world. Listen closely." For the next twenty minutes, Cheng showed the men how to make small batches of fentanyl, telling them that the steps would double in more controlled, indoor conditions.

They all wore respirators and eye goggles as Cheng demonstrated how to make fentanyl in twenty-gallon vats. He carefully measured and mixed, pouring powder, water, and various liquids into the bubbling vat, white smoke curling straight up and drifting towards the hard blue sky. A golden eagle, with a seven-foot wingspan, soared two hundred feet above the men, the bird's shadow moving slowly over them.

Cheng was methodical, explaining and demonstrating the order of the chemicals, how and why they're mixed. "This is piperidine. It is a big part of the secret sauce of the white dragon. It feeds the fire of the beast and, in turn, feeds the craving of the addicts. Once the dragon enters their blood, they have a strong desire to keep the beast there. They can't live without dragon milk." He chuckled, stepping away from the fire, removing his respirator, grinning, and taking a sip of water from a plastic bottle.

He placed the respirator back on his face, returning to the bubbling caldron. The liquid in the vat was turning black and thickening—a dark oatmeal consistency, with white smoke popping up through the bubbles and air pockets, like gases rising from boiling volcanic lava. Cheng used a small wooden boat paddle to mix the substance, turning clockwise.

In Spanish, one of the trainees, eyes wide, said, "It's like a witches' brew."

Another man, belly stretching his T-shirt, nodded. "It's a candy for the sweet tooth of the addicts. It looks like heroin, the black goat."

Cheng shook his head. "This mix is at least one hundred times more powerful than heroin. We'll use ladles to scoop out and pour the fentanyl into the plastic storage trays. We must carefully weigh them." He gestured to the dozens of plastic containers, resembling canisters used to store food. They were stacked on two long foldout tables.

Cheng picked up a shiny ladle from a smaller table. The ladle had an extended handle, three feet in length. He scooped out two cups of the cooling mixture, which he slowly poured into a hard-plastic storage container positioned on one of the portable scales. When he finished, he set the ladle back into the caldron.

Cheng looked up, his eyes lively through the goggles. "That's how it is done. We will cook a half dozen more vats today, each man getting turns at every step of the process. You only become a great cook by doing it over and over. Practice and patience. The Chinese way."

He looked to his far left, something catching his eye. A late model Ford-150 pickup truck was coming down the dirt road, a rooster tail of dust billowing up behind the rear wheels. The men paused what they were doing. Some mumbling. Others silent.

They recognized the truck, knew who owned it. And they knew he usually didn't make an appearance at the mobile labs out in the country. One reason was the potential danger from rival gangs. The other was the possibility of an arrest, should the area be under surveillance by a new police chief who hadn't been bought off yet, someone who might be working undercover with America's DEA.

One of the new cooks said, "Maybe they come here to check the quality of our work."

Another man wearing a Don Julio Tequila T-shirt shook his head. "No, he never comes to the mobile labs. Why is he here today? Whatever it is … I don't think it's a good thing."

TEN

I looked at Wynona and then at Clint, the lyrics of a Van Morrison song playing somewhere in the back of my mind. I could just hear the blues crooner singing, *Well, my mama told me there'd be days like this.* I wanted to help my old friend. I could feel his pain. When you spend long days and nights, much of that time in and around combat, the rest of the time trying not to step on a land mine, you grow a special bond with your military brothers. For life.

I glanced through the screened porch at the backyard, the river flat and dark as oil. Angela sat on the wooden seat of the rope swing hanging from a thick, moss-covered limb of a large live oak. Max was about ten feet away from her. I heard Angela say, "Max, I wish you could stand up and push me."

I knew it wouldn't be long before Angela asked Wynona or me to push her in the swing a couple of times. After that, after the break from gravity, she could keep the momentum going on her own.

Clint cleared his throat. "Sean, are you still working as a PI?"

"Yes. Most often I'm trying to help people recover things that were illegally taken from them. Crooked attorneys operating beyond the law. Cold cases. Unsolved homicides. They come to me by referral, and I'm usually their last resort after trying everything else they could."

"Andy was taken from me and his mother. And there was nothing legal about the way they took him from us."

I said nothing.

Clint inhaled a deep breath through his nostrils, jawline hard. "Not too long ago, if someone wanted to buy prescription pills and not deal with a legitimate doctor and pharmacy, they'd buy them from a pill mill or some back-alley drug dealer. Easy access on the internet, however, has changed that. More people are buying this junk on social media sites. I'm told that they often communicate with dealers using emojis, for example, showing an electrical cord plug for wanting to get *plugged in* with some drug. A snowman for cocaine. It's crazy."

"And it's deadly." Wynona sat back in her chair, adjusting one of the floral pillows behind her. "Clint, you said Andy told his girlfriend that he thought he'd bought oxy for the pain in his shoulder. I wonder how much of the pill he took was oxy and how much was other drugs, like fentanyl?"

"The police forensic lab report indicates that half the ingredients were oxy. The rest included morphine, and the deadliest … fentanyl. The lab techs said there were at least two milligrams of fentanyl in each of the pills. Andy ordered a dozen. Eleven were left in the bottle. He only took one pill. Two milligrams of fentanyl, the weight of a mosquito, can kill a person."

Wynona listened closely, her years of criminal investigation experience coming through in the questions she asked and how she asked them. Real empathy. Real concern. "Most police departments, especially one the size of Gainesville PD with more than fifty-thousand students and many permanent residents in the city, have excellent internet forensics departments. What are they telling you?"

"Not much. The police took Andy's computer from his apartment. The lead detective, Winston Porter, tells me they couldn't find a lot. Andy's girlfriend, Brittany, said he told her that he'd bought the pills using an app on Instagram that disappears after a short while. Sort of like the chat history and transaction go through a digital paper shredder."

Wynona nodded. "One of my former colleagues with the FBI told me that social media algorithms work like tossing gas on a fire. These algorithms are very good at suggesting content to users, even to people occasionally active online. This can create an open window for drug dealers to connect with potential customers—or in Andy's case, victims, in a matter of a few clicks of a mouse."

"And it amounts to playing a deadly game of Russian roulette. What's the difference between walking up behind someone, putting a gun to his or her head and pulling the trigger, or shipping lethal drugs that can cause death from one pill?"

"It's often easier to prove intent in a murder by shooting or stabbing than it is when someone dies from a drug overdose. However, in Florida, drug dealers can be charged with murder or manslaughter if their customers die after taking a lethal drug."

Clint looked toward the river. "Evil is part of it. Maybe not in the immediate area … but lurking in the shadows somewhere is the dealer with the black hoodie, grinning, and counting his blood money. These people must be held accountable. Andy didn't die from abusing and overdosing on drugs. He died from taking one pill, never knowing it was fake and that there was fentanyl in it."

I nodded. "Agreed. If the local PD has run out of options in their investigation, maybe somebody with the DEA can help you."

"If the local police make the request, maybe. The DEA is swamped with hundreds of cases across the nation. I'm told the feds are seizing thousands of lethal pills all along the border from California to Texas. The fentanyl problem is now an epidemic. It's like the Black plague, and it's primarily descending on our kids. At least a 100,000 people in this country alone are dying from fentanyl overdoses each year. It's coming across our southern border in record numbers."

"Daddy, Mama … can you push me?" I heard Angela ask, sitting in the motionless swing.

Clint looked across the yard at Angela in the mottled sunlight under the massive oak. "When Andy was her age, we'd walk to the park down the street, and I'd push him on the swing." He turned his head to us. "It seems like it was yesterday. When I look at young kids like Angela, I get the feeling that God hasn't given up on mankind."

Wynona smiled. "Even after what Angela went through, I hope that the power and essence of who she is, the loving home she now has, will rekindle the spirit of the innocent child inside her. And it's my prayer that, as Angela grows up and into a woman, she'll develop the best parts of who she was before those traffickers entered her world. Sean and I don't want her scarred and defined by the hand of evil that briefly rocked her cradle."

Clint nodded. "Amen to that. My son had a normal, loving childhood, and yet, somehow, evil snuffed out his life like a candle. I feel Andy's presence in so many places we used to go, in the things we used to do together. All I have left are memories. My heart aches. When my wife, Lauren, arrived at Andy's door, before she knew he was dead, she touched the doorknob and felt an intense feeling in her gut that something was horribly wrong inside."

Wynona looked at him through her caring, soft brown eyes. "I'm so sorry." She glanced over at me.

I stood, touching Clint on his shoulder. "Duty calls. Let me give Angela a push to provide her with some momentum. You two can get to know each other a little better as I swing into action." I left the porch, heading fifty feet toward the large oak and a little girl sitting alone on the wooden swing that we'd both painted red. Max greeted me as if the party was now getting started.

Angela looked up as I approached, a wide smile on beaming her face. "Daddy, can you push me high, to the leaves on the branches?"

"I'm not sure the swing will reach that far. But I can build you a treehouse, and then you can see the birds up close."

"Yippee! Can I help, like we did when we painted the seat for the swing?"

"Of course. You and Max are my little helpers. Now put both of your hands on the ropes. Hold on tight, and I'll get you going."

"Okay." She clutched the ropes, looking down the sloping back yard, through the orange and tangerine trees, to the river.

I gave her a gentle push. On her return, I pushed a little bit harder.

"Higher, Daddy. I want to fly like Tinkerbell."

"Okay, Tink. Hold tight."

Max turned a half circle before sitting on her haunches, head moving back and forth like she was watching a tennis match. I gave Angela another push. "Okay, you're flying now."

"I feel like a bird, and I don't even have wings."

"You're soaring in the sky like an eagle."

"I can really see the river up here. I wish Max could swing, too."

"She can't hold the ropes with her paws, but she can be your cheerleader as you swing."

"Yep."

"Can you take it from here and keep swinging?"

"Just one more push, okay?"

"Okay." I watched her lean into the pendulum-like movement of the swing, knees bent and then her legs extended, leaning back, giggling.

I stepped a few feet away, parallel to her. She looked over at me, smiling, singing one of the songs that Wynona had taught her, *Old MacDonald had a Farm*.

Two gunshots rang out.

It came from somewhere deep within the Ocala National Forest. I could tell the shots were from a high-powered rifle. Probably a poacher shooting deer or gators. For a moment, the sound of gunfire took me back to Afghanistan, to the time and place when I managed to escape from a compound made from mudbricks, running into the night toward the rugged Tora Bora Mountains. I was followed by a half dozen Taliban warriors. Three days later, that number would be reduced to one man, one final bridge I had to cross.

As I watched Angela, the back-and-forth movement of the swing seemed to go into a slow-motion effect for a few seconds. It was as if I could see the smallest detail, her dark hair barely cascading in the wind, the pink under her fingernails as her hands gripped the ropes, Winnie the Pooh's smiling round face on her yellow tennis shoes. Her laughing sounded far away, as if the wind took it and turned the laughter into a canned whisper. I could hear Clint's voice as if he was standing next to me. *I feel Andy's presence in so many places we used to go, in the things we used to do together. All I have left is memories. My heart aches.*

I blinked my eyes. Everything was restored. My heart beating faster. Angela's swinging was in real time. Her laugher was back. Max's bark returned. There was a third distant gunshot. I could smell wood smoke coming from a southeast breeze. Clint had asked for my help. It was in that moment, watching my little girl fly like Tinkerbell, that I made my decision.

Walking back up to the cabin, thinking about Wynona planning our wedding, the Van Morrison song seemed to follow me. *Mama said there'd be days like this.*

In my case, my mother never said it. I grew up without her. Eventually, I found and got to know her a few years ago, not long before her death. The decision she was forced to make when I was a baby was the most difficult any mother could make. What she told me confirmed the internal compass that had guided me since I was a boy. Although, to no fault of hers, I didn't have the benefit of her wisdom and guidance growing up. But I did share her blood and spirit. Like the invisible wind in the sails of a boat, it pushed and challenged me to cross boundaries—mostly manmade.

I thought about one of the last things she told me before her death: *Sean, just because the horizon is always in front of you, it doesn't mean you stop going forward. It gives you a reason to do it. Don't sit too long, or you'll turn to stone.*

ELEVEN

Hu Cheng looked at the gurgling sludge inside the galvanized tub. "Let us continue. You do not want the fentanyl to be in this state for too long, or you might cook out its strength, turning the dragon into a toothless iguana." He pointed to one man. "You, fill some of the containers."

The man nodded, picking up a ladle, filling and weighing the plastic tins. During his second attempt, he glanced a hundred feet away where the driver in the pickup truck had stopped. Three men got out of the Ford. The man with the ladle spilled some of the mixture over the side of the tray. He looked at Cheng who said, "Be careful! We cannot use the spillage because there may be dust on the table. We do not want our mix to be compromised."

"I'm sorry," the man said in Spanish. "It was an accident." He filled the receptacle a half inch from the top and weighed it before sealing it with the plastic cover.

The three men who left the truck put on new respirators and eye protection as they approached the cooking area. One man, the passenger, was the obvious leader, walking with the swagger money often bought, making quick inquires in Spanish, asking how the cooking sessions were going. He didn't wait for complete answers from his men, getting the gist of what they were saying. He was medium height with a small mouth and protruding ears. Even through the glass of the goggles, his black eyes were cool and detached.

The boss looked over at Hu Cheng and said, "I see some of the fentanyl is spilled on the table. How did that happen?"

"It was a simple accident. It can occur when men are learning to cook."

"That mess, maybe half a cup, would bring five-thousand dollars across the border. Scoop it up and put it back with the rest."

Cheng started to protest but thought differently after spotting a 9mm Ruger wedged under the driver's belt. The man, in his early thirties, wore a Houston Astros ball cap, a diamond stud earring in his right ear, and a tattoo of a fanged, red-eyed wolf on his left forearm. Cheng stood back from the vat. "Welcome gentlemen. The training and cooking processes are going well. I would expect us to fill more than two hundred plastic trays by the end of the day."

The three men who just arrived said nothing. They watched the procedure, the cry of a golden eagle at the ridgeline.

The man with the ladle set it back down. He tried not to make eye contact with the new arrivals. He used a wooden spoon to scoop up the spilled mixture of fentanyl, putting it back in the ladle. After he got most of it up, he looked over at Cheng. "Do you want me to put it back in the big pot?"

Cheng shook his head. "No, we will keep it aside and use it as part of the next mix." Cheng used the boat oar to continue mixing the fentanyl, adjusting the propane flame, turning it down a notch. He didn't look over at the boss and his associates.

The boss was Diego Navarro. He was the oldest son of legendary drug runner Sergio Navarro, the leader of the Durango cartel, one of the top five operating in Mexico. The cartel, which made more than five billion dollars last year in drug sales and human trafficking, was known for its ruthless bloodshed. Their enforcement tactics included beheadings, hangings, and mass shootings—always leaving the bodies where they fell. They fought hard to keep gangs from the Durango territory and its drug distribution routes through Mexico, across the border, and into the United States.

The man who'd spilled some of the fentanyl removed his yellow rubber gloves, the type often used to wash dishes. He stepped back over to the other men, all watching as Cheng continued with his instructions, adding a bit more water to the mix.

Navarro stood twenty feet from the men, the gurgling vat, and the smoke. He surveyed the plastic trays already filled, looked at his watch before glancing at the sun as a cloud moved across it. He leaned over, whispering something into the ear of his lieutenant, a man who had worked with the family for more than ten years. He had proven his value and loyalty often. The man nodded and walked back to the pickup truck, removing something from a toolbox in the truck bed.

The ring of new cooks had their backs turned to them as the men watched and listened to Hu Cheng. Another man began to ladle out the fentanyl and fill the plastic trays. He was assisted by one of the other men, both wearing rubber gloves, goggles, and respirators.

The trusted associate came back to Navarro's side, carrying a machete, its long blade sharp, the sunlight reflecting off the hard blue steel. Navarro whispered something to the two men. They nodded, walking quietly over to the men with their backs turned toward him. Navarro's men grabbed the trainee who had spilled the fentanyl, pulling him from the others, pushing him through wet cow dung toward a gnarled mesquite tree. Navarro came up behind them. In Spanish, he shouted. "You have made a very bad mistake, Juan Garcia."

Garcia, eyes frightened through the goggles, raised his hands. "I am sorry I spilled the fentanyl. It didn't fall to the ground and go to waste. There is very little that is lost."

"I am not talking about the fentanyl. You, Garcia, work for the Americans—the DEA. You are here as a spy. You have infiltrated our family, our brothers." Navarro motioned toward the rest of the men in the background. "You are here to learn, not to divulge information. We have brought in the best chemist in all of China, a man revered for his keen abilities to mix and cook the best fentanyl in the world. You want to let the DEA know what we're doing?"

"No! You're wrong. It is a mistake. I work for you and your family. I am a loyal soldier."

Navarro shook his head. He glanced back at the two men standing on either side of Garcia. "Santiago, tell us: what did you and Roberto see?"

Santiago, a man with a stringy black beard and slits for eyes said, "We saw Garcia sitting at a back table in the Cantina de Pepe. He was sipping cervezas with one man, an American—someone we know is an American agent with the DEA."

"No!" shouted Garcia. "It is a mistake. I was never there. Maybe it was somebody who looks like me."

Navarro shook his head. "In that case, no one will ever look like you again." He nodded to his two henchmen. They grabbed Garcia, throwing him to the ground. He fought hard, but the two men were vicious, overpowering, one landing a strong blow to Garcia's lower jaw, knocking him out. Navarro pointed to a fallen log, a downed mesquite tree.

His men nodded, pulling Garcia next to the log. They lifted him up, allowing his neck to rest on the log. The strongest of the two assassins stood over Garcia, raising the machete high above his head, a crow calling out in the foothills.

The man brought the machete down hard, the sharp blade cutting through muscle, bone, and cartilage, slicing Garcia's head from his body. The executioner reached down, picking up the decapitated head by the hair. He held it in an outstretched arm for the frightened men to see. Blood dripped onto a large cactus plant, hitting the green stem at the base of a single red flower, the trickling of blood appearing as if it came from the flower.

The men standing at the cookfire with Cheng looked on in horror. All of them had been farmers, never frontline enforcers or assassins. One of the youngest, a man in his mid-twenties, placed a hand on his throat. He sprinted fifty feet to a stand of scrub oats, removed his goggles and respirator, and vomited at the base of the trees.

The killer with the machete wiped the blade on the dead man's pants. He carried the severed head, dangling, as the two killers followed Navarro back to where all his men stood staring. They were almost too afraid to take a breath. Navarro used one finger to clear the blood spatter from the glass on his goggles.

"Let this be a warning to all of you. If anyone defects, works with our sworn enemies, or America's DEA, this is what will happen to you. We will cut off your head and leave it at your front door for your family to find when they wake up in the morning. It is not a pleasant thing for them to see before breakfast."

He turned to Cheng. "When these plastic trays are all filled, bring them to the warehouse on Francisco Street. Come through the back alley." Navarro nodded toward the two men who participated in the slaughter, walking back toward the truck, throwing the bloody goggles and respirator in the bushes. Two black vultures soared in spirals high above the men.

TWELVE

I was opening the door to the screened porch when Angela and Max caught up with me. "Daddy, I picked three tangerines. One for you, one for Mama, and one for your friend, Clint. She handed two tangerines to me and pulled a third, smaller one from her pocket.

"Thank you. That's very thoughtful. How about you and Max? Did you pick a tangerine for you two to share?"

"No, we're going back to the trees to pick one more."

"Okay."

"We saw a bumblebee flying around the flowers on one of the orange trees."

"That's a good sign. The bees help plants, trees, and flowers to grow."

She nodded. "Yep. You told me that bees are our friends." She turned, running off, Max at her side.

When I opened the porch door, looking at Clint and Wynona, I knew something had changed. Not so much with Clint but with Wynona. She was nodding as Clint spoke, listening closely, like the many times she did as a former FBI agent when talking with crime victims. Now, she was looking through the prism of good and evil from the perspective of a devoted and protective mother. Although always compassionate to victims and their families, something that made Wynona very good in law enforcement, the fact we also had a child, I thought, built a natural bond—a bridge of empathy to Clint considering his horrific loss.

Wynona smiled as I entered carrying the tangerines. "These gifts are from our daughter. She picked them all by herself, making sure Mom and Dad got a tangerine and that our friend received one, too." I handed each a tangerine.

48

Clint smiled. "This is the best gift I've had all week. When Angela comes back up here, I'll thank her." He set the tangerine on a table beside his wicker chair.

Wynona held her tangerine, glancing at Angela and Max in the small citrus grove. "Sean, Clint and I have been discussing what happened to Andy, the known players, and the available evidence." She took a deep breath, setting the tangerine in her lap. "I can see why the Gainesville PD hasn't found a suspect. Because these drugs are bought and sold by phantoms on the internet and the deadly goods are mailed to customers or sent through UPS or FedEx, the physical contact between victims and perps is, for the most part, nonexistent."

I nodded. "There could be trace evidence, maybe, on the packaging or even the bottles."

Clint cleared his throat. "Unfortunately, the police or their forensic lab couldn't find any. No prints. No DNA. These thugs—drug dealers have got their business model down pat. Every damn thing done online. Untraceable."

I shook my head. "Tracks are left. Even in the digital world. Drug peddlers usually aren't the sharpest knives in the drawer. They will make mistakes. Investigators must think out of the box to find the perps in a virtual world with no boxes, no corners, no straight lines, and no physical angles. Lots of zeros and ones, and that can lead to all corners of the world."

"I wouldn't know where to look. In Delta Force, Sean, we were taught to track the enemy—someone who usually leaves human signs behind. But I do remember times over there when the guys in our squad couldn't find a speck of the enemy. Living on black coffee and freeze-dried food in the field, most of us were ready to give up, pack it in, and wait for them to come out of their caves to do something. You, my friend, didn't wait. You kept looking for signs, tracking, ready to poke the bear in the cave. You were relentless."

"Just like you, Clint, I did what I had to do. Nothing more. Nothing less."

He shook his head, half smiling, looking from me to Wynona. "This man of yours, he's too humble. You probably have no idea what he did in Afghanistan."

"You're right. I don't. The war is something Sean doesn't care to talk about."

"That's understandable." He eyed me. "All that time our forces were there … twenty years. I hate how the soldiers were pulled out of there—left a bad taste in my mouth. Do you ever think about it, the way we left, the sacrifices all of us made over there? The guys who came back home with their legs blown off. Or worse … in flag-draped coffins?"

"I try hard not to think about it. Let's discuss your situation, Clint."

Wynona smiled. "That's what we were doing while you were pushing Angela in the swing. I know we're planning our wedding, but if you decide to help Clint, maybe we can manage to squeeze a wedding date in between whatever your investigation might entail."

Clint lifted one hand. "I don't want to interfere with your wedding plans. Could you do both, Sean, work the case, and set a date to get married?"

"You mean can I multitask?"

Wynona chuckled. "Yes, Clint, he can. On the surface, it appears like most of the probe would center in and around Gainesville. It's not like the large metropolis of Miami or Tampa. Maybe you could find the perp or perps in the Gainesville area, assuming they're meeting and preying on naïve college kids, supplying them with Adderall for pulling all-nighters and Xanax for coming down after cramming for finals."

I said nothing, allowing Wynona to finish her thoughts.

She shrugged. "I know, it's a lot different from the time we were in college." She looked at Angela in the yard, Wynona's face pensive. "What will it be like when our daughter is ready to go off to a university. Maybe she'll take online courses." Wynona eyed me. "If you want to take the case, I'm fine with it. Knowing how you work, I imagine it shouldn't be too long before you have real leads to follow or whether you're just going down a lot of dead-end trails."

I nodded. "That, of course, could be the situation, unless the fallen dominoes lead back to a larger picture, as they did when I agreed to take the child abduction and human trafficking case."

She looked from me to Clint, managing a sincere smile. Because Andy's investigation was on the police department's back burner, Wynona was willing to trade places and put our wedding plans on hold as I peeled back the layers of Andy's case. It could take a few weeks or longer. She didn't know, of course, but she wasn't going to let that cloud her thoughts.

She was altruistic by nature, always looking to find a way to squeeze a better sense of fairness out of life. It made her a great cop, an outstanding mother, and eventually, a marvelous wife. I knew that whatever I may decide to do, take the case or not, Wynona would honor that decision.

I looked at Clint. "I don't want you to have any illusions. There's a good chance that I can't get any further than the police have as they worked Andy's case."

"I understand that."

"As we've discussed, his death is not a direct crime of passion resulting in a murder. Killings, nine times out of ten, involve what we used to call in Miami-Dade PD as the 'four L's.' That boils down to love, lust, loathing, and loot. The rare exception is the work of serial killers. Often their only motive is the sickening thrill of the kill. Most of the time, they don't even know their victims, at least not very well. In Andy's case, from the things you've told us, none of what I just said, except for one, fits in his death."

Clint nodded. "Okay, which one?"

"Loot. Or greed. For the drug dealer, it's all about money—the next score. Deaths, in their slimy world, are collateral damage. For the most part, the internet makes it a faceless crime. The thread to follow, if one can be found, is the communication before the delivery or deliveries. This is the routing of the money, IP addresses, cell phone numbers, and texts. With some of today's sales apps, a lot of that transactional information goes up in digital smoke. I would have to find the genie before he's out of the bottle."

"I understand. I know it won't be a walk in the park."

I smiled, remembering how Clint used that phrase when we were about to enter military combat. "You're right. It won't. I just don't want you to get your hopes up and then be let down if I can't find anything or enough evidence for a DA to take it to trial or a grand jury."

"Sean, all I can ask is that you do the best you can. Knowing you as well as I do, I've never seen you give anything less than your best effort. I'm just appreciative that you and Wynona let me insert a comma—a pause, in your life. You're both putting your plans on hold, taking an off ramp to help me and my wife, Lauren. I'm happy to pay you what you charge for things like this."

I shook my head. "I'm doing this for you and Lauren … and for Andy. In the rare chance that I hit unforeseen expenses, such as some kind of international travel, I'll let you know, and we can settle when the job's done."

"Fair enough. I don't think you'd travel much beyond Gainesville. Maybe the dealers are in Jacksonville, Orlando, Tampa, or Miami. I can't see your investigation taking you out of Florida."

We stood. I shook Clint's hand. Angela came up the wooden steps and tried to press the button on the screen door handle. "Mama, my hands are sticky. Can you open the door?"

"I can do that for you and Max." She opened the door, Angela and Max entering the porch like two swashbuckling pals. There was tangerine juice over part of Angela's face, dress, and hands. Max appeared clean. "Let's head for the bathroom to get you cleaned up."

Angela nodded.

Clint looked at her and said, "Thank you very much for my tangerine. When I eat it, I bet I get sticky fingers, too."

She beamed. "It comes off with soap and water."

"Yes, it does."

Wynona gave Clint a hug before she and Angela left the porch. I walked with him around the side of the cabin to the driveway. He shook my hand. "I can't thank you enough."

"Thank me when the job's done. Text me with all the information you have. This includes the contact information for Andy's girlfriend and contacts for any close friends or enemies he may have had. I'll need a sixty-day printout of Andy's call and text logs and the address of the place he lived. Did the police return his computer and phone?"

"Yes. They downloaded or took whatever they could get from both. Wasn't much."

He nodded, turned, and walked down the driveway, his posture a little straighter than when he first arrived. He was a man walking with a renewed sense of pride and hope. I wanted to keep his hope alive, but I had no illusions that I could do that.

At least not yet.

THIRTEEN

From a distance, there was nothing ominous about the building. Up close it was a different story. A barbed-wire fence surrounded the cinderblock building in the center of a large lot four miles north of Daytona Beach, Florida. The structure was painted a pale shade of gray, with iron burglar bars on the exterior of all the windows and weeds sprouting through the potholes and cracks in the asphalt parking lot. Oil stains, some the size of pizzas, covered much of the area. It was large enough to handle twenty cars. But there were no cars parked here.

Only motorcycles.

All Harleys. Eight were parked in a neat row, polished chrome reflecting the hot midday sun. In the distance was the rumble of more motorcycles, coming closer. Within a half-minute, seven additional cycles stopped at the closed gate. The bikers all wore leather or denim jackets. No one wore a helmet. Each man sported a beard, most as ragged as Spanish moss hanging from their faces. Lots of ink on their arms, hands, and necks; the wink of gold from rings and chains around their necks.

The man in the center of the pack had the road name Hawk. He wore a red pirate's bandana and dark wrap-around sunglasses. Three small tattoos, dark blue teardrops, were just below his left eye. A week's worth of stubble on his face, his goatee streaked with black and white whiskers like long piano keys.

Some of the men revved their engines, waiting for the gate across the entrance to open. Seconds later, the motor behind the fence screeched, the gate slowly opening. Hawk was the first to enter the premises. The rest of the bikers followed him, motors rumbling. They parked and walked toward the front door of the building. The gate closed behind them.

Hawk stood next to his Harley, stretching his long frame, looking past the barbed wire fence at the surrounding neighborhood. It was industrial. Rundown warehouses. Businesses included an auto parts store, a plumbing contractor, a roofing company, and a dive bar—Ralph's. Half a block south was a strip club, Blue Moon.

Hawk wedged a small cigar in one corner of his mouth. He lit it with a tarnished Zippo lighter, puffing the cigar, eyeing a man with the street name Axle. Hawk grunted. "Look's clear. Let's take the candy inside."

Axle grinned, one of his lower teeth missing. Sleepy eyes. Face shaved close to his ruddy skin. A few pitted scars, pockmarks on his cheeks. A diamond stud earring in one ear. "I got the candy in both of my saddlebags. Only reason I have the bags on my bike is to deliver the merchandise here to the club."

Axle put an unlit cigarette behind one ear, took off his sunglass, and opened both saddlebags on his motorcycle. He reached in and lifted out what looked like grocery sacks, brown paper, the bags stapled at the top. "This candy will blow the sweet tooths outta customers up and down the state."

"Let's get it inside. We got orders to fill. Time's wastin' standin' out here in the parking lot."

The men stood in a near semicircle at the front door to the clubhouse. On the back of each jacket, leather, or denim, were patches designed with the club's colors, red and black, sewn into the material. Three patches were on each jacket. The top one was the name of the motorcycle club, *Iron Fist*. In the center was an image of a clenched human fist, large knuckles, a silver-gray metallic look. Below that was their region, Florida.

The gang had chapters and clubhouses in five states, mostly in the South and Texas. The FBI estimated there were about five hundred members. They were territorial, battling rival biker gangs that tried to move into their regions and take business away from them. In Tampa last year, they fought a gang called the Mongrels. When the smoke cleared, three bikers were dead. Two Mongrels and one member of the Fist.

Their only business was crime. Drug and weapons trafficking, extortion, prostitution, money laundering, arson, murder for hire, and human smuggling. From the clubhouse near Daytona Beach, members of the Iron Fist moved millions of dollars in illicit drugs across Florida and north into Georgia and South Carolina.

But it was Florida, with its massive human tidal influx of tourists, domestic and international, that was the most lucrative. From college kids vacationing for a month during spring break to the events that attracted massive crowds, such as the Daytona 500 and Bike Week, to huge seasonal festivals under the tropical sun, people in Florida were in a party mood. Many chose to start the party off with drugs.

Cocaine was still the number one drug of choice. However, opioids, simple and easy to swallow with a sip of beer, wine, or a shot of whiskey, were gaining in popularity. The Iron Fist, along with dozens of other motorcycle gangs across the nation, was happy to accommodate.

Hawk and the rest of the biker gang entered the clubhouse, a Guns N' Roses song, *Welcome to the Jungle*, coming from speakers near the bar to the far left of the room. Most of the men joined the other members of the club. Slapping high-fives, trash talking. Some were sitting at tables, a few in chairs, mostly recliners, nursing beers. Three sat at the bar.

The bartender's face was gaunt, leathery, ashen gray whiskers, snowy hair hanging over his ears. The large room smelled of burnt marijuana, beer, and testosterone. The bartender looked over at Hawk and nodded, popping the top off a bottle of beer, lifting it in his direction before taking a long pull. He signaled for Hawk to approach the bar.

"Looks like Digger's got somethin' on his mind," Axle said.

Hawk nodded. "Let's go see what the ol' man wants." They strolled over to the bar. "What's happening, Digger?"

"Just wanna give you boys a heads up. Tank is in one of those dark moods. Maybe it's on account of his PTSD stuff. Last night, down at the Blue Moon, he was leaving the joint when a dude came around from a pickup truck. He had a baseball bat and threatened to kill Tank for bangin' one of the strippers … the guy's old lady. Welder was the only witness. He said the pissed off husband came at Tank with the bat raised up above his head. Tank snatched it in mid-swing, broke the bat over his knee like a toothpick, and commenced to beat the livin' dog shit outta the dude. Last I heard, the fella is on life support at Halifax Hospital."

"No other witnesses. No sweat."

"Sometimes it ain't that easy. The stripper probably knows it was Tank. Whether or not she points the cops his way is anybody's guess."

"My guess, if she was doin' Tank, she's got some pent-up anger toward her hubby. Probably hopes he doesn't come outta the hospital alive. Gimme a beer. Heineken if you got one back there."

"Sound good." He cut his eyes over to Axle. "Whatcha drinking, Ax?"

"Got any Blue Moon in the cooler?"

"Sure do." He pulled the beers from a stainless-steel refrigerator and popped the tops, setting the cold bottles in front of the men. They both took long pulls, Axle finishing half his beer in a couple of large swallows, his face reddening, shiny. Digger glanced at the paper bags. "Looks like y'all been busy."

Hawk nodded. "Just takin' care of business." The music changed to a Lynyrd Skynyrd song, *Sweet Home Alabama*.

Digger used a paper towel to wipe condensation from the bar. "Tank rode downtown to meet with the club's attorney."

Hawk snorted. "Is Tucker around here?"

"Haven't see him."

"We'll just sit here and drink 'til Tank gets his ass back to the club."

"If the cops come around lookin' for Tank, he's gonna claim self-defense. In the meantime, he left in one bad ass mood. Maybe the new candy y'all brought will cheer him up. Nothin' like the smell of money to take a man's mind off his troubles."

FOURTEEN

It was almost sunset when the text I was expecting arrived on my phone with a soft *ping*. I stood near the end of my dock, looking out over the St. Johns River and watching a snowy egret sail just above the surface. Max was nearby, sniffing along the aged wood. The bird's image reflected off the dark surface, giving the illusion that two egrets were flying at the same time, in unison, like aerial acrobatics. The bird soared across the river, vanishing into the Ocala National Forest.

I read the text from Clint Ward. *Sean, here's the info. Not a lot, unfortunately. I've attached the tox report, phone logs, and contact names and numbers for every person I could remember. Andy had lots of friends. No enemies that I could find. Wish I had more for you to go on, but it's as if he was killed by a stray bullet. His bullet was fentanyl. Somebody fired it, and now my son is gone. – Clint.*

I scanned the contact list, less than a dozen names. It included Andy's girlfriend and what appeared to be people, probably students, within Andy's inner circle at the university. Clint included the name and number of Andy's landlord. There was contact information for the police investigators and the coroner.

I looked up at the fiery western sky. Beyond the wide oxbow, the river seemed to go on forever, meandering and melting into an infinity of colors painted across the horizon. The water's surface reflected brushstrokes of red, crimson, and pink; the sky still a vivid blue in small patches high above the vista. Caught in a pocket of fading sunlight, about fifty feet away, I could see gnats swarming near a weeping willow tree at the river's edge. A great blue heron followed the watery trail.

What was the trail that would lead me to the person who sold Andy the killer pills?

Often, a detective is only as good as the crime trail that he or she must follow. In the initial walk, it doesn't always lead to the killer. But, if I'm lucky, it will meander like the old river before me, to a bigger destination—a target.

Along the path, it's often a process of elimination. Excluding people who, with circumstantial evidence, might appear to be the perpetrator. When it's too easy, often they weren't the killers. He or she sometimes would be in plain sight but never visible as a real prospect. They were people on the fringe—on the fringe of the victim's life. Ex-boyfriends, former husbands or wives, past business partners. The perps were those people who'd been associated with the victim through relationships—emotional, financial. What remained was some glue, usually cracked and brittle, that still managed to connect them.

That probably wasn't the case in the death of Andy Ward.

I stared at the sunset, my thoughts drifting to the time when I was in the Delta Force and serving a tour in Syria. Our unit, on the hunt for ISIS, hired an elderly man who was a legendary tracker. Not an easy job considering the shifting sands of a desert terrain. He was a Bedouin, face weathered and lined from the sun, skin the color and toughness of scuffed cowboy boots. He wore a red-checkered headscarf and full white tunic.

"You must learn how to see things as they should be, not as they are," Kadeem told me as he squatted down in the hot desert sand, looking up at the horizon and the many points in between, from a few feet in front of his sandals to the craggy mountains in the distance. Just above a throaty whisper he said, "When I follow their tracks long enough, I begin to see their faces. Use the sunlight, in shifting sands, to look for slight dimples that twelve hours ago were full footprints."

Even though the desert landscape could quickly change, Kadeem had faint signs to look for in his tracking. Granted, much of his skill was intuitive, a compass in his DNA from centuries of Bedouin desert survival. But, between the sand, the rocks, and the sky, there was something physical for him to put into perspective, a subtle lead to follow.

For me to track down the person or persons who provided Andy with deadly drugs, I'd have to backtrack, to follow tracks that could have been created by multiple people long before Andy opened the bottle of pills. Who sent the package? Who delivered it? Was it a standard shipping company? Was the source the original manufacturer of the drugs or layers of people in between—the middlemen, all taking a cut to get the product from manufacturing to consumption?

If multiple hands were involved, could they all be complicit, or was it only the person or persons who made the lethal drugs and shipped them out into the world where unknowing consumers played a deadly game of Russian roulette with each pill they swallowed? Which bullet would the revolver hammer strike, firing the fatal round into the bloodstream of the person who took it? I watched the sun lowering to the cusp of the distant tree line, the western sky blooming in shades of deep red, soft pinks, and golden light.

***

Some of the neon lights inside the Iron Fist clubhouse were now glowing. Vintage beer signs mostly. Miller. Coors. Blatz. Lone Star. Dixie. As a few more members of the biker gang entered, the conversation level was growing. The main room was a man cave on steroids—a seventy-inch, widescreen TV mounted to a wall; a pool table under a shaded fluorescent light; dart boards; a smaller TV screen for video games; and black leather couches and chairs.

Behind the bar was a velvet painting of a nude blonde woman on a motorcycle. Iron Fist patches from the various chapters across the nation were displayed under glass in a shadow box. Directly below the wall of patches was a closed coffin, wood shiny and polished.

There were two doors on each side of the room, each door led to a half dozen other rooms. Some were used as offices. One was for shipping and receiving. There were two bedrooms. Beyond a gunmetal gray door was a garage area where the members could wash and clean their motorcycles or work on the engines.

"What's happening, Hawk?" asked a man approaching the bar where Hawk and Axle sat. The man was wearing a cut-off denim jacket, black T-shirt, his thick biceps the size of cantaloupes. His road name was Snake. Flat eyes like a reptile, an animal that never blinks. He had no visible eyelashes. He wore a gold hoop earring and had a tat of a rattlesnake on his left forearm.

"Snake, you stayin' out of trouble?" Hawk asked.

"I was born into trouble. When I came outta my mama's womb, I was holdin' up my middle finger on both fists. And, all these years later, I'm in the Iron Fist." He laughed, looking over at Axle, the two paper bags next to him at the corner of the bar. "Looks like y'all been shoppin' for the good stuff."

Axle didn't respond. Hawk said, "Picked it up from one of our distributors, straight outta Texas. Best stuff in the Southeast. This shit is changing a lot of our business model. Right there, by Axle's side, is a cool quarter of a million in merchandise."

Snake's head bobbed left to right like a cobra following the movement of a snake charmer's flute. He looked up at the bartender. "Digger, you mind pourin' me a generous shot of Jack?"

Digger nodded. "Sure."

He poured the drink, setting the glass in front of Snake. Glancing at Hawk, Axle, and the bag of drugs. Digger smiled and said, "So much has changed since I joined the club. In my day, we'd be off-loading bales of pot from a shrimp boat and puttin' the weed into plastic bags for distribution. Nowadays, marijuana is pretty much legal and available anywhere. We moved shitloads of coke and heroin. Now, this new generation gets its kicks from all kinds of pills. When I was a teenager, I'd have to steal a couple of tranquilizers from the bottle in my pop's medicine cabinet. I'd take the pills, lie out in the backyard, and watch the shootin' stars. We lived on a farm, and sometimes I'd wake up to a cow staring me in the face."

"It sure as hell beats a bull that doesn't do mornings well." Hawk said, sipping his beer.

The club door opened, and a man stood at the threshold for a second, as if he was surveying the place. He almost had to duck under the door frame. At six-six, a shaved and shined head, 320 pounds, barrel chest, dark beard, Tank made an impression without saying a word. His real name was Simon Hogan. Some of the club members looked his way, all aware of what went down. The music changed from a Tom Petty Song, *Runnin' Down a Dream,* to music from CCR, *Bad Moon Rising.* Tank entered and headed toward the bar. Hawk drained the last of his beer as he and Axle waited for the club president to arrive.

Tank lumbered up to them, mouth turned down. The neon light on the wall directly behind him crested around his bald head, making the diffused light look like a blood red halo. His voice was gruff and sounded like he'd smoked a dozen cigars and drank a quart of whiskey. "Digger, pour me a double bourbon."

FIFTEEN

Max made one of her playful barks. It was more of a greeting she offered to her friends. I turned around to see Wynona and Angela walking down the backyard holding hands. Soft sunlight, the tint of sliced peaches, poured through the boughs of the live oaks, making it appear like Wynona and Angela were walking into diffused spotlights on a stage of dark green grass.

"Daddy, what are you doing?" They were now on the dock, which comprised of eighty feet of timber and board that stretched from the shore to where Max and I stood at its end. Max ran toward them, tail a blur.

"I'm thinking while watching the sunset. Come see. It's different every night."

Angela grinned, running to meet Max halfway, the two of them turning around and racing down the dock toward me. Wynona smiled and shook her head. "Unbridled enthusiasm. I wish I could bottle it and give it away in my antique store."

I laughed. "Old antiques mixed with the exuberance of youth; what a combo package to offer customers."

We sat on one of the two wooden benches I'd installed at the end of the dock. One faced east, a spot to watch spectacular sunrises over the river, while the other gave us a western view of the river, the oxbow and far beyond, where the St. Johns was swallowed by the mossy green of the forest and the endless vista. It was here where the twilights became magical most nights.

Angela sat between us. I lifted Max to my lap. We were silent for a moment, simply watching the kaleidoscope of nature, the feathery cherry red stratus clouds, the cumulus turning pink and tangerine colors, like masses of coral reefs floating high above the horizon.

"Look at that!" Angela pointed to the silhouette of an alligator crossing the river, the veiled eyes, snout, and its knotty back just visible above the surface. "It's an alligator!"

Wynona said, "He or she is probably crossing the river over to the forest where the alligator can get a good night's sleep."

I chuckled. "Maybe. But since gators are often nocturnal, meaning they like to hunt for food in the dark, that gator might be hunting for its dinner."

"What do they eat, Daddy?"

"Whatever they can catch. Fish, birds, and small animals."

Angela looked down at Max. "They better not try to eat Max."

"As long as she stays up here on the dock and doesn't go down by the river's edge, she'll be fine."

Angela nodded. "I'll watch her."

The gator, probably at least eight feet long, moved its large tail and was soon lost in the dark shadows on the far riverbank. The sun disappeared behind the horizon, its last light backlighting the low-hanging clouds in soft colors. The tall cypress trees along the shore were in silhouette, a breeze teasing the drooping beards of moss, the scent of night blooming jasmine already in the cooling air.

Wynona pointed to a cloud in the distance. "That pink cloud looks like it has ears. Sort of like a giant hot air balloon. Looks a little bit like Dumbo the elephant."

"I see it," Angela said. "Hi, Dumbo."

Max looked up at Angela and cocked her head, doxie ears rising as high as they could go.

Wynona took a deep breath. "I never tire of these sunsets. No two are alike." She looked at Angela. "But now that the sun has gone to bed, it's time for your bath. Your bedtime is coming up soon." Wynona stood, glancing down at me. "I can tell you have something on your mind besides all this beauty. Want to talk about it after you read Angela a bedtime story?"

"Clint sent a text. I was just thinking about it as you two joined me for this spectacular evening show of colors."

"Let's talk on the porch after our little beauty becomes sleeping beauty."

***

In a state that's often hit by hurricanes, another storm was brewing in Florida's Panama City. This one wouldn't blow down buildings or homes. But it would be devasting in terms of the loss of human life. It was spring break along Florida's Gulf Coast. For many years, the beaches stretching west from Apalachicola to Destin were known by the locals as the *Forgotten Coast*. They enjoyed the title. Last thing they wanted was a Miami Beach.

College spring breakers had discovered the area before the major developers did. But now, beachfront property is bringing record prices. Ritzy homes are replacing the bungalows and ranch-style homes that have been fixtures since the 1940s. Panama City Beach, known to college kids as PCB, was ground zero when it came to spring breakers looking for a closer and more affordable destination.

Five young men from the University of Michigan pooled their money and rented an Airbnb house with a partial view of the beach. It was a grand old home, Victorian, two stories, large front porch, and six bedrooms. The place was used as a vacation rental for the last twenty years. The students, all between the ages of eighteen and twenty-one, had the house for five days.

The first day was ending. They had hung out on the beach with hundreds of college kids from across the country. Most from colleges and universities in the Eastern and Midwest sections of the nation. They drank beer on the beach, tossed Frisbees, and rented jet skis and surf boards. And they did their very best to charm the bikini-clad women.

And they met a drug dealer. Online shopping. With all the drinking and smoking weed on the beach, the buy was easy. But, before the first day came to an end at midnight, nothing would be easy or the same again. Ever.

SIXTEEN

Their plans were in place. No one knew just how deadly those plans were. Later that night, the guys were going to hang out with a few of the girls at their beachfront condo. Six young women from the University of Georgia, average age nineteen, rented a three-bedroom condo on the third floor of the building. It had a balcony with a spectacular oceanfront view. The guys were coming with a beer keg, tequila, and margarita mix.

Bruce Cooper would be bringing the drugs.

Of the five students from Michigan, he came from a long line of family money going back to the Gilded Age—the flamboyance of the Gatsby era. Old money from the auto industry and real estate. Cooper, tall, black hair, a face that made women linger on until they managed to look away, could afford the drugs. *Doesn't make much difference*, he thought. *A good deal is a good deal. Cooper men, all entrepreneurs, were known for their talent at striking good deals.*

***

Earlier in the day, a guy on the beach with the drugs in his backpack had arrived via a referral. The referral came from an online source. Someone Cooper knew and whose opinion he valued. Cooper used his phone to place the order through social media—Instagram. The dealer on the beach rode a bicycle with fat tires, staying in the area where the sand was hard and wet from the receding surf.

They'd met near the pier and a jet ski rental stand. Lots of activity. Lots of noise—the sounds of small engines and rock music. The dealer was a little older than most of the students. He wore dark glasses. Shaggy black beard, deep tan, long hair, a gold hoop earring, red bandana, and a tattoo of a tall-masted schooner on his upper arm. Cooper thought the guy looked like a pirate on a bicycle.

The man grinned, nodding in the warm sun. "You said you had a blue tank top and yellow shorts, your college colors. You gotta be my man, Brice."

Cooper smiled. "It's Bruce."

"Sorry, dude."

"You said your name's Charlie, right?"

"Just like Charlie Brown. That was the name my mama wanted to give me 'cause she was nuts for Peanuts. She loved those damn comics. I never got into them, but I sure as hell got Charlie Brown's name for life."

"Is Brown your last name?"

"Of course. Common name for a regular dude." He glanced around the area, hundreds of students hanging out, some openly drinking. No sign of cops. The smell of burning weed and sunblock mixing with the salty sea breeze. He reached in a side pocket of the backpack, pulling out a Ziploc bag. There were ten pills inside. "These are gonna get you laid."

"You think?"

"Hell yeah. Gals love 'em because these pills completely eliminate their inhibitions."

Cooper smiled and glanced around, two girls walking by wearing string bikinis, a banner plane flying three hundred feet over the churning breakers. The plane pulled a sign advertising a buck 'n beer happy hour at a local bar. Cooper chuckled, squinting in the sun. "I haven't seen a whole lot of inhibitions from any of the girls down here. I think spring break has a way to loosen any inhibitions."

"When a gal takes one of these, she'll go all night. Trust me on this one, okay?"

"Okay."

"You got the skeeters?"

"Skeeters?"

"I don't do Square or PayPal out here."

Cooper reached inside his pocket, pulling out a wad of bills. "I'm willing to buy more, but not for the price you quoted me. You said eight at fifty dollars each. I'll do fifteen at forty-five each."

The dealer glanced down at the roll of bills, a seagull snickering in the air above them. "All right. You got yourself a deal. You're getting the best love potion known to man. These blue beauties ought to be called horny pills when it comes to settin' the mood. You and your pals are gonna score all week long, Brice."

"Bruce."

"Right. Gotcha. Lemme refill your prescription, dude."

***

Later that night, Bruce Cooper and four of his best friends from college were partying in the condo that the girls rented. Two beer kegs were set up on the kitchen table next to a gallon of rum, two bottles of tequila, margarita mix, and a large open bag of ice in the sink. A dozen marijuana cigarettes lay in a neat pile on the table. The guys from the University of Michigan partied with the girls from the University of Georgia.

The college girls were all pretty—wide smiles, bright eyes, skin glowing from spending their first day of spring break on the beach. There were two blondes, three brunettes, and one girl with long auburn hair, her face bright pink from too much sun. They'd all showered and slipped into casual clothes—tight jeans or shorts, knit shirts, push-up bras, lots of skin showing.

Music blared from an Alexa speaker in one corner—a vintage song recorded long before any of the college kids were born, Jimi Hendrix singing *All Along the Watch Tower*. During a guitar solo, one of the guys, an eighteen-year-old kid from Detroit, baseball cap worn backwards, Michigan T-shirt, stood on a chair playing an air guitar, hitting the riffs perfectly. His head bobbing, "That's one of my dad's favorite songs. Today's music sucks."

Within an hour, most of the students were drunk or close to it, moving with exaggerated body language, talking, and laughing loudly. Bruce Cooper had his eyes on a shapely blonde who sipped a rum and coke from a red plastic Solo cup. She stood next to the open sliding glass door leading to the outside balcony, curtains on either side of the frame barely moving in the sea breeze. She wore a white shirt, tanned midriff showing.

Cooper walked up to her, smiling. "Hello."

"Hi."

"Sorry, I know hello's kind of overused when you meet someone. How about this … I don't know what's more beautiful, you or the moonlight over the ocean."

67

She looked up at him and smiled. Her eyes were the greenest that Cooper had ever seen, like sunlight through emeralds. "Well, aren't you sweet?"

"Most of the time." He grinned. "I'm Bruce Cooper. What's your name?"

"Shelly Robinson. It's nice to meet you, Bruce Cooper. You sort of favor that actor, Bradley Cooper. Is he your brother?"

"Not that I know of."

"I just loved him opposite Lady Gaga in *A Star is Born*. What a good movie. My mother says the version with Barbara Streisand and Kris Kristofferson was better."

Cooper smiled and sipped his beer. "I sure love the way you talk."

"You mean my Southern drawl?"

"Yeah. It's so cool. I'm hanging onto every word you say because I really like the way you say it."

Shelly batted her eyes. "Are you sincere or are you just makin' fun of the way I talk?"

"I'm serious." He licked his wet lips. "Can I see the view you guys have from up here?"

"Sure, but in case you haven't noticed ... we're not guys." Shelly moistened her full lips.

"That's so true, no mistaking the real deal." They stepped out and into the night on the balcony, a soft breeze from the ocean warm against their faces. Cooper stood next to a wrought iron railing, watching people on the beach. "When I first saw you in the kitchen, I said to myself, self, that girl is the prettiest one here tonight. And now outside in the moonlight, you're even prettier."

"You don't have to compliment me again. You had me at hello." She turned and looked at the sea, the sound of the waves like whispers, the rolling of the breakers were ribbons of white in the moonlight.

"What are you drinking?"

"Rum and coke as in Coca-Cola." She smiled.

"I have something that'll go great with what you're drinking."

"What?"

He reached in his jeans pocket and pulled out the Ziploc bag. These little blue boys are the food of the gods. Take one and you'll be brave and sing karaoke at the top of your lungs."

"That doesn't scare me. I sing in church. My sister thinks I ought to try out for American Idol or The Voice. What's in those pills?"

"Only the best ingredients. Just a little muscle relaxer. It's a great high."

"Are you gonna take one?"

"Oh, hell yeah." He opened the bag, popped a pill into his mouth, chasing it down with a long swallow of beer from his Solo cup. Cooper opened the bag, extending it in front of Shelly, smiling, moonlight trapped in his blue eyes.

Shelly reached in the bag, took out a pill, held it between her manicured fingernails before placing it on her tongue, slowly, sipping her drink, swallowing it. Cooper watched her, wondering how long the pill would take to affect her. He said, "Let's seal it with a kiss." He leaned in, kissing her. It would be the last kiss for both.

SEVENTEEN

After the kiss, Shelly inhaled a deep breath, taking the salty air into her lungs. "If these magic pills are so special, we ought to share them with our friends. C'mon." They walked back inside the condo, a John Mellencamp song, *Pink Houses,* coming from the speaker. Shelly stood on a leather ottoman. "Listen up, y'all." Everyone in the beach-themed living room looked her way. "My friend, Bradley Cooper … sorry, Bruce Cooper, brought us some magic pills. I just took one and so did he. From what I can see in that lil' plastic baggie of his, there are more than enough to go around."

"What's in the pills?" asked one of the girls.

Cooper said, "Sort of a mild muscle relaxer. You can take it with booze and nothing bad happens. What does happen is the magic. A mild high. You don't hallucinate, but you'll lose any sort of inhibitions—you know, the stuff our parents put on us. C'mon! How often in our lives do we experience spring break? Let's really soak it in so that fifty years from now we'll relive it in our rockin' chairs."

"Gimme one, Coop," said a sunburned guy.

Cooper opened the bag and walked around the room. All the students except the girl with auburn hair, took a pill from the bag. She would be the only one physically able to call for emergency medical help.

***

Thirty minutes later, two of the girls were having seizures. "Help!" shouted one. "I can't breathe!" The other girl laid in the fetal position on the couch, clutching her chest, crying, and calling for her mother. "Mama … please hold me … Mama." Some of the guys were vomiting in the toilets and planters, whatever they could crawl to before their hearts stopped beating.

Shelly and Bruce Cooper were in the bedroom, clothes off, when the fentanyl hit their bloodstreams, skin cold and clammy, lips turning blue. Neither one had the strength to stand. "What's happening to me?" Shelly whispered, coughing. "What's in those pills?"

Cooper was too weak to answer. He lay sprawled on the bed, staring into her green eyes. He thought they were the most beautiful eyes he'd ever seen. That was his final thought as his heart stopped, his last breath spilling from destroyed lungs, blood at the corner of his mouth.

***

"911 … what's your emergency?"

The girl with auburn hair barely could hold the phone to her ear, hands shaking, tears rolling down her freckled face. "Help! People are sick! I'm afraid they're gonna die. Please send ambulances. It's horrible!"

"Ma'am. How many people?"

"I don't know! Maybe a dozen! All college students."

"What's the address?"

"It's the Catalina Condos on Driftwood Street. Third floor. Condo 1632."

***

Within a few minutes, five ambulances, two fire trucks, and four police cars arrived at the Catalina Condominiums. The paramedics, fire department medics, and police officers ran toward the building. Some used the elevators to go to the third floor. Others ran up the stairway, taking two steps at a time, quickly finding unit 1632. The door was unlocked. They entered and, what the fire chief later would tell news media, walked into the worst spring break disaster he'd seen in his twenty-three-year career.

The girl with the auburn hair was in the kitchen. She was in a corner, hugging her upper arms, tears flowing, the body of one of the young men on the floor. He died lying on his back, eyes locked on the slow-turning ceiling fan above him. A female police officer went up to the girl. "What happened?"

One paramedic squatted down next to the body. He shook his head. "No pulse."

"Let's try to resuscitate," said another paramedic.

One of the first officers to enter, a veteran with a dozen years on the force, stood near the door leading from the kitchen into the rest of the condo. He said, "If you're going to resuscitate, you have a lot of people to work on in here. They're scattered all over the rooms."

The girl in the kitchen corner could barely speak, her body trembling. She looked at the female officer standing in front of her. "They took pills. Half an hour later, people were throwing up, most having trouble breathing. I think all my friends are dead. Some are unconscious, barely breathing." She sobbed, the officer's eyes misting as she reached out, holding the girl like she was her own daughter.

EIGHTEEN

Angela fell asleep before I could finish reading a story to her. I set the book, *Sleeping Beauty*, on a bedside nightstand. I tucked the soft blanket around her small body before turning out the light, leaving her door open. Max followed me from Angela's bedroom, through the cabin, to the back porch.

Wynona and I settled on the porch as heat lightning rumbled in the distance over the national forest. We sat in the wicker chairs, Max between us, dark clouds smothering the starlight, a chorus of frogs yodeling at the river's edge. The night air carried the scent of orange blossoms. In the soft light from the kitchen window, I looked up at the middle rafter where I'd set the Sig. It was hidden behind the oak timber.

Wynona glanced over at me, a glass of red wine in one hand. "What's on your mind?"

"If possible, I want to help Clint. But based on what he's shared with me, the information from his text, the death of his son isn't a typical crime in the sense of a homicide. Clint texted that Andy's death was akin to him being hit by a stray bullet. He may be right. Andy was certainly a victim, his death no accident in the traditional sense. It's as if he was an indirect target caught in the crossroads of some gang banger's fight. If not, Andy may have been deliberately chosen to die by the perp or perps. But who would do that to a college kid—someone well-liked, had no known enemies, and was about to head out from Gainesville to a new life?"

"All you can do is the best you can do. Clint isn't asking for anything more. Andy was by no means an anomaly. Unfortunately, many young people are dying in record numbers from fentanyl overdoses. I can only imagine the kind of investigative challenges this epidemic is causing within the FBI and the DEA."

"And yet, the people and drugs flow across the southern border with near impunity."

The rumble of thunder was coming closer, the air cooler, a whiff of rain in the distance. I stirred my drink, vodka over ice.

Wynona sipped her wine, watching the pulse of lightning a few miles over the national forest. She looked back at me. "In Andy's case, maybe there will be evidence no one has found yet that will give you a path to follow. My Seminole grandfather used to say that, after we're gone, we'll be remembered by the tracks we leave behind … good or bad."

"I'm not sure those responsible for Andy's death left visible tracks."

"No doubt that you'll be searching for near invisible footsteps. But I know you, Sean, you'll find a way or make one. That's the only part of what you do that frightens me."

"What do you mean?"

"You won't quit when it appears that the investigation has ended. Sometimes, trails simply come to a dead end."

I said nothing. The breeze stopped. A great horned owl called out from across the river. I sipped the drink.

Wynona reached over to me. "Just give it your best. Clint will appreciate that."

"Earlier today, down on the dock, before you and Angela joined me, I was thinking back about one of my tours of duty in Syria. Our Delta Force unit hired a scout, a tracker, as we were hunting for members of ISIS in the desert sand and mountains. The old man was a Bedouin with fifty years of tracking experience. That, combined with the generations of nomadic life in his DNA, gave him an extraordinary skill level to see and distinguish the subtle signs of the desert. I learned a lot from spending time with him, including the right way to ride a camel."

"Did you find ISIS?"

"Yes." I didn't elaborate.

"Good."

"One of the things the old man said to me about tracking was this: *truth will walk through the world unharmed.* He was right. It doesn't make it any less challenging to find it, but when you do, it will be absolute."

Wynona was quiet for a moment. "When you're done, we'll set a wedding date and stick to it." She squeezed my hand. "I can't wait to see

Angela dressed as a flower girl. If Nick Cronus attends in something other than a T-shirt, shorts, and flip-flops, I'm not sure that I'd recognize him." Wynona smiled and sipped her wine.

The floodlights at one corner of the porch came on, tripped by the motion detector. The lights illuminated a large swath of the backyard. I stood, watching a racoon waddle through the grass. "It's a racoon. A well-fed one at that." I sat back down, sipped my drink, the floodlights continuing to burn into the night, moths orbiting the light.

Wynona watched them for a moment, intrigued. "I look at those moths and think about the expression: *like a moth to a flame.* They are attracted to a flame even though the heat can kill them."

"I'm betting they'll survive the floodlight."

"Think about it, Sean, what's the difference between these two: a moth attracted to light and a human addicted to the light from the screen of his or her phone or computer? Many people spend more time in a virtual world rather than a real one. It's a form of addiction. Andy Ward would probably be alive right now had he not trusted that virtual world with his life. And, like the moth that comes too close to the flame, he suffered the worst fate."

Thunder clapped causing Max to raise her head. Simultaneously, the timer on the floodlights went out. Beyond the periphery of the porch, it was pure black. The solid blackness came like an instant veil over the eyes but carried with it a sense of the way pure things are—a mystery of the universe felt in the core of your soul. It gave the moths freedom to flutter through the night like unseen whispers flickering in the dark.

Rain began to fall, creating a plopping sound on the tin roof. In seconds, it was a steady drone. I picked Max up and placed her in my lap while holding Wynona's hand.

Tomorrow, in the wash of morning light, I would begin my investigation into the death of Andy Ward. I thought about the old Bedouin's comment, how truth walks through the world unharmed. Maybe so. But it doesn't make it any easier to find that truth. Sometimes it's elusive, just like evil standing in the shadows near you. Often, you don't see it until it wants to be seen.

NINETEEN

Tony Salazar had to travel through a dark place to speak with the loves of his life. He glanced at his watch, calibrating the time zone differences between where he was in Mexico and his family back home in California. He was in his rental house, the sound of someone on a moped buzzing by outside. He made the calls to his family by going through the DEA's portal on the dark web. It wasn't the easiest way to call home, but it was the most secure.

Salazar sat at his computer in the small kitchen, the refrigerator humming, his curtains drawn. He made the video call, a half minute later the image on the screen was that of his wife, Nicole. She was blonde with eyes so blue they popped with color through the computer screen. She smiled, "Hello, handsome hubby. How about that for a poor attempt at alliteration?"

"It's excellent. But that's coming from a guy who had to go to night school to learn English. You teach English grammar to high school kids."

"And, all these years later, your English is so good you can pass for someone who grew up in America's Midwest."

Salazar smiled. "Now that I'm back in Mexico, I might gain the accent again."

"How's it going? Are you getting the reinforcements you need?"

"No, at least not yet. The future doesn't look too bright. Some of our operations are pretty much at a standstill. We're more than willing to share intel with our Mexican counterparts, but it's not a two-way street today. They're getting hesitant to engage with us because they fear consequences from their own government if they are caught working with the DEA. In the meantime, the leaders of the cartels strut around with near impunity."

"It's as if you're trying to do a dangerous job with one hand tied behind your back. It sounds like our president needs to have a serious talk with Mexico's president. If there's very little in the commitment from the Mexican government to do their part to fight the illegal drug trade, why is the DEA even down there? I just wish you'd come home and fight the bad guys on this side of the border."

"I know, but if we could bust them—really stop them here, there would be much less of a drug problem on the American side of the border. That's what keeps me going, believing we can make a difference."

"The kids are done with their dinner and ready to talk with you." Nicole leaned forward, kissed two fingers, and placed them close to the camera lens. "Here's my virtual kiss. I love you."

"Love you, too."

She got up from her chair, and seconds later, a teenage boy and an eight-year-old girl were on screen. "Hi Daddy," said the girl.

"How's it going down there?" asked the boy. "Are you busting the bad guys?"

Salazar smiled. "I'm trying. I miss you two. How's school?"

"I love it!" said his daughter, Eva.

"School pretty much sucks. Books are boring," said his son, Lucas.

"Do you really think that books are boring?"

"A lot of them."

"A book is nothing but an object until it is opened and read. School is only dull until you open your mind and allow it to learn, to become curious. Otherwise, you will never know what you don't know. Teachers can open the classroom door, but you must walk inside. Lucas, it's not about learning a lot of facts. It's about learning how to think. Does that make sense to you?"

"Yes, I guess so."

Eva leaned closer to the screen. "When are you coming home, Daddy?"

"In a few weeks. I'll be home for about a month before coming back down here."

"I miss you soooo much." She grinned, a tooth missing at the top and one at the bottom.

"I miss you both even more."

Salazar's phone buzzed on the kitchen table. He glanced at the screen, recognizing the caller ID. He looked back up at his children. "Hey guys, I need to take a call. Help Mom with the dishes, okay?"

They both nodded.

"Talk to you soon. Love you."

"Love you."

He clicked off, picking up his phone and answering. "Hey, Manuel, didn't expect to hear from you so soon. What's up?"

The man spoke English with a heavy Hispanic accent. "Tony, I wish I did not have to be the one who delivers bad news to you—"

"What is it?"

"It's Juan Garcia. He's dead. I am so sorry. I know he was more than an asset to you. He was your close friend."

Salazar said nothing, looking at the blank computer screen, his thoughts racing. After a few seconds, he took a deep breath. "How did it happen? Who did it?"

"Diego Navarro ordered it. My contact told me that Navarro and his men came to a cattle ranch he owns, one of the places where they cook the fentanyl. Navarro showed up with two of his henchmen. They beat Juan. When he was knocked unconscious, they put his neck over a log and used a machete to cut off his head. Before they killed him, Navarro told Juan that he was seen speaking with a DEA agent. That could only be you. Tony, you need to relocate—maybe Mexico City or somewhere. And do it fast. They may know where you live. Get out of there."

"I have to make some calls. Thanks, Manuel." Salazar clicked off, walking to the front window, using one finger to slightly move the drapes over the iron-barred window. A car sped down the street, followed by a dilapidated pickup truck. Salazar looked up beyond the Mexican fan palm trees, to the inky sky, a cloud parting over a moon with a crooked smile.

***

I stood at the kitchen sink, looking at the moon through the boughs of the cypress trees. Max was near my feet, making a short whimper. It was more of a command. She had very little patience when it comes to two things: food and her outdoor bathroom needs. She trotted a few feet away across the wooden floor, stopping to look back at me. Her expression was this: *will you hurry up?*

Wynona came down the hall from Angela's bedroom. She looked at Max and over at me near the sink. "Your dog calls. It's that little bladder talking."

I smiled. "Why is she my dog when it comes to taking her outside?"

"I don't handle mosquito bites as well as you do."

"Oh, of course. It could be a mosquito-free night. Winds are from the southwest, blowing across the national forest. I looked down at Max, who snorted, walking to the screened porch. We went outside, heading down toward the dock.

Max stopped to pee and then stopped every ten feet to sniff something in the damp grass. The night carried the scent of orange blossoms and wet oak bark. She looked over at me and then stared up into the sky, stars intense, a meteor blazing a trail through the dark.

As we walked to the end of the dock, listening to crickets and frogs sing, I heard a splash near the weeping willow tree at the edge of the riverbank. The big gator was in silhouette as it swam near the surface of the dark water, reflecting starlight and the crescent moon. I thought about how the light and dark complement each other. But it's the light that we yearn for because it speaks in a comforting silence. Without it, what is our world? From moths to humans, we are drawn to it.

I looked up at the cosmos, the clear night sky teeming with raw energy. It is always the purest art in its most beautiful form. Primitive and complex. It touches all the senses in a visceral way, hanging above us, whispering in a way that is felt, not heard. It was as if there was a subtle vibration in the stillness beyond the veil of the heavens. During times like this, the universe on fire, I felt as if I could hear a distant throb, a calling from somewhere deep within the cosmos—a song for the eyes.

But it was the dark where I had to journey to find Andy Ward's killer. I picked up Max and looked at the pulsating light of the Milky Way. I stared at Sirius, brightest star in the galaxy, and thought about what Wynona said when the moths were circling our floodlights. *They are attracted to a flame even though the heat can kill them.*

TWENTY

The device looked like a narrow slot machine found in casinos. But it wasn't in a casino. It was on a long table in a backroom of the Iron Fist motorcycle club. The machine was a pill counter. Large pharmacies, those filling hundreds of orders per day, sometimes used them. The device could count twenty pills in a second at one hundred percent accuracy.

Hawk and Axle stood near the table with the machines on it. At the top, the counter had a metal container curved like a small shovel. Pills were placed in there. Midway down was a digital screen that displayed the number and total weight of the product. The counter was plugged into an electrical outlet, two red lights, like eyes, blinking at the base.

At the back of the room was a high-tech workspace with state-of-the-art computers and two widescreen monitors. A man with a military haircut and a diamond stud earring sat in profile reading something on the screens. The bikers called him Trucker. Seconds later, he tapped the keyboard, grinning. He had a curved nose—an eagle's beak, and four days' worth of whiskers shadowing his face. The name on his driver's license was Gary Beck.

Trucker was a former IT manager who worked for a major trucking company. When he got bored in front of computer screens, he moved to a job behind the wheel as a long-haul truck driver. Within two months, he was recruited by the Iron Fist to transport drugs to dealers waiting in the dark backlots of selected truck stops. After he was arrested, convicted, and served three years of a seven-year sentence, he began working full time for the biker gang in online sales and distribution of illegal drugs.

Across from Trucker was a closed door that opened to a small workstation, a lab where the quality of counterfeit drugs was tested. They also were stored there, which was why the door always was locked. Only two people had keys. Tank and a man who used to work as a pharmacist before joining the Iron Fist. His real name was Kevin Webster, with the biker alias Doc.

A man, who the club members called Popeye, was standing behind the table, both paper bags on top of it. The only thing average about Popeye was his height. He wore a cut-off denim jacket. Tats covering both arms. A tattoo on one of his upper arms was not an image or a word. It was a symbol: 1%. Between the knuckles on his right hand was the word *VITA* tattooed on his four fingers, one letter on each. The tat on left hand spelled out *MORS*. In Latin, vita means life. Mors is death.

His right eye was askew—cockeyed, forever stuck in a locked position to the left, the result from a fight around a pool table. His attacker, a man now dead, had swung a cue stick across Popeye's face. That was two years ago. Today, behind him, music came from speakers mounted on one wall, Chris Stapleton singing *The Devil Always Made Me Think Twice.*

On the other side of the office, Tank sat behind a wooden desk with a glass top. Two lines of cocaine, both three inches long, were in front of him. He stuck a rolled dollar bill in one nostril, pressing a finger—black dirt under the nail, against the opposite nostril. He leaned over to the desktop, snorting a line of coke into his nasal cavity. He blinked twice, sticking the bill in the other nostril, repeating. He sat back in his chair, closing his eyes for a few seconds, fingers tapping the table to the beat of the music, shaved head pink and shiny under the ceiling lights.

Tank grunted, looking over at his men. "Let's get this show on the road, boys. We got orders to fill."

Popeye grinned, his lips red and wet. Smoke from a half-smoked cigar curled from a seashell serving as an ashtray. He reached over and took a puff off the stogie. "All right, fellas. Somebody wanna get Doc's skinny ass back here to give us a read on the samples?"

Tank cut his eyes over to Axle. "Go find Doc. Did he bring his old lady to the club? What's her name? Lucy or Legs? Somethin' like that."

Axle shrugged. "I saw 'em with a big bucket of fried chicken she'd brought over. Her name's Lashes. She got those long eyelashes with 'em big ol' brown doe eyes." He rotated his left shoulder, popping knuckles against the palm of one hand. "I'll go see where Doc's hangin'. He could be doin' his old lady in one of the backrooms."

Tank shook his glossy head. "He's supposed to be doin' his job back here, giving us the word on the pills. If it's not what it's supposed to be, we got a problem. And, more than that, our supplier will have a bigger problem."

Hawk shook his head. "We haven't been cheated yet. Their product has always been top notch."

Tank pulled out a pocketknife, opening it, using the tip of one blade to scrape dirt from underneath his fingernails. He was a Gulf War veteran who had wrestled professionally for two years following his discharge from the Army. After serving five months in jail for aggravated assault, he joined the Iron Fist, taking five years to work his way up to chapter president. But he had no plans to stop at the local or regional level. He was determined to serve as president over the entire Iron Fist biker gang. Whatever it took, he'd exceed expectations. He did it in the war. In his view, he was still fighting a war. Always would be.

Axle returned with Doc following him.

"Where the hell you been?" barked Tank.

Doc cleared his throat. "Sorry, man. Didn't know y'all were back here and ready for me." Doc was in his mid-thirties. Stringy blonde beard. Mouth turned down at the corners. Dark circles under droopy eyes. "I can get started right now and give y'all a readout in just a few minutes."

Using one of his wide hands, Tank wiped the fingernail dirt off the top of his desk. "Let's do a count first. We can randomly pull a pill from each batch. You test it for the quality Iron Fist is known for, and Trucker can start filling orders. "We need to hit goals that'll take us higher than other chapters across the country. That means our supply chain can't have a weak link in any part of the operation."

Hawk nodded. "Amen. Hey, Tank, if we produce more sales than the other clubs, do you think the Dallas chapter will give us an all-expenses-paid vacation to the islands?"

"You'll have more money in your pocket to take your own damn vacation." He looked across at Popeye. "Start the count. We got spring breakers arriving and orders to fill. First rule of business, make sure you got the inventory. Don't want to lose customers to the competition."

Hawk nodded. "How 'bout the customers who might OD?"

"They ought to follow instructions. If not, they're collateral damage. Speaking of dying, I want you to take Razor and ride over to a trailer park. The dude who tried to crack a Louisville slugger against my skull, he may or may not come out of his coma. He shares a trailer with a stripper. Name's Tracey Hall. She loves meth. I banged her a couple times. As a dancer, she goes by Mona. Her trailer is at 1719 Seahorse Lane. She drives a white Toyota. Don't know if her boyfriend's truck is gonna be there. It's a black Ford 150."

Hawk ran his tongue inside his left cheek. "What you want us to do with her?"

"Scare the livin' shit outta her. Tell her if she mentions my name to the cops, we'll let Razor use his razor, and he'll start removing her body parts. They'll find what's left of Tracey scattered on her linoleum kitchen floor."

Hawk nodded. "We can do that.

He looked at Popeye. "Let's count this candy."

TWENTY-ONE

He resembled a bird of prey looking for a rabbit. Popeye angled his head, stationary eye locked in the direction of Tank who was sitting behind his desk. Popeye snorted, his good eye focused on Axle, Hawk, and Doc. "I know we don't have many rules here at the clubhouse, but back in this area, with new product coming in all the time, we need to take extra precautions. As much as we hate masks, we gotta do it. Fentanyl, depending on how it's cooked, cut, and mixed, can be like radiation pellets if not done right. Great product with a real bad side. Nasty stuff."

He reached in a drawer behind the table, pulling out six high-end surgical masks, giving one to every man in the room. "Trucker, come get yours. I'm not walkin' my ass back there."

Trucker got up from behind the computers, catching a mask that Popeye tossed to him. He walked twenty feet back to his work area, settling in front of the computers, hands on the keyboard. The glow of the screens reflected off his gold hoop earring; his red bandana pulled low on his forehead; his eyes transfixed, like a buccaneer staring at a blue moonrise across the sea.

Popeye put on a pair of latex gloves, opened the two paper bags, and weighed each bag on a separate scale that was so sensitive and accurate it could weigh pills down to one-hundredth of a gram. The plastic bags, filled with light blue pills, were about the size of bags that would cover a large loaf of bread.

Popeye was silent, turning the machine on, carefully pouring a third of the content from the first plastic bag into the scoop container at the top. The machine hummed and rattled as the drugs poured through its internal structure. Seconds later, the drugs came out a chute, spilling into another rounded tray, the metal holder larger than the one at the top.

84

He repeated the procedure four times, until the last few pills rolled out of the chute, plopping into the container.

Tank watched, shifting his eyes over to Hawk and Axle, both men standing a few feet from the table, a Cody Jinks song, *Loud and Heavy*, coming from the speakers. When Popeye finished the counting, he looked at the reading on the digital screen, writing something on a yellow legal pad. He raised his eyes to Tank. "It comes to three-thousand pills even."

"Count the other one."

Popeye grunted and repeated the inventory with the second bag. After a few minutes, he said, "This one comes out less. To be exact, there are two thousand, nine hundred and eighty. So, it looks like a shortage of twenty pills."

Tank leaned forward in his chair. "You sure?"

"Yep. Never seen the machine make a mistake. I can count 'em again."

"No. At fifty bucks a pill on the street, that's a grand we're gonna lose."

Hawk scratched his beard. "You think our suppliers shorted us?"

"Maybe. I'll make a call while Doc does his thing." He eyed Doc. "Test 'em."

"Okay." He put on a pair of latex gloves, picked up one pill from each plastic bin, and headed to the back of the room for the door that opened to the makeshift lab.

Tank cut his eyes to Axle and Hawk. "Axle, you go on back with him. We need you to intern with Doc, learn how he does his thing. If Doc's sick and can't come to the clubhouse, we need a backup man to do the quality control testing."

The office door opened, and another biker entered. He was almost as large as Tank. The man had a handlebar moustache and steroid biceps and wore his gray hair pulled back in a ponytail. "Tank, can I have a word with you? Alone."

***

Doc used his key to open a deadlock, Axle standing next to him. The room was long and narrow, lit by florescent bulbs in a fixture near the ceiling. Against one wall was a metal table. It was filled with glass jars and beakers, two scales, hot plates, a butane burner, rubber hoses, microscope, a bottle of acetone, and sulfuric acid. A sink was to the left of the table. The room had the acrid smell of ammonia, lye, and urine, like the odor of a cat litter box. Shelves held plastic bags full of drugs.

Doc flipped a switch and a large window fan started turning, sucking the stale air outside. He picked up two separate glass containers. "All right, here are some basics for testing the fentanyl and the amount that may or may not be in the pills. We want a little bit, but we don't want pills so damn toxic they'll kill our customers."

"No shit." Axle grinned.

Doc turned on a light connected to a gooseneck lamp. He picked up each pill separately, using a magnifying glass to examine them. He grunted. "I'm blown away at how real these fakes look. Even with my years of experience as a pharmacist in my previous life, I couldn't spot this as anything but the real thing. The pill presses they're using down in ol' Mexico are impressive. Good as Big Pharma companies like Pfizer or Merck."

"Yeah, they do look like legit oxy pills, the big *M* on one side and the number *30* on the other."

"We put each pill into a small plastic bag, use a hammer to give them a few wallops." He did that, taking a hammer from a hook on the wall. "Gotta make sure we have good granulation, like sugar. Then we pour the powder into each glass container."

"All right." Axle crossed his arms.

"We put two shots of water into each glass, add a half ounce of pure rubbing alcohol to the mix, and then add three drops of acetone." He lowered a test strip into the first container before doing the same with the other. "This will tell us if there is the presence of fentanyl. The spectrometer will measure how much is in each pill."

Axle looked at the test strip closest to him. "I see a red line."

"And there's one in the other glass, too. Means fentanyl." He used an eyedropper to remove some of the liquid from one jar, placing it into the spectrometer. "This will tell us how much." Doc ran the test for both samples. "There are two milligrams of fentanyl in each pill. It's only a small portion of the whole oxy pill, but it's enough to keep our clients coming back."

TWENTY-TWO

When Axle and Doc approached Tank, Axle sensed that something had changed for the worse while he was in the lab with Doc. Three bikers stood near the door like they were guarding it. No one to enter and no one to leave. Thick arms folded. Frowns.

Tank took a deep breath and scratched a fresh scab on his forearm. He looked at the largest man in the room. "Search him for a wire."

"What?" Axle raised his palms in disbelief. "What the hell you talkin' about?"

"Arms straight out," ordered the man. He ripped Axle's shirt open, looking for a wire, padded him down from shoulders to his boots. He lifted a phone from Axle's back pocket, looked at it before setting the phone on Tank's desk. "It's not recording unless they do it remotely?"

"Who the hell is *they*?" Axle asked, his face flustered.

Tank snorted. "Why don't you tell us, Axle? You were seen coming out of a coffee shop with a known FBI agent from the Orlando office."

"That's bullshit! I'm not a snitch and never will be. Who's sayin' this shit about me?"

Tank lifted a plastic bag off the desk. It was a Ziploc, the kind of bag used to keep sandwiches fresh. He held it in the air. There were light blue pills inside it. "Axle, guess where these came from."

"I got no idea."

"They came from one of the bags. It's the missing inventory. I called Texas and had 'em check their records. Supposed to have been two shipments with three thousand pills in each bag. The mistake is not on their part. So, after I hung up, I asked Razor to check your bike. He found a fake bottom in one saddle bag. Under it was this bag of pills. Twenty. We're missing twenty. A thousand bucks in this little baggie. Is this the evidence you were gonna take to the FBI?"

"Whoa! Tank, I'm being set up. I had no idea the shit was in there." He looked over at Hawk who was poker-faced.

"That's bullshit! I'm loyal." A nerve began twitching under his left eye.

Tank looked at his men and said, "Y'all hold Axle while I teach him a lesson."

Axle shook his head. "No! You got this wrong. It's a set up!"

"Sure, it is." Tank nodded at his men. Within seconds, the three of them held Axle, keeping his arms and legs from moving. Axle fought hard to get out of their grasp, but it was too much muscle. Tank stepped up to him, opening his pocketknife. "Doc, hold his head."

Doc placed both of his hands on either side of Axle's head, holding tightly. Tank looked at Axle's cheek like he was deciding how to carve into a steak. He glanced over at Razor who was holding back Axle's left arm. "Razor, my knife ought to be sharp enough, but if it's not, are you carrying your straight razor today."

"Never leave home without it. Got two of 'em in my pockets. One's a backup."

Tank took a deep breath, his jawline hard, nostrils flaring. He used the knife, carving a wide X into Axle's cheek, making quick, deliberate strokes that went from the cheekbone to lower jawbone.

Axle's head shook, his eyes burning, disbelieving, blood trickling out of the cut dripping off his chin onto his chest. Tank wiped his knife across Axle's shirt, spitting in his face. Popeye tilted his head, his locked eye looking at the blood, like a praying mantis studying the striking distance to an insect.

Tank grinned. "Axle, you're a branded man. Now and forever more. That X will scar up good, which means bad for you. It'll let everybody know that you're a snitch and a loser. X marks the spot for a Judas. No club will take you in … ever. Maybe you can join the FBI in their freak division. But you gotta survive your midnight swim."

Axle said nothing, his breathing fast, more blood pouring out, red drops the size of quarters on the floor. Tank looked at the men. "Carry Axle out to the Tomoka swamps. Teach him to swim. Maybe a gator will stuff him in a hole."

They manhandled Axle across the room toward the exit door. "Tank, you're the big man with your soldiers all around you. I'll find you when you're all alone. Payback will be hell!"

"Get that piece of shit away from me and this clubhouse." From the speakers came a song from the Rolling Stones, *Gimme Shelter*.

They jostled Axle out, leaving a trail of blood across the laminate wood floor.

TWENTY-THREE

I stepped onto the red oak floor inside our cabin. The hardwood was cool on my bare feet. I didn't want to wake Wynona as I got up from our bed. It had been a restless night of drifting in and out of sleep, and my T-shirt was damp from night sweats. This happened when my subconscious mind replayed experiences that I'd tried hard to bury.

The episodes, many from the war, were buried. But that didn't mean their ghosts would stay in graves with worn headstones. Sometimes the nightmares were so vivid, even in my sleep, that I thought I could detect the metallic scent of the battlefield in the drifting smoke and coppery smell of fresh blood. The screams. The horror. No balm could soothe the ugliness of war, and those egocentrics who label war a necessary evil have never spent time in combat.

My internal clock told me it was near 3:30 a.m. I'd walk into the kitchen to see if it was accurate. I stood in our bedroom a moment, watching the soft moonlight coming through the window. As I started to leave, Max raised her head like a curious but sleepy prairie dog, eyes half-closed. She was in the center of the bed, her little head rising from a fold in the blanket. I stepped over and touched her, whispering, "Go back to sleep." She laid her head down and watched me leave.

I entered the kitchen. The clock above the stove read 3:31. I walked quietly down the hall to Angela's bedroom. I paused a few feet from the edge of her bed where an angel slept. Diffused moonlight came through her bedroom curtains, falling softly on her sweet face. In sleep, she looked so innocent. So much like the little girl that she was.

Angela was lucky to be alive. Far too often, children caught in human sex trafficking rings are used until there is nothing more to use. No more child left inside the shell, no more innocence. Nothing but a numbed and frightened soul, one longing to escape the physical and emotional torture that their young minds could not begin to grasp.

Angela slept with her favorite stuffed toy in the crook of her arm. It was a small teddy bear with large brown eyes. She had named her bear Cuddles, often taking it around the house and into the backyard for walks and talks with Max. They became a trio in search of adventure, the Three Musketeers bound together by a shared fantasy—a quest for discovery and an unbreakable friendship of trust.

Leaning down, I adjusted Angela's blanket on her shoulder, kissed her forehead, and watched her sleep for a moment. Yes, she was lucky to be alive, and we were just as fortunate to have her in our lives. After my first wife Sherri died, I thought I wouldn't become a father. After I met Wynona and she became pregnant with our baby, I felt a joy I'd never known. But, when she lost the baby from a gunshot inflicted by a madman, I felt something inside me vanish. A lock was broken, and stolen was my hope of fatherhood.

For Wynona, I believe the loss of our baby was even more devastating. She'd studied and worked hard to go through the FBI's academy—Quantico, graduating at the top of her class, and afterward, pursuing a career with the Bureau. There had been so many sacrifices of time and commitment. She fought evil, a foe that never sleeps. As the birthdays slipped by, she told me that any thoughts she had of becoming a mother slid away as well.

Then she was pregnant. For six months. And then she wasn't. All gone.

Until Angela came into our life.

As I watched Angela sleep, a tiny smile began working at one corner of her mouth. I wanted to know what she was dreaming—wanted her to share those happy thoughts with me, even if they only lasted for a fleeting moment. It was in the confines of Angela's good dreams where her privacy hadn't been violated. It was her safe harbor, a place of refuge after absolute evil tried to hijack her innocence. And now, we were all fortunate.

Maybe Wynona and I could pick up the pieces of Angela's stuffing, restore as much of her innocence as possible, and build on the good. I looked at Cuddles. He stared at me in the moonlight. No words were needed. I knew that the human body, its organs, blood vessels, and skin had a remarkable ability to recover and restore after an injury or sickness. But how about the human mind—the soul? Could the mind recover as well, or could we only hope the internal wounds would scab, not leaving permanent scars? I looked at Angela's peaceful face, the faraway hooting of an owl calling me to join him in the darkest hour, the hour before sunrise.

TWENTY-FOUR

It was one of their favorite places to dump a body. In this case, the body wasn't dead, at least not yet. Axle was in the bed of a pickup truck, hands bound behind his back, a chain around his feet and bolted to the truck's inner side panel. A heavy plastic tarp was covering him as the truck driver turned off the main road, Old Dixie Highway, west of Ormond Beach.

Axle heard two motorcycles riding behind the truck. It was dark, and he could barely make out the bounce of the biker's headlights as they followed, meandering down a bumpy dirt road, the smell of dust and exhaust in the night air.

He knew where they were taking him, and the thought caused his body to pump adrenaline. They were heading for the Tomoka River. Although it was less than twenty miles in length, the river has one of the most diverse wildlife populations in the state of Florida. The last three miles of the river, due to its open proximity to the ocean, has animals that live in briny water. Manatees, crabs, and alligators. Bull sharks would swim upriver into the cusp of fresh water to give live birth. After a bull shark delivered her young, she was on the prowl, hungry.

Axle closed his eyes. Tried to remember the last time he prayed. He couldn't. He jerked at the rope around his wrists. Kicked at the chain anchoring his legs to the truck panel. "God, you get my sorry ass outta this one, I'm gonna turn my life around for the better. I swear."

In less than a minute, the truck came to a stop. The motorcycles pulled up behind the rear and went silent, lights out. Axle heard the truck doors open and close. In seconds, the tailgate was down, and the tarp yanked off him.

"You pissed in your pants yet?" asked one of the bikers.

Axle ignored him.

"Let's get this shit over with," said Popeye. "Unlock the iron around his legs. He can walk to the shoreline."

One of the bikers used a key to unlock the chains, two others grabbed Axle's legs, pulling him from the truck bed. Popeye lifted a .22 Ruger from his belt, pointing the gun at Axle's face. "Walk! Toward the river."

Axle shook his head. "Y'all don't have to do this. Just lemme go. I need a doctor. After I get sewed up, I'll take my bike and head across the country to California. You guys know I'm not a snitch. And I don't take what's not mine. I didn't steal any pills."

"Shut up!" Popeye pointed the end of the barrel less than three feet from Axle's forehead. One of the bikers shoved Axle toward the river. It was fifty feet beyond the front of the truck. They all walked in that direction, four men following Axle. No one talking, the sound of something scurrying into the dark underbrush. In thirty seconds, they stood near the riverbank, the reflection of the moon off the dark and silent water, mosquitos orbiting the men.

Axle thought they would shoot him in the back of the head and push him into the river. He'd be eaten by something before his body could bloat and rise to the surface. He couldn't turn around and run against them. He had one option. Get to the river and dive in before a bullet entered his brain. He knew they wouldn't follow him into the water. They're fearless guys, but nobody in Florida jumps into a remote river in the middle of the damn night.

Less than ten feet from the riverbank, Axle bolted. He ran hard, diving into the water. Although his hands were tied behind his back, he could still use his legs and feet. He swam down. It was cool, deep. Bullets pierced the surface, coming very close to him. He held his breath, trying to swim far enough down to survive.

Axle swam underwater with the current. A minute later, his lungs were on fire. He couldn't hold his breath any longer, the open cuts on his cheek were burning in the river. He opened his eyes beneath the water, following the moonlight coming through the surface, slowly emerging. He tried to breathe shallow breaths to keep from being heard.

But Axle heard the men. They were eighty feet upriver, cursing and using the flashlights on their phones to shine over the dark surface. He was too far away for the small lights to find him. He had to get out of the river before one of the alligators, some more than twelve feet long, took him under.

He kicked with his feet below the water, swimming quietly toward cypress trees and canopies of limbs hanging above the river. When he got close, it was still too deep to stand. He grabbed a willow branch by his teeth, holding on to keep from sinking. As he caught his breath, he looked over his shoulder upriver to where the men still stood, their swearing getting louder.

He heard something splash into the river from the opposite shoreline. By the loud sound, he knew it was a big gator. Axle opened his month, releasing the limb. He kicked underwater and soon felt the knotty wooden cypress knees—the roots protruding up and out of the river. He crawled over the hard stumps into shallow water, managing to stand and limp from the river. With his hands tied, he couldn't slap the mosquitoes landing on his face and neck. He leaned into a cypress tree and pressed his face against the bark of the trunk to keep the biting insects from alighting on the deep cuts.

* * *

I sat in one of the white wicker chairs on the back porch, the night air cool and crisp from the fresh scent of rain, the dark clouds moving on, leaving a world drenched in the promise of a new day. I listened to the wise old owl and his friends whoop it up from across the St. Johns as a mist rose in the moonlight from the river's surface. I thought about some of what Clint said to us when he came to our home. *I feel Andy's presence in so many places we used to go, in the things we used to do together. All I have left is memories. It cuts like a knife … my heart aches.*

Somewhere out there in the dark, far beyond the fog, was the person who tipped the first domino, knocking down the others and creating a twisty trail that led to Andy's door. But it didn't stop until Andy opened the package and took a pill that he thought would ease the lingering pain of a torn muscle in his shoulder.

I remembered Andy as a boy, the time that Clint invited me to attend a little league game where Andy was to be the starting pitcher. He was fourteen and already had a strong arm. But it was not just the strength of his throw. It also was his talent to change it up and throw balls that would challenge every player who stepped up to the plate with a bat.

I watched a soft pink glow of sunrise in the eastern sky over the wide river. The owls stopped their conversation, yielding the forest to the cardinals and mourning doves. The glow of the sunrise sliced through the fog billowing above the river. It was as if the clouds had decided the heavens were down here instead of high above my cabin in the woods.

I wanted to look beyond the fog, deep into the mystery of Andy Ward's death. I would have to stare past the obvious, searching the murky chasm, until I could remove the cloak, the camouflage of the monster who thought he was hidden in plain sight.

TWENTY-FIVE

Durango, Mexico

Sleep didn't come easy to Tony Salazar. After hearing the news of the death of his friend and DEA asset, Juan Garcia, Salazar spent part of the night making phone calls to other agents, securing a new place to stay and a more protected office for work. He'd packed two suitcases and three cardboard boxes, all the possessions he had in the rental house. It was his plan to leave at first light to drive straight to Mexico City for relocation and strategy sessions with his constituents at the DEA headquarters in Virginia.

Salazar had slept sitting up in a chair. He'd moved it to the corner of his small living room, away from the windows. Before he finally drifted off, he'd walked around the inside of the house, peering out the windows, through the burglar bars, to the street in front and the gravel drive at the rear of the house. The night was calm; there was very little traffic. The only movement he saw was a black cat strolling in the moonlight across the intersection at 3:00 a.m.

He woke in the chair, tired and sore, his neck slightly stiff from the angle he'd slept. Salazar brushed his teeth in the bathroom, thinking this was the final time he'd do so, knowing the abrupt change was often one of the few things permanent in the life of an undercover federal agent. He thought about that—the job, the ongoing challenge he'd accepted without reservation. Field work was driven by a passion to combat those who chose a criminal life.

The survival side of the job was propelled by suspicions, rumor, anxiety, and adrenaline fueled by fear—fear that came from courage to live driven by the courage to die if it came to that. It was a creed. A personal oath. There was no turning back. He'd faced the same situation serving in the Army. In combat, you followed command. Followed your instincts and hoped the two matched when the smoke cleared.

Salazar tucked his 9mm Glock in his belt, opening the front door as daylight was breaking through the Mexican fan palm trees. Traffic was very light, a delivery truck sputtering white exhaust fumes and moving through the intersection. Salazar looked at the Honda in the driveway. He stood in the doorway, aimed the remote to start the engine. There was no explosion, the engine began purring.

He loaded his suitcases and cardboard boxes into the car. As he turned to go back to the front door to lock it, two men came around from both sides of the house. One pointed a shotgun at him. The other held a .44 magnum revolver, the gun trained directly at Salazar's chest. If it was just one man, Salazar thought he might have a chance to draw on him. But with a 12-gauge shotgun aimed at him, he would die on the spot.

In Spanish, the man holding the revolver barked, "Hands in the air!"

Salazar complied. He heard a vehicle stop behind him, pulling into the driveway. The two men with the guns came closer. The man with the handgun was about ten feet away from Salazar when he said, "Lift up your shirt, and use your left hand to remove your piece. Toss it in in the grass."

Salazar nodded, a visual of his son on screen from the computer phone call entering his mind. *Dad, are you busting the bad guys?* Salazar took a deep breath through his nostrils, and he did what the man ordered, tossing the Glock into the weedy yard. He looked at both men. "What do you want? Money?"

The man with the .44 shook his round head. "We don't want money. We want you. Turn around and walk to the van behind you. Go to the side door."

Salazar kept his hands up, walking around his car, the motor running, to the left side of the van. He looked at the driver. The man's face was complacent—a jaded delivery driver picking up yet another order to be distributed somewhere. Salazar stood next to the van's closed doors. The man with the revolver stuck the gun under his belt, while the other man leveled the shotgun at Salazar.

"Hands behind your back," ordered the guy with the .44. "Now!"

Salazar complied. The man used zip ties to handcuff him, opening the side panel door. He reached into Salazar's pocket and lifted out a phone. "Get in!" Salazar stepped up on the running board and got inside the van. "Move to the far side," came another order. The man with the shotgun got in the front passenger side. His partner with the handgun pulled it from his belt and climbed onto the bench seat, sitting a few feet away from Salazar.

He removed a handheld device, using a wire to connect it to Salazar's phone. He watched the screen on his device as digital data was being transferred. He looked up at Salazar and grinned. "Did you think only the DEA uses this? It is a UFED—a universal forensic extraction device. We now have everything on your phone, all of your photos, texts, phone numbers, and files. Nothing escapes us."

Salazar didn't respond.

The driver put the van in reverse, backing out of the driveway. The hired gun sitting in the back with Salazar pointed the .44 at him. "Hope you pissed before you came outside. We got a long ride, and there is no stopping to piss on the side of the road."

Salazar looked at the man's pitted face and flat eyes. His breath smelled of decay. "Where are we going?"

"Someplace where the DEA won't find you."

"Who do you work for?"

"We're independent contractors." He laughed.

"How long have you worked for Diego Navarro?"

"You're a DEA agent. You ask too many questions. Let me give you some answers perhaps you would prefer not to hear." The driver glanced up on the rearview mirror, his eyes empty. The man with the .44 chuckled. "The last time a DEA agent was taken, I was only a teenager. But I heard the stories. El Chapo was just a foot soldier in Guadalajara working for the family … drug lords as Americans like to call them. They partied for two days while torturing the DEA agent. When his heart stopped, they had a doctor there with a hypodermic needle and a drug that would resuscitate the American so he could experience more torture."

He paused and pursed his lips, his bloodshot eyes running over Salazar's face. "Will they do that to you?" He shrugged, lifting his shoulders. "Perhaps. One thing is certain. You will never go back to the U.S. standing up."

Salazar didn't react. He looked through the van's front windshield, streaked from dust and bug guts. They pulled a black bag over his head and drove west, toward the heart of the city. Salazar thought about the last conversation he held with his family. Would he ever see them again? His daughter's question echoing through his head. *When are you coming home, Daddy?*

TWENTY-SIX

Breakfast was beginning, and Max watched her every move. Using her stealth dachshund skills, Max got into the catch position, knowing the odds were good that Angela would drop pieces of pancake or scrambled egg while eating. She sat on the floor next to Angela's chair, eagerly waiting. She wouldn't be disappointed. I enjoyed breakfast with the family, all of us around the small table near the kitchen, the morning sunlight streaming through the window with a view of the river.

Wynona made blueberry pancakes, link sausage, and scrambled eggs. She'd placed three fresh-cut red roses from the garden in a vase at the center of the table, the fragrance of the roses mixing with the rich scent of coffee. We ate and talked about our plans for the day. When I was working a PI job, I never discussed any of the details in front of Angela. Not now. Maybe never.

Wynona sipped her coffee. "I didn't hear you get out of bed last night."

"Max heard me, but she chose to go back to sleep."

"I don't blame her. What time was that?"

"Around 3:30."

"Was it more of those heavy dreams?"

I glanced from Wynona to Angela. "What I want to know is what was Angela dreaming? I walked into your bedroom very early this morning and guess what?"

"What, Daddy?"

"I saw you smiling in your sleep. It looked like Cuddles was smiling, too. Maybe you two were sharing the same dream."

She looked up from her pancake. "We were."

"What dream was that?" Wynona asked.

"One about flying with Dumbo. Before Daddy read me a story last night, when I was brushing my teeth, I remembered what we said about the clouds over the river. One was like Dumbo. I was holding Cuddles, and we were flying with Dumbo. Max was with us."

"Was she flying, too?" I asked.

"Yep. Her ears were sticking out in the wind just like Dumbo's ears do."

Wynona laughed. "That must have been a fun sight … Dumbo with his big ears, and Max with her long ears, soaring in the air with you. Where'd you three go?"

"To the end of the rainbow." Angela giggled.

"I always wanted to go there."

"Come with us, Mama. All you have to do is close your eyes and dream."

"I can do that." Wynona closed her eyes, smiling. After a few seconds, she said, "I can see the rainbow. All the colors make it so beautiful. And there goes Dumbo flying by me … somewhere over the rainbow, just like the song."

Angela grinned. "Sing that song to me."

Wynona opened her eyes. "I will on the way to the store. We need to leave in half an hour. Make sure you brush your teeth before we go." She looked over at me. "Sandy is coming to the store for a few hours this morning. That gives me the time to homeschool Angela in the back office. We have her little desk set up across from mine. It's quiet in there and works well."

"I can't wait to see your one-room schoolhouse."

We finished breakfast, Angela trotting off to the bathroom to brush her teeth, Max right behind her. I helped Wynona clear the table and do the dishes.

"Are you starting your investigation today?" she asked.

"That's the plan."

"Where will you begin?"

"I'm not sure. I'll look at everything Clint sent to me, take some notes, and go from there. Where it takes me … that could be a few twists and turns. I have something I want to run by Dave Collins, so I'll head over to the marina."

"Can you take Max? Sometimes, it's a challenge to keep Angela's attention while homeschooling. She gets distracted by Max's curiosity when someone comes into the shop."

"No problem. Let's see if we can catch the weather forecast." I used a TV remote to turn on the small television at the end of the kitchen counter. I flipped through the channels and caught a morning newscast out of Orlando.

From a studio, the news anchorman said, "Tragedy in Panama City Beach. It's reported that eight college students visiting the area for Spring Break have died. Although the cause of the deaths is not conclusive at this time, it's believed that the students died from an overdose of drugs. Live from the scene is Channel Four's Erin Fields."

Wynona stared at the screen, drying a dish. She whispered, "Eight college kids … dear God."

The shot cut to a night scene at a high-rise condominium complex, more than a dozen police and emergency vehicles—red, blue, and white lights pulsating, the responders frantically moving around the premises. While spectators were being held behind the yellow crime scene tape, TV news personnel angled at pushing the boundaries.

The reporter began. "This video captures the intense emergency last night as police and paramedics worked to save the lives of eleven college students. They were inside this beachfront condo, the Catalina, when a 911 call came into police headquarters. The caller was one of the few to survive what authorities believe were drug overdoses. The horrific scene left eight of the eleven students dead. Two are hospitalized and listed in critical condition."

The video cut to detectives speaking with a college-aged female, her face wet from tears. The reporter continued. "Nineteen-year-old, Sonia Reece, was not affected. She told police that she was the only one in the condo who didn't take one of the pills that were being passed around inside. Reece was too traumatized to go on camera, but police say she told them that one of the male students brought the drugs and started handing them out to the others. Police detective, Lindsey Owen, is the lead investigator."

The shot cut to a woman dressed in a white shirt, dark jacket, and pants. Her brown hair was just above her shoulders. Yellow crime scene tape crisscrossed the front entrance to the condo. "We did find some pills. They resembled OxyContin. However, that doesn't explain the deaths because, according to our witness, each person took one pill. The drugs are most likely fake pills, made in a clandestine lab, and mixed with fentanyl. We will know more after they're tested in the lab and when we get the results back from the autopsy reports."

The images cut to some of the victims laying on gurneys, paramedics trying hard to resuscitate them as they loaded the students into awaiting ambulances. The reporter said, "Emergency medical personnel fought hard to resuscitate those students who were unconscious. Police will be checking security cameras to see if someone may have delivered the pills to the one student who was said to have handed them out … or maybe he had brought the drugs to the party. We do know that he and four of his friends are students from the University of Michigan and the girls from the University of Georgia."

The shot cut to the reporter standing near the entrance to the condominium complex. It was morning. Four police vehicles were still on the scene, police and detectives coming in and out of the building, collecting evidence.

As the stark images appeared on screen, the reporter continued. "Never in the history of college spring break in Florida has there been a tragedy on this scale. But in past years, the prevalence of fentanyl—if that proves to be the cause of these deaths—has never been as easy to get as it is today. If lab reports reveal it was fentanyl that led to the deaths, these students become sad statistics in a drug epidemic that's sweeping our nation. Police will release the names of the victims pending notification of family. Again, eight college students are dead, two in critical condition in the hospital's ICU. From Panama City Beach, this is Erin Fields."

Wynona looked up at me. I could tell by her eyes that she knew the scope of my investigation just got much deeper. She set a dry plate in the cupboard and turned back to me. "Panama City Beach isn't that far from Gainesville. I'm sure there are University of Florida students over there for spring break."

"Probably."

I looked back at the images on the screen of the college kids lying on gurneys and watched in sorrow as they were placed either into ambulances or coroner's vans. Wynona looked up at me and said, "As I think of our little girl, Angela, I feel so bad for the parents of the victims. They're receiving phone calls this morning that no parent should ever face … the death of their child. A parent should never have to bury his or her child. There's no moving on from that … I'm not sure you can even move forward."

"I see it in the anguish on Clint Ward's face. Nothing we experienced in war affected him like son's death." We could hear Angela singing in the bathroom, her soft voice on key as she sang *Old McDonald*.

Wynona leaned against the kitchen counter. She looked at the bay window toward the river, the morning sky pastel blue. "When I was with the Bureau, after we caught a serial killer—the perp was a civil engineer who left bodies in three states, I spoke to the mother of one of the dead girls, whose daughter was a freshman in college. The mother told me that the pain of birthing her daughter led to amazing joy, but the pain she endured burying her and since then has been horrendous. She said the finality of death was smothering, especially when she'd pick up the phone to call her, stopping when she heard the first ring. She'd hang up and cry."

I said nothing, letting Wynona finish her thoughts.

She took a deep breath. "Although I wasn't fortunate enough to give birth, I was pregnant for more than six months. I felt our baby, our daughter, moving inside me. Before I lost her, I remember how she would become more active when you came into the room. When she heard your voice, Sean, it was as if she had some cosmic connection to you, her father." Wynona's eyes welled with tears. "I didn't get the joy of giving birth … but I did go through the pain of losing our baby girl who'd spent six months, two weeks, and three days inside me. My heart aches for those parents."

I reached out and held her. After a moment, Wynona pulled a tissue from a box on the counter. She looked up at me and said, "I have a feeling that this will be one of the toughest cases you'll ever face. The link between Andy Ward's death and those eight other college kids seems to be fentanyl. Maybe it came through the same distribution channel. Meaning the same inhumane creature is producing and selling that poison. Whoever he is, Sean, he's not alone."

TWENTY-SEVEN

Ponce Marina is a head trip of sorts. And I mean that in a good way. For me, and probably for Max, the marina, with its salty scents, boats, and boat people, is a form of mental therapy. Maybe it's due to the water—the cyclical rise and fall of the tide, the location just north of Ponce Inlet, and its open door to the Atlantic Ocean and the world.

I pulled my Jeep across the gravel and crushed oyster shell parking lot, Max sticking her head out the open passenger window, her black nose quivering with anticipation. I parked in the shade of three cabbage palm trees, picked up Max, and got out. The midday sun was hot, the shadows from the trees just moving in the breeze coming across the Atlantic. Before I set Max down, I looked at the cars and pickup trucks in the lot. Nine cars. Two trucks and two motorcycles. I scanned the nearest license plates. One Dade County tag.

Max made a beeline for the screen door leading to maybe her favorite place on the planet—inside the Ponce Tiki Bar and Restaurant. The exterior looked like it was built from materials strewn behind by a hurricane. The building, which overlooked the marina, was supported by massive cypress timbers. The outside walls were cobbled together with weathered wood from a barn in South Georgia. The thatched roof was made from dried palmetto palm fronds, its peak christened by pelicans that roosted there every night. Perhaps it was because they liked sitting on a roof near a weathervane shaped like a pelican, affectionately known by the boaters as Pelican Pete.

When Max and I entered, we were greeted by the smell of blackened grouper, fried hushpuppies, and onion rings. There was no holding her back. She became a greyhound, running across the beer-stained wooden floor, small legs trotting and hopping at the same time.

106

I scanned the interior. I guessed there were at least sixteen people sitting around the tables made from discarded wooden spools that power companies used to haul cable and wire. The tables, all turned vertical, were shellacked with a lacquer the color of honey.

Most of the lunchtime diners appeared to be tourists—faces glowing from the sun, lots of T-shirts with Florida roots, Gatorland, Daytona 500, Sloppy Joes—Key West. A vintage jukebox, a Wurlitzer, played a Jack Johnson song, *One Step Ahead.*

There were four people at a bar that accommodated a dozen stools. The Tiki Bar was decorated with a nautical theme. Lots of sailing and maritime souvenirs—a rusted anchor in one corner, portholes, a sextant, oars, and a large compass mounted on the walls. Behind the bar was a brass diving helmet, the kind used by divers in Florida before SCUBA tanks. It was next to a wooden wheel from a schooner that went down in the Atlantic five miles off Ponce Inlet in 1897.

The Tiki Bar's windows, during operating hours, were isinglass. Most of the time they were wide open, the sea breeze entering from the east—the Atlantic side, exiting out the windows to the right, the bar's west side. The breeze, as it encircled the marina with more than 150 boats, was the best form of advertising. The aromatic smells of the grilling food beckoned hungry sailors like the covert song of sirens, calling them to dinner.

"Hot Dawg!" Nick Cronus was one of the four people sitting at the bar. As he sipped beer from a frosty mug, Max came trotting up to him, stopped near the flipflops he wore, and propped up on the stool's bottom rung. Nick reached down with one big hand, scooping Max up and setting her in his lap. He wore a tank top and faded red swimsuit trunks.

"Look what the wind blew in … my man, Sean O'Brien." He grinned, his thick moustache lifting, dark eyes bright and playful, crinkling at the edges. His skin was the shade of creosote. Forever tanned from working as a fisherman. Before that, back in his home country of Greece, he dove for sponges as a teenager. Now, in his mid-forties, America was his home. Nick was one of at least fifty people who were full-time, live-a-boards at the marina.

I smiled. "How are you doing, Nick?"

"Better now that you and Hot Dawg are here. How's the family?"

"Good. Wynona and Angela are doing well. They're in the middle of homeschooling. Wynona does it inside her antique store in a backroom. Angela is an excellent student."

"Good." He nodded. "That little girl's a great kid. Are you taking *Jupiter* out today?"

"No. And it's one of those rare times that I'm not coming to the marina to replace a boat part or fix something on *Jupiter*. She's a great old boat, just showing her age a little more."

"You still got that gorgeous sailboat, *Dragonfly*, down in the islands. I can't believe that couple gave it to you after you saved their lives."

"After what they went through, sailing was the last thing they ever wanted to do again. Too bad. She's a fine boat, and they are good people. Just burned and scarred from what happened." I glanced at a widescreen TV mounted up on the wall, the sound off.

"Are you gonna sell her?"

"Maybe. But not now. A friend of mine is using her for a while. He and his family are sailing through the Caribbean. I have no idea where they are at any given time."

"Hope you get *Dragonfly* back."

"I will, and she'll be in better shape than what she was when I let him borrow her."

"This guy sounds like a helluva sailor."

I smiled. "Let's just say that he pays close attention to detail."

Nick nodded and sipped his beer. Max propped her front paws up against the weathered bar, her tail wagging.

"Is that my favorite little dog in all the world?" asked Flo Spencer, coming from an open door at the far end of the bar, heading toward us. Flo, late fifties, black and gray hair pinned up in the back, owned the Tiki Bar. She had a smile that would have put her on the covers of magazines in her youth. Today, her smile often broke up fights before they started between commercial fisherman, the guys who sometimes drank too much when they came back from a week at sea, thirsting for cold beer and itching for a fight.

"Hey, Maxine," Flo said, reaching over the bar to pet Max. "Sean, it's good to see you. How's Wynona and Angela?"

"Good. How's business, Flo?"

"Can't complain. I keep trying to talk Nick into working as my head chef. Nobody, and I mean nobody, can cook a grouper like he can."

Nick grinned. "That's cause I'm Nick the Greek. For thousands of years, the Greeks lived on seafood. If I get a cut, I bleed salty seawater."

Flo's head went back, braying one of her unbridled laughs that carried across the restaurant. After a misty moment, she said, "Sean, are you and Miss Max gonna have lunch?"

"Maybe later."

She eyed me, wiping her hands on a white towel. "I bet you're working a new case."

I said nothing.

She motioned toward the TV. "Did y'all see the news this morning?"

Nick shook his head. "I have a TV on my boat, but I didn't catch the news."

Flo lowered her voice, leaning closer, the wooden bar between us. "The story is that eight college kids in Panama City Beach died due to some tainted drug overdose."

Nick used the back of his calloused hand to wipe the beer foam off his bushy moustache. "What a shame. Something like that happened to some college kids on spring break down near Fort Lauderdale. These kids, many away from home for the first time … sand, sun, and booze. And then … bam!" He clapped his hands together. Max looked confused.

Flo's dark, pencil-drawn eyebrows lifted on her forehead. "I remember something like that happening to a college student at the University of Florida in Gainesville. Must have been a couple months ago. Danny Sullivan, a retired cop, said …. Do you know Danny, Sean?"

"No."

"Nick knows him because Danny has lunch here a couple of days a week. Anyway, he was saying they haven't arrested anyone in that case. He said it'll probably be a cold case if it's not already one." She eyed me. "Don't you work cold cases?"

"Sometimes." From outside in the parking lot, I could hear the rumble of motorcycle engines—all bellowing the distinct sound of Harley-Davidsons.

TWENTY-EIGHT

There was a drop in the noise level. The normal chatter and drone of conversations in the Tiki Bar dipped for a few seconds, as if all the customers ran out of something to say at the same time. Rare for a place filled with vacationing tourists enjoying tropical drinks. The only loud sounds came the clatter of a high school student busing a table and a song coming from the jukebox, Otis Redding singing, *Dock of the Bay*.

The normal noise level returned. I didn't have to turn around to see the initial source of their distraction. I glanced at the smoky mirror behind the bottles of liquor elevated on shelves near the wall. I could see four bikers enter, walking between the round tables and heading to a table in the back corner. Lots of leather and ink. One man looked like someone you'd see in a wrestling ring. As they sat at the table, I saw the club patches or colors on the denim back of one biker as he sat. *Iron Fist*.

Flo smiled. "Well, let me give a hushpuppy to my favorite pup." She signaled to the bartender, a muscular former Marine in a T-shirt with the image of a doe-eyed oyster on the front. The caption read:

Eat 'em raw
Tiki Bar, Ponce Marina, Fla.

The seasoned bartender worked the bar with a trained sense of rhythm, like a juggler handling orders. "Whatcha need, Flo?" he asked, popping the cap off a Corona bottle, setting it on a server's tray next to a bloody Mary.

"Stan, do you mind going into the kitchen and bringing out one hot hushpuppy? Eddie just cooked up two dozen more."

"No problem."

110

"Thanks." Flo stepped a few feet away to greet a new customer. I recognized him. He was a shrimp boat captain who kept his boat docked at Ponce Marina.

Nick petted Max and looked over at me. "This new case you're working on …." He paused and sniffed a quick breath through his nostrils. "What's the case about? You don't have to go into any confidential details, but you know I've always got your back."

Flo returned as the bartender brought a single hushpuppy on a paper plate and handed it to her. "Here you go."

She smiled. "Thanks, Stan." He nodded and walked to the opposite end of the bar to serve a customer. Max sat up, tilting her head, looking from the hushpuppy to Flo's smiling face. Flo cut the hushpuppy into quarters and let it cool for a minute before sliding the plate in front of Nick. Max stood in his lap, paws on the bar, quickly eating the food. She looked up at Flo for more.

I said, "That's enough kiddo. If Wynona smells hushpuppy on your breath, we'll both be in the doghouse."

Nick snorted, almost spitting out a mouthful of beer. "Sean, have a seat, man. Lemme buy you a beer. You work too hard. Whatever your new case is, you can make time for a cold one."

"I appreciate it, but I'm on the clock. I need to talk to Dave. Have you seen him today?"

"I saw him a couple of hours ago. He was carrying a bag of groceries down the dock to his boat."

"Come on, Max. If you stay here much longer, you'll give up eating dog food."

Nick chuckled. "You can always leave her with me. She'll sit right here on the stool by my side. Max has a way with women, especially the tourists. She's the ultimate ice breaker. Not that I've ever really needed an ice breaker."

"Oh, good Lord, Nicky," Flo said, shaking her head, walking to the end of the bar to greet a new customer.

Nick glanced at the images on the TV screen. It was an entertainment talk show, some actor on camera pitching his new movie. Even with the sound off, I could tell the actor was just going through the motions. On a PR tour because it was in his contract.

Nick glanced back at the parking lot entrance to the Tiki Bar. "Sean, the first time I ever met you was right out there." He motioned with one hand. "It was in the lot between the Tiki and the marina office. I'm only thinking about it because hearing the roar of those biker motorcycles when they got here reminded me of that night. You remember it like I do?"

"I remember it well."

"It was a few years ago, but sometimes sights and sounds … even smells, bring back what happened that night. I'd had a bit too much whiskey, and before I could walk to my boat, one of the biker dudes accused me of making a pass at his girlfriend when he went to take a piss. One thing led to another. Outside, they jumped me, three of 'em. I put up a pretty good fight 'til they broke out the knives. After hitting me in the head with a pipe, they were about five seconds away from slitting my throat and pushing me into the palmetto bushes to die. Man, you came outta nowhere. I remember seeing you hitting them so hard and fast, they didn't know what happened."

"I managed to surprise them."

"When you dropped the first one, a big fella, the other two looked dumbfounded. Before they could collect their thoughts, down came biker number two, then biker number three. I heard two of the three were in the hospital for a couple of days."

I looked at the bar mirror, glancing toward the four bikers at the back table. "That's history, Nick."

"Maybe so, but you gave me a new lease on the future. When you save a man's life, and this thinking comes from the ancient Greeks, you are brothers for life. Thick and thin. Come what may. You stand by that?"

"That's one of the reasons I took this new case."

"Really?" Nick's thick eyebrows rose, he finished his beer.

"Yes. You asked me about the case. I didn't want to say much in front of Flo. I share some things with you and Dave because I know you will keep it in confidence."

"That's for damn sure."

"The case has to do with the death of a college student due to illicit drugs."

"Wow. You didn't let on one bit when Flo mentioned it."

"The University of Florida kid who died of a drug overdose in Gainesville … I served in the Delta Force with his father in Syria and

Afghanistan. During one of our hunts for ISIS members, we'd managed to rout out ten of them in the village of Jazrah, southwest of Raqqah. It was a hard and heavy firefight. After the smoke cleared, when all had gone silent around the abandoned buildings, I was trying to help a team member who was hit by a round to his left leg, hitting the femoral artery. Through the blood and dust, I didn't see one more hostile on a roof of a three-story building. He was a sniper and was sighting down on me."

"What happened?"

"One of our squad members saw the sniper and hit him in the chest with a round before the shooter could pull the trigger. That move probably saved my life. And now, years later, that team member lost his only son. He's dead because an internet drug dealer sold him a product that was supposed to alleviate the shoulder pain in his rotator cuff. He took one pill and died. It was laced with fentanyl."

Nick wrapped his brown arms protectively around Max. "I'm sorry to hear that. I guess there aren't a lot of suspects if you have the case. The cops just give up or what?"

"No, they ran out of leads. I think it's going to take a lot of effort to track and trace on the internet. Maybe I'll find some physical evidence or someone who knows someone who knows something about his death."

"That's a lot of *some*, but to sum it up, you gotta get lucky and pull this one out of your hat like a magician."

"Yes, but in this case, there are no illusions. No tricks. Real forensic evidence, if I can find some, doesn't lie."

Nick glanced up at the TV screen. He motioned toward the bartender. "Hey, Stan, you got the remote back there. There's something on the news."

The bartender nodded, picking up the TV remote control and sliding it across the bar to Nick. He picked it up and quickly hit the mute button. The sound was back. A news reporter was standing on the side of a rural road, thick woods in the background. The reporter, a woman with light brown hair, looked at the camera and said, "Police are searching for a suspect in a bizarre case. Here's cell phone video of a man found walking out of an alligator-infested swamp this morning, the Tomoka Marsh Preserve, off Old Dixie Highway. A plumber stopped his van when he saw a bloodied man come out of a swampy area. He was covered in mud suffering from insect bites, cuts, and bruises, including his face where an X was slashed into his cheek."

The video cut to a closer image of the man's face, the X on his cheek was bloody and appeared infected. I spotted a unique tattoo on his upper arm. As the news promo was ending, I looked at the bar mirror, watching the four bikers. The reporter concluded, "This story and more coming up on Channel Four's Midday Report."

The bikers knew him. No doubt. Their body language broadcast their recognition. One man, the largest, with tats, ink, and fur, pointed across the restaurant to the big screen. He shook his head in what appeared to be disbelief. The other three were nodding, shrugging their meaty shoulders. One man knocked back three-fingers worth of whiskey in his glass. The largest man stared at the screen even after the news promo ended, like he'd seen a ghost.

Was the injured man a friend of theirs, maybe a biker, someone who rode with them, or did they put him in the swamps?

TWENTY-NINE

Before they pulled a hood over Tony Salazar's head, he glanced at his watch. Without the use of his eyes, he tried to get a rudimentary picture of what faced him. Inside the van, he attempted to calibrate the average speed of the driver. Even without the use of his sight, he knew they were leaving the city.

After they abducted him, after taking his phone and pulling out of his driveway, the men stopped the van somewhere in the inner city, one man getting out and removing something from the back of the van, slamming the hatch door. He returned in less than five minutes.

The man in the front seat opposite the driver was smoking. He kept his window partially open. That allowed Salazar to listen to sounds as the driver stopped at traffic lights or slowed to cross railroad tracks. In his mind, he was trying to draw a map—to be able to retrace the direction or, if he found the opportunity, to get a message to DEA headquarters in Mexico City.

He made mental notes when the driver turned in tandem with honking horns, church bells ringing, the sound of a train, and traffic with the undercurrent of man-made noises. Using the training he'd received for survival in kidnapping and hostage situations, Salazar was trying to form a picture in his mind of where his abductors were taking him. Within twenty minutes, the urban noises of the city faded.

The only sound now was wind noise coming through a window that was lowered a few inches. Someone in the front seat turned on the car radio, flipping through the dials, settling for pop music. When the song ended, in Spanish, the disc jockey said, "Don't forget to get your tickets for the upcoming Mexicana Music Fest. It's in ten days at the WTC, in the heart of Mexico City. Time now in Durango is nine o'clock."

Thirty minutes later, steady driving northeast, the disc jockey gave the time before introducing the next song as the radio signal was breaking up with static. Salazar listened to the mumbled conversation of the three men, trying to pick up on keywords, before someone found another station on the radio. After a song ended, the new disc jockey said, "We're welcoming back Torreón's favorite son—Santiago Alverez, appearing at the Municipal Arena for one night only. Get your tickets online. Information's on our website."

The radio shut off, the driver making a right turn, heading in a direction that Salazar thought was due east. Within thirty minutes, the van slowed. Salazar could smell dust and cow manure. He heard cattle mooing somewhere, the van driving over gravel, loose pebbles striking the undercarriage. A few minutes later, the van came to a stop. The men said nothing as they opened the doors. When the side panel door slid open, the man with the .44 grabbed Salazar by the arm. "Get out! More your ass!"

Salazar, hands still cuffed behind his back, shimmied across the seat, managing to get out of the van without falling. Someone pushed him in the center of his back. "Walk straight ahead." Salazar followed the directions, taking small steps, aware that he could be walking into a hole—a grave.

After he'd walked what he assumed to be at least fifty yards, one of the men grabbed him by the upper arm, leading him somewhere. A door opened, the hinges squeaking; it seemed heavy and large. The sunlight suddenly faded, and Salazar knew he was inside a building. But it wasn't air-conditioned. It was warm and smelled of hay, animal feed, and manure. One of the men kicked him hard in the center of his back, sending Salazar face-down onto the hardpacked dirt floor. The blow almost knocked the air out of his lungs.

"Stand up!" someone ordered.

Salazar, flat on his stomach, turned over, slowly standing. The hood was jerked off his face. He stared into a backdrop of sunlight at the wide barn door. There was a silhouette of another man in the swathe of sunlight. Salazar blinked, trying to adjust to the light. He couldn't make out the man's features, but he could see that the man carried something in one hand. It looked like a rope.

The man in silhouette entered. He walked fifty feet past a half dozen horse stalls, harnesses near each stall. He stood within ten feet of Salazar, and now he recognized him—Diego Navarro—the eldest son of drug lord Sergio Navarro. And the rope he carried in his right hand wasn't a rope. It was a whip—a leather bullwhip.

"Welcome to my hacienda," Navarro said in Spanish. "This is one of our horse stables. The casa is on top of the hill. From there, I can look for miles in any direction to see what my grandfather called the federales. Today, that's your DEA … one of the most corrupt organizations the American government runs."

Salazar studied Navarro's face a moment, the contempt in his eyes, the small white scar under his left eye that looked like a comma. "What do you want, Diego?"

He chuckled. "I truly want for nothing. What I desire is altogether another thing. And that desire is for me to be left alone as I build and run my various business interests."

"Which includes drug running, human trafficking, extortion, and murder, to name just a few."

Navarro laughed. "You have quite the imagination, Antonio Salazar. Our commodities fill a human need. Our business model is not that different from any Fortune 500 company. We simply operate without the corporate bureaucracy. We constantly innovate, anticipating what the public wants before they even know it. We're like Apple with its iPhone. We also build brand loyalty."

"That's not hard, considering most of your customer base is stoned or high."

Navarro smiled, stepping closer. "You Americans are so damn sanctimonious and hypocritical. Your government, the system you sold your soul to, is just as corrupt as anyone within Mexico's government. Your politicians manage to hide their fraud better. That's all."

"If by abducting me, you plan to use that to negotiate with the DEA, it won't work. Regardless of your perception of the U.S. government, we don't negotiate with terrorists. It won't happen. Either kill me or let me go."

Navarro glanced down at the whip in his hand. He lifted his eyes to meet Salazar's. "So, you dictate two options to me … kill you or let you go. And you think of my business as a terrorist organization." He shook his head, black eyes filled with disdain. He turned to one of his men. "Take his picture."

The man nodded and used his phone to take a picture of Salazar, then stepped back.

Navarro slammed the wooden handle of the bullwhip across Salazar's mouth. The blow knocked his head back, stunning Salazar for a moment, blood oozing from a cut lip and a loose tooth. Navarro turned back to the man holding his phone. "Take another picture."

The man did as ordered. Salazar stared at the camera phone, blood dripping from his chin onto his shirt. Navarro grinned. "You are quite the bleeder. Perhaps you need a diet of more fruits and vegetables. You could be deficient in vitamin K. You can get vitamin K from foods, such as avocados. We have plenty of them here in Mexico. In the state of Durango, we own the avocado market. And you, Antonio, thought it was only about drugs."

Salazar spit out blood. "Why am I here? What do you want?"

"The release of my father from the American prison. You for him."

"It won't happen."

"Then we will send them your head in a box."

"And they will come for you."

"No, they won't. Let's put our cards on the table, face up, okay? Since your government opened the border, pretty much enticing people from all over the world to wade across the Rio Grande, our business his tripled. We don't have to smuggle drugs across. We walk them across in backpacks or in small boats. It's almost too easy. Doesn't that marginalize the presence of you and other DEA agents in our country? What's the point? Why are you even here?"

Salazar said nothing, blood spattering on the top of his left shoe.

"I wanted to send a personal, handwritten letter to your president thanking him, and perhaps even nominating him for businessman of the year. However, sometimes the U.S. Border Patrol is allowed to make a few arrests. It is mostly for show or grandstanding as the Americans call it. We want these arrests to happen to our competition. Let's call it what it is … selective enforcement of border patrol, immigration, and drug laws. I know that you are aware of where the Sinaloa and Jalisco operations run their merchandise across the border. I want your government to make arrests in those areas and hold news conferences. On your national news, you can show the faces of the coyotes and the leaders of the Sinaloa and

Jalisco cartels. In the meantime, I want sovereignty along the areas of the Rio Grande where we operate, from Terlingua in the west to Del Rio in the east."

"It will never happen."

"Of course it will. We will work as silent partners with your puppet—your director of Homeland Security. It will be a six-month agreement. We will keep you alive with the assurance that we will release you in six months if the terms of the agreement are met. This can be a confidential arrangement. No media coverage. Just between us and the top people in the DEA and Homeland Security. At the end of the period, my father is released, you go back to your family, and we conclude the agreement with no further stipulations. It will allow us to dominate market share while giving the DEA and Border Patrol some positive news. You'll be perpetuating the façade that your border is secure and that the U.S. is drastically slowing the flow of drugs. This is a win-win."

"Our country doesn't negotiate with terrorists."

"Bad answer." He turned to his men, "Remove his shirt and tie him to that post near the wall."

The men did as ordered, cutting off Salazar's handcuffs and tying his hands to a metal railroad spike drilled into a timber eight feet from the ground. He was positioned with his face toward the beam and his back to the barn's entrance. Navarro walked a few feet away, holding the handle of the bullwhip. Using skills he developed herding cattle years ago, he cracked the tip of the leather whip across Salazar's back. The first strike raised a severe red welt.

Salazar gnashed his teeth, eyes closed as the whip ripped through his flesh a second and third time, the slashes cutting skin, blood mixing with leather. He thought of his family—Nicole, Lucas, and Eva—as Diego Navarro brought the whip down again with such fervor that spittle flew from his mouth. Then Navarro dropped the whip onto the hardpacked ground, turned, and walked back toward the sunlight.

THIRTY

From the distance of a hundred feet, it was hard to tell if he was home. However, it wouldn't be any easier the closer we came. His home was a 42-foot Grand Banks trawler named *Gibraltar*. Dave Collins lived aboard full time. The bow of the yacht faced L-dock, where my boat *Jupiter* also was moored, but in the last slip at the end.

As Nick, Max, and I walked down L-dock, Max in the lead, coming closer to *Gibraltar,* I thought of Angela. I pictured her in my backyard with Max and Cuddles, the three little musketeers in search of adventure.

Ponce Marina, south of Daytona Beach, was just a mile north of Ponce Inlet and its gateway into the Atlantic Ocean. The marina was on the Halifax River, part of the Intracoastal Waterway. There were a dozen long docks—through N-dock. More than 150 boats, varying in sizes and types, were moored there. The Tiki Bar, along with the marina office, was near the main dock.

As we chatted and walked, white pelicans soared over the masts of the sailboats, the smell of fresh paint and varnish in the salty air. Nick gestured toward the cockpit of a 60-foot Hatteras. Brand new. Gleaming white. But it wasn't the yacht that caught his attention. It was the woman in a red bikini, lounging in the sun, a glass of white wine in one hand, her phone in the other, reading something on the screen. She wore dark sunglasses, her body curvy and tanned. The name on the transom was *Endless Summer*. It was from Annapolis, Maryland.

As we got closer, I could hear music coming from the yacht, Kenny Chesney singing *Pirate Song*. The woman looked up. Nick flashed one of his charming smiles. "That Hatteras looks good on you."

It was his amiable way of saying this: *you look beautiful sitting on that yacht.* She smiled and said, "Thank you. Your little dog is so cute."

120

Nick winked at me, whispering, "See what I mean. The ladies love Hot Dawg."

The woman sipped her wine and said, "I've always loved dachshunds. My best friend had one. She liked it so much that she got a second one."

Nick stopped walking. Max looked back at him, cocking her head, ears up. "Max is more of a loner dog. Not sure if she'd share her space with another dachshund."

"Max. That's in interesting name for a female dog."

Nick lifted one finger to his lips. "Shhh … she doesn't know she's a d—o—g."

"Is she your d—o—g or your friend's pup?"

"My man, Sean, owns her, or she owns him. I'm not quite sure."

She smiled. "Back in Maryland, you don't see a lot of big men with small dogs." The woman crossed her legs at the ankles and looked at me. "I'd picture you with a bigger dog."

I smiled. "Max has a big heart. That's enough for me."

Nick laughed, taking a couple of steps closer to the Hatteras. "Welcome to Florida and Ponce Marina. I'm Nick Cronus, the official ambassador of Ponce Marina. My pal here is Sean O'Brien, and you've already met Max. My boat, *St. Michael,* is moored near the end of L-dock. She's got the lines of the seafaring ships that the ancient Greeks sailed."

"Oh, really?"

At that moment, the door from the cockpit to the main salon opened, and a man stepped onto the teak deck. Shirtless. Swim trunks. Slip-on sneakers. He was probably twenty years older than the woman. His thick white hair was neatly combed. Fleshy neck beginning to sag. Gut stretching the elastic lining of the trunks. He carried a cocktail in one hand, and from where I stood, it looked to be scotch. No ice cubes visible in his glass.

Nick nodded. "Welcome to our little marina. I've never been to Annapolis. Hope to get up there one day."

The man smiled, sitting in a deck chair beside the woman. He said, "Annapolis is the sailing capital of the world."

Nick grinned, his moustache rising. "Well, you folks have a good day."

Max saw a brown pelican alight on a post. She picked up her pace, ignoring us.

The woman smiled. The man sipped his drink. We left, walking down the dock, following Max. Nick chuckled. "Maybe, while they're here, the lady will run out of wine and tip toe down to my boat to borrow a bottle."

I shook my head. "Nick, you'll always be a player."

"C'mon. Give me a break. I just got back to port yesterday after spending nine days at sea. Caught a lot of snapper and grouper. On Mykonos, women used to come down to the docks every day to see if their men were returning from the sea."

"But the woman on the Hatteras doesn't quite fit that bill."

"A man can dream."

Nick's boat, *St. Michael*, was moored on the opposite side of the dock from Dave's boat, *Gibraltar*. As Nick mentioned to the woman on the Hatteras, *St. Michael* looked like it could have been sailed by the Ancient Mariner. The boat had a high bow for fishing in blue water. Its wheelhouse was ten feet higher, giving Nick a superb view of his fishing grounds in the Atlantic. The cockpit was filled with fishing rods, bait tanks, and coolers.

Dave's boat, by contrast, was a stately trawler, a Grand Banks. You couldn't see the cockpit from the dock. The transom was pointed in the opposite direction. *Gibraltar* was spotless, all ropes and hoses perfectly coiled and in place. The boat was waxed. Chrome polished. The windows were tinted, meaning it was hard to see inside the yacht unless the sun was over your shoulder and shining onto the glass.

Max looked back at us before making a left turn to walk down the small secondary dock that led to *Gibraltar's* stern. Nick laughed. "Hot Dawg knows her way around here. She didn't even walk on farther to your boat."

"No, she didn't." I looked another fifty feet down the dock where my boat, *Jupiter*, a 38-foot Bayliner, was moored. All seemed well from here. I'd inspect her before going back to the river cabin.

As Max vanished around the corner, heading down the auxiliary dock toward *Gibraltar's* stern, I heard the rumble of Harley engines in the parking lot. I recalled the look on the faces of the bikers. I glanced at my watch. The noon news was coming on in half an hour. If Dave was in his boat, we could catch the news together.

Something that happened in the Tiki Bar made me curious.

THIRTY-ONE

"Well, look who came to see me. It's my gal pal, Miss Max," Dave Collins bellowed from somewhere on his trawler. Max stood at the far end of the smaller dock, barking twice, looking into the cockpit. "Did you come alone Max or are you escorting others as well?"

Nick and I approached the cockpit, his flipflops, slapping the hard dock. He laughed. "Hey, Dave, look who I found wanderin' into the Tiki, Sean O'Brien. We came to watch TV with you."

Dave grinned, his pale blue eyes curious. "Perhaps I should feel a sense of honor. Although I would prefer a game of chess over TV." He lifted Max from the dock to the deck. "Come aboard, gentlemen. Nick, despite my reservations, I'm including you in that category." Dave wore an untucked tropical print shirt, shorts, and sandals.

Nick shook his head, grinning. "You keep that up, old man, and I might forget you when you want some of the freshest fish that ever swam in the deep blue sea."

Dave chuckled, eyes lively in the sunlight. He was in good shape for a man in his late sixties. Muscle definition still in his chest and arms. No gut, despite his love for craft beers and foods cooked in butter and wine, a taste he never lost from the time he worked with the CIA in Paris. He had cotton-white hair and a trimmed beard to match, skin tanned. "Sean, how's Wynona and little Angela?"

"Good, thanks."

He looked at me for a moment before glancing toward the Ponce Lighthouse a mile away, his thoughts distant and private. We'd become close friends through the years. There were many days when I'd spent more time aboard *Jupiter* than I did at the river cabin. After working twenty-five years in the CIA, all that time as an agency officer stationed in many parts of Europe, Dave retired and moved from Virginia to a beachfront condo in Florida. His wife of twenty-eight years made it nine months before filing for divorce and going back north.

They split the money from the sale of the condo, stocks, and bonds—Dave buying the Grand Banks and moving *Gibraltar* up from Boca Raton to Ponce Inlet. Dave's only child, a grown daughter, lived with her husband in London. Today, the marina community—the live-aboard boaters, with its cast of eccentrics, were Dave's family. I was fortunate to be included.

The divorce caught Dave off guard, and that was rare for a man who'd spent his professional life being observant, looking for anomalies in people and situations. Over drinks, he sometimes talked about it, the wound of divorce after a long marriage never quite healing. He didn't dwell on it, but in self-reflection, he tried to objectively look at the fault line in the relationship.

I wasn't sure what had been worse for him, being oblivious to what was obvious or existing within the reality of a loveless marriage. I believe we can become unaware of the gradual decay and loss in our lives and yet, somehow, conscious of the haunting feeling it breathes through our souls on those lonely mornings when we stare into the mirror, not recognizing the image gazing back at us.

"What's this about TV?" Dave asked, bushy white eyebrows rising. "Sean, in your text, you said you had a new case and wanted to run something by me. If a side note isn't TV, Nick must be wanting to catch a soccer game."

Nick lifted both hands, palms out. "Nope. But Greece is gonna be in the World Cup."

Dave eyed me. "Well, how about a cooling libation as we settle in the salon to watch a round of Jeopardy or whatever?"

I nodded. "The whatever is the local news. There are a lot of people finding themselves in jeopardy as a tsunami of drugs washes across the nation. That's what I want to talk about with you, Dave. The case I'm working on, I believe, is related to it."

"Is this case going to be on the TV news?"

"It was a couple of months ago up in Gainesville. But yesterday, a group of college kids died from drug overdoses at a rented condo in

Panama City Beach. The common ingredient between the death of the young man I'm investigating and those college kids in Panama City could be fentanyl. We know it was found in the blood of my client's son. Toxicology reports will tell if it killed eight kids and put two more on life support."

"Good God," Dave mumbled. "What a tragedy."

"In the Tiki Bar, Nick and I caught a news promo about a victim of violence, a man who walked out of a local swamp in very bad shape. He was bloodied and shirtless. When the news flashed this man's image on screen, I noticed a small tattoo on his left upper arm. It's the tattoo of a one percent image—the number one and the percentage sign."

"What the hell does that mean?" Nick asked.

"I believe I know what Sean's referencing. An accountant friend of mine, a part-time biker, enlightened me about bikers and their tattoos. It's fascinating, to some degree. The one percent is a tattoo you'll see on only a few members of motorcycle gangs. These specific tats refer to a statement put out years ago by the American Motorcycle Association. The AMA suggested that ninety-nine percent of motorcyclists were law-abiding citizens, implying that the last one percent were indeed outliers and outlaws. Am I correct, Sean?"

"That's exactly want it means. However, for some of the few who wear the patch or the tattoo, they have stepped even further over the outlaw line. They've killed at least one person."

Nick asked, "Does this have something to do with those bikers who came into the Tiki?"

"When the news clip came on, I glanced at the bar mirror. I could see more than a casual recognition on the faces of the bikers. They knew him well."

Nick shrugged. "No big deal, Daytona Beach is full of bikers. Hell, Bike Week brings 'em all down here by the thousands."

"Bike Week, for the most part, attracts people who have a love and passion for riding and owning motorcycles. That doesn't mean you'll see the Hells Angels, Bandidos, Pagans, or any others hanging out at the same bars and strip clubs. These guys are all about their territory, protecting their sphere of influence and business interests."

Dave nodded. "Let's sit in the shade of the salon and drill down. I want to hear the details of your new case. You know, in a vicarious way, I enjoy my role as an armchair sleuth. You, Sean, do the heavy lifting while I get to ponder the what ifs as you knock on door number one, two, and three. I have a pot of clam chowder simmering. It'll go well with the fresh French baguettes I bought warm from the bakery this morning."

The three of us sat around a table in the salon, eating, the doors and windows open, a light breeze from the east carrying the smell of barnacles drying on dock posts in the receding tide. Soft jazz played from speakers in the background, the TV on but the sound muted. Max sat close to Nick as he handed a small piece of baguette to her.

I told Dave what I knew about Andy Ward's death. Finishing, I added, "So you guys can see I have very little to go on. Clint Ward said the detectives have spoken more than once to Andy's girlfriend, Brittany Harmon. She's telling police and the Ward family that, before she left Andy's apartment, she saw him use a knife to cut one of the pills in half and swallow only one half. The police report indicates that the other half of the pill wasn't found, and there were nine left in a bottle of ten."

Dave nodded. "So, it appears as if Andy took the second half of the pill after his girlfriend left the apartment."

"Possibly."

"Meaning that the two combined halves packed enough fentanyl to kill him."

"On the surface, that's exactly what it means."

Nick blew out a deep breath, handing Max a small piece of bread. "Where'd they find the kid's body?"

"In his bedroom. His left arm was outstretched, appearing as if he was trying to reach the phone on his nightstand when he died. His mom arrived a few hours later to take him shopping to buy something for his dad's birthday. Andy's body was found shortly after that."

Dave pushed back from the table, watching a brown pelican alight on a dock post just to the port side of *Gibraltar*. "I had a lot of challenges during my career in the CIA. In dealing with covert intelligence, it's about being in the people business—engaging people, winning their trust, recruiting assets in hostile countries, and flushing out deception by analyzing targets, often face-to-face. Sure, we gathered a lot of intel from the internet, but the old-fashioned way of spying versus spying today seemed more productive … less convoluted or spread out. Not so with what you're facing in this case."

Nick finished his chowder, "What do you mean?"

"These illicit drugs are being bought and sold online, often using apps designed to make the transactions untraceable. And it's mostly on popular social media platforms where the buying and selling is taking place. Physical forensic evidence, by its usual definition—blood spatter, fingerprints, fiber, DNA, etcetera, is non-existent on the internet. Digital evidence often can't prove a physical connection to a crime like murder."

Nick gestured to the widescreen TV, which was muted on the wall behind the salon's bar. "News is on the tube."

Dave reached for a remote on the table, turning up the sound.

THIRTY-TWO

The body language was clear even with the sound off. Slightly angling his body, leaning into the camera, and wrinkling his brow, the TV news anchorman's face took on a serious look as he led into the story. "Police are saying a Volusia County man is lucky to be alive today. The man apparently was thrown into alligator infested waters with his hands tied behind his back, and he lived to talk about it. But he's not saying much. Jackie Campbell has more on the story."

The image cut to an aerial shot of a river with a surface the color of a blackbird's wing. The reporter began, "From Channel Four's drone shot, you can see the twisting Tomoka River west of Ormond Beach. What you can't see are some of the very large alligators that roam the river. Down here you can." The video cut to images of gators sunning on the riverbank before cutting to a scene of police questioning a shirtless man on the side of a rural road, his jeans so drenched the pants were barely hanging onto his waist.

The reporter continued. "This is Robert Holloway, a thirty-two-year-old man who managed to somehow swim out of the Tomoka River with his hands tied behind his back. He told police that he was abducted near his home by four men and taken here. Holloway said the men jumped and beat him before tying him up, chaining him to the bed of a pickup truck late last night and driving to a remote section of the Tomoka River. He feared for his life, saying they were about to shoot him when he ran and jumped in the river. Holloway added that he managed to stay under long enough, to swim beneath the water, emerging downriver where the men couldn't find him. He swam to the opposite shore and got out, walking two miles to the Old Dixie Highway where a plumber on his way to work pulled over to help. Holloway's hands were still tied behind his back."

The shot cut to a man standing next to a plumbing truck, the morning sun exposing the lines in his craggy face. "I almost spilled my coffee when I spotted this fella walking down the road. He looked in pretty awful shape. His pants were soaked and caked in mud, and he was covered in gashes, bruises, and bug bites. He told me some bad dudes tried to kill him and throw his body in the river."

The image cut to paramedics loading Holloway into an ambulance, lights flashing, the sound of a semi-truck barreling down the highway. The reporter said, "Bad dudes indeed. Holloway is telling police that he didn't recognize any of the four men who allegedly kidnapped him from outside a trailer where he lives alone in a rural area of Volusia County."

The shot cut to a seasoned investigator in his mid-forties with sagging jowls. "The victim isn't giving us a lot of details because he says it was a surprise attack in his backyard. *Why* these perpetrators would rob Mr. Holloway, chain him in a pickup truck, try to shoot him, and plan to leave his body in the river, doesn't make a lot of sense considering the crime of robbery. He has a severe wound on his cheek, a cut in the shape of an X. He didn't get that from swimming in the river."

The shot cut to the reporter standing in a wooded area along the Tomoka River. "Robert Holloway was treated at a local hospital where he received more than two hundred stiches to close the wound on his face. Police are saying that rarely is a mugging victim kidnapped and driven away from the original crime scene to an area, such as a remote river, to be killed unless there is more to the apparent story than currently known. Also, what is not known is whether Holloway will press charges against the perpetrators if police find them. Live from the Tomoka River Preserve, this is Jackie Campbell."

Dave used the remote to mute the sound. "Well, it appears to me, and obviously to that detective interviewed, that there is a lot more to this bizarre crime than what this guy Holloway is willing to say. The question is *why?*"

Nick grunted. "He's scared of those bad dudes comin' back and finishing the job."

Dave eyed me. "Do you think this, in a remote way, could be connected to your case?"

"Maybe. I think some of those referenced *bad dudes* were just in the Tiki Bar. From what I saw on the back of one leather jacket, they are members of the Iron Fist biker gang. And from the tats on this guy Holloway, especially the one percent image, I'd suggest he is or was a member of the gang, too. But something happened to have the others turn on him."

"Wonder what the hell he did?" Nick asked.

Dave shrugged his wide shoulders. "Could be anything the gang believes grossly violates their code of ethics as oxymoronic as that may sound. How far did this guy step over the line to be sentenced to a late-night swim in an alligator-infested river? What do you think, Sean?"

"I think the X carved into his cheek is a dead giveaway that Holloway is forever ostracized from the Iron Fist gang. He'll have self-induced amnesia when it comes to giving police details of the crime. He knows that if he IDs any members of the gang, not only will they kill him but also his immediate family, including the dog if he has one. They'll all be in danger of reprisal."

Dave got up from the table and went behind his bar to remove the cork from a bottle of red wine that had been opened. He poured a small amount into a glass and sipped, watching a 56-foot Oyster sailboat motor from its berth on N-dock and head out to the Intracoastal and Ponce Inlet. He looked at me. "What do you see on the horizon? When I asked you if this biker gang could be tied to your case, you said maybe. Something cross your mind? I've heard Wynona call your skills of observation a 'Spidey sense,' not that I believe creatures with eight legs possess any intuitive talent except for how to spin a web. I think some politicians have a similar capacity—if webs of deceit count."

"I read a news article last year called the *Wild West of the Rio Grande.* It was about illegal border crossings from Mexico, primarily along the states of Texas and New Mexico. Part of the story dealt with the coyotes that are hired by the Mexican cartels to smuggle people and drugs over the border. Once here, the article illustrated how human trafficking and drugs fan out across the nation. One of those ways of distribution involves motorcycle gangs. The Iron Fist has a presence in the Rio Grande Valley from Las Cruces to San Antonio."

Nick wiped a spot of chowder off his mustache. "The Iron Fist is like the long arm of the lawless. Texas, Florida … wherever they run operations."

Dave set a water bowl down for Max and returned to the table. "The local Iron Fist chapters in Florida could be part of the supply chain, selling pills brought across the border by billion-dollar drug cartels, bought by dealers, such as biker gangs, and distributed to their dealers or sold online, or both. Perhaps their sales model is akin to a pyramid scheme, recruit people to sell and the higher ups get a cut. Police and the FBI know some biker gangs make a fortune in drug distribution. Is the death of Andy Ward somehow connected? Who knows—could be a futile lead. This is not going to be easy to crack."

Nick shook his head and looked across the table at me. "Maybe you just share your thoughts with the cops and let them start interrogating members of the biker gangs."

I said nothing.

Nick tossed Max a bite of bread. Dave said, "Perhaps the police will find forensic evidence on the packaging material—the box or envelope used to ship the drugs to Andy, or the bottle, perhaps even the pills themselves. How about tracking the shipping destination?"

"According to Clint, the police tell him there wasn't a speck of forensic evidence on the small box used for shipping, the bottle, or the pills. Delivery was done through the postal service. No return address and no postmark since the sender used postage from a personal computer. These perps could send it UPS or FedEx and still maintain anonymity. Drug traffickers work social media sites like magicians. Visible one minute, invisible the next. Algorithms designed to make them concealed when they want to be."

Nick stood to get a beer from the bar. He popped the top. "So, what the hell do you do?"

"I don't know." I glanced at Dave. "In the CIA, did you liaise with the DEA occasionally?"

"Sometimes. The CIA, DEA, and FBI do share information when mutually beneficial. However, each agency likes to hold its cards close to the chest, ensuring more caseloads, thus the greater justification for increased funding in each year's budget. In that sense, crime pays. Why do you ask?"

"Because, after seeing the news footage of the deaths of the eight college kids in Panama City Beach, what happened to West Point students in Fort Lauderdale when they overdosed, and of course Andy Ward, I'm looking at this in a much broader perspective."

"You mean biker gangs?" Nick asked.

"If there's any connection, they could be just a cog in this illegal enterprise."

He sipped his beer. "All you gotta do is find the creep who sold and shipped the pills to Andy. Let the feds, the DEA, and the rest of the alphabet soup agencies carry the big load."

"In the last year alone, more than 100,000 of America's youth died per year from drugs laced with fentanyl. Where does that river of drugs start? Like most natural rivers, it usually begins in higher elevations—a steady stream, working its way down to a basin where other tributaries join the flow. The headwaters are the *source* of the drugs. The creeks are the dealers. The river itself is the drug flow. If I find the headwaters of this thing, I find the original source."

Nick's eyebrows rose. "Whoa, you're talking about one dangerous journey upstream. It'll be like traveling the Amazon—against the current, piranhas in the water, bugs that lay eggs into your skin, and headhunters along the river."

Dave removed his bifocals, cleaning them with a soft cloth. He looked over at me. "With this country facing so many deaths every year from fentanyl, where do you begin to solve a local case that was apparently consummated online?"

"I'll do what I can, starting around Gainesville, where Andy lived." I motioned to the TV screen. "I want to talk to the guy on the news, Robert Holloway. If he was a member of Iron Fist, I'm sure he used a street name. He isn't saying much to the police. I'll see if he'll talk to me."

THIRTY-THREE

Ciudad Lerdo, Mexico

Many of the devotees call her Saint Death. The more formal name of this female figure is Santa Muerte. Some in Mexico refer to her as the saint of last resort. Shrines dedicated to what a growing number of people in Mexico call Our Lady of the Most Holy Death are more visible than ever before. Dozens of altars are in back rooms of shops across Mexico, stores that sell images of Santa Muerte. Others are larger buildings, chapels, or sanctuaries often built from drug cartel money.

In the shadowy world of cartels and crime, it's no surprise that a variant religion would bubble up from dark crevices to satisfy the spiritual needs of those who see nothing wrong with an evil value system that rewards personal gain over everything. How that advantage is achieved often results from destroying others along the way. Crime and the occult can be a deadly combination. Inside many prisoners' jail cells in Mexico and the U.S., convicts keep small statuettes of Santa Muerte.

In the public areas, from Mexico City down to some of the smallest villages, the effigy of Santa Muerte is the centerpiece, eerily placed among the burning candles on semi-dark altars. The figure is usually life-size. But there is nothing about life represented in the imagery. It's all about death with the suggestion of a better life if certain conditions are met, including leaving donations and gifts.

Santa Muerte is often depicted as a human skeleton dressed in a long robe, cape, or a flowing bridal gown, the head area of the skull covered in a veil, the skeletal face always revealed. Traditionally, she is holding a scythe in one boney hand and a globe of the world in the other. The Grim Reaper among idols.

Diego Navarro doesn't worship anything but money and the power it buys. He does believe that Santa Muerte possesses a spiritual power of the underworld that offers him protection if he serves her well. Navarro is one of an estimated twelve million followers of Santa Muerte. Although he belongs to a large devotion group, very few in those masses do what he does—operate one of Mexico's most feared drug cartels. His deal with the Angel of Death is to bring her the finest gifts while she ensures his cartel will be the largest in history.

That's why he visits Santa Muerte the first Wednesday of each month. To pray for success and protection. To count on Santa Muerte is to allow him to get away with murder and still go to heaven. He is a firm believer— a believer that this purported saint will protect him no matter what he does … if he offers atonement and gifts. Especially the gifts.

Navarro was entering the shrine today to pay homage to the dark patron and to ask for her blessing, protection, and guidance. On this day, however, he had one more request. His driver parked the black Ford Expedition with tinted windows near the sanctuary, a dull white adobe building that once was a Catholic church. After the structure was partially damaged in a fire, the Durango cartel paid to have it rebuilt, not as a church but rather as a shrine to Santa Muerte. In Spanish, the building was now called Catedral de Lerdo.

It was in the heart of the city, Ciudad Lerdo, surrounded by shops, open-air markets, and street vendors cooking under colorful umbrellas. The smell of tostadas and quesadillas being grilled over mesquite wood permeated the air. Music blared from the speakers of boom boxes at almost every booth.

Before Navarro got out of the SUV, his bodyguards preceded him. There were two, both men dressed in jeans and untucked long shirts. Two pistols each under their shirts. They wore sunglasses, eyes scanning the roofs of buildings, alleys, and the adjoining street. Mopeds and small cars chugged by, exhaust fumes drifting as they passed. Navarro got out of the vehicle carrying a cardboard box. He headed toward the entrance to the shrine, dark glasses on, ignoring stares from some customers buying food at the street vendors' stands.

His men waited outside the entrance as Navarro walked down the cobblestone pathway to the doorway. A woman and her skinny, mixed breed dog stood near the wrought iron bars blocking the front door. Ariana Garza was almost fifty and grateful she had lived that long in a place where violent death is an everyday occurrence. She was wearing a long red robe draped with a white sash, silver hoop earrings, and a charm bracelet, her graying hair pulled back into a tight bun. Ariana's face was etched with lines from years working as a field laborer—a picker in the hot sun, dark circles beneath tired eyes. But those days of field labor were finally behind her.

She attributes her longevity to having prayed to Santa Muerte. Ariana made a prayer the day before she was abducted by human traffickers twenty years ago. For no apparent reason, as they were about to take her and seven other women across the border into the U.S., her captives let her go. She believed it was because she'd asked for protection from Santa Muerte. In a land where violent death is so commonplace, Ariana chose to follow a dark spirit that embodies death.

And, today, she is the high priestess and curator of the shrine.

In Spanish, she greeted Navarro. "Blessings, sir. It is good to see you again. The shrine has been reserved only for you this afternoon. Our Lady of the Most Holy Death awaits you."

THIRTY-FOUR

Outside the shrine, a woman was stopped in her tracks. As she approached the entrance, one of Navarro's guards stepped in front of her. She was a small woman, less than five feet tall, in her early sixties, with wispy gray hair. She wore a long black dress with a fringed poncho thrown over her hunched shoulders. She looked at the guard. He shook his head. In Spanish he said, "Come back later, señora."

"I am only here for a little while today. My grandson brought me here to the shrine. Please—I do not have—"

"Come back later."

She stared up at his angry eyes and mumbled words under her breath. "Men who deny an old woman prayer can be cursed … that includes your boss." She turned and walked away.

The guard smirked. "You're just an old, dried-up witch."

***

Diego Navarro removed his sunglasses, staring at the keeper of the shrine for a moment. He reached in his pocket and removed a wad of folded bills, more than two thousand pesos. He handed the money to Ariana. "Take this and buy some more clothes. The high priestess of this sanctuary must be the best dressed in all of Ciudad Lerdo."

She reached for the money, pausing to kiss the back of his hand. Ariana looked up at him. "Thank you. May your blessings be many and your protection against those who would wish to do you harm be repelled like an umbrella repels the rain." She put the cash in the pocket of her robe and stepped aside, allowing Navarro to enter. Her dog sat in the shade of a guava tree.

Inside the shrine was a large room, a few hard wooden pews for sitting, candles flickering in every corner and across much of the altar,

136

shadows dancing over the walls. The room smelled of fresh linen, burning candles, roses, and oiled wood. Along the right and left sides of the altar were red roses, daisies, and rosary beads. A large brass plate was partially filled with money, unsmoked cigars, small bottles of unopened perfume, chocolates, and tequila.

In the center, directly behind the altar, was what Navarro came to see. It was believed by locals that the skeleton, dressed in a long white wedding dress with a matching veil, was that of a human skeleton. She was said to have been one of the many victims of human trafficking, her body left in the Chihuahua Desert, flesh devoured by scavengers, bones bleached white from the scorching sun.

Navarro stood in front of the skeleton, setting the cardboard box on the altar. He stared at the boney face for half a minute, saying nothing, the candlelight curling across the figure's facial bones, entering the twin black holes—the eye sockets, as if the light could somehow illuminate the darkness inside.

He lit a cigar, blowing smoke up toward the ceiling. He ran his tongue along the inside of one cheek. His Spanish slow and deliberate, words carefully chosen. "You are in a much better place now. On earth you were used by too many people. In death, though, you have real life … a better life. You are the saint of the dead, a woman who is empowered to escort the believers to heaven."

A smile worked at the corner of his mouth, a rooster crowing somewhere behind the building. "The question is this: once there, will we be allowed inside? With your help, I believe it is possible. We did not create this world, nor did we ask to come here. We were born into it … the good, bad, and ugly. My mother always said the meek shall inherit the earth. I do not believe that. It is truly the rule of the jungle. Eat or be eaten. You must be ruthless to survive. But, is it more than physical strength, or is it the power of the mind?"

He blew a smoke ring, the sphere wobbling toward the top of the skeleton's veil like a smoky halo. "It is not only the power of the mind, but also a man's ability to anticipate change, like storms beyond the horizon, and prepare for their arrival. Some say it is about adapting to those things around you. I believe it is more like seeing what doesn't exist, creating those things, and forcing others to adapt or perish. I have learned that from you, my holy angel of death. Humans are fascinated about the mystery of death because it is the most traumatic event and the last thing we will ever experience in this life. Poof, and we are no more." He exhaled a mouthful of smoke.

Navarro paused, his eyes filled with veiled thoughts. He held the cigar between his fingers, starring at the red-hot ash, the smoke barely curling as it rose to the ceiling in the stale and unmoving air. "I do not come here, Santa Muerte, to ask for things. I do not need things. I need your shield. I have been a benefit to this town and region, giving money to the poor, doing good in a land of bad. However, I do seek your shelter and guidance as me and my men move forward with some of our most ambitious plans."

Ariana stood in the shadows of the vestibule and passageway, quietly listening. She looked back at the closed and locked iron bars in front of the entrance, her dog now sleeping under a fan palm tree bordering the pathway.

Navarro stepped closer to the altar. "You helped to open the door at the American border. It would be foolish of us if we did not enter. I ask for your protection as we export more drugs in history into the soul of the gringos—the Americans. They are hungry for it, no? Someone must fill that need. It might as well be me. I ask for the release of my father." He puffed his cigar, his left eye closing in the smoke.

"My prayer is for you, my angel of death, to protect us as we strive to be the top provider of drugs and people into the United States. Provide us with the best migration routes, keeping our competitors away. Guide us to the safest new areas to cross the Rio Grande and for passage into that country." He paused staring at the face of the skeleton. "One last thing … some generals win the war by taking no prisoners. I think the opposite can be true in certain situations. A prisoner is a pawn in this game—a negotiating tool. You have helped us capture this pawn. In your holy name, I humbly ask that we use him to your advantage."

He pushed one hand into his pocket, pulling out a small knife. He stuck the cigar in the corner of his mouth as he opened one of the folding blades, using the knife to slice through the plastic packaging tape that sealed the cardboard box. He opened the four flaps, looked up at the skeleton's hollow face. "For you, Santa Muerte, because you request us to make sacrifices so our prayers will be fulfilled. Here is my contribution to your altar."

He reached into the box, grabbing something with his left hand, pulling out a man's decapitated head. Navarro held it by the thick black hair, the dead man's eyes open, candlelight playing over the ashen face— the light pulled into the lifeless eyes, dried blood at one side of his mouth.

Navarro held the severed head up higher in the air, toward the skeleton. "Behold! This is the sacrifice I make to you. In your name, I ask that my requests be granted." He lowered the head onto the center of the brass plate, resting it on Mexican pesos and chocolate mints.

Ariana walked quietly toward the entrance, waiting at the iron bar door. She used her key to unlock it as Navarro came down the hall from the altar. He paused at the door, his black eyes studying her face. "High Priestess, I suggest that you close the shrine to anyone else for the rest of the day. As night falls, you should remove the sacrifice I found on the altar. Bury it somewhere where your dog will not dig up."

She said nothing, nodding and folding her arms across her breasts.

He turned and walked away as the rooster crowed again.

THIRTY-FIVE

The following day I went to meet a man who didn't have a desire to speak with me. As I was driving to Gainesville to talk with Detective Winston Porter, I placed a call to the Panama City Beach PD. When I'd watched the TV news story about the spring break tragedy—eight college kids who died in a rented condo on Panama City Beach, I made a mental note. I remembered the name of the detective who was interviewed. And I remembered her demeanor. Her name was Lindsey Owen, and I could tell she was emotionally affected by what she faced.

The PD receptionist, a woman with a monotone voice, said, "I think Detective Owen is at her desk this morning. May I ask what your call is in reference to, sir?"

"Of course. It's in reference to the deaths of the eight college students. Do I need to say more?"

"No, sir. Please hold."

Thirty seconds later, another woman came on the line. The voice much more pleasant. "This is Detective Owen. I understand you have some information."

"Good morning, Detective Owen. My name is Sean O'Brien. I happened to see your TV news interview the other day when you were on the scene investigating the deaths of those college students. I have a case that might be related."

"Oh, really. Are you in law enforcement?"

"Used to be. I spent eight years working homicide with Miami-Dade PD. I've seen more than my share of drug overdoses. Usually from heroin. But that's all changed since fentanyl became the drug of choice for pushers and users."

"That's the sad truth. So, you fought the good fight at ground zero in Miami. What are you doing now?"

"Still fighting the good fight, but without as many rules and regulations. And I only do it when the victim or the victim's family request my services."

"What would those services be?"

"I try hard to find answers, and in some small way, bring closure."

"Don't we all in this line of work?"

"I'd like to think that. Sometimes, due to case overloads, time, manpower restraints, and lack of physical evidence, cases might fall through the cracks. I only do what I do by request … when it seems the light at the end of the tunnel has gone dark."

"Are you a PI?"

"Yes. I work to put the pieces together on cold cases. The case I mentioned isn't that cold, it's simply at a standstill. Before the horrific scene that you're investigating, a University of Florida student, the son of a close friend of mine, died from an overdose. One pill. Not what I'd call an overdose. It's more like a single shot to the heart—a pill laced with fentanyl."

"Do you think your case and what happened on Panama City Beach are related?"

"If fentanyl is the link, they might be."

She said nothing for a few seconds. "As a matter of fact, we just got the tox reports in this morning. The ME put an extreme rush on getting the results, considering the circumstances and intense national news coverage. This was the worst thing to happen since college kids have been coming to Florida for spring break over the last fifty years. Fentanyl was in the blood of the eight students who died, and it was in the blood of the two who survived. They are still in the hospital. What can you tell me about the case that you're investigating?"

"I hope to have more I can share with you in a few hours. I'm driving to Gainesville from Ponce Inlet to speak with the lead detective. Now that I know fentanyl is the common denominator in the death of my friend's son and those deaths in your investigation, I'll look for a hidden path between the two."

"That's assuming there is one. Unfortunately, fentanyl is killing a lot of young people nowadays. And that's all across the country, year-round, not just during spring break."

"There may be no connection. Andy Ward bought his pills online. Bought them for pain. All it took was one to kill him. Whomever brought the drugs to the party at the condo in the case you're investigating could have used the same online dealer that Andy used. Were the pills bought in Panama City Beach, or did one of the kids bring them from home? Do you know how the drugs were delivered … by a dealer or FedEx?"

"We don't know that yet. Does Gainesville PD have those answers in Andy Ward's death?"

"They know how the drugs arrived—through the mail. But as far as who sent them … no, not yet. That's what they're telling Andy's parents. I suspect it's accurate. Maybe the lead detective will corroborate that with me."

"I'll reach out to Gainesville PD as well to see where they stand, to see if there may be something that'll connect the cases. I'll also ask if they have any other cases similar since it is a college town." The tone of her voice changed slightly. Less affable. More reserved. "Thanks for your call, Mr. O'Brien."

"You have children, don't you?"

"Yes, a son and a daughter. Why?"

"Watching the TV interview with you, I could see the compassion on your face—the empathy that parents feel for other parents who've lost a child, especially when the death is caused by a killer."

"Right now, the deaths of the eight students appear to have been caused by the young man who brought the drugs to the party. His name was Bruce Cooper. Unfortunately, he died as well. Whomever Cooper bought the drugs from certainly bears major responsibility. The five college men were from Michigan. Did Cooper buy them from a dealer up there? If so, the investigation would need to expand beyond Panama City."

"Maybe they were bought in Panama City."

"We hope to find out. There's a whole daisy chain from the dealer on up to the people who make this poison. I want to find the last link in the chain—the dealer who sold or gave the pill bottle to Bruce Cooper. Mr. O'Brien, I need to take a meeting."

"Is there a chapter of the Iron Fist motorcycle gang in Panama City?"

"No. There could be members, but as far as I'm aware, there's no organized group. Maybe in Pensacola. It's not that far away. Why? Is this gang pushing fentanyl?"

"I don't know. I do know that the Iron Fist has a presence in two of the states bordering Mexico—Texas and New Mexico. A lot of drugs are crossing the border. Once here, the Mexican cartels use distributors to get the stuff into the rest of the nation. The Iron Fist, according to the FBI, sells everything from guns to drugs to people."

"Thanks for your call, Mr. O'Brien. If you hear anything else, please don't hesitate to get in touch."

"One last thing. The news reports indicated one of the college kids didn't take the pills. Maybe this person knows where Bruce Cooper bought the drugs."

"We'll be sure to ask her. Thank you." She clicked off.

I set my phone on the seat beside me. As I drove my Jeep north along the Florida Turnpike, the tread on the off-road tires hummed against the pavement, adding to the cadence on the radio. In two hours, I would be in Gainesville—the place where Andy Ward died. Detective Owen called the possible links to Andy's death a daisy chain. Daisy chains are made by tying the stems together producing a circle. A perfect circle is said to have no starting point, or ending, for that matter. But it does have a center. The location formula is as easy as A-B-C. To find the center of a circle, you can use a triangle. Let two points, A and B touch the inner part of the circle. The top or apex of the triangle will be in the exact center.

In Andy's case, that's where the trail of the lethal drugs begins. In the center of a circle.

That would be my destination.

There is an old blues and country hymn called *Will the Circle be Unbroken*. In the circle of death that encompasses lethal drugs, there's only one way to fix it.

Break it.

THIRTY-SIX

Robert Holloway—Axle, was a desperate man. He feared staying at his trailer in rural Volusia County. After his cheek was cleaned, stitched, and bandaged, he'd hitched a ride from the hospital to his trailer. He was there long enough to get some money he had stashed in the freezer, a pistol, rounds of ammo, and drugs. His friend, Drywall, left Axle's motorcycle in the yard.

He walked into his bathroom to get a bottle of Adderall, cupping his hands to drink water from the sink, swallowing a pill. He looked in the mirror, staring at the bandage on his face, anger rising in his gut. "Tank, come hell or high water, I'm gonna track your fat ass down. Payback is sweet." In less than two minutes, he was out of his trailer.

Axle cranked his twenty-year-old Dodge Ram pickup truck, peeling rubber, getting out of his driveway. He drove the speed limit fifteen miles away to a friend's house, a former biker, now retired—a man who made a living as a welder when he felt like working. On the way there, Axle constantly looked in the truck's mirrors, watching for members of the Iron Fist who Tank may have ordered to find him. *Maybe they were done*, he thought. *Too much news coverage. Doesn't jibe with the bullshit images of bikers doin' stuff to help Toys for Tots.*

Axle felt the drug in his system. He lowered the driver's window, the musty smell of fresh-turned earth coming from where a farmer on a tractor was pulling a chisel plow through a field, clouds of dust rising. Axle drove with his Ruger pistol next to him on the truck's bench seat. He slowed as he came to a dirt driveway leading to a small ranch-style brick house two hundred feet from the road. Behind it was a barn, a gray horse at the wire fence.

Axle turned onto the drive, parking near a newer truck under the shade of a leafy oak tree. He got out and jogged to the front door almost hidden behind two cabbage palm trees. He banged on the door with one fist. He waited ten seconds before knocking again. He saw the curtain part in an adjacent window, and moments later, the door opened.

A wiry man in his mid-fifties stepped onto the concrete porch. He had a cagey look new prisoners often have while mixing with the general population in the prison yard. His nose was scarred, bowed from a bar fight twenty years ago. He glanced over Axle's shoulder to the road. His name was George Tyler, street name, Welder. "What the hell are you doing here, Axle?"

"That's a damn fine way to greet an old friend. Look, Welder, I need to crash on your couch for a couple of days. Gotta lay low. Some crap went down at the clubhouse, nothin' that was my fault. Tank went ape-shit crazy. That happens when he gets deep into the snow. Anyway, the asshole had four members try to shoot and dump me in the Tomoka River. I took a leap of faith and jumped in before they could pull the trigger. Even with my hands tied behind my back, somehow, I got outta that mess. It'll all blow over in a few days. In the meantime, I need a place to crash."

Welder lifted a Camel cigarette from a pack in his pocket, using a plastic Bic to light an unfiltered cigarette. He took a long drag, smoke curling from his crooked nostrils, spitting a sliver of tobacco. "As much as I'd like to help you, man, I can't take the chance. I've been out of the biker's life for goin' on five years. Before my retirement, I suffered three broken bones, a concussion, and a stabbing from more fights than I can count. My brain bled from the time that peckerwood, Ronnie Flathead Weaver, broke a pool stick over my skull. I can't risk Tank and his boys sniffing around my place."

"It'll only be for a night or two."

Welder took another drag, shaking his head. "My old lady would pitch a fit so bad that it'd make her periods look like pattycake if I let you stay here."

"Welder, I got nowhere else to go."

"Man, I'm sorry, okay?"

"In hard times, you know who your real friends are." He turned to leave.

"Wait a second. You can pull your truck inside the barn and sleep in the hayloft. I keep a wool blanket up there. I'll bring you some food.

You just gotta keep out of sight. Understand? No gettin' in your truck and runnin' down to the 7-Eleven for smokes."

"Thanks, Welder."

"Three days tops. Then you land somewhere else, and you're somebody else's problem."

***

As I drove into the Gainesville city limits, Dave Collins' name popped up on my phone screen. I answered his call. "Where are you, Sean?"

"Gainesville. Driving to the PD."

"Good. That means you're sitting down."

"And that means you have bad news."

"More of a good news bad news scenario, or perhaps, it simply is news of confirmation."

"What do you have?"

"I spoke with one of my former CIA contacts. He's a field agent who worked out of Mexico City for three years before moving to Caracas. Santiago has a lot of DEA contacts in and out of Mexico. I spoke with him on the phone, asking a few questions relating to this explosion of drugs across the border—especially fentanyl. He told me that, in the last two years, the Iron Fist motorcycle gang is suspected of being a major trafficker, working directly in concert with the second largest cartel in Mexico, the Durango Cartel."

"Interesting."

"He said that the Iron Fist is distributing drugs into some southern states—Louisiana, Mississippi, Georgia, parts of Texas, and the most profitable on the list—Florida. So, you were right about your assumption of a possible connection between our southern border and the vast influx of fentanyl into Florida. A huge chunk of it is being delivered here, courtesy of the Iron Fist."

"Thanks, Dave. That's good to know."

"That revelation, as unsurprising as it appears to be, is the good news in terms of an exposé. The bad news is that it seems as if these bikers, since fentanyl hit the nation, rarely are busted. Are they that good, or are they good at intimidating members of law enforcement who might be choosing not to penetrate their circle of influence?"

"The FBI had agents infiltrating some of these gangs like the Outlaws, Pagans, Bandidos, and probably others over the last few years. Maybe that's the case with the Iron Fist. In the meantime, I must work harder to see if there's a connection between the Iron Fist and the death of Andy Ward."

"There's a slight problem with that scenario, Sean. It means that you will have no one to watch your back. It will be analogous to you walking in shorts and barefoot inside a den of rattlesnakes. At least rattlesnakes give you a warning before they strike."

THIRTY-SEVEN

Central Mexico

Tony Salazar usually prayed for others, especially for his wife, Nicole, son Lucas, and little Eva. Today, Salazar whispered a prayer for himself. He assumed, without some kind of divine intervention, he'd never leave the stable alive. The men left hours ago, closing the stable door. Salazar's hands were still tied by a rope to a roughhewn beam above his head. He could hear a horse shuffle in its stall. Seconds later, the horse made a loud whinny.

And he could hear the flies. They seemed to enter through cracks in the wood, smelling blood and raw flesh. They were horseflies and blowflies. He could feel the insects alighting on his back, crawling, scratching at the torn flesh and open sores. Salazar didn't know whether they were drinking his blood or laying eggs in the lacerations. Regardless, tied to the wide timber, he couldn't swat them or turn around and place his back to the wood. He had to endure the bites, the gnawing, the relentless attack.

He stood there, thinking about the conversation with Diego Navarro. The man epitomized how vast money gained with little or no consequences could turn someone like him into a monster. These extremists relish power, believing that the myths they spin make them into legends. Unfortunately, it also delivers legions of shady followers. Salazar knew that Navarro truly believed that the only thing separating him from his admirers, competitors, and most of Mexico, for that matter, was his mind, bravado, and willingness to take calculated risks—to see what others didn't. Navarro's psychosis led him to believe he was untouchable. He could live by the sword on the killing fields like great warriors before him, but he would be the greatest.

Salazar thought about the extreme narcissism that is in the DNA of many of Mexico's drug lords. Life is not sacred. Death is the leverage they use for instilling fear, compliance, and conformity. They were the kings, defending their turf and territory in wars going back to the days of the Aztecs and Mayans.

He looked up at his hands. The men had tied rope around his wrists in the same method a rodeo cowboy ties the legs of a calf. From there, another rope was tied to a timber near the stable's ceiling, keeping his hands and arms suspended high over his head and lifting him on the balls of his feet. His fingers were becoming numb from the loss of movement and reduced blood circulation.

He closed his eyes and thought about his options. Since they'd taken his phone, there was no way the DEA in Mexico could track him. And there was no way he could call them unless he somehow managed to take a phone off one of the men.

He looked around the stable. There were tools hanging from the wall near the last stall to his right. The tools included a handsaw, shovels, rakes, two pitchforks, hammers, augers, and wire cutters for fence mending. He pulled at the ropes, the fibers only digging further into his chaffed skin.

***

DEA agent Byron Lopez made the call for the fifth time. No answer. Tall, close-cropped hair, he stood in his office at the U.S. consulate building in Guadalajara, looking out the third-story window at the street vendors. Most were selling fruits and vegetables. Some offered fresh baked breads, tacos, tamales, gorditas, and other Mexican staples. The crowd was light for an early Friday afternoon. He used his desk phone to make another call. "Cedro, it's Byron. I was expecting Tony Salazar here yesterday. He's not answering his phone. How far are you from his house?"

"Twenty minutes."

"You mind running by there to see if he's home. See if his car is in the driveway?"

"No problem."

"Thanks." He clicked off and made another call. This one was to the DEA's Mexican headquarters in Mexico City. "Carlos, it's Byron Lopez."

"Hey, buddy, what's up?"

"It's Tony Salazar. His asset was breached recently. The guy was embedded with the Durango cartel, trying to keep a close eye on Diego Navarro. The asset was killed. Before he died, he might have been tortured and forced to tell Navarro and his men where to find Tony."

"I heard about that. Didn't get the full details yet. You think Navarro would go after Tony?"

"I don't know. It depends on what Navarro thinks that Tony knows … or it could be that Navarro, knowing where a DEA agent lives, might want to harass him, or he could send someone to put a bullet in Tony's head."

"That doesn't seem like a smart move, considering the state of things in Mexico. The Narcos aren't getting a lot of pressure from the government, military, or police. Many in those groups are owned by the cartels. Doesn't make a lot of sense to kill a DEA agent and risk the wrath of the agency and the U.S. government. Why rock the boat when there's smooth sailing in the illegal drug business right now?"

"Tony isn't answering his phone. That's not like him. No text messages. Nothing. We need to run a trace. You have the number. Let's see if we can find a GPS location, and if that's the case, maybe that's where we'll find Tony. And, if we find him … let's hope he's still alive."

THIRTY-EIGHT

I often considered the contradiction of terms with the words law enforcement. When I was a detective, I didn't enforce the law. Everything we did in the police department was a reaction to someone breaking the law. Laws weren't enforced. Penalties for violations were. Sometimes. The job, or a case, can end up becoming a double-edged sword. Maybe that's because of the human psychology that goes into catching lawbreakers. Police are trained to receive information, but they're hesitant to share. Striking the right balance is an art, and it can lead to making or breaking a case. I thought about that as I entered the Gainesville PD.

Of course, there can be good reason for concealment in an open criminal investigation. But how about a closed one or an investigation that has moved to the back burner and the gas is shut off? Unfortunately, there are detectives who cling to their cases regardless of whether the investigation is stale or closed. If selfishness, greed, or tightfisted egos can cause a nation most of its problems, those same reasons can keep a cold case turning in circles or frozen in time.

That's often the situation when it comes to detectives talking with private investigators. The PIs were usually hired by victims' families, primarily when they felt the local police weren't on track to solve the case. Many detectives view a PI as someone who wants to be in law enforcement but can't play by the rules.

As a former detective, I played by the rules. Most of the time. But there were situations where rules didn't apply. During a hunt, to get into a criminal's head, you must think like one in order to view the world from their selfish perspective. When you do that, you begin to see what their next move might be. You bait traps. You anticipate intersections in trails they follow and the routines they develop. You look for patterns and anomalies, trying hard to anticipate the next move a sociopath might make.

It's very time-consuming, detailed work lethargic detectives prefer not to pursue. There are detectives who look at an investigating PI as someone of value, a person who eases their caseload if the criminal is found. Conversely, there are others who look at PIs as flies around their picnic table. After my phone call to Detective Winston Porter with the Gainesville PD, I thought the fly scenario would fit.

I was right.

He agreed to meet with me. Not in his office, but rather in the department's lobby. Even at 11:00 a.m., his blue tie was loosened a notch or two, sleeves on his white shirt rolled up to the center of his meaty forearms. Eyes puffy. After our initial greeting, me restating why I was there, and clarifying what I was looking for, he shook his head.

"Wish I could help you, Mr. O'Brien. But the fact of the matter is, there are no witnesses in the actual death of Andy Ward. His girlfriend left and went to the gym. Her alibi checks out. We have no physical or forensic evidence to process. Nothing but the package, the pill bottle, and the pills. There is not a thing traceable on those items."

"How about people in the apartment complex? Someone who might have seen something?"

He shook his head. "Like I said, there are no witnesses. We knocked on all the doors. Talked to residents. There are no surveillance cameras in the direct vicinity of Ward's apartment. So, what we have is a postal delivery, one of hundreds that day for the carrier, and a benign, anonymous package that, unfortunately, had ten little bombs inside. Ten light blue pills containing fentanyl as part of the mix."

"Any idea where the pills were made?"

"Not in the slightest. They could be traceable to a pill press, but where do you go for that with no suspects? Those drugs could have come from some clandestine back-alley neighborhood lab in a basement, like a meth-cooking house, or they could have come from out of state. Maybe out of the country, all the way from Mexico. We don't know."

"What about the online connections? The point of sale?"

"What about it? Our IT team has gone through Andy Ward's laptop. They couldn't find a thing in reference to a drug sale. Nothing in his emails, Twitter, Instagram, Snapchat, Facebook, the whole slew of social media garbage. Regardless, we do know that most pills are bought and sold today from online sources. Just a couple of years ago, illegal drugs were sold on the dark web. Now, dealers and buyers are using emojis in place of keywords. They use *code words* more than keywords. It's hard to trace. But can't say we didn't try."

"Maybe what killed Andy Ward is traceable to what and who killed those eight college kids over in Panama City Beach. Those pills, just like the ones that Andy bought, were cut with fentanyl. All could be coming from the same supply chain."

"Possibly. Our office will touch base with Panama City PD."

"A good contact is Detective Lindsey Owen, the lead investigator. She's the one who told me that fentanyl was what killed those students. Just like Andy Ward, light blue pills, the number 30 on one side, the letter M on the other. And inside, the same poison—fentanyl."

Detective Porter rocked slightly in his large laced-up shoes. "Why would you call Panama City Beach PD?"

"Because I saw the story on TV, and I was curious as to the cause of those deaths. If it was fentanyl, I wanted to share that information with you."

He took a deep breath, looking across the lobby to a memorial on one wall. Framed photos of uniformed police officers who died in the line of duty. "Mr. O'Brien, on the phone, you told me you are friends with the Ward family. Because of that, and since you are trying to help, I don't mind sharing with you some of the facts surrounding our investigation into what killed Andy Ward."

"I appreciate that."

"But you need to stay on the rails. Stay within boundaries. Last thing I need is some PI interfering. By the way, this is not a homicide investigation. The ME ruled it as an accidental drug overdose. That doesn't mean we're not hunting for whoever sold Ward the drugs, but it doesn't fit the standard requisites for homicide"

I said nothing, the sound of a phone buzzing in the reception area.

Porter cleared his throat, turning to leave. "Detective, I'm aware that this is not your only case, and you're probably stretched thin. But, when Andy Ward, a strong and healthy young man, dies from one pill with fentanyl in it, when eight more kids die in the same way in Panama City, and when West Point students overdose during spring break in South

Florida … these aren't accidental overdoses. When 100,000 young people died last year in America from fentanyl overdoses, I'd suggest we have an epidemic on our hands, and that's no accident. You say these deaths don't fit the standard requisite for homicide. You can remove the word accidental from the ME's report and insert these words … intentional overdose caused by an unknown person. And, under Florida state law, if a dealer sells a drug that kills the customer, that dealer can be charged with murder."

"Have a good day, O'Brien."

"If someone knowingly sells or gives a deadly product to another person for ingesting, and if the result of that is death, it's murder. That is the focus of my investigation. These killer dealers, using the internet, don't operate within boundaries. They don't use a standard requisite in their world of crime, greed, and egos. To find them, to level the playing field, there are no boundaries."

I turned and walked out the door.

THIRTY-NINE

Cedro Alvarez didn't know which might be better news: Tony Salazar's car in his driveway or arriving and seeing it gone. If the car was there, it should mean that Tony was home as well. *But why the loss of communications? If the car was gone, where the hell was Tony?* He was supposed to be in Guadalajara by now. Alvarez, shaggy black hair, a week's worth of whiskers, wearing dark glasses, drove his Ford Escape less than a block from Salazar's house.

He stopped at a red light and watched the traffic at an intersection in the downtown area, cars and motorcycles coming and going. Most of the buildings in the city block stood at least two stories. Some had balconies. A black SUV, a Lincoln Navigator, pulled up in the adjacent lane, next to Alvarez's car. He glanced at it, looking at the dark, tinted windows, knowing the SUV was owned by the Durango cartel. Alvarez reached in the center console, his hand on the grip of a 9mm gun.

He looked back at the traffic light. Red. He was at a crossroads— physically and mentally, deciding his next ten-second move. Could it be coincidental that a driver for the cartel was in the next lane waiting for the light to change? Or were they tracking him, too? He glanced back at the Lincoln. He didn't know how many men were inside, but he did know that if one of the windows facing his car came down, he was going through the red light, assuming there was a gap in traffic.

Alvarez felt a slight pain in his stomach. No breakfast, too much black coffee, and the stress of a job as advisor to the DEA. The pay was excellent. Benefits good. Risks were always on his mind. He managed to keep a relatively low profile as he did intel work for the DEA. The job came with baggage. He thought about that as he drummed his fingers on the steering wheel. Making a quick, casual glance at the Lincoln, he could barely see someone sitting in the backseat. That meant there were at least three people inside.

Although he never talked about his part-time affiliation with the DEA, he knew that a few family members were aware of it. Word gets out and rarely escapes the big ears of the cartel. Even though the DEA was fighting the drug war, some people in Mexico looked at the presence of the agency as a foreign police force within their sovereign country. It was a strange contrast—the drug cartels were making billions of dollars in profits, and most Mexican citizens were poor. Yet, a lot of people had a repressed admiration for the drug lords. Robin Hoods.

The light changed to green, and Alvarez stepped on the accelerator pedal. He drove quickly through the intersection, glancing in the rearview and side-view mirrors. The black Lincoln moved slowly, the driver staying under the speed limit. Alvarez leveled off his speed. He was coming closer to the small house that Tony Salazar rented.

He watched in his side-view mirror, the afternoon shade from the buildings and apartments falling across the street. He was almost to Tony's house, and from a couple of hundred feet, he could see Tony's car in the driveway. Alvarez didn't hit the brakes as he got closer. He continued past the house for a block, taking a left at the next street, rolling through a stop sign. If the Lincoln turned, Alvarez would take a series of turns through the city he knew like the back of his hand.

The driver in the Lincoln didn't turn, the SUV heading in the opposite direction. Alvarez took a deep breath, lowering the 9mm back in the console. He drove around the block and came to Tony's house, parking behind his car. Alvarez shoved his pistol under his belt beneath his untucked shirt and got out of his Ford. He walked up to Tony's car, trying the driver's side door handle. It was unlocked. He opened the doors, spotting cardboard boxes in the back seat.

He opened the car's rear door, looking into one of the boxes. It was filled with neatly folded clothes. A second box contained shoes and a framed photo of Tony's family. Alvarez stood straighter, quietly closing the car doors, glancing around the neighborhood. An elderly man was sitting in a metal chair on his front porch directly across the street from the house. The man sat like a statue, staring beyond his weedy yard.

Alvarez went to Tony's front door, knocking. No response. "Tony, you home?" Nothing. He opened the door while reaching inside his shirt for his pistol. The inside of the house had the smell of old carpet and bleach. A window air-conditioner unit hummed in another room. "Tony! You home? It's Cedro." Alvarez paused, listening.

He searched the house—two bedrooms, kitchen and one bathroom. No sign of anyone and no indication that there had been a break-in or the violence often associated with an abduction—furniture knocked over or something broken indicating a struggle.

Alvarez put his pistol under his shirt and walked back outside into the bright light. He spotted the elderly man across the street and walked quickly toward him. His cinderblock home was unassuming and painted a dark green. The man's face was creased with deep lines, one eye opaque at the iris, his hands scarred. Alvarez greeted him with a quick smile. In Spanish he said, "My friend lives across the street. Do you know him?"

The man shook his gray head, spitting tobacco juice into an open coffee can—Folgers. Alvarez continued. "I'm afraid my good friend might be in trouble. Have you seen anyone at his house today?"

The old man licked his wet lips, a spot of brown tobacco juice in one corner. "Yes. Three men came. One was in a van. The other two came from around the sides of your friend's house while he was taking boxes and things to his car. They had guns on him."

"What happened? What'd they do?'

"They grabbed him and forced your friend into their van. Then they drove away. I believe the men are part of the cartel."

"Do you know the make—the model of the van?"

"No."

"What color was it?"

"Dark blue."

"Did the van go left or right leaving the house?"

The old man thought for a moment, a dog barked behind his house. He pointed to the east. "That way."

"Can you describe the men?"

He shook his head. "Too far. But from here, they looked big. And they looked mean."

"Did you or anyone in your house call the police."

The man looked up, one good eye curious, the other milky. "What would they do? Many of them take money from the cartel. When I was young, everyone worked. We were proud, and the spirit of Mexico wasn't stolen from its people."

"Thank you." As Alvarez was heading to his car, the old man called out. "May Jesus walk with your friend."

Alvarez pulled out his phone, calling Byron Lopez. "I'm at Tony's place. A neighbor across the street—an old man, said he saw three men abduct Tony this morning and drive away in a dark blue van. Tony's car is in his driveway, and it's filled with boxes of his stuff."

"Grab Tony's things from his car so no one can rifle through it. We'll store it at the office." Lopez stood from his desk, holding the phone, and rubbing his temples. "Headquarters just picked up a trace on Tony's phone."

"Which direction is it moving?"

"It's stationary. That either means they tossed Tony's phone, or it's on his body. I'll have three more agents meet you at the location. Looks to be a single-story warehouse in the downtown area."

FORTY

It's hard to gauge deception over the phone. When the visual body language is removed, you only have the tonal quality of the words, the inflections, and the hesitancy that happens when a liar must think about his or her answers. Speaking the truth doesn't require a rehearsal. Spontaneity is not the liar's friend. I thought about that as I drove to the address I had for Andy's best friend in college, Jason Parker.

On the phone, Jason was not too forthcoming about Andy's death. I didn't know whether he was hiding something, or he simply had nothing to hide and was just a scared college kid whose best friend would never graduate with him. Before I left my cabin, I called Jason, leaving a message, mentioning that I was working for Andy's parents. He returned the call. We agreed to meet after his tennis session in a small park next to the university's tennis courts.

I stood near one of the wrought iron benches under the shade of moss-draped oaks, squirrels playing chase, racquets striking tennis balls on the nearby courts. Jason approached wearing all white, including his sweatband. His racquet, zipped in a bag, was slung over his shoulder. He was tall and lanky with dark curly hair, thick black eyebrows, and wary hazel eyes. "Hi, Jason. I'm Sean O'Brien. Thanks for agreeing to meet with me."

He nodded, unsmiling. "No problem. If I can do something more to help Andy's family, I'll always do it."

"I understand you two grew up together."

"We were best friends since second grade. As kids, we spent a lot of time at each other's homes. Andy's mom and dad were like a second set of parents to me. My dad traveled a lot for work."

"His parents told me that Andy's girlfriend mentioned he bought the drugs from the same online site you used. What site was that?"

159

He made a dry swallow. "Andy and I were both having pain from reoccurring sports injuries. His was in his rotator cuff. Mine is in my right elbow and left knee. The cortisone shots wore off, and the pain kept coming back. We didn't want to go into our final games hurting."

"I understand. Where'd you buy the drugs online? Who sold them to you guys?"

"On my laptop, I put in keywords like hydromorphone and oxycodone, looking for something strong enough to knock out the pain."

"Why didn't you go to a doctor and get a prescription?"

"I don't have a doctor. My family didn't have much money when I was growing up. If any of us kids got really sick, we went to the ER. I'm here on a scholarship. So, I can't let the pain keep me from playing tennis. The pills you buy online are supposed to be the same as those you'd get in a brick-and-mortar pharmacy like CVS. But a whole lot cheaper. Like ten percent of what you'd pay at a pharmacy."

"What happened when you entered the keywords?"

Jason looked around the small park before focusing on two nearby picnic tables, then on the short nature trail that wove around the trees. Slowly, he turned his attention back to me. "It didn't take long to get responses. These dealers advertise on social media sites in disappearing posts. They come. Then they're gone. One keyword leads to another, and soon you're walking through a virtual sidewalk sale of online pharmacies. Most looked real legit. Good graphics. Professional. The one that we used was called RX-SaveMore.net. For twenty-five dollars, you can get ten pills of oxy."

"What happens when you pay."

"What do you mean?"

"Do you get a receipt or confirmation?"

He moved his tennis bag to his other shoulder. "You get a confirmation number with a delivery date."

"How do you pay?"

"Money is transferred online. You can use stuff like Zelle, Venmo, CashApp, Remitly."

"Did you try to use the confirmation number ... to see if it gave you any more delivery information?"

Jason shook his head. "Nope. It said thank you for you order and gave an estimated delivery date. No tracking numbers, though. That was fine with me 'cause the package showed up in two days."

"How was it delivered."

"UPS."

"You mentioned the site *was* called RX-SaveMore.net rather saying that the site *is* called that name. Have you tried to go back to the site again?"

"I went there the day Andy died. The site was down, changed, or moved around. Another RX site popped. There are hundreds of them on the internet. It's freaking crazy."

"Did you print out the confirmation number?"

"No, but I wrote it down. Still have it in my wallet. It starts with the letters RX and ends with an emoji. I'd never seen that before. The emoji was smiling and wearing a halo."

"May I see it?"

"Sure."

He opened his wallet, handing me a small slip of paper. His handwriting was neat and done in ink: *RX-SaveMore-1512*

"Did you tell the police about this online site?"

"They never asked. From what Andy's parents and Brittany told me, once the autopsy report came back saying Andy died from a drug overdose, it seems like the police sort of lost interest. I don't think they're looking too hard for a drug dealer. Maybe they believe Andy's death was his own fault. Like he should have known better. He couldn't have known better because nobody thinks fentanyl is being mixed inside a pain pill."

"Did you take any of the pills you received?"

"No. Andy took his first and …." Jason's voice choked. As his eyes welled, he took a deep breath, looking toward the tennis courts, touching his right elbow. The pain in his arm and heart was showing. I believe the eyes, for most people, work two ways—viewing or taking in a visual. And they project emotions. Love. Pain. Jason's eyes were projecting a deep sorrow.

"We'll need to make sure the pills you have get tested." My next stop would be to examine Andy's apartment and question Andy's girlfriend, Brittany Harmon.

FORTY-ONE

Durango, Mexico

Six men moved around an abandoned warehouse in Durango as if there was a bomb in the one-story building. They walked with the rhythm of the city, trying hard not to draw attention. There were no street vendors in this area of town. Mostly industrial. Brick buildings, some with faded signs advertising wholesale prices for fresh fruit and vegetables.

The men were all DEA agents, and Cedro Alvarez was the lead agent. Under their street clothes, they wore body armor. The men were there because the GPS location signal indicated that Tony Salazar's phone was inside. They didn't know if he was with the phone. And if he was there, could the Durango cartel be holding Salazar hostage?

No one in the cartel had yet to make any outside contact with the DEA, the Mexican military, or the police. The DEA followed the tracer signal and was ready to breach the building. Each man holstered two 9mm Glocks under his shirt. Two of the men, Alvarez and one man—a muscular agent, stood near the entrance. The other three agents walked around the perimeter, returning in less than a minute.

The tallest of the group said, "No vehicles in the back parking area. There are no utility wires attached to the building. It looks like this place has been abandoned and boarded up for years. According to the faded lettering above the entrance, it used to be an avocado packing warehouse."

Alvarez pointed to the double front door. "There's a chain between the door handles, but the lock is open and just hanging from one of the links. I'd guess they want us to walk right in."

"And we could be walking into a trap. Maybe a firefight. Or a bomb,"

"Something about this place smells like isolation. It's as if people haven't come and gone in years. We know Tony's phone is in there. The only way to know if he's with it is to go inside." He looked around the periphery, noting any nearby activity—a man zooming by on a motorcycle and a farm tractor loaded with cantaloupes puttering and belching black exhaust from a rusted tailpipe.

Alvarez stepped up to the door, lifted the open padlock, and quietly removed the heavy chain from the door handles. He turned to the other five men. "Let's move." They opened the doors, running into the warehouse. Each man was back-to-back, pistols drawn and pointed, the Glocks sweeping the interior.

The layout was an open warehouse with a small office and a shipping and receiving counter adjacent to the wall by the door. Cobwebs hung from the ceiling, and the dust, like fine gray sand, layered the floor and counters. Beyond the shipping area, toward the interior of the building, stacks of wooden pallets were in a corner, opposite a painter's ladder. In the middle of the room stood another half dozen pallets with two-by-six boards placed across the top. Something was propped in the center.

"Clear!" shouted two of the men, still holding their pistols in both hands.

"What's that odor?" asked the youngest agent. "Smells like garbage."

Alvarez nodded. "It's the smell of decomp. A body."

The men walked further into the interior. The air was hot and stale, a mouse scampering to hide under some cardboard boxes. The sound of flies buzzing. Alvarez motioned with his Glock. "What the hell's sitting on the board?"

The men came closer, moving in a semicircle, glancing around, broken windows near the rafters, bats hanging from the wooden beams at the ceiling. "Shit!" said one of the men. "It's a head."

Alvarez stepped closer. "It's not Tony's head, but his phone is next to it. There's a paper under the phone."

The men came nearer, the odor stronger, green blowflies crawling in and out of the nostrils and ears on the decapitated head, the face opaque—the color of smoky clouds. "I don't know who the hell that poor guy was," said Alvarez. He holstered his gun using one gloved hand to pick up the phone and paper.

"Looks like it's in English," said one of the agents.

Alvarez nodded. "Undoubtably for us. It says:

This is the fate your fellow agent Antonio Salazar will suffer if you do not cooperate with us. We will release Salazar if the following conditions are met. First, you quietly release Sergio Navarro from the American prison. Return him to Mexico. You work exclusively with the Durango cartel at the border, allowing us to cross while enforcing your laws against our competitors. This will be good public relations for you. You will keep this a quiet and confidential arrangement for six months. If the terms of the agreement are kept, Salazar will be released back to you unharmed. If not, you will receive his head. We will be in touch.

Alvarez looked up from the note. "Gentlemen, we got one helluva problem."

FORTY-TWO

When I worked as a detective, I often thought that some houses suffered a form of death. Not by neglect, termites, or age. But rather when its owner had died and left bits of his or her personality in a home that was vacant. Empty homes sometimes echo the silence of their departed owners or former occupants, especially when there are personal items left behind. That was the case when I used the key that Clint gave me to unlock the door of Andy's apartment.

I remembered what Clint told Wynona and I when his wife Lauren had arrived at Andy's door the day they found his body. *When my wife, Lauren, arrived at Andy's door, before she knew he was dead, she touched the doorknob and felt an intense feeling in her gut that something was horribly wrong inside.*

As I turned the key to Andy's apartment door and stepped inside, my reaction was one of sorrow because a palpable grief still hung in the room like a fog that was felt but not seen. I could feel it in one corner where Andy's tennis racquet and baseball mitt were kept. I could sense it from the framed photo of Andy and his family still on an end table near the couch with a slight depression in one cushion to the left where Andy probably sat during the last four years doing his homework.

Clint told Wynona and me that Andy's rent had been paid through the end of next month. He and Lauren wouldn't be moving the belongings out for now, leaving the apartment as it is to give detectives the freedom to come and go as their investigation warranted. From where I stood, looking around the apartment, I didn't feel that Detective Porter, or his colleagues, ever came back after their initial investigation and release of the coroner's report.

I slowly walked through the apartment, looking around the kitchen before heading down the hallway. I stepped into the bathroom and opened the medicine cabinet above the sink. Nothing. I walked into one of the two bedrooms. This one had a daybed in it along with more of Andy's sports equipment, including two bats, a basket of tennis balls, and two more racquets. A guitar was propped against the foot of the daybed.

I crossed the hall and opened the door to Andy's bedroom. The bed was unmade, left like it was when Clint and Lauren found their son's body. On one shelf were sports trophies, award plaques, and an album with a collection of baseball cards. I looked in drawers, hunting for something—anything that might give a better insight into the days leading up to Andy's death.

On one side of the bedroom was a small table or work desk. A paperclip was in one corner, two dried water rings to the left where a cup or glass had been. I pulled the wooden chair out, looking in the area where Andy would have sat. I spotted something.

It was a piece of paper lying on the carpet under the desk near the wall, as if the paper had fallen from the rear of the desk, through the half-inch gap. I knelt further down, picking up the paper. There was something written on it. In Andy's handwriting was what appeared to be a confirmation code. Below it, a phone number, and the letters C. B.

The confirmation code was similar to what Jason Parker shared with me, but the digits were different: *RX-SaveMore-1738*

The phone number had a Florida area code, 850. I knew it covered much of Florida's Panhandle. Was the phone number and confirmation code connected? Whose phone number was on the paper? A drug dealer or a friend? I knew it wasn't Jason Parker's, and it wasn't Brittany Harmon's number either.

I set the paper on the desk, using my phone to run a Google search for a possible name—a person's name or that of a company. The search came back with no results, which was a result, just not the one I wanted. I didn't want to use my phone to call the number and leave a trail.

I called Dave Collins and said, "I'm still up in Gainesville." I updated Dave and added, "The piece of paper I found behind Andy's desk has a confirmation code similar to the one Jason Parker has for his drug order. The phone number I mentioned has the Northeast Florida area code of 850. If I give you the full number, can you run it through your computer's software filters to make the call while blocking your identity?"

"Of course. Sean, you need to give me greater challenges. Do you want to wait while I do the research?"

"I don't want to be late for an appointment I have with Andy's former girlfriend, Brittany Harmon. Call me when you know something. Thanks."

"You got it. Oh, before you go, I caught the local news, and the reporter said that the biker who had a midnight swim the Tomoka River, courtesy of his abductors, is or was a member of the Iron Fist biker gang. The story indicated that this guy, Robert Holloway, whose street name is Axle, is refusing to press charges should the police find the culprits who abducted him at gunpoint."

"Sounds like he's afraid of retaliation from the gang."

"No doubt. The reporter said that the police aren't sure where Holloway is now. He seems to have gone off the radar. Imagine that. So, in the unlikely event that you still want to have a little chat with him, he'll be even more difficult to find. And, if you find him, I don't believe the gentleman will be cooperative or forthcoming."

"You think? If that biker gang is running fentanyl, and it's being sold in Gainesville via an online source, maybe that phone number you have might offer a hint. If so, and if it points to the biker gang, I'll try to find Holloway, because I imagine, under the right circumstances, he might talk."

"Not unless he enters a witness protection program. And you, Sean, as altruistic as you are, can't offer that option." Dave chuckled.

"Then I suppose there will have to be another option on the table."

He made a slight grunt, the kind of sound Dave sometimes uttered when he was about to share a poignant idea. "The strange irony of online crime, such as in purchasing illegal drugs, is that today it's done with the element of digital magic. What you see is not always what's there. Vanishing apps and dead-end websites create an illusion. But there still is a criminal behind the curtain, a wizard, who thinks he's smarter than everyone else."

I walked out of Andy's bedroom. "Ego and greed make a bad combo."

"Indeed. Although the digital criminal may hide behind a virtual curtain, to catch him, you must do it the old-fashioned way. Hunt and trap the quarry. That's where the illusion ends, and the reality of combat begins. I sincerely hope your investigation in Gainesville and the horrible deaths in Panama City Beach don't point to a biker gang. Because, if it does, where would you find that kind of backup if you're coming down the last mile?"

"I don't know."

"I'll call you as soon as I run this number through everything I have … and then some."

"Thanks." I clicked off and walked out the front door. As I turned to lock it, a man was standing to my left.

FORTY-THREE

I lowered my eyes to his hands. A laptop computer in one hand, a ring of keys in the other. He looked like a graduate student or a guy who'd spent the last couple of nights finishing his PhD thesis in metaphysics. Late twenties with a scruffy blonde beard, dark raccoon eyes, long hair that appeared to have been styled by static electricity—the Einstein look. "Hi," he said with an unsmiling nod, fidgeting. Anxious. Maybe some form of Asperger's syndrome.

I nodded back. "How are you?"

"Good."

"Glad to hear it."

Nothing.

I smiled. "Did you know Andy Ward?"

"Not very well. It's hard to believe that he died."

"Do you live in the complex?"

"Three doors down. Are you a cop?"

"No, I'm a friend of the family."

"Did the police find who did it?" More fidgeting.

"Andy died from a drug overdose. Do you think there was an ulterior motive … something more than that?"

"I don't really know. Maybe."

"Why would that be the case?"

"It might have been an accident. A week before he died, I did see someone deliver a package to his door. I was returning from the library when a man parked his motorcycle next to my Prius, then walked over to Andy's door. The man was carrying a small package."

"Did Andy answer the door?"

"Yes. They spoke, maybe thirty seconds. It looked like Andy gave him money at the door. When I was walking to my apartment, I heard Andy laugh and say, *'you're the man, Charlie Brown,'* and that was all I heard."

"Can you describe him—this man Andy called Charlie Brown?"

"Yes. He didn't wear a motorcycle helmet. He was very tanned, like he spent all day on the beach. He had a black beard and a gold hoop earring about the size of a quarter. There was a red banana on his head. And he had a tattoo of a sailing ship on his upper arm, the kind of ships that pirates sailed."

I nodded. "You have a remarkable memory for details."

"It's photographic. I wish sometimes I could forget things. But that is hard to do."

"Did you mention this to the police?"

"No. They never knocked on my door. At least I never saw them. But I might not have been home when they were here."

"They could always return to speak with nearby residents."

He looked down at his sandals and then up at me. "I should be going."

"Thank you for the information."

He said nothing. As he walked around me, I asked, "You mentioned that you'd just returned from the library when you saw the guy get off his motorcycle. Do you know if he was riding a Harley-Davidson?"

"No. It was a Triumph."

I smiled. "What's your name?"

"Jonathan Bennett."

"I'm Sean O'Brien. What are you studying?"

"I'm finishing my doctorate in philosophy and its relation to cosmology." He nodded and left.

As I walked back to my Jeep, I took out the paper in my shirt pocket. I stared at Andy's handwriting. The letters C.B., I now believe, stood for Charlie Brown. I was curious to find out if Brittany Harmon knew Charlie Brown. I got in my Jeep and lifted Andy Ward's file folder from between the seats. I glanced at the phone number again on the crinkled paper before taking out the two printed pages of phone calls from Andy's phone records. I scanned for the area code first, and then the number.

I quickly found the area code and then the number. It was a match. The call was made from Andy's phone two weeks before he died. The call was for thirty-seven seconds. There were no text messages matching that number. The next number on the phone log came an hour later, and it was from an incoming call. The area code was 888, a toll-free area code with no specific location in the nation. The 888-area code was most often used by scammers.

On the way to meet Brittany Harmon, I thought about how she might help narrow down the field in my hunt for Charlie Brown. I didn't want to do anything that would put Brittany in immediate jeopardy or come back to haunt her later. I decided to try Detective Winston Porter again. I made the call, spoke to the receptionist, and was put through to his office.

"Detective Porter, homicide."

"Hi, detective, it's Sean O'Brien. I wanted to reach out to you because I think that Andy Ward—"

"O'Brien, the last thing I need at this moment is a sideline coach calling plays and sending them into my huddle. I am the quarterback. I decide how this game is played. Last thing I need is an overzealous PI calling the shots. Won't happen in my city."

"I understand. Using your sports metaphor, I have something that might put points on the board for you."

"Whatcha got?"

"A phone number that could be connected to the person who sold Andy Ward the lethal drugs. Guy's name is Charlie Brown."

"Like the cartoon character from the Peanuts gang?"

"Yeah, like that. I found the number on a crumpled slip of paper under the desk in Andy's room."

"We must have missed that."

"The desk or the room?"

"I don't have to put up with this bullshit. I'm hanging up, O'Brien—"

"Just trying to inject some humor into the homicide division. The number on the paper matches a call on the phone log from Andy's phone. I believe it's linked to this Charlie Brown, a guy that one of Andy's neighbors, Jonathan Bennett, saw delivering a package to Andy's apartment a couple of weeks before Andy received the second package with the fentanyl. I think the first delivery was Prozac, or a knock-off of the drug. It was the second package with the alleged oxy that killed Andy."

"Did you hear yourself, O'Brien. You said his death was caused by counterfeit oxy not by a killer holding a gun. You're looking for ghosts. Andy Ward consumed those pills with nobody forcing him to do so."

"I find semantics never work in a homicide investigation. Murder doesn't come in shades of gray. Maybe a jury would conclude that Andy didn't die a violent death, but he died because he was provided a pill made with fentanyl. In Florida, that's murder. Now, detective, do you want Charlie Brown's number?"

"Give it to me."

I gave him the number and added, "I don't want to clash with you. I'm only sharing information. If you choose not to do anything with it … I will. I hope you view this as a homicide matter and not just a college kid with an accidental overdose from *one damn* pill."

He hung up on me. I guess that was his answer. As I drove to meet Brittany, I put in a call to Panama City Beach Detective, Lindsey Owen. When she answered, I told her about finding the crumpled note with the name Charlie Brown and the phone number. I let her know what Andy's neighbor saw and shared with me. I added, "In your digital forensics check, have you run across this name … Charlie Brown?"

"In all fairness, I can't share that in a yes or no answer, Mr. O'Brien. Suffice to say that name doesn't ring a bell. It sounds like an alias, too."

"Maybe it is. I'll give you the number on the paper in the event you might see something that could connect to Charlie Brown."

"Okay."

I gave her the number. "Detective Owen, if this is his name, even as an alias, he could be a dealer working the college campuses from Gainesville to Tallahassee."

"Since you gave me that name, I want to offer a quid pro quo. I spoke with the sole surviving male college student from that horrible scene. Name's Rudy Connor. He's still in the hospital. The student who bought the pills, Bruce Cooper, was Connor's best friend. He told me that Cooper met some guy on the beach to do the buy."

"Maybe this guy is Charlie Brown."

"Who knows?"

"Did Rudy Connor know where on the beach that his friend bought the fentanyl?"

"He said it was near the pier and a jet ski rental."

"Are there beach cams there?"

"Yes."

"Live feeds or recorded?"

"Both. The live feeds are archived for seven days in the cloud. We'll check the cameras to see what we can see."

"You know what Bruce Cooper looked like. If the sale was caught on camera, you might know what the dealer looks like. Maybe it will be our elusive Charlie Brown."

"Thanks, O'Brien. Gotta go." She clicked off.

At least she was more receptive than Detective Winston Porter. With his guard held high, protecting his territory through this one case—Andy's, has kept it from being as active as it could be. I knew his department would continue to disregard me. So, I needed a plan B, maybe even a plan C, if I was going to get answers for Clint and Lauren Ward.

As I drove closer to where I was to meet Brittany, I came upon a city park. The sign indicated it was Depot Park. It overlooked a large pond, lots of playground swings, seesaws, merry-go-round, monkey bars, and more. There were pavilions and picnic tables. With the exception of a few oak trees, the park was wide open.

It would serve well for the next thing I had in mind. And I only thought of it because I knew Detective Porter wasn't going to break a sweat 'looking for ghosts.' Charlie Brown was a ghost. And, unlike the cartoon character, he wasn't a loveable loser. He was a killer.

And I would find him.

FORTY-FOUR

DEA Headquarters, Springfield VA

The DEA was experiencing a crisis that stretched back almost four decades. From the agency's offices in Mexico City, to its headquarters near Washington, D.C., the news of Tony Salazar's abduction was somber, sobering, and frightening. The last time a DEA agent was captured by a Mexican drug cartel was in 1985.

The story, the brutal treatment of Enrique Camarena, was spoken about often as new recruits went through training. It was drilled even harder into the minds of junior agents that were going to be working undercover in foreign countries. Camarena's fate, his valiant fight, was legendary in the agency.

It didn't end well.

He was abducted by members of the Guadalajara cartel and taken to one of the houses the drug lords frequented. Once there, he was relentlessly questioned about DEA activity and agents in Mexico. Witnesses, those rank-and-file cartel members who were there, later would say that Camarena gave up no information. Maybe he had none to give, but it would cost Camarena his life.

He fought hard, as hard as a man can do with his hands tied behind his back. He was repeatedly beaten, burned, knocked out cold, revived and put through the same torture, time and time again. His attackers kept at it for more than thirty hours before one of the cartel members used a piece of steel rebar to punch a hole through Camarena's skull and brain.

This history was going through the minds of two groups of people—the DEA agents gathered in a conference room at the agency's Mexico City offices and the senior agents and directors at the agency's

174

headquarters in Springfield, Virginia. They sat around conference tables, connected by closed-circuit, encrypted satellite feeds to widescreen monitors in both locations.

DEA Administrator Christina Bowman opened the meeting. She wore a dark business suit, auburn hair to her shoulders, vivid green eyes visible through the camera lens. She had an open file folder on the table in front of her. There were six people in the room, four men and another woman. All were senior leadership, some agency veterans with years in the field. Bowman leaned forward, looking into the camera. "What's the situation, Byron? Any changes?"

In the Mexico City conference room, Byron Lopez cleared his throat. "Not since we spoke over the phone. Diego Navarro is calling every shot. The Durango cartel is believed to have at least a dozen hideouts in that state—many are hidden in the Sierra Madre mountains. Tony's asset, a man who was embedded in the cartel, was beheaded."

Bowman nodded. "Was our asset's head found near Tony's phone?"

"No, but the resemblance was there. We guess it may have been a family member to send a wider message. Unfortunately, decapitation seems to be Navarro's preferred statement to his enemies, competitors, and anyone who interferes with his vast operations. He has an enormous ego and vows not to make the same mistake that plagued his father. Navarro also knows how to work the Mexican political system."

The assistant administrator at the DEA headquarters, a man sitting near Bowman, said, "Not only does Navarro know the political spectrum in Mexico, but we also believe he's primarily responsible for the Mexican government ending the issuance of visas to our agents, dramatically curtailing our visible staff in the country."

Bowman glanced down at the file folder to a photo of Tony Salazar on one page and a smaller picture of Diego Navarro on the other. She looked up. "I was reviewing Tony Salazar's background. Before joining the DEA, he was a member of an elite group of the Delta Force—one they internally called *The Compromisers*. The name comes from when these men were deployed into hostile situations. They usually managed to compromise the threat and restore a degree of order—often achieved by using extreme measures. That's a quote from information in his bio. What this tells me is that Tony, due to his survival skills, might be in a unique position to escape, given the slightest possibility to do so."

Lopez shook his head. "Christina, that possibility is doubtful because the Durango cartel has a lot of well-trained members, guys guarding Tony 24-7. Navarro has hired ex-cops, former Mexican military, mercenaries, and a lot of psychopaths who look at killing people as a sport."

Bowman said, "When the southern border was allowed to become much more open, Diego Navarro became a lot more emboldened. He's a sociopath who views his illegal business as a Fortune 500 company, and he wants the same kind of admiration and respect given to many of those companies."

The assistant administrator nodded. "Navarro's mind is warped. He's believing his own PR rants. And now, he wants us to release his father, then turn our backs to give his drug and human smuggling operations easier access into our country and, at the same time, intensify enforcement against his competitors, the Sinaloa, Juarez, and Tijuana cartels. That guy has some big cojones."

Bowman eyed him sharply. "Let's move on. Our nation doesn't negotiate with terrorists. Once we start, once we compromise, cave in, and meet their demands, the flood gates open, and it becomes nonstop hostage-taking. From my view, the only way to rescue Tony Salazar out of there is to go in and bring him out." She paused, looking through the camera at Lopez. "From your perspective, Byron, since you are down there … how do we do that?"

Lopez cleared his throat. "If we knew where the cartel is hiding Tony, we could send in a team. There would, no doubt, be a substantial number of casualties on both sides. It'd be hard to pull off a surprise attack because Navarro has a lot of paid ears and eyes. The state of Durango is almost fifty-thousand square miles. Much of it is mountainous, including vast areas of forests. There are a few larger cities and lots of small towns. For the most part, the people living in the villages view Navarro as a modern-day Pancho Villa, a gutsy guy who isn't afraid of its powerful northern neighbor, and someone who shares some of the spoils of his illegal operations with them."

Bowman looked down at Navarro's photo in the file folder. "He's not a Robin Hood figure. He doesn't rob from the rich and give to the poor. He's a ruthless sociopath with no regard for human life. For his human trafficking operation, this guy views the women and girls as livestock. Navarro is a parasite, preying on the sick minds of drug addicts. It's a vicious cycle. And now that we have drug dealers in the U.S. using the internet to find customers, sell products, and ship like Amazon, that brings a whole new dynamic to a growing equation." She paused, leaning back in her chair. "Somebody knows where Navarro is holding Tony."

Lopez nodded. "We'll rattle a lot of cages down here to see what we can find. According to the note the cartel left under Tony's phone, it said that Navarro will be in touch. Maybe we'll receive a message through one of our offices here in Mexico. Or they could send a text through Tony's phone. We have it."

Another senior DEA agent at the conference table at headquarters, a woman, said, "Since they left Tony's phone, we can assume they gleaned the data from it. We know the cartels are using UFED devices to download data. Let's just hope there wasn't a lot for them to retrieve from Tony's personal phone."

Lopez said, "Most of his sensitive calls were made using encrypted phones and computers in our offices. But sometimes, as we all know, our agents must use what they have in the field. I don't like being in a standby mode, waiting to see what Navarro's next move—his next demand, might be. But considering the tenuous circumstances, we don't have much of a choice."

Bowman asked, "Have you spoken with Tony's wife?"

"Yes. As you would expect, Nicole's devastated. Tony's parents are flying to San Diego to be with her."

"Good. Maybe we can bring them some better news soon. I don't want Navarro calling the shots. Somehow, we need to perform an extraction—to find where these people are holding Tony and pull a surprise attack to rescue him."

Lopez took a deep breath, measuring his words. "Christina, I want Tony out of there as much as you do. Not only is he an excellent agent, he's also my friend. But I think we need to play along with Navarro to buy us some time. We'll need to pretend that we might consider his demands, all the while trying to narrow in on where they have Tony."

She stared at Tony Salazar's photo before looking back in the camera. "None of us was working at the DEA when the Guadalajara cartel abducted agent Enrique 'Kiki' Camarena. He was so badly tortured that it was difficult to ID what was left of his body. None of the cartels have repeated that scenario since then because they don't want the wrath of America breathing down their throats. And then along comes cocky Diego Navarro."

"What do we do about him?" asked one of the agents sitting next to Lopez.

Bowman closed the file folder. "For some reason, Diego Navarro has burned the playbook. The longer that fanatic has Tony stashed away in some mountain compound, the greater the chances are that what happened to Camarena will happen to Tony. In this case, according to what Navarro left in his note, Tony's head is literally on the line. That's a line in the sand that none of us want to cross." She paused and looked through the camera at Lopez. "Byron, you said your team can rattle some cages. See if you can do that without letting the snakes out."

FORTY-FIVE

Brittany Harmon wasn't hard to spot. On the phone, we'd agreed to meet after her shift in the coffee shop where she worked part-time. She was sitting at a corner table when I arrived. Her honey-blonde hair caught the sunlight through the windows, pretty, bright blue eyes. She sat with her backpack on the floor near her feet, pink sneakers, laptop open. There were ten other customers in the shop, the scent of fresh-ground coffee beans welcoming.

I smiled as I approached her table. "Hi, Brittany, I'm Sean. May I have a seat?"

"Sure. Of all these people in here, how'd you know which person was me?"

"Because when I entered the coffee shop, only one other person looked my way. He's a guy with his pal at a center table. You looked up twice, the second time you involuntarily scratched your left forearm, as if you had an itch. On the other hand, maybe me picking you out of everyone could have been just a lucky guess."

Brittany stared at me, not sure how to respond or what to say. She managed a smile. "I don't remember scratching my arm. It's not like I have a mosquito bite or something."

"Can I buy you a cup of coffee?"

She shook her head. "Believe it or not, even though I work in a coffee shop, I don't drink the stuff. I'm more into smoothies."

"Do they serve them here?"

"Yes."

I signaled for a server, another college girl in black jeans and a red T-shirt with the words *Java Hut* on the front. She approached the table. I sat down. "A smoothie for the lady and coffee for me. Black. Thanks."

The server looked at Brittany. "You want mixed berries, Brit?"

"That'd be great."

The server left. "Do you prefer to be called Brit or Brittany?"

She shrugged. "Doesn't matter."

"Okay. I'll choose Brittany. That's a pretty name."

She smiled, dimples popping on both cheeks. "You look a little like the actor … can't think of his name. Sorry. I'm a bit nervous."

"No need to be. I'm a friend of Andy's family."

"Yes, when you called, you said you were old friends with Andy's father. Did you guys go to college together?"

"We served overseas. Army."

"I never knew Andy's dad was in the Army."

"We did tours of duty in the Middle East and other places."

"Did you know Andy?"

"We'd met a few times, especially when he was younger and winning little league games on the pitcher's mound."

"Yeah, he played baseball and tennis at school. I think that's why his shoulder hurt so much. I'm not sure I have anything that's going help you. I answered every question the police asked me."

"Maybe there is a question they didn't ask you."

"What would that be?"

"Was Andy depressed?"

Brittany looked up, hesitation in her eyes. "How'd you know that? He wasn't depressed most of the time. He had mood swings. But I guess most people get depressed sometimes."

"But most people don't order Prozac from questionable online pharmacies … places that pretend to be pharmacies. He did, didn't he?"

Brittany adjusted her weight in the wooden chair as the server brought my coffee and her smoothie to the table. I paid with cash. "Keep the change."

"Thanks!" she said, folding a ten-dollar bill and leaving.

I sipped my coffee and looked at Brittany. She said, "Yes, he was depressed from time to time."

"Tell me a little about your relationship with Andy. Were you two engaged?"

She smiled. "Not officially, but we'd talked about the future—a future together as a couple. He hadn't proposed to me yet, but I felt in my heart that it was just a matter of time. You know, graduating, trying to move on to careers and stuff."

"So, you loved Andy?"

"Yes. Very much. And he loved me. He was smart, and he treated me like a princess."

"Why was Andy depressed?"

"Because the baseball scouts weren't giving him options. When he wasn't getting any offers to try out for the major leagues, Andy got like real moody. We almost broke up over it a while back. But he said he'd work hard to beat the depression."

"Is that when he started taking Prozac?"

She stirred her smoothie with a straw. "No, a little later, maybe a couple of weeks before he died. But it wasn't the Prozac that killed him. It was the other stuff he ordered for the pain in his shoulder."

"Did Charlie Brown ever come by Andy's apartment?"

"Who?"

"Charlie Brown."

She smiled. "The only Charlie Brown I ever heard of is the animated character. Who are you talking about?"

"That's the question I'd like to have answered. Think back … can you remember Andy ever mentioning someone called Charlie Brown?"

"No. That's an easy name to remember."

"The pills Andy ordered online to fight his depression, did he say how they were delivered? Maybe by this guy Charlie Brown or someone with the initials C.B."

She drank through her straw, eyes pensive. "I can't remember Andy talking about how those pills were delivered. Speaking of depression, the cartoon Charlie Brown always seemed to have lots of issues. I think Snoopy was the only one in the bunch who had his head on straight. Because of Snoopy, I wanted a beagle when I was a kid, but my mom bought us a poodle. She was cool."

"Your mom or the poodle?"

"The poodle, but my mom's cool, too." Brittany laughed and sipped from her smoothie.

My phone buzzed on the table. I looked at the caller ID. Dave Collins. "Excuse me, Brittany. I need to take this."

"Okay. And I need to go to the bathroom. Be right back."

She left, and I took Dave's call. "Sean, the phone number you gave me is registered to Gulf Stream Carrier. Checking with the corporation data on file with the state, there is no physical address, only a post office box number in Tallahassee. The only name associated with the incorporation papers is Charles B. Dean, president."

"Did you call the number?"

"Yes. The voicemail prompt is not that of a man, but rather a woman's voice. The greeting is this: *You've reached Gulf Stream Carrier. Please leave a message, and we'll get back with you as soon as possible.*" Dave chuckled. The initials for Charles B. Dean are CBD. Seems appropriate, considering the source and circumstances. I blocked my number, and I didn't leave a message, of course. I thought I'd reserve that step for you and however you choose to contact this person or persons."

"I wonder what, if any significance, the name of this bogus company, Gulf Steam Carrier, plays into the distribution of drugs. The Gulf Stream begins off the eastern coast of Mexico in the Gulf of Mexico. As you know, it flows near the coasts of Texas, Louisiana, Mississippi, Alabama, and Florida before heading north into the Atlantic. From there, it moves up America's eastern seashore, continues off the coast of Canada, and makes a sweep right, flowing east to Europe."

"Indeed. Not unlike the flow of drugs from Mexico, through the states, into Canada before moving on to Europe. The first known mention of the Gulf Stream came from Spanish sailor Ponce De Leon. In his captain's log, he wrote that the current in this unknown ocean river is so strong, it defied the power of the wind in his ship's sails. If the name, Gulf Stream Carrier, is a metaphor, it sounds like whomever CBD is, he has an intrepid sense of satire. Perhaps he's subtly thumbing his nose at the drug enforcement authorities. It's not unlike the movie, *Catch Me if You Can,* starring Leonardo DiCaprio."

"In real life, and in the movie, he was caught."

"Which brings us back around to the option I alluded to earlier. You managed to find that number on a crinkled piece of paper in Andy Ward's bedroom, and now you know what greets the person who calls the number … what's your next step."

I watched Brittany walking back across the coffee shop. "My next move will involve Andy's girlfriend. In India, goats have been tied up to attract man-eating tigers. The goats bleat, and then tigers come and are shot by the farmers. I will see if Brittany will make a call and set the trap for me."

Dave paused before responding. I could hear a boat horn in the background. "She would be the perfect customer, college-aged, female. And her voice left on voicemail could probably get a response. That would, of course, depend on what she says and how good of an actress she can become. You, Sean, must make sure the young goat tied to the stake doesn't become a sacrificial lamb in an arena where the players take no prisoners."

FORTY-SIX

I thought the noise in the coffee shop would add a feel of reality. The sound of steam from brewing cappuccinos, the pop music playing from ceiling speakers, the drone of conversation, and the cacophony of sounds would give an air of authenticity—a sincere person making a legitimate call. If I left a message, whomever Charlie Brown was might think that I sounded like a middle-aged detective or the father of one of the overdose victims.

Not the case with Brittany Harmon.

She sat down and stirred her smoothie, taking a sip. I could smell the scent of flowery soap on her hands. "Brittany, I admire you for trying to help Andy's family find some form of closure. I can tell that you cared a lot about Andy and care about them as well."

"I do. I might grieve in a different way, but it's like my heart has been squeezed, pushing the breath out of my chest."

"I don't think we're just supposed to *get on* after the death of a loved one. Instead, we're to move forward with the memory of that person forever welded to our heart. The gamble of love—real love is the chance of loss. And the result of a loss is grief and mourning. But love is worth the risks, because to deny yourself of it is to allow a shadow of the past to follow you. There is pain and hurting from the death of someone you love, but there is another kind of pain from never taking a chance on love."

"I understand. I will always treasure the gift of time that I had with Andy. After he died, I called my mom and talked for a long time, like we hadn't talked in years. She's helping me to accept what seems unacceptable." Brittany moistened her lips, her eyes misty.

"I found a number in Andy's apartment. I want to show it to you to see if you recognize it. Okay?"

"Okay."

I reached in my pocket and took out the paper with the number, name, and confirmation code on it. "The phone number starts with the area code 850. Take a good look at it and tell me if you recognize it."

She stared at the phone number for a few seconds, her eyes drifting to the other information that Andy had left. I could tell that just by seeing his handwriting, it had affected her. She blinked rapidly, clearing her eyes and shaking her head. "No, I don't recognize it."

"It may be Charlie Brown's number. I think he's a drug dealer, a guy who works the college campuses, maybe from here in Gainesville to Florida State University in Tallahassee."

"Are you going to give it to the police?"

"Yes. But I'd like to give them more evidence. What I'd like for you to do is to use your phone to call the number. The call will go to voicemail. The prompt will say this ... *you've reached Gulf Stream Carrier. Please leave a message, and we'll get back with you as soon as possible.* I want you to leave a message."

She made a dry swallow. "What do you want me to say?"

"Just be quick and to the point. Say your name and the reason for your call. The reason is this: let them know that you're a college student cramming for midterms. You're in the market for something to help you get through—something like Adderall. You can leave your number and add that you're reachable online, too. What social media sites are you on now?"

"Facebook, Instagram, Twitter, and Tik Tok."

"Good."

"Do I tell them how I have their number?"

"Just say a close friend referred you." I paused and looked at her eyes. "Do you think that you can do it and sound real?"

"Yes. Theater-dance almost was my major before switching to tourism and hospitality."

"Okay. Here's the number again. Make the call."

She nodded, taking a deep breath, using her thumbs to punch numbers on her keyboard. She held the phone to her ear. I could barely hear the ringing and the prompt message on the other line. When it ended, she began. "Hi, this is Brittany Harmon. I'm a senior at University of Florida. I'm cramming for midterm exams in a couple of days. I hate coffee, at least most coffees. My friend referred me to your company. Maybe I can order something from you to help me study."

She left her phone number, quickly adding, "Oh, you can reach me on Twitter, Brit at Brittany Harmon, or Facebook, Instagram and TikTok. Hope to hear from you soon. Bye." She pressed the end-call button and looked over at me, releasing a deep breath. "That wasn't so hard."

"No, but the next part might be a little harder. That's the scene when they contact you."

"What do I do?"

"That depends on how they contact you. If it's by phone, most likely it will be from an 888-area code, let it go to your voicemail. See if they'll leave a message. Should they reach out to you on social media, I want you to call me, let me know what they said, and I'll tell you how to respond."

"Okay."

"Under no circumstances are you to give them your address or any personal information, such as a credit card number."

"If they reach out to me and leave a message or something on social media, when I call you, what will you do?"

"I want to question this guy, Charlie Brown, if that's his real name. But, at this point, it doesn't matter whether that's his real name or not. I'd like to talk with him."

"Do you think he's dangerous?"

"I don't know, but I do know the drugs he sells can be very dangerous. I'd like to find out where he's getting them. I'm going to write down my number. Don't hesitate to call or text me the minute that you're contacted. Get in touch with me anytime, even if it's three in the morning. Okay?"

"Okay. I'm just a little bit afraid."

I smiled. "You'll be fine. These people are like cockroaches, they run in the light. Sometimes, it's good to be a little afraid because it makes you more cautious."

"Now, I'm scared."

FORTY-SEVEN

He was developing a bad case of cabin fever. After three days of living in a barn, sleeping in the hayloft, and eating peanut butter and jelly sandwiches on white bread, Axle was going stir crazy. His stitched-up cheek was itching as the wound started to heal. He thought his body odor was getting worse than that of the old mare, Maggie, who slept in her stall below him.

During the last few days, he refused to answer his phone or make calls. He didn't think that the Iron Fist was using cell phone pinging technology like the cops, but he didn't want to take the chance that someone was calling to get him to leave his hiding place. *Gotta lay low*, he kept telling himself. *It'll all blow over soon.*

That couldn't happen soon enough.

And then came a call from Hank Newton, his closest friend in the biker gang—the one member who stood up to Tank and refused to follow orders to eliminate Axle. Newton's road name was Drywall, a name he got from a long history of hanging drywall. When he called late into the third day, Axle looked at his phone screen and decided to take the risk. "What's up, Drywall?"

"Man, I'm glad to hear your voice. I hope you got to a doctor to stitch up that cut."

"Yeah, I did. Got a shit load of stitches."

"Look, Axle, word got back to Tank that you're not pressing charges. That made a helluva difference."

"How's that?"

"It took some of the piss 'n vinegar outta Tank's gut. He's called back the order to have you popped. You won't be back in the club, but you still got your life."

"How do I know that Tank's not holding a gun to your head right now, making you tell me that stuff?"

"We've been friends a long time, even before we joined the Fist. I hope it will remain that way when we're sittin' in our rockers at the home of old fart bikers. I was the only one in the club that stood up for you when Tank had you hustled out. I had your back then, and I got it now."

Axle moved in front of one of the barn windows, which overlooked a 100-acre plowed field all the way up to the road. Chickens strutted and picked at bits of grain on the hard-packed earth around the barn. "It never should have come to this. For Tank and the others to believe I'm a federal agent or cop who's pretending to be a biker in the club is pure horse shit. Somebody must have planted that thought into his crazy brain."

"From what I hear, it was Birddog who was pissin' that stuff about you in Tank's ear."

"Dog's got an axe to grind. His old lady, Rhonda, hit on me a few months ago in the side parking lot of the Silver Dollar Saloon. After smokin' some weed with her, she leaned up against a palm tree and asked me if my balls were as big as the coconuts in the tree."

"I had to say, hell yeah, you wanna see? She grinned and told me I needed to have big ones if I wanted to do her behind the building. Since the place was crawlin' with bikers, my better judgment somehow kicked in, and I told her maybe some other time."

"What happened then?"

"She told me I had no idea what I was missing and that all I had in common with the coconut tree was me bein' a nut for turning her down. I laughed and started to leave. She lifted her middle finger. The next thing I know is that she told Birddog I came on to her. I had to talk that dickhead off the ledge."

"Yeah, I remember a little about that, but I didn't have the skinny on it."

"Nothing was ever square between Birddog and me after that. I think because his old lady wanted me to bang her, it really messed with him, so he talked shit about me to Tank. And here I am today, sleepin' with a mare, and I got a f-in' scar on my cheek that looks like the twenty-fourth letter in the alphabet."

"I don't want to ask you where you are right now ... I just wanted to let you know that you don't have to hide in some stripper's backroom.

You can go about your business without lookin' over your shoulder. Nobody's comin' after you."

Axle glanced at the gray mare, Maggie. "I wish I was in a stripper's backroom. No matter what, Drywall, after the crap I went through, I'll always be lookin' over my shoulder. Not only will I be scarred for life 'cause of Tank, but he carved a big ol' cut into the heart of my reputation. He made me into something I'm not—a rat, a cop in disguise. I won't let that slide."

"I understand how you feel, I really do. But you gotta let the air outta your pride and move on. If you don't, and if you come sniffin' around the clubhouse, or if Tank hears word on the street that you're gunnin' for him, he'll hunt you down. And the home chapter in San Antonio might give him a blood patch for doin' it."

Axle spit out a sliver of tobacco from the tip of his tongue. "Maybe I'll join the Bandidos and crash Tank's next party. If nothin' else, I can kick Birddog's lyin' ass."

"That won't work well for either of you. Be smart, man. It ain't worth it. Sometimes this stuff comes with the territory. Shit happens. You know that."

"Yeah, I do. If you see Tank, tell him I'm goin' to a priest to confess my sins, seek penance, and ask for forgiveness before I bomb the clubhouse. Thanks for the call. Take care of yourself, Drywall. You're a stand-up guy. One of the damn few left."

Axle disconnected. He climbed the short wooden ladder up to the hayloft, pulled back a dark green Army blanket, and picked up his pistol. He stowed it in his belt, descended, and walked over to the large barn door. He paused a moment, taking a deep breath, a barn swallow flittering from the rafters. Axle opened the heavy door, the rusted hinges creaking, sunlight pouring in and over his face. The bright light illuminated the wound, pink, swollen, the stitches resembling a zipper in the form of an X.

Axle opened his truck door and looked over to the mare. "Nice hangin' with you, Maggie." He got into his truck and drove from the barn, heading down the long gravel drive toward the road. He glanced over at Welder's farmhouse, the screen door opening, and Welder coming out, wearing a black T-shirt and jeans. In his bare feet, he showed no signs of discomfort as he walked across crushed rock and gravel. He lifted his hand, signaling for Axle to stop.

Welder walked around to Axle's side of the truck. "Whoa, bro. You leaving or just out for a Sunday drive in the country?"

"I got to go, Welder. Thanks for the hospitality. I need to move on with my life. I can't live in a barn with a horse anymore."

"What about Tank?"

"What about him?"

"Last I heard, his guys were lookin' for you. Dead or alive."

"Well, I got news just now that he's backed off. He knows I refused to press charges. There won't be a kidnapping and attempted murder case. My pal, a guy still in the club, says that Tank is having second thoughts about me being a federal agent. Seems like his original source, a guy with a hard on for me 'cause his old lady wanted me to do her, he's the one spreading the bullshit."

"Where are you gonna go?"

"I don't know. I'd like to sell my trailer and all the crap in it. I'd hit the road and stay along the backroads across the country. Maybe I'll wind up in Texas, helping the Bandidos kick Iron Fist's ass."

"Before you pull outta here, can I give you some advice? Don't know if you'll take it, Axle. But I think you ought to hear it."

"All right."

"Bury the hatchet. I've fought like cats and dogs in club turf wars. Kickin' ass and takin' names for what, really? To play the game in that world is foolish. You gain nothing but more swagger 'til somebody sticks a cold shank in your gut and rips it up to your heart. I found the Lord, buried my ego, and put all that behind me. There are two rare things in my new world … old bikers and compassion. You gotta have nine lives to hang in there for the long haul. I'd say you done used up eight of 'em by now. The question you need to ask, son, is this: if time is stackin' the deck against you, do you still want to stay in the game?"

FORTY-EIGHT

I watched Angela's face as she took a bite of the homemade mac 'n cheese. Her eyes opened wide, as if the flavors of her favorite meal were being experienced for the first time, again. That's one of the advantages that comes from watching a child develop his or her tastes in life—from food, fun, hobbies, and work ethic to the way they treat others. Witnessing and being part of it was a benefit of fatherhood I was enjoying.

We sat at the small, round table on the back porch and ate dinner. During the last few weeks, Wynona had tried three mac 'n' cheese recipes before we, as a family, settled on the one we thought was best for all of us. It's worth mentioning, though, that I was outvoted—two to one. I suppose the recipe with garlic was a little too pungent.

Max sat to the left of Angela's chair. If Max had voted, I had the feeling it would have been three females to me. The cheesier it is, the better for Max. Might as well call it Max 'n' cheese. I know when to lay down my cards. In addition to the macaroni, Wynona made a large garden salad and baked bread served hot out of the oven. I expected Max to do cartwheels from the aromatic scents despite the fact we fed her first.

Wynona watched Angela try a slice of cucumber and said, "We had a very good day today with homeschool. Did you tell Daddy about your grade?"

Angela looked at me and smiled. "I made one hundred percent on my spelling."

"That's great. What are some of the words you learned to spell?"

"Lots. I can spell apple, grape, and orange."

Wynona said, "We are learning to spell members of the fruit family. Tomorrow, we move to vegetables."

191

I nodded. "I'm impressed. Speaking of fruit, there are ripe oranges in the yard that we can go pick and make fresh-squeezed orange juice. And maybe we can freeze some for orange pops."

"Yeah! I have these new things that can freeze the popsicles into animal shapes," said Angela, dropping a small piece of macaroni from her fork. Max caught the cheesy noodle before it could hit the floor.

After lunch, Max and Angela played in the backyard. They put Cuddles in the middle of the swing seat and pushed, Cuddles toppling off onto the grass each time. "You have to hold tighter," Angela said, trying to teach her plush friend with large eyes and a permanent smile.

Wynona and I sat on the porch, watching them play. A blue butterfly—an Atala—alighted on the other side of the screened porch. Wynona watched it before the butterfly sailed off toward the river and the national forest. She said, "That's such a beautiful butterfly, the dark blue wings with their light blue spots and the red body, wow. The colors are so vivid."

"It's called an Atala. They're rare, and they only live in Florida."

She smiled. "You, Sean O'Brien, are quite the entomologist. How'd you know it's an Atala butterfly."

"An old friend's daughter used to release the Atala butterflies into the wild." I motioned to the river. "In the national forest, you can find a fern-like plant called the coontie. To most critters, the plant's resin is toxic. But not to the Atala. It's their ambrosia. These butterflies, almost extinct at one time, are making a comeback."

"It sounds like it's because of the efforts of people like your friend's daughter."

I said nothing, watching Angela at the rope swing.

Max barked twice. Angela laughed as she tried to balance the stuffed bear on the swing seat. Wynona watched them, her voice soft and reflective. "The butterfly's story is symbolic and hopeful ... that a human being can be immersed in darkness and still become beautiful—still emerge into the world and fly."

"It's easier when loving people are there to be the wind beneath their wings. With the proper support, that first solo flight out of the cocoon is where someone who's been abused can find their wings. From darkness into the light of the world—it's a rebirth of the spirit."

Wynona smiled, the serenade of a cardinal coming from the oak tree above Angela and Max. Earlier in the day, I had shared the results thus far of my investigation into Andy's death. And now, Wynona looked over at me. "You told me about Andy's girlfriend, Brittany Harmon. In just a blink of our eyes, Angela will be in college, trying to figure out her passion in this world. Do you think Brittany has the internal strength to handle a call, a text, or a social media solicitation from a drug dealer?"

"Yes. She comes across as a young woman with a strong, uncompromising spirit. A lot of grit. Probably like you when you were her age."

"I don't know. It took me years to grow into what I am, and I still can't define that." She smiled.

"Brittany doesn't need to have face-to-face contact with this guy, Charlie Brown, if that's his real name. She just must let me know if, when, and how he tries to connect with her. I will take it from there. And, if she can get enough information, I might track him down."

"Do you think this Charlie Brown sold the lethal pills, oxy spiked with fentanyl, to Andy?"

"I don't know. But I do think Brown delivered the Prozac to him. Clint said a bottle of twenty Prozac pills, or knockoffs, were found in Andy's bathroom. Ten pills were left. Forensic tests couldn't find any indication of fentanyl. That's apparently reserved for the painkillers, not the mood killers."

"And police think the pills with the fentanyl were delivered in a plain brown cardboard box through the mail or one of the carrier services, correct?"

"Yes. According to Brittany, Andy said the box was left at the door."

"Maybe Charlie Brown left that one, too. Do you think this guy is the dealer who provided the drugs to those college kids in Panama City Beach?"

"I think it's a good possibility. The lead detective in the case, Lindsey Owen, said there is no evidence thus far in terms of a name. No reference to a Charlie Brown on the phones of the dead kids or their social media contacts. Charlie Brown is probably an alias."

"If Brown is the point of contact for these college kids, who's he getting the drugs from? Are they the people making the stuff, or are they the distributors suppling Northeast Florida with illegal drugs? Is the Iron Fist biker gang bringing the stuff in from the Texas-Mexico border?"

"I wish I had answers for all of that. What we know is that Andy Ward and this Charlie Brown character met. Did it put Andy in the crosshairs of a lethal drug overdose? Most likely. If I can find Charlie Brown, I might get some answers. I gave the guy's name and number to Detective Porter with the Gainesville PD. Maybe it'll fire up their dormant investigation and bring closure to Clint and Lauren and their son's strong but emotionally drained girlfriend, Brittany Harmon."

Wynona looked from me to Angela and Max playing, Cuddles left behind in the center of the wooden swing seat. "Sean, what if this guy, Charlie Brown, is just a cog in the wheel of this drug operation? Even if he is the point-of-contact, the guy who sold the drugs to Andy, do you step away, not be involved anymore as Gainesville PD pursues the investigation, or do you stay with it?"

"I suppose that would depend on whether the PD moves on it. If they continue to look at Andy's death as unfortunate, just another college kid overdosing on illegal drugs, and they don't attempt to question or arrest Charlie Brown, I will intervene. I can't arrest him, obviously, but I can question him. At that point, I believe my initial questioning might reveal something that the Gainesville PD can hang their hat on. Then I can step away, letting justice take its new course."

"And then, we can plan our simple wedding ceremony and stick to that date. It would be great if Angela could be a flower girl while she's still a little girl." Wynona laughed.

"Sounds like a good plan."

My phone buzzed on the table. I looked at the caller ID. I had a feeling that what she had to say was going to cause me to go back to Gainesville. What I didn't know was where I might have to go from there. I looked over at Wynona. "It's Brittany Harmon calling."

FORTY-NINE

It was a phone call I hoped would lead to a degree of closure for Clint and Lauren Ward. I answered and Brittany Harmon blurted out, "I heard from him!"

"Charlie Brown?"

"Yes. He texted me and said this, hold on, I want to read it to you."

"All right."

"Okay … here it is. He wrote … *Hi, Brit. Got your message. We know how it is, cramming for college midterm exams. Glad you don't drink coffee. Not healthy. We'll call you from another # within 15 minutes to discuss prices, ordering, and delivery options. Thx!*"

"Brittany, send that text to me."

"Okay. What do I do?"

"Text back and tell him you can take the call."

"What do I say?"

"Mostly you listen. Our goal is to see if Charlie Brown will deliver to you." I looked at my watch. "Brittany, it'll take me about an hour and forty minutes to drive to Gainesville. I'll meet you outside the coffee shop and take you to where I'd like for this guy to come to you."

"Where?"

"I don't want him arriving at your apartment. There's a park near the university. It's called Depot Park. It's wide open with a playground, performance stage, and pavilions overlooking a pond. Try to set up an exchange with this guy at a picnic table under one of the pavilions that face Southeast 4th Street. That location will be safe and allow me to be close to you when he shows up. Okay?"

"Okay. Southeast 4th Street, right?"

"Yes. He'll want money—cash. I will bring that for you."

TOM LOWE

"Okay. What are you going to do, like jump out of the bushes and grab him?"

"No. That wouldn't serve the purpose we need. I want to follow him. See where he goes and who, if anyone, he meets with after he leaves you. At some point during this time, I will have a discussion with him."

"Okay."

"See if he can meet you at four o'clock today. If so, we'll get you there early. Before the time you're to meet, I want you to hit the audio record button on your phone. Have the phone in your purse. Unzip or unfasten it. Position the phone so the microphone spot is facing toward the top of your purse."

"What if he wants me to go online to actually buy the stuff?"

"We know he makes deliveries. That's probably because he'd prefer a cash sale. And that's what we want, too. Broad daylight in an open park where kids are playing in the background. That'll make it safe for you."

"Okay."

"Are you nervous?"

"Just a little."

"That's normal. I will make this promise. I won't let anything bad happen to you on my watch. Understand?"

"Yes. I'm doing this for Andy and his parents, and I guess, in a way, for me, too."

"I appreciate that. I want you to call me the minute you're off the line with him. I need to know what he said and whether he'll be there at four or wants to reschedule for some other time."

"Okay."

"Take a few deep breaths and let them out slowly. You can do this."

"I can. I am strong."

"See you soon." I clicked off and looked across the table at Wynona. "Well, you heard what I said to Brittany. I'll bet you can guess what she was saying at the other end of the line."

"I just hope it goes down well. Buying illegal drugs from a dealer can get messy."

"When I was a detective, the real mess came after drug dealers and their suppliers got into arguments about money. Most often, it was one of the perps putting his greedy thumb on the scale, and other times, it was a turf war. Rarely did a neighborhood dealer hurt a client unless that client shorted him or owed money for extended credit. That's not going to be the case with Brittany. A quick and easy exchange. I'll watch and follow this guy to wherever rats go after they snatch the cheese."

Wynona reached across the table with both of her hands. She held my hand. "The detectives may rebuke you, Sean, for taking the hard road. But deep down, they wish they had the courage to do the same. Call me when the mist clears."

***

Brittany Harmon was in her car, parking at the coffee shop when she received the call. She looked at the screen for a caller ID. The number had an 888-area code. She answered. "Hello."

"Hey, Brit. I'm calling from Gulf Stream Carrier. How are you?"

"Okay." The guy on the line didn't identify himself.

"Good … really good. Listen up. Here's the deal. We can offer speedy delivery to you. A bottle of thirty "adds" at five milligram each for just $140 cash. Online payment is $160. If you went to the pharmacy, you'd pay $8 per pill—meaning thirty pills would come to $240. Ouch! Who needs that? We're here to make an affordable difference. How and where would you like delivery and mode of payment?"

"You said that you can deliver it to me at a cash price of $140, right?"

"You got it, and what a special that is. Nobody beats our prices and speed of delivery. We can be your DoorDash for meds. We'll get you through college and on the dean's list." He laughed.

"I don't know about that. Okay, I'll go with the $140 cash."

"Spot on! Excellent choice. Where's your place?"

"I'd rather you not try to deliver to the dorms. I'm going to be at Depot Park this afternoon, saying bye to my aunt and her little girl. That's at 3:30. Can you meet me there at four o'clock? I'll be sitting at a picnic table under the pavilion closest to Southeast 4th Street. I'm wearing a blue sundress."

"We're on it. We'll see you at four."

"Oh, before you go … you know my name. But I don't know yours."

"You can call me Charlie or CB. Take your pick."

"I'm not into initials. What's the B stand for in CB?"

"Brown. Gotta go." He clicked off.

Brittany lowered her phone to her lap. She looked down at her trembling hands and wondered if she was making the right decision.

FIFTY

I was less than five miles from Gainesville when I got an unexpected phone call. The area code was 850, the same as Charlie Brown's, but this call wasn't coming from a criminal. It was coming from a cop. Panama City Beach Detective Lindsey Owen on the line. I answered and she said, "Mr. O'Brien, I wanted to let you know that this office did find beach-cam footage of a man meeting the student, Bruce Cooper, for what appears to be a drug sale."

"Where was the location?"

"Close to where Cooper's surviving friend said it would be, near the pier. Although there are hundreds of people, mostly college kids on the beach, in the video, the guy who sold Cooper the fentanyl stands out. He's on a bicycle, wearing a bright red pirate's bandana. He's in a swimsuit. No shirt and with a blue backpack. He's got a scruffy beard and one of those deep tans a lifeguard gets, like a guy who works the beach often."

"Can you email the video to me?"

"I can do that."

"Good. Thanks. You might want to share it with Detective Winston Porter. It'll look better coming from your office."

"I understand."

"I really appreciate you taking the time to call me." I gave her my email. "If I hear of anything more in the Gainesville area, I'll let you know."

"Thanks." She clicked off.

I pulled over to the side of the road and opened my email. I wanted to study the guy's antics, his face—if the video was close enough. I played it, watching people on the beach tossing Frisbees, footballs, and zipping past the pier on Jet Skis. A few seconds later, a guy on a bike peddled into the video frame.

Even in the crowd of people not much younger than he was, this man stood out. Skin the color of brown hazelnuts. Blood red bandana. Gold necklace and earring. A windblown Viking beard. He rode near the breakers where the sand was hardpacked, gulls scattering out of his way.

I watched him survey the beachgoers. Even behind his dark glasses, I could see his visual radar scanning. He appeared to be wearing earbuds, his head bobbing, like a peacock pecking at seeds. Then he spotted his quarry. The guy on the bike came to a stop, the pier less than one hundred feet away. He got off his bike and pushed it through the white sand, carving the kind of wavy trail a slithering snake would leave.

He came up to a tall college kid and made what appeared to be small talk, the guy with the red bandana was animated, lots of hand gestures, wide smiles, looking around the area. On guard. After a minute, he opened his backpack and took out something. It was hard to see from the angle and distance, but it looked like the size of a prescription bottle. The fresh-faced, wide-eyed college kid, Bruce Cooper, pulled out a wad of money and peeled off a few of the bills, giving them to the dealer.

They made the fatal exchange. I looked at the date and time in the lower part of the screen. By my calculations, the deadly pills were bought the day that the college kids would later meet that night in the condo. After the deal was done, Bruce Cooper walked away. The guy got back on his bike watching two girls in bikinis stroll by him. He said something to the girls. They appeared to laugh and shake their heads in a "no thanks" response.

He got on his bike and started to ride away, his eyes still following the girls. I stopped the video and zoomed in as close as possible before the image became pixilated. I could see a leering smile on his face and a tattoo on his upper arm. Now I knew what the drug dealer looked like. Since Andy and his friend Jason had used a number with an 850-area code, I wondered if the dealer lived in that area or if he was from that area? And was the guy on the bike Charlie Brown?

Later today, I hoped to find out.

FIFTY-ONE

Tony Salazar was forced to stare at a slow death. A man hung, dying, on one timbered wall in the stables, across from where Salazar was chained to a large girder. Blood oozed from his hands, which were nailed to the wood. He had been hanging there, crucifixion-style, for the last five hours.

Earlier in the day, the man had stared at Salazar through pleading, helpless eyes after Diego Navarro's men left him nailed to one wall of the stables. His bare feet were suspended from the floor, blood dripping off his toes into flowers of red beneath him.

Salazar desperately wanted to help, but with the tight rope on his hands and arms, he could barely move. As the man's breathing became shallower, Salazar cleared his throat and said in Spanish, "Can I pray for you brother?"

The man managed to lift his head slightly, face swollen the color of plums, one eye closed from a severe beating. He nodded. "Si."

Salazar began to recite Psalms 23 in Spanish. When he got to the part, "Even though I walk through the darkest valley, I shall fear no evil," the man cried. When Salazar finished, the man took a final breath and was still. The blood stopped dripping. Within a few seconds, a blowfly alighted on his torn face.

***

At DEA headquarters in Mexico City, a half dozen agents were in the conference room with lead agent, Byron Lopez. They sipped water from bottles, waiting for headquarters in Virginia to come on the satellite feed. Seconds later, DEA administrator Christina Bowman was on the screen. Next to her was the assistant administrator. To his left was a woman with dark hair, pearl earrings, and hazel eyes. Silvia Geller was the agency's media relations director.

Bowman looked at the camera. "Byron, I just came back from the White House. The president is adamant. He will not, nor will he allow us to negotiate—to make a deal with the cartel. The president says there is no difference between them and the most radical Islamic extremist groups with a hatred for America."

Lopez nodded. "I assumed as much. A least you gave it your best shot. Did he offer a suggestion as to how his administration wants to deal with getting Tony the hell out of there?"

"Yes. It was something that I strongly disagreed with when it was mentioned. However, with five key members of his staff, including two cabinet members, I was overruled. Before we get into that, have you heard from Navarro again?"

"Yes. We received another text message from him on Tony's phone."

"What did he write?"

"Basically, that he's growing impatient, and we have forty-eight hours to decide. If we won't decide in his favor for what he calls a six-month pact and the release of his father, or if we choose simply not to communicate back with him, he said Tony's head will be put on display at the top of the spire at the Nuestra Senora Santa Ana cathedral. It's one of the most well-known cathedrals in all of Mexico."

Bowman leaned back in her chair, looking away from the screen for a few seconds. She released a deep breath. "The president wants us to let the news media know what happened."

"That's insane! Why?" Lopez shifted in his chair.

"He believes the media will find out anyway. But, when it comes from us, we can control the messaging." She gestured to the woman with the pearl earrings. "That's why Silvia Geller is here. She will write the news release, be the agency's spokesperson, and field questions from the news media."

Lopez shook his head. "I think we're playing with fire. Navarro can't be intimidated."

"The president and most of his top staff feel that, if the spotlight is shone on Navarro, if Americans and people around the world can see what's happened, to see who Tony is, a good man with a wife and two children, a guy just trying to do his job, the PR response would be huge. The White House believes that the public outcry will put Navarro in a place he doesn't want to be and portray him for who he really is … a power-hungry, demonic psychopath."

Lopez eyed a few of the men in the room with him. "Gabriel Perez knows Navarro better than anyone in the room. He lived in the same town and grew up across the proverbial tracks from the Navarro family. What's your take on this, Gabe? Do you think the international exposure will be the leverage we need to have Navarro let Tony out of there alive?"

Gabriel Perez appeared older than his age of thirty-seven. The crow's feet around his black eyes were distinct. He placed his wide palms on the table and shook his head. "I think it's a bad idea. Diego Navarro is a man with no conscience. People only represent a monetary value, something he can barter, trade, or sell. He has no empathy and is without remorse."

"Sounds like people we deal with most of the time," Bowman said.

"Yes," agreed Perez. "The big exception is Navarro's vast wealth and his connection within the Mexican government and military. He may not have a conscience, but he does have one horrible personality trait that I have seen, even when he was a teenager. He is quick to anger. If he feels something has been taken from him, regardless of whether it was his, he comes out with fists flying. He will push back against the president because Navarro has no respect for him, and he does not fear him. Diego Navarro will kill Tony Salazar, and he'll find a way to blame it on America's intrusion into Mexico."

Lopez nodded. "From the profiles we have of Navarro, and from talking to people who know him, I believe you're right. In Navarro's last text, he said he needs an answer in forty-eight hours, or he'll kill Tony. Maybe we should hold off on any press release and bide our time, trying to come up with a viable extraction plan, and then go public if we can't get Tony out of there."

The media relations director, Silvia Geller, said, "I'm not so sure that's the direction we want to go. The president gave us marching orders. I suggest we follow them and do it now."

"We should take advantage of the forty-eight-hour window. If we don't, Nicole Salazar will become a widow and their two children will be fatherless. There won't be enough of Tony's body left to ship home for burial. If you write your press release, it could be writing his epitaph."

FIFTY-TWO

Even from across the coffee shop parking lot, I could see the anxiety on her face. As I walked closer, Brittany grinned, standing straighter, the breeze in her hair. I smiled. "Thanks for doing this. If you change your mind, just let me know. Okay?"

"Okay. I'm going to be in a city park with other people. He's making a delivery, and I'm paying him. This was probably how it happened with Andy. The difference is that, after this guy leaves, I won't be taking any of his stupid pills. And I know you'll be there watching."

"Tell me as much as you can remember of your phone conversation with him."

We stood in the shade of a blooming mimosa tree, its red blossoms giving off a scent like honey and straw. Brittany told me the complete conversation she had with the man. She added, "He really didn't want to give me his name, which makes me think it's his real name because, if it was fake, he wouldn't care. I think he'd rather be called CB than Charlie Brown. Just a hunch."

"You may be right. I can tell you have good deductive reasoning skills. Not many people your age do. Some never do, regardless of age."

"When I was a little girl, in the first and second grades, my mom used to say I had an old soul."

"I'd say you have a wise soul."

"Thanks."

"Here's more on the plan. Follow me to Depot Park. Once there, I want you to park your car at least a block away. After you've parked, you can walk the rest of the way down 4th Street. The pavilions are easy to see from the road. Since it's not the weekend, I doubt if anyone is having a barbecue or using the picnic tables. There are seven of them. Sit on a table bench closest to the street. I will be parked across the street, watching everything he does."

"Okay." She made a dry swallow.

"Give me your phone and purse." She took her purse strap from her shoulder, handing her phone and purse. I unzipped it, placing the phone vertical and in the upside-down position. "Keep this on your lap when you're talking with him. You want your purse between you and Charlie Brown. I have the cash for you. Keep it near your phone in the purse so you can easily get the money out. We want him to admit he's doing an illegal transaction."

"How do we do that?"

"You chat first. Make him feel comfortable. Talk about the weather or the park. Then you say something like … okay I have the money for the Adderall. You said $140 dollars, right? He should say yes. If he only nods, then ask the question—was it $140 or $160? He may say $160. I am giving you two hundred dollars, a hundred-dollar bill and the rest in twenties. When you pay him, count it out. When you finish, say something like … okay that's a total of whatever it is, and add this question … where is the Adderall?"

"Okay."

"He should give it to you and have a closing comment or two. Brittany, I have no idea if this guy knows that Andy is dead. If he doesn't, he might be more forthcoming than he would otherwise."

"What do you mean?"

"If he's not aware of Andy's death, which could be a good possibility since drug overdoses don't often get the news media coverage as do murders, he might have something to say. Clint Ward told me that the local paper printed a short news story. That was followed a week later by Andy's obituary. Charlie Brown might admit that Andy was a customer if approached the right way."

"What do I say?"

"After the exchange of money, not before, say that you were referred to Gulf Stream Carrier by a friend. He probably will ask you who your friend is. Just smile and say Andy Ward. You don't have to add another word after that. See what he says. Gauge his response. Watch his face for any signs of deception."

"What do I look for?"

"Darting eyes. Eyes that look up before he answers a question. Vagueness in his answers. Repeating a question before answering. The pretense of indifference—seeming bored, shrugging. Most importantly, just trust your instincts, which will be heightened because of the circumstances. Ready to do this?"

"Yes. I'll just be glad when it's over."

"When the guy leaves, start walking back to your car. Don't go to your apartment. Just go back to the coffee shop and call me as you're driving there. I want to know everything he says. Okay?"

"Okay."

***

Twenty minutes later, Brittany was sitting at one of the picnic tables. I sat in my Jeep across the street, window down, a clear view of Brittany. Behind her were children and moms, mostly. People enjoying the playground. Some used a concrete path to walk around the pond, the perimeter dotted with leafy oaks, two white swans near the center of the pond. Across the area from where Brittany sat was a stage and bandstand. Despite what she was doing, Brittany appeared calm. She read or pretended to be reading a paperback book.

I looked at my watch. It was a few minutes until four o'clock. The traffic was light. I watched each car and truck that passed the park, looking for a tapping of brake lights or the slowing down as the drivers approached the park. All appeared normal.

Until a man on a bicycle appeared.

He seemed to simply materialize on the sidewalk, as if he rode in from a blacktop road, emerging through the mirage and haze of a shimmering heat wave. He stopped about a hundred feet before the center of the park, close enough for him to surveil the surroundings and spot anything that seemed out of the ordinary. I could see him looking in Brittany's direction. Then he watched a landscaper using hedge shears to prune low-hanging branches from a magnolia tree.

The guy on the bike came closer, like a predator stalking prey and trying not to be seen. He appeared to be in his late twenties. He wore sunglasses and a backpack, and his face was lean and pointed like an axe.

His unkempt black beard and long hair were the color of a walnut. I could see the sun wink on a gold hoop earring in his right ear. A dark red bandana was on his head. And from where he was now, I could see a tattoo of a tall-masted schooner on his upper right arm. He rode his bike from the sidewalk to within twenty feet of Brittany. I knew Charlie Brown was approaching.

She looked up and smiled.

He used one foot to push down the bike's kickstand, walking with a swagger to the picnic table under the pavilion.

Brittany pressed the audio record button on her phone.

FIFTY-THREE

The dress rehearsals in her mind were about to become the real thing, trying to spot deception from a man with the same name as a cartoon character, Charlie Brown. Brittany had gone over what she was supposed to do in the conversation and exchange. What she didn't know was whether she should speak first or let him say something. She decided to take the initiative, to appear friendly and approachable.

"Are you Charlie?"

"Is that a lucky guess or do you think I look like a Charlie?"

"I'm not sure what a Charlie is supposed to look like. I know what Charlie Sheen and Charlie Daniels look like. You don't resemble them, and you certainly don't look like the animated character, Charlie Brown. Maybe you look more like a Charles than a Charlie."

Brown smiled. "Long as I don't look like Charles Manson."

"I'd say more like Charlie the pirate."

"Aargh." He laughed.

Brittany smiled, glancing down at her unzipped purse. "I feel kind of weird buying Adderall, but if I don't pass these midterms, I might lose my scholarship. If that happened, I'd have to leave school and go back home to Tampa, facing my parents with my head hanging low."

"You got too pretty of a head to let it hang low. Face like yours ought to greet the morning sun like the new blossom on a rose bush." He grinned, his eyes bright, like a dog happy to see its owner.

"I bet you say that to all your female customers."

"No. Trust me on that one."

She smiled. "Okay."

"Did you bring the glue?"

"Glue?"

"The stuff that holds a deal together."

"You mean money?"

"For a college girl, you catch on fast." Wide smile, his eyes taking in her entire body.

"But I'm not great with numbers. Did you say a bottle of thirty Adderall was for $140 or $160?"

"With a tip, it can come to $160. You'd tip the pizza delivery person, right?"

"Where's the Adderall?"

"In here." He unzipped his backpack and took out what resembled a prescription bottle, handing it to Brittany. She looked at the bottle, the label, twisting open the top, staring at the pills. He grinned. "Savvy girl. Checking out the merchandise."

"Nothing is in here but Adderall, right?"

"Absolutely. Only the best. Can't have you losing your scholarship. Where's the glue?"

She reached in her purse, counting the money out loud, stopping at $160. "That's your tip." She handed him the cash and added. "You come highly recommended. Andy Ward referred you to me."

He glanced up from folding the bills. "Who? Andy Ward?" He looked away, pursing his thin lips. "Nah, never heard of him. But I got a lot of freaking customers. Can't remember all their names off the top of my head."

"That's weird because Andy highly recommends you. He said you're like a pirate philosopher on two wheels. Laidback outlook on life and always something funny to say, plus the best prices on the internet. He liked the fact that you deliver to his apartment on West University Avenue."

Brown cocked his head. "What'd you say the dude's name is?"

"Andy Ward."

"What's he look like?"

"Tall. Handsome. A beautiful smile."

"You just described me." He chuckled. "Yeah, I think I know him. He's a jock, right? Got some pulled muscle problems. Wasn't nothin' Doctor Charlie couldn't fix. I took care of him. Is this guy your boyfriend?"

"No."

"When you see him again, let the dude know he can get ten percent off his next order from his referral. Customer loyalty is everything. Well, I gotta go. Thanks for the biz, and good luck on those midterms."

As he turned to walk back to his bike, Brittany felt a recessed anger well up inside her heart. It was like a caged wild animal pacing behind bars. "He used to be my boyfriend."

Brown stopped and turned to face her. "If y'all are trying to get back together, tell him I got some magic pills. A love potion in fifty milligram doses. Guaranteed to put the lead back in his libido. Sometimes even jocks sing the blues. Know what I mean?"

"No, I don't. He's no longer my boyfriend because Andy's dead."

"Dead?"

"Are you surprised or is it just part of your act? He died from one pill. Not an overdose. It was one oxy pill made with fentanyl."

Brown wasn't sure what to say, the sound of children's laughter in the background, the chop of the hedge shears across the pond. "Hey, what is this … a setup? I'm no different than any online pharmacy—but I deliver. He looked around the park, eyes darting, lower jaw hard. Brown used one finger to scratch the skin under his scraggly beard. "I don't sell bad oxy. My stuff isn't pressed with fentanyl. He must have bought it from someplace else. If this is an ambush, I'm gonna come back and hurt you like you've never been hurt before."

Brown turned and jumped on his bike, peddling through the grass and bushes to the sidewalk. He headed in a northeast direction, peddling fast, the wind blowing his beard, head low, back arched like a pirate looking over the gunwale of a galleon at sea, caught in the pull of the Gulf Stream.

FIFTY-FOUR

I made a U-turn in the street. Brittany walked southeast, in the opposite direction from Charlie Brown and his bicycle. I watched her out of my side-view mirror. I wasn't sure if she was crying. But she held her head up, walking with a sense of pride as though whatever was said between her and the guy fleeing on the bike, Brittany had the last word.

That worried me.

I followed the bike at a distance, watching Charlie Brown go from the sidewalk to the street and back again. Choosing the path of least resistance in terms of obstacles—people, traffic. I picked up my phone and called Brittany. "Are you okay?"

"Yes. That guy is a narcissist, like somebody with ice water for blood."

"Check the conversation to make sure it recorded on your phone."

"I did that walking to my car. It's there."

"Tell me everything he said. Try to remember every word. I'll listen to the audio recording later."

"Okay. We started out chitchatting. All the time, he kept looking around, over my shoulders, toward the stage area and across the little lake, like he was trying to find cops hiding in the bushes." She told me the conversation and added, "Maybe I shouldn't have said anything about Andy being dead, but this guy had such arrogance that I wanted him to know it was the poison he sold that killed Andy."

I said nothing, driving, watching the pirate on a bike ride the wind for another two blocks. He turned his head, a gust blowing his sunglasses off. He didn't stop to pick them up. I saw where the glasses tumbled in a weedy area next to a live oak, its roots cracking and raising the sidewalk.

Brittany let out a pent-up breath. "Do you think I made a mistake mentioning Andy's death?"

"Yes. I'm just counting on it being one that I can deflate very quickly. Send the audio recording to my phone."

"Okay. Are you going to take it to the police?"

"Probably. It depends on what I learn from Charlie Brown. Call you back as soon as I can." I clicked off. As I drove slowly down the tree-lined street, I spotted Brown pulling his bike up to the back of a parked van. It was a new van, white with heavy-duty shocks and an engine made for hauling and towing. I pulled over behind a parked car, watching as he opened the van's two doors in the rear and quickly putting his bike inside. He ran to the drivers' side, got in and sped away.

I followed not knowing if I'd be in for a long ride to Tallahassee or somewhere here in Gainesville.

Either way, I knew he'd keep a sharp eye, looking in all the van's mirrors. I stayed behind traffic, driving and glancing at the digital map of the area on my phone screen. I turned off, taking a side road that I knew ran adjacent to Southeast 4th Street. From half a block over, I watched the van and looked at the map. Earlier, if he noticed my Jeep at a distance, he'd see that it was gone. Rather than following from behind the van, I drove parallel to it. I could do this for three more blocks before I had to take a left and continue the tail on 4th Street.

I spotted him shifting lanes, moving to the left as the van came to a stop at a traffic light. I sped through the neighborhood, squealing tires at a stop sign, pulling onto 4th Street, just catching the yellow light as it was turning to red. Charlie Brown's van was at least a quarter mile ahead of me.

My phone buzzed. I read the text message from Brittany. *Here's the audio file.* As I followed Brown from a distance, I played the recording. I was amazed at how well Brittany had relayed the conversation back to me. Almost word-for-word. *Yeah, I know him. He's a jock, right? Got some pulled muscle problems. Wasn't nothin' Doctor Charlie couldn't fix. I took care of him. Is this guy your boyfriend?*

I couldn't help but smile. "Gotcha." Within five minutes, the van was turning. No turn signal at the traffic light, but still turning right. I waited for the light to change back to red, stopping and allowing Brown to gain a little distance before I took a right on red and soon saw him about two hundred yards ahead of me. Around the next bend, he turned off the road. As I approached the gravel drive, I kept at the same speed. His van was pulling up to a red brick house set off the road and under moss-draped oaks. The house was ranch style, probably built in the eighties.

I drove past, stopping when my Jeep was out of the direct line of sight. I pulled over to the side of the road, accessing satellite maps near my location. Within seconds, I could see a clear aerial view of the house. I zoomed in for a closer look. There were no other buildings on the property. Heatherbrae Lane ran behind the house. I followed the directions, soon turning onto Heatherbrae Lane and backtracking toward the house.

I parked off the side of the road behind a gumbo-limbo tree with branches so twisted and gnarled it appeared to have a form of flora arthritis. I got my Glock from the Jeep's console, shoving the pistol under my belt, shirttail out. I jumped over a shallow drainage ditch, water the color of black tar, mosquito larvae wriggling like alien life forms at the surface. I walked through the scrub brush, sandspurs sticking to my jeans at the cuffs, the scent of milkweed in the motionless air, butterflies scattering.

In less than a minute, I was approaching the back side of the house. The yard wasn't much better than the field I had just walked through, sand and pockets of straw-colored weeds. There were three windows. Curtains drawn tight. A sagging powerline hung between the back of the house and a utility pole.

I looked for security cameras. There weren't any, at least not on this side of the house. I walked up to the back door, the brass knob dulled from exposure. I tried the door. Locked. I used my shirttail to wipe off my fingerprints, the sound of rock music coming from somewhere inside the house.

I walked around to the left side, where one of the windows near the garage was slightly open, the rock music louder, Def Leppard belting out *Pour Some Sugar on Me*. I heard a diesel truck coming up the gravel driveway. I moved from the edge of the house to stand behind a massive water oak, its bark turning creamy white in areas from blight and rot.

It was a UPS truck. Brown and boxy, the driver wearing dark glasses. He parked behind the van, leaving his engine running and exiting from the driver's seat. He sprinted up to the door, left a cardboard box on the porch, snapped a photo, and jogged back to the truck. All in under forty seconds. With the rock music so loud, I doubted whether Charlie Brown heard the truck. I walked up to the front porch and used my camera to take a picture of the label and any tracking or reference numbers.

I knocked loud on the door, leaving the package where I found it, stepping back behind the scraggly crape myrtles. Maybe Charlie Brown would come to the door, see the package, and walk outside.

I'd be there to greet him.

FIFTY-FIVE

It was the only part of the job that he didn't like. Attorney General Edwin Rubin, the top appointed official in the U.S. Department of Justice, was uncomfortable under the bright lights of TV cameras and the assessing eyes of the national news media. He stood behind the DOJ podium in the media center, the room filled with reporters and recording gear. His mouth was tight and turned down as if his lips were glued together.

Rubin's suit hung from his bony structure. He was tall and gangly, wore bifocals, and his silver hair was parted high on his head, making him look more like a member of a barbershop quartet rather than the nation's top cop.

He blinked under the lights. "Thank you for coming," he began after clearing his throat. "As some of you may already have heard, there has been an incident on the other side of our southern border in Mexico that we are dealing with at this moment. A veteran member of the U.S. Drug Enforcement Agency, Anthony Salazar, has been abducted from where he lived in the town of Durango and taken to an unknown location. At least it's unknown to us. What is apparent is the note left behind by the leader of the notorious Durango cartel, Diego Navarro. In the note, he admits to kidnapping Tony Salazar and holding him hostage while issuing unreasonable demands. He wants us to release his father from federal prison in Colorado in exchange for Tony Salazar. And he wants us to turn a blind eye toward his cartel, allowing them to move with an air of impunity across our border while stepping up the arrests of his competitors—smugglers in the other cartels."

The reporters in the room scribbled notes, cameramen rolling video. Rubin continued. "Navarro and his gang of thugs are some of the most ruthless in Mexico. They smuggle billions of dollars' worth of illegal drugs around the world, not just through our southern border, but into many countries. However, it's an increasing problem in the U.S. The cartel also is one of the largest in terms of human trafficking, including the sex trafficking of minors."

Rubin shifted his weight behind the podium, glancing down at the notes his staff prepared for him. "Navarro is delusional. A madman. Our president, of course, has a firm policy to not open any doors of negotiation with terrorists. He puts Navarro and his gang in that category. We are, however, working diligently behind the scenes with the Mexican government to convince Navarro it will be in his best interest to free Tony and let him return to his family. Suffice to say, if Navarro chooses otherwise, he will suffer the consequences. We'll have updates on this changing situation when we get them. Thank you for coming."

"Attorney General Rubin," shouted a reporter from a cable news network. "What will those consequences be should Diego Navarro choose not to release Agent Salazar?"

"This office is not at liberty to say what we would or would not do to a drug cartel that takes the life of a DEA agent."

Another reporter, a woman wearing a blue suit with blonde hair down to her shoulders, said, "It appears odd on the surface that even someone like Diego Navarro would think he could receive some degree of exemption at the border. How did he hope to pull that off? Or is it because there are people flooding across the border, and he sees much less enforcement by the Border Patrol?"

"First, and foremost, your statement isn't accurate. There is no flood across the border. Our immigration policies are being challenged, and we're managing the influx. But that's another topic for another day. I can't see into the dark thoughts in Navarro's mind. He assumed, per his demands, that our office would not make this public. The DEA will do everything in its power, in and out of Mexico, to bring Tony Salazar home safely. That's all the time I have for now. Thank you all for coming."

As he turned to leave, a reporter in a wrinkled white dress shirt and red and teal striped tie barked another question. "Was Tony Salazar investigating the Durango cartel?"

No answer.

"What specifically is the Mexican government doing to help facilitate the safe return of Salazar?" asked another reporter with the New York Times.

Rubin ignored the barrage of follow-up questions as he and two senior members of his staff headed for a door in the wings of the room behind the small stage.

***

I waited less than a minute for Charlie Brown to open the door. I hit the audio record button on my phone, slipping it into the front pocket of my jeans. I assumed Brown looked through the peephole before I heard the click and turning of the deadbolt, followed by the clacking of the brass chain lock, the door opening with creaking hinges. I could see his profile as he stepped barefoot onto the concrete slab porch.

When he leaned over to pick up the box, I was there, my shadow falling across the top of the box. He looked up, the sun in his face, hazel eyes like yellow-green marbles in the sunlight. He slowly stood as if he didn't know what to say or do. Brown, just under six feet with prominent cheekbones, tilted his head slightly, his gold hoop earring flashing in the late afternoon light. Trying hard not to reveal fear in his eyes, he squeezed his right hand into a fist.

He sneered. "You don't look like the UPS man. Who are you?"

FIFTY-SIX

In the distance, I could hear the distinct sound of a Harley-Davidson motorcycle coming down the road in front of Charlie Brown's house. I watched his wary eyes. He glanced toward the end of his driveway. *Recognition.* I could tell the motorcycle rider stopped, the engine rumbling in neutral. Someone watching us. Seconds later, the Harley was leaving, the growl of its motor growing thin, the sound of a mockingbird returning in the pine trees.

I stared at Brown. "I'm not the UPS man. But because I don't wear a brown uniform doesn't mean I can't deliver. Like you, Charlie, I deliver. But not drugs. I can deliver grief. Not in the good grief, Charlie Brown, but in the bad stuff."

"You're trespassing! There's a 'Private Property Keep Out' sign at the end of the driveway. Move your ass off my property."

"Didn't come up your driveway. So, I didn't see it. Here's what I do see … a scared drug dealer. A guy who is facing a murder charge in the death of Andy Ward. But that's just the beginning. You're the same lowlife who sold Bruce Cooper fentanyl on Panama City Beach."

"I got no idea what you're talking about."

"Really? My Spidey sense is feeling deception. Before you do your drug deals, you should know if there are security cameras in the area." I pulled the phone out of my pocket. On the screen was the image of Brown near the beach pier, standing next to Cooper. "That's Bruce, the young man who had a bright future. He's dead, as are seven of his friends because of you."

"You can't pin that shit on me."

"Your whole drug deal is on the beach cam. Not only did you sell fentanyl to Andy Ward, killing him, you sold the poison to Bruce

218

Cooper, resulting in the deaths of eight college kids who came to the beach for spring break. You, Charlie Brown, are on the hook for murder … nine murders. That puts you up there with guys like Bundy and Manson. At this point, you can say, good grief, Charlie Brown, you're screwed for life. That's if you don't get the death penalty."

"Bullshit! I was just chatting with a dude on the beach. That's it. Leave or—"

"Or what? You'll blow pixie dust in my face and turn me into a stone statue."

"You're not a cop. Who the hell are you?"

"Andy Ward's family friend. I watched him play little league as a kid, followed his path to playing college ball, and being scouted by the pros. You took that away from him, and you took Andy away from his family and fiancée."

"That bitch!"

He threw the box at me, turning, scrambling back into his house. Before he could slam and lock the door, I shoved it open, barging inside. He picked up a baseball bat in one corner, holding it like a pro player hovering over first base. Brown charged me. I calculated his speed and timing of the swing. He drew further back and swung the bat at my head. I ducked, crouching low, the swoosh of the wind in my ears.

At that point, he was slightly off balance. Slightly was all I needed. I grabbed his right arm, knocking the bat out of his grip. He swung at me with his left hand. Another miss. I drove my fist hard into his head, the blow landing above his left eye, skin splitting, blood dripping down his face. He was dazed. He spat blood and charged me again. This time I brought my right knee up into his chin. The blow knocking him backwards.

I stared at his dazed face, thinking about the motorcycle that had almost turned into Brown's driveway. The next thirty seconds would be a form of closure for Clint and Lauren Ward, or it could be a turning point.

Every homicide detective arrives there.

I used to call it the crossroads. It was a point in the investigation when you saw the layers of the onion peeling back further into multiple levels of possible complicity. Do you simply take an axe and cut down the diseased tree of evil, or do you cut it down and pull the roots out of the earth? Do you scorch the fallen seeds—the spores of the criminal mind?

Looking at the dazed and flat eyes of Charlie Brown, I knew there would be enough evidence for the two police agencies to file charges, but would they dig deeper to find the *source* of the poison?

I doubted it.

Dust your hands and move on. Crime solved.

I thought of what Clint said as he watched Angela on her rope swing under the mossy oak. *I remember when Andy was her age. When I look at young kids like Angela, I get the feeling the God hasn't given up on mankind.* Wynona's words on the back porch with the rain falling on our tin roof were like a whisper in my ear. *All you can do, Sean, is the best you can do. Clint isn't asking for anything more.*

He shouldn't have had to ask for it, I thought, approaching Charlie Brown.

FIFTY-SEVEN

I leaned over, picking Brown off the floor, pushing him up against the wall. "Here's the deal, Charlie." His head bobbled, eyes blinking. I let go of his shirt. He slid down the wall, staring up at me through watery eyes, blood dripping off his chin. "Having a hard time focusing, are you? Well, focus on this." I lifted my shirt and pulled the Glock from my belt. I pressed the muzzle against his forehead.

"Hey, man!" He tried to push back against the wall, shoes slipping in blood.

"Talk!"

"Okay! I sold the pills to 'em."

"Who is them?"

"That dude you mentioned … Andy Ward."

"You sold it to Bruce Cooper, too. But it's nice to hear you admit it." I pressed harder.

"Okay! I sold it to that guy, too … the Bruce Cooper dude. Look, man. I had no idea the pills had fentanyl in 'em. They're supposed to be oxy."

"Take me through the daisy chain."

"Huh?"

"Where are you getting the drugs? Who's the distributor?"

He shook his head, using the back of his hand to wipe a drop of blood from the tip of his chin. "You really don't want to go there."

"Where?"

"A place you won't get out of alive."

"Where?" I moved the steel of the muzzle between his eyebrows. "Who and where?"

"The Iron Fist biker gang. Those dudes own the state of Florida and Georgia, just to name a few territories. If you even attempt to put a stop to their business, they'll skin you alive. You don't mess with those guys. I'm probably dead by telling you."

"Where is their main distribution hub?"

"They got satellite points of distribution all over the state. The Iron Fist moves most of the product outta their clubhouse near Daytona beach."

"The guy on the Harley … was he bringing drugs to you?"

"Yeah. But then he saw you. He's probably on the phone back to his guys."

"Where do they get the drugs?"

"They used to press a lot of the pills themselves. Then things changed along the Mexican border. It got a lot easier to work with the cartels. The Iron Fist is big in Texas."

"How are they bringing it into Florida?"

"Lots of ways. Easiest is from their stash houses. They're in remote parts of Texas a few miles over the border. They use trucks and vans to move the stuff. Man, that's all I know."

"Which cartel are they working with in Mexico?"

"Durango. They're bad asses … worse than the Iron fist … if that's even possible."

I pulled the Glock away from his head, lifting the phone out of my pocket. "Charlie, your confession is recorded. Don't even think of back peddling. Remember this … I found you when the police couldn't. I can find you again. Promise. The woman you referred to as 'the bitch,' if you or any of your pals come near her, I will come near you. Very up-close and personal."

He stared at me through loathing eyes. "You're a dead man."

"Here's what you're going to do. When the police arrive, you will tell them what you told me. I'm going to hang out with you until they arrive. Then I'm gone. I'll give you some advice. You aren't pressing the pills, not putting gunpowder in the bullets. You may have some wiggle room."

"What the shit does that mean?"

"It means you might be able to cut a deal. As a retailer, you're selling something you're buying from someone else—the middleman or manufacturer. If you turn state's witness, you might get a greatly reduced sentence or serve no time if you can implicate members of the Iron Fist."

He looked at me through incredulous eyes, shaking his head. "While I'm at it, why don't I just go on and testify against the Durango cartel, huh? That's the ultimate death wish for psychos like you. What the hell are you smokin'? If I testify against the Iron Fist, they'll slit my throat in jail or out. Don't matter. There won't be any place I can hide."

"Cockroaches can always find a garbage can to crawl into." I held my Glock in my right hand as I used my left hand to tap Detective Winston Porter's number. "Detective, I met a guy with an interesting story he wants to tell you. Goes by the name Charlie Brown. Charlie, in a moment of clarity, admits to selling the fentanyl to Andy Ward. Charlie tells me that he didn't know the pills were mixed with fentanyl. I suppose you can straighten that out. He admits to selling lethal pills to Bruce Cooper on Panama City Beach. You know what happened after that. I'm sure Detective Lindsey Owen would like to have a discussion with Charlie, too."

"Where are you, O'Brien?"

I remembered the UPS address on the box label. "I'm inside a brick house, 8957 Cloverleaf Lane, just outside the city. I'll keep Charlie company until your team can arrive."

"We'll be there in fifteen minutes." He clicked off.

I called Detective Lindsey Owen and told her what happened. "I suppose you and Detective Porter can divvy out how you want to file charges and prosecute."

"How'd you track down this guy?"

"Just sort of followed my instincts. That photo you sent me helped."

"You have a talent, Mr. O'Brien, that I've never seen in a PI, and I've met a lot."

"Sometimes you get lucky. Charlie Brown tells me he's just the last stem in the daisy chain of blame. Maybe between you and Gainesville PD, your departments can dig even further. If not, Charlie will be replaced on the street before he's arraigned."

"Will see how it all plays out. I suppose you've done what you've been hired to do. Do you have a next case pending?"

"Maybe. You never know what'll walk through the door. I do know that I'm not finished with this one."

She said nothing for a moment. In the background, I could hear the buzz of an office phone, the drone of a detective division working. "I'll call Detective Porter and speak with our prosecutor. My immediate interest is questioning this man, Charlie Brown. If he's the one on the beach cam, that's all I need. Since you have his confession on tape, I'm sure we'll get it in our interrogation. This will bring some closure to eight families going to funerals."

"Does that mean you close the book on those cases?"

"I didn't say that. But I will say, in prosecuting drug dealers, how far down the rope—the supply chain, do you go to flush out each person who had something to do with the manufacture, distribution, and sale of a drug?"

"That depends on how serious you are about stopping this." I heard her sigh.

"In the case of fentanyl, since most of the ingredients for making the stuff are coming from China, imported into Mexico by the cartels, then manufactured and sent to the U.S., do you file charges against people in China, which boils down to the Chinese Communist Party? That's out of my jurisdiction. My job is to arrest and prosecute drug dealers in Bay County. Again, how far down the rope do you go?"

"To the end of the rope."

***

A half hour later, after Detective Porter arrived at Charlie Brown's house with seven police officers, I gave them my statement. As they questioned Brown, I stood near the front door, within earshot, listening. He admitted to Porter what he'd said to me. They read Brown his rights and walked him past me, handcuffed, toward one of the waiting squad cars, blue and red lights pulsing.

As Brown walked by, he turned and said, "I heard 'em say your name's Sean O'Brien. You best have your last will and testament in order, O'Brien. The people you're messin' with live to die. It's in their blood, like a pack of wolves and mongrels."

"Let's go," said one of the two officers on either side of Brown, hustling him to the car.

Detective Porter watched them for a moment before saying, "O'Brien, I suppose you'll be heading back home. Your vigilante mission is over. We appreciate the tip, but we have a Crime Line phone number for that. One part of me wants to bust you for interference of a police investigation."

"You must be investigating a case to give that any validity." I turned to walk away.

He said, "I'll speak with the Ward family. Let them know we have a suspect in custody."

"Suspect? He admitted to selling Andy the fentanyl. There is no presumption of innocence under those circumstances."

"That's why we have courts and juries. We arrest. Prosecutors prosecute. Juries decide."

I paused, turning back toward him. "There should be no need for a jury trial in a plea—an admission of guilt. The judge can hear the facts in a summary judgment unless you, detective, or the prosecutor, offer Brown a plea deal to bring down the kingpins."

"Like I said, juries decide."

"The decision you should make is whether you're going to look for the *source* of the drugs that killed Andy and those kids in Panama City Beach. But I believe you've already made that decision. And now I'll make mine."

FIFTY-EIGHT

It was a call I was about to make with mixed emotions. Since I agreed to help Clint and Lauren Ward find out who sent or delivered the fentanyl to Andy, I looked forward to sharing some good news with them. At the start, I didn't know if I'd find any. But now that I found a gold nugget in the muddy water, I wanted to see if there were more. Not in terms of treasure, but rather as salvation.

I made the call. "Clint, have you heard from Detective Porter?"

"No. Should I? What's going on, Sean?"

"They've arrested the person who sold and delivered the fentanyl to Andy's apartment."

He said nothing, only the sound of his breathing coming over the phone. "Hold on. You mind if I put you on speakerphone? I'm in the kitchen with Lauren. I want her to hear this."

"Okay."

"All right, Sean. We're listening."

"Okay. Hi, Lauren. I have some good news."

"Thank God," she said. I could hear the anxiety in her voice.

"Here's what happened." I explained to them everything that had occurred up to now. I could hear Lauren crying in the background. I added, "I'm not sure how the two police agencies and their respective prosecutors will co-op their investigation and cases. I would assume that Charlie Brown will be tried in a Gainesville court for Andy's death and then face what should be eight counts of murder over in Panama City."

Lauren cleared her throat. "They can bring murder charges against this guy, right?"

"Yes. And they should."

"Good. Maybe he'll get the death penalty here in Florida."

Clint said, "We can't thank you enough for what you did and how quickly you found this guy. The police should have done it weeks ago. If they had, maybe the college kids in Panama City would still be alive. Did this piece of garbage, Charlie Brown, act alone, or did he have a chemist in the background, like those guys who operate in the meth labs? A couple of guys making the poison and others distributing it."

"Brown is the last cog in the gears of this operation. A biker gang, one that is known in a half dozen states for drug running, human trafficking— among other crimes, is the distributor. They're called the Iron Fist."

"I've heard of them," said Clint. "From some of the news clips I've seen in the last couple of years, these guys muscle in and run other biker gangs out of an area and take that territory over to commit their crimes."

"They're not into profit sharing. I told the lead detectives in both police departments that Brown was a low-level dealer. There are probably at least a dozen like him that the Iron Fist uses in Florida to hustle fentanyl and other junk. I'd bet the DEA has no clue how much this group delivers through traditional carriers, such as UPS, compared to the smaller percentage delivered to your door by dealers, like a pizza in a cardboard box."

Lauren said, "Based on what you told us, I think that Brittany is a very brave young woman to have agreed to meet this guy in the city park."

"Yes, she is brave and very resourceful, able to quickly think on her feet. I can see why Andy was drawn to her."

"Do you think Brittany is in danger?" asked Clint.

"Not in an immediate sense. Her involvement, outside of being Andy's girlfriend, is the fact of what she heard Brown say during the drug buy in the park. All of that, as I mentioned, was recorded on audio. The police have it. Brittany can testify if called to the stand. But it may not come to that."

"What do you mean?" Lauren asked.

"Through Brown, the police can drill down to the source of the fentanyl operation. If he cooperates by providing names and details, helping the local police and the DEA in Florida bring down the head honchos calling the shots, they might offer him a lighter sentence. In addition to Florida, the Iron Fist operates in other southern states. Brown said the bikers are working with the drug cartels in Mexico to distribute into America. He said the Iron Fist delivers for the Durango cartel."

"And now our son, and those kids in Panama City Beach, are part of the statistics—100,000 dead from fentanyl in the U.S. last year alone. It's the plague that doesn't make the headlines. Sean, do you think the police in Gainesville or Panama City Beach will take it to the next level? Will they work with the DEA or the FBI to bust these bikers who think they're above the law?"

"I doubt they'll take it beyond Charlie Brown's arrest."

"Why?" Lauren asked.

"Most of the time, biker gangs keep a low profile. The police need much more than probable cause when dealing with them. They need provable reasons and evidence. Organized gangs involved in illegal operations allocate money toward retaining talented and pricey defense attorneys, people who like to tie a small town like Panama City Beach or Gainesville into expensive lawsuits. Knowing that certain gangs are heavily into criminal activity and finding evidence to stand up in court for convictions are two different things. But it can be done."

"With so many young people having died last year, and probably more will by the end of this year, law enforcement ought to be willing to put in the work."

"I've often found that it's easier for people, those who say something can't be done, interrupt people who are already doing it." I drove out of Gainesville and headed south toward my river cabin and my girls—Wynona, Angela, and Max. Clint and Lauren were quiet. "If you two want me to look beyond Charlie Brown to see if I can track down the source of the fentanyl, I will."

"The source," Clint said, "would be somewhere in Mexico. We'd never ask you to do that unless the U.S. government gave you an army."

"But I can visit our friendly neighborhood biker bars to see what I can find out. It wouldn't be my first time and probably not my last."

"We don't want to put you in danger," Lauren said.

"It's part of the job."

Clint said, "Sean, we served together in places a hell of a lot worse than infiltrating a biker gang. I can go with you. Be like old times. I'm still in pretty good shape. Nothing like you, of course. Must be your diet and exercise. But I can hold my own, and I can still hit a target from five hundred yards."

"These targets will be up close and very impersonal. Moving targets. I don't think it'll come to a shootout. My goal is to find a way into the inner sanctum of the Iron Fist, learn the players, and see how and where they're getting the fentanyl. And, beyond Charlie Brown, who else is working for them?"

I heard Clint release a deep breath. "You don't have to do this."

"Yes, I do."

"Where will you start?"

"I'll track down a guy they tossed out when they threw him into an alligator infested river late at night. I bet, under the right circumstances, he'll have a good story to tell."

"I will pray for your protection," Lauren said.

FIFTY-NINE

They appeared in my rearview mirror, emerging from the shimmering road heat—a grainy Easy Rider film clip out of the past. As I drove south in Florida down I-75, I caught a glimpse of two guys on motorcycles pulling ahead of the traffic behind me. I glanced down at my Glock in the Jeep's center console. Based on what I knew, there was no reason to be concerned. Not yet.

When the biker came to Charlie Brown's house, my Jeep was parked on a street behind his home, which was blocked from view by a stand of pine trees. I didn't think the biker saw my Jeep or the license plate. And, if he circled the area, I don't think he would have made the connection. Brown, facing potential murder or manslaughter charges, was probably still sitting in a police interrogation room. After that, he'd most likely spend his phone call on an attorney or a family member who could get a lawyer. Had he called the Iron Fist? Didn't think so.

Unless Charlie Brown's closest family *was* the Iron Fist. Would he ask them for legal help? I doubted that was the case. The last place a biker gang would want to spend money is defending someone who is not a member of their vetted club. The band of bad brothers. Although potential members often are willing to commit a felony as part of initiation rites, I didn't think Brown fit the bill. I glanced back in the rearview mirror.

The motorcycles were getting closer.

I picked up my phone and called Dave. He said, "My wayfaring friend, are you traveling on foot? Perhaps, like Hannibal crossing the Pyrenees, although there are no mountains in the sunshine state. It's about time that I heard from you. How are things between Gainesville and Panama City Beach?"

I brought Dave up to speed and added, "Charlie Brown, and guys like him, are considered disposable by close-knit biker gangs who traffic millions of dollars in drugs, guns, and human beings. Brown was the last hand in the supply chain that killed Andy and those other kids."

"Do you think he'll turn state's witness in exchange for a lighter sentence or maybe a witness relocation program depending on what he has to say?"

"Don't know. I do know that he's scared—no, terrified at the thought of facing the Iron Fist. Would he take the fall for them? Depends on whether he thinks hard time in a state prison is worse than taking his chances with the biker gang."

"Although you told Clint and Lauren that you would indeed take your chances with the biker gang, I'm not sure if the trade out is equitable for you, Sean. What's your approach?"

"Don't know how far I'll get, but I have a feeling that the guy on the news—the biker who came out of a forced midnight river swim, might have a grudge to settle."

The bikers behind my Jeep were coming closer. There are three southbound lanes on I-75. I was in the center lane. Steady speed of seventy-five.

Dave cleared his throat. "And you think this exiled biker might consider sharing that information with you, correct?"

"I suppose it would depend on how I ask. I'll just need to remember to say please and thank you."

"Have you told Wynona that your investigation is expanding from a drug dealer in Gainesville and the Florida Panhandle to a biker gang running drugs all over Florida and other states?"

"Not yet. That's not a conversation for over the phone. I want to be with Wynona when I tell her. Hold on a minute, Dave. I need to put the phone down and pick up my gun."

"What? Why?"

"Just in case things go south as I'm heading south. I'm at mile-marker 334 on I-75 near the Ocala exit. I have two guys on Harleys less than thirty feet from by rear bumper, and I'm doing seventy-five." I set the phone down on the opposite seat, reaching for my Glock. At that moment, the bikers started to pass me. One passing on the left side. The other on the right.

I gripped my pistol.

They passed me in a loud roar of motors and exhaust, both bikers holding onto their raised handlebars, the wind whipping their beards. I watched them for a few seconds. Neither man moving his head to look into the rearview mirrors. They wore sleeveless jean jackets, denim pants, and boots. No biker club colors or lettering on the back of their jackets. I set the Glock down, picking up the phone.

"I'm back."

"That noise sounded like a 757-jet taking off."

"They passed me on the left and right sides of my Jeep. Harley humor I suppose. If they're part of a biker gang, they weren't wearing jackets to identify their clubs. I don't think that Charlie Brown, under police custody, had time or the opportunity to alert anyone … not yet."

"So, ol' Charlie Brown, like the cartoon character, has the weight of the underworld on his shoulders. Based on your description, I don't picture him as the Greek god Atlas, holding up the world of biker gangs and Mexican drug cartels."

"He's not."

"Speaking of Greek, Nick is coming over the gunwale into *Gibraltar's* cockpit with some fresh redfish. Shall we put one on the grill for you?"

"I'm not heading to the marina. Driving home. Can you check a UPS tracking number for me? I took a picture of a shipping label on a box delivered to Brown's house."

"Of course. What is it?"

I pulled up the photo and read the number to Dave.

He repeated it back to me and said, "You want to hold the phone while I check?"

"Sure. You said Nick is there. Can you put him on the line?"

Nick said, "What's happening, Sean? You still in Gainesville?"

"I'm heading back home. Dave can fill you on what I shared with him. I wanted to follow up on your text message. You said the dockmaster, Roger Thornton, overheard those bikers the day we saw them at the Tiki, right?"

"Yeah. Roger said their motorcycles were parked in the lot near his office window. He had the front and back windows open to catch the sea breeze. Roger's not a fan of AC. Anyway, he said he heard 'em arguing. So, he got up from his desk to look out the window. He said the largest biker was really pissed, saying stuff like *'I gave you a job to do, and you screwed up. How the hell do you miss a shot at a guy's head standing right in front of you with his hands tied behind his back?'* Roger said the big guy used the heel of his hand to pop one of them in the middle of his forehead, knocking him on his butt in the oyster shell lot. He overheard one biker calling the big guy Tank. I guess he's the leader."

"Did Roger hear the leader of the pack or any of the others mention the man's name that they were talking about? They man they were supposed to shoot?"

"I asked him if that conversation might be traced back to the TV news story about the guy who walked out of the river and was picked up on the side of the road by a plumber. Roger said he didn't hear them bring up the guy's name. And they didn't say anything about the river. But I'd bet a bushel of oysters that he's the same person."

"Probably."

"Here's Dave."

Dave came back on the line. "That reference number is linked to an address in Daytona Beach."

"Can you text the address to me?"

"Yes. As you and Nick were talking, I used satellite maps to see what's at that address. It appears to be in an industrial district of the city. Warehouses. An auto parts store. Electric contractors, plumbing, and so on. The street level view simply shows the front of an aged brick building. No sign out front. It could be a bogus address, an abandoned place where no business has existed in years. Or it might be a location from where the biker gang ships its illegal drugs."

"There's only one way to find out. I need to go there. Thanks, Dave."

SIXTY

One of the things that first attracted me to Wynona was her emotional intelligence. I could see how it had made her an excellent FBI agent. It is a combination of deductive reasoning with the compassion that empowers the rational to restore justice—to right a wrong. Emotional intelligence makes people better listeners. They are more empathetic. It gives them a greater perspective into the emotions of others, skilled at reading and responding to subtle signs—able to connect with people. It makes them more human.

I thought about that trait Wynona had in spades as we finished dinner on the back porch, the air soft and carrying the scent of citrus, frogs crooning in baritone tunes down by the river. I'd grilled snapper using white-hot mesquite wood the way that Nick taught me to grill. The snapper wasn't as good as his, but it was good enough for Angela. She liked her fish with ketchup and her fries without ketchup. As I grilled earlier in the evening, I shared with Wynona everything that had happened in Gainesville, telling her about my interaction with Panama City Beach PD as well.

I could tell she was processing what I said.

And now, at dinner, our conversation included things that she and Angela had done and planned to do. Angela looked up at me as she used her fork to swirl a piece of grilled fish in the ketchup on her plate, Max squatting next to Angela's chair. "Daddy, when we were fishing in the river, you let the fish go. Who caught these ones?"

"I don't know. Mom bought them in the grocery store."

"I still like hamburgers more better." She sipped her chocolate milk.

Wynona smiled. "Angela, when you're describing how you like something, you don't have to say more better. You can just say I like hamburgers better. Better by itself works best. Understand?"

"Yep. It's better." She giggled.

After the dinner table was cleared, Angela and Max played in the twilight, chasing fireflies, laughing, barking, and enjoying a warm summer evening under a sprinkling of stars just becoming visible. Wynona and I shared a cabernet. She looked over at me. "You did what Clint asked you to do when he came here. Based on what you told me, Charlie Brown might cut a deal with the prosecutor's office. They could convene a grand jury and open an investigation into the Iron Fist."

"I don't believe Brown will risk it. I think, rather than cop a plea, he'll do time at Raiford, keep his mouth shut, and hope he's released early by being a model prisoner."

"From my perspective as a former federal agent, I would think that investigating a biker gang believed to be the prime distributor of fentanyl in five southern states, the DEA would become more proactive. Since the early days, the FBI has infiltrated motorcycle clubs, like Hells Angels, with agents who passed the bar, so to speak, to be accepted by the gang. And that's exactly what they are … gangs."

"Maybe the FBI or the DEA has an agent or two embedded in the Iron Fist, perhaps in Texas and here in Florida. It's possible the Iron Fist mistook the guy in the news story for a federal agent, beat and left him for dead in the Tomoka River."

"If so, would members of a motorcycle club be willing to risk the wrath of the full FBI by murdering a suspected agent rather than breaking his legs and ostracizing him from the club?"

"If it sent a strong signal back to the FBI, maybe. Who knows at what corrupt levels the criminal mind can go? The biker mentality is a lot like lynch mob thinking. It is groupthink. You remove the collective mindset, and you find that individually, most of them wouldn't be uncoiling the hangman's rope."

Wynona sipped her wine, her eyes filled with thoughts that were pulling at her gift of emotional intelligence. Perhaps, when deep emotions, such as love, coalesce around a perceived situation—a threat, there is a tug of war between emotional intelligence and the rationale of the brain, the intellect.

"Sean, when I was working criminal cases, not just with the Bureau, but during my time as a detective with the Seminole PD, I found that during the questioning of witnesses or suspects, most often suspects in the interrogation rooms, to get into someone's head, I had to enter their heart. But there were cases where the suspect's heart was so dark and evil, it was like speaking to Satan across the table from me. If you choose to investigate the Iron Fist, you'll be looking into those cold, collective eyes you talked about. What you will see staring back at you is going to be that lynch mob. Many of these people share forms of mental illness … antisocial behavior, and bipolar. These often are men filled with rage."

"I've spent time in those situations, occasionally with bikers or wannabe bikers. I choose not to acknowledge the chip on their shoulder. During military service, I learned that, if someone angered me, at least on an emotional or reactive level, I was giving them permission to leverage control over me. If I allowed them to make me visibly angry, I was training them how to turn the screw harder. I didn't want to be that kind of trainer."

"Did you tell Clint you would follow the fentanyl trail to a biker gang?"

"Yes. But not alone. Depending on what I find by poking around, I can relay that information to the local police and the DEA. If I can point the way with evidence that offers convictions, people with badges on their belts can make the arrests. Charlie Brown was the pawn, the one who dropped off the drugs. The Iron Fist supplies the stuff. The drug cartels in Mexico make it."

Wynona was quiet for half a minute. She sipped her wine, turning to me. "How will you penetrate a biker club? FBI agents take on the look, everything from tattoos to the unwashed hair, tangled beards, and the swagger. You are clean shaven. You have no tattoos, and your body language doesn't say get out of my way."

"I might not have tattoos, but I have plenty of scars. They're a form of tattoo that I never asked for. I have no plans to attempt to embed with a biker gang. I wouldn't get very far. But I can seek out dissention among the ranks. Look for unhappy soldiers and see if someone might be in a retaliatory mood to offer some insight into the structure of the Iron Fist."

"How would you find unhappy soldiers, assuming they exist?"

"The first would be the guy on the news. If his mouth wasn't wired shut from a beating, he might be in the mood to talk. And he could know others who have come and gone from the biker gang, exiting because they ruffled the feathers of protocol. These gangs enforce strict club rules of hierarchy. Not unlike the miliary. But they're more like soldiers of misfortune."

"These bikers often sport the do-or-die maxim. They appear to have no boundaries. Non-conformists. Aren't you fearful of walking into a lion's den?"

"The only place in the world where fear exists is in the mind. That doesn't mean I let my guard down. It means I won't allow justice for Andy and the other kids to be curtailed by fear or possible intimidation. When those walls don't exist in your mind's eye, you see a clearer path."

"But you're one man."

"On a fact-finding mission. You mentioned how these guys appear. To me they're not true non-conformists. I think they struggle over self-esteem. By trying hard to appear as non-conformists, they follow a hierarchy from their club rules to the leather uniforms of dissention, right down to the badges and patches they wear on their jackets, not unlike medals earned by a conformist reward system. I will be the sole outsider among a den of like-minded thieves."

Wynona watched Angela and Max walking back toward the porch steps. "You said fear doesn't exist anywhere on earth outside the mind. When I look at Angela, I have a mama bear fear for her safety. And as you begin the next phase of your investigation, that feeling will be on high alert because you're about to poke a stick into a hornets' nest. Antisocial gangs don't color within the lines. They smear the colors, break the crayons, and leave colorful-sounding graffiti. Then they rip the pages out of the coloring book."

SIXTY-ONE

The deadline had come and gone. In its aftermath, Diego Navarro was not a happy man. He sat outside at one of the painted white wrought iron tables. The tables and chairs were on the patio of his 10,000-square foot home, a Mediterranean-style with a red tile roof, a secluded pool, and stone balconies overlooking the Sierra Madre Mountains in the distance. Navarro was having breakfast with his wife, Sophie, and their two small children, a son and daughter. The patio was surrounded by a lush garden blooming in gardenias and roses, the throb of bees working the flowers.

Sophie, his wife of ten years, was a striking brunette, the previous winner of the Miss Ciudad de México beauty pageant. As breakfast was ending, in Spanish, she said to her son, "Miguel, go inside with your sister and wash your hands before playing with any toys. You both have blueberry jelly on your hands."

When the kids left, she sipped black coffee from a handmade porcelain cup imported from Germany and looked at her husband. "Diego, I have and always will be the dutiful wife. I know how hard you work and how you try to make a difference in the Durango towns and villages. But capturing an American DEA agent will do more harm than good. Can you release him? I am fearful that, if you do not, something very bad will happen to our family."

He looked over at her through cold black eyes. "I try very hard to separate my family from the business I run. I employ hundreds of people directly while providing money and gifts to many more. These people would have nothing if it were not for me. I am like a god to them. They worship me. You should too, Sophie." He leaned in closer. "Never question me about the way I run my business—a business that has been in the Navarro family long before you came into it. Do you understand?"

"Yes. I do not want to appear that I am trying to say you are doing something wrong. However, I went to mass and prayed hard over this. I bring a message from that … from my time kneeling at the altar with rosary beads in my hand and Jesus in my heart. The message is that, if you release the American, you will show good faith cooperation and your business will benefit even more in the future."

"And, if not, what then?"

She shook her head. "It will not be good."

Navarro tossed his linen napkin on the table. "I cannot control the future. I can control the moment, and those decisions will make the future what I envision. A man doesn't just dream it—he gets up and does it."

She reached across the table, touching his hand. "It is because I love you that my heart fills with fear. No one is forcing you to make the business the largest cartel in Mexico. Our life is blessed, fulfilled, and good. The children are happy. As you said, you have helped many people. I know one of your boyhood heroes was Santa Anna, a man who marched into Texas with his troops and took victory at the Alamo. Today, the issues are so much larger than Texas. The American politicians will make you out to be a modern-day Hitler rather than the good and decent man that you are—the man I sleep with at night. I beg you, Diego, let the U.S. agent go. You already have proven your point with the DEA. You are, perhaps, the most powerful man in all of Mexico."

He started to respond when one of his men walked past a stoic server from the kitchen, a middle-aged woman, an apron around her waist, standing in one corner of the patio under the shade of a blooming red bougainvillea. A tray set on a serving stand had a silver coffee pot on it. The man didn't acknowledge the woman as he approached Navarro's table.

"I'm sorry to interrupt your breakfast, Diego."

"What is it, Jose?" Navarro pushed back in his chair and looked up at the man, the morning sunlight breaking over a tall banyan tree in the yard at the edge of the patio.

"It is the news. All the networks—Televisa, Las Estrellas, Groupe TV … they all are broadcasting news about the DEA agent we are holding."

"What! What are they saying?"

"They are playing video footage of a news conference held in Washington, D.C., by the DEA. The stories are all about how the

Durango cartel brutally kidnapped and is holding a DEA agent hostage. They are showing pictures of his face, some of the photos include him with his family. The TV presenters are saying Salazar was a decorated war hero who fought for his country before taking a job with the DEA. The U.S. president answered reporters' questions as he was getting onto a plane. He said his administration is working closely with the Mexican government to have Antonio Salazar released unharmed."

"I told the DEA that our negotiations must remain confidential and to not turn this into a political chess game. And I warned them that, if they went to the news media with their agenda, there would be hell to pay. They should know, with no more issuances of visas, the Mexican government does not want additional DEA agents walking around Mexico like secret ambassadors with diplomatic immunity." He stood. "That ends with Anthony Salazar."

Sophie said, "Diego, perhaps this is an opportunity—a divine intervention, to show your disgust for America placing federal agents in our sovereign nation, and that you will release Salazar unharmed because of your good faith that altruism sets an example."

The man standing near the table appeared uncomfortable, as if he'd walked into a domestic situation between Navarro and his wife that should remain confidential. Navarro looked at Sophie with the lidless eyes of a toad. "I made a pact with Santa Muerte. Our Lady of Holy Death has opened many doors for me. She guides me in everything I do. I will bring her the head of Anthony Salazar."

"No!"

He turned and left. The man followed him. Sophie held her left hand to her heart, the five-carat diamond on her ring finger catching the morning light. She stared at the diamond, suddenly seeing it as something repulsive, bought with money made from drug addicts, and women, girls, and boys trapped in lives of forced sexual slavery. She whispered a prayer.

SIXTY-TWO

Wynona, Angela, and Max had already left for the antique shop in DeLand. I would spend my day in Daytona. I finished the last of my coffee, closed my laptop, and headed out the door. The traffic was light, so I made the drive in good time.

Turning onto a side street, I wondered if the building was more like a Hollywood façade. Movie set designers can use façades to give the illusion of reality. Anything outside of the camera frame is not part of the deception. I thought about that as I drove slowly by the building in downtown Daytona Beach that was linked to the address on the box delivered to Charlie Brown's porch. Was it made to look abandoned, or was it, in fact, vacant?

The building had the disheveled look of neglect, not unlike some older people who have been made to feel like they are a burden. Made of brick and cinderblock, the two-story building had four street-level windows near the entrance, all of which were covered in grime. I drove past the building. It sat in an industrial block among equipment supply houses, a bar called Snookers, and a place to rent everything from chainsaws to stump grinders.

I parked a block north of the building and removed my lockpicking kit from the console. The zipped leather kit, about half the size of my hand, had small pockets for five tools. In picking a lock, I would always need at least two. I locked the Jeep and doubled back to the building on foot. I looked for surveillance cameras on the businesses and across the street, including Snookers. There were none, at least none that could be seen. I walked to the front of the building and looked through the grime on the windows. From what I could see, there was a reception area with a desk. No other furniture. Nothing was on top of the desk. No papers and no phone lines or power cords running to it.

To have a better look, I took some leaves, crouched, and cleared the dirt from an inconspicuous corner of a window. I spotted half a dozen dead cockroaches lying on their backs. One was barely moving, crawling across the floor with its hind leg dangling, useless. I assumed the building recently had been sprayed for insects. Maybe it wasn't as abandoned as it appeared. Insects, like maggots on a dead body, tell a story.

I strolled down the sidewalk and took a left to go to the back of the building. There were no cars, trucks, or motorcycles in the small parking lot. Weeds grew through cracks in the asphalt. There was a small loading dock and a large roll-up door that was wide enough for a pickup truck to drive through had the door been opened.

I could see the shine of oil and transmission stains between the parking spaces. The painted white lines marking the spots were faded. I knelt and studied the stains, some about the diameter of a doughnut. I rubbed a bit of oil between my finger and thumb, feeling the viscosity and then sniffing it. It was a synthetic oil often used in Harley-Davidson motorcycles. And it was fresh.

I walked to the right side of the building, looked at the electric meter, expecting it to be disconnected. The wheel inside the glass casing was slowly turning. I went back to the large, roll-up metal door, put on latex gloves, and tried pulling the center handle. It was locked. I glanced around the perimeter of the adjacent buildings. Some of the back parking lots had pickup trucks and cars in them. Employees probably. I couldn't see anyone moving about in or around the various lots and alleyways.

I approached a regular-sized door and tried the handle. It turned but wouldn't open because a deadbolt lock was a few inches above it. Most of the tools in my lockpicking kit were about the size of bobby pins. My go-to tools for picking a deadbolt lock were the small tension wrench and a pick called a rake. It had three raised sections, each less than a quarter inch from the one before it. The design of the pin and tumbler lock has been around for a century. These locks give the illusion of protection.

I inserted the tension wrench into the bottom of the lock's keyhole, applying only a slight bit of pressure. Then I pushed the humped-back rake tool into the top portion. After that, it's more art than science. You feel for the pins being lifted and know when to put a bit more pressure on the wrench.

In less than thirty seconds, the deadbolt turned to the right and unlocked. I put the tools back in the kit and opened the door.

***

The stable doors opened, causing Tony Salazar to lift his head as Diego Navarro walked through the shafts of morning sunlight. He was followed by his top honcho, the man who had brought Navarro the news of the DEA's decision to go public with the abduction and their refusal to barter. Two more of Navarro's men entered the stables. One held a long rope with a hangman's noose at the end.

Navarro moved over to where Salazar was handcuffed and chained to a support timber. "Your people have abandoned you, Anthony."

No response. A horsefly buzzed above one of the empty stalls.

Navarro took measure of Salazar, like a man deciding whether to peel an apple or bite into it. "Not only have they abandoned you, but the DEA is using you to justify their presence and aggression in the sovereign nation of Mexico."

Salazar looked at him hard, one eye partially swollen. "I told you that the U.S. government does not negotiate or barter with terrorists."

"Your government does it all the time. Not only do the negotiate with people who, when examined closely, are the very definition of terrorists, but they also pour money into the coffers of dictators they control. Then they call it nation-building. I am helping to build the nation of Mexico into one of the most powerful and respected countries in the world."

"Just like Hitler did. In the end, he shot himself."

Navarro ran his palm along one of the timbers, the sound was like sandpaper against his skin. "I am building an army. Every time I get another loser addicted to fentanyl, I *own* that person. They will trade me their very soul to have a steady supply of a drug that makes them feel like the person they will never become. I am a soul collector. That is why I have protection from Santa Muerte in this life and into the next. She places her cloak of security over me."

Salazar shook his head. "You're a sick man, and you need help."

"Since your president wants to use you as a poster boy for corrupt politicians to push agendas that give them under-the-table kickbacks, let us send them a picture of you to use." Navarro nodded toward the man with the rope. The man grunted, tossing one end of the line over a rafter near the stable's ceiling. Two of the other men held the end of the rope. The third man slipped the hangman's noose over Salazar's head.

They pushed and dragged him closer to one of the wooden walls, making the rope taut against his neck. Navarro unfolded a pocketknife, slicing through the cords that bound Salazar's hands behind his back. "How long can you hold the noose before you finally give out and hang yourself? Most people can only go about five minutes. In a way, it becomes a form of suicide. You know there will be no hope of life as you wiggle from the rope like a worm on a hook. At one point, you will finally give in, removing your hands and have the air choked out of your lungs. I hear it is a very painful way to die. Like drowning but without the comfort of water."

He motioned to his men with his head, and they began pulling the rope, lifting Salazar more than two feet above the ground. A horse in one of the stalls whinnied as Salazar kicked and fought, his shoes striking the wall behind him. His hands gripped the rope tearing into his neck, pressing against his carotid artery, larynx, cartilage, and the cervical spine in the back of his neck.

Navarro climbed onto a stepladder so he could look Salazar in the eyes as the man struggled for his life—face crimson, spittle flying from his mouth, jugular vein knotting and blue, snot dripping from his nostrils, gurgling sounds coming from his voice box. He kicked as his body swayed side-to-side in a pendulum motion, suspended above the ground like a bale of hay being pulley-loaded into the loft.

Navarro watched with merry light in his dark eyes. "Soon I will have your soul, too, Anthony. I will be the last person on earth you see as your heart beats one final time." He used a phone to take a picture of Salazar before gesturing to his men. They lowered the rope. Salazar's feet touched the ground, and he crumpled to the floor. He pulled at the noose, gasping for air, lying on his back and coughing, bile trickling out of his mouth.

Navarro watched him like a sadistic hunter would watch a deer with a gunshot wound slowly dying at the edge of a cornfield in winter. Navarro laughed. "The next time will be the last time. I will send this photo to the DEA. Perhaps it will encourage them to rethink their negotiation policy before I really become a terrorist." He looked at his men. "Tie him up. I am running out of patience."

He folded the blade into the pocketknife and walked toward the sunlight.

SIXTY-THREE

I walked through the open door to the building, wondering if I needed a hazmat suit and oxygen. I paused a few feet inside, remembering that fentanyl, like deadly carbon monoxide and arsenic is odorless and tasteless. Enough light came through the back door and the grimy windows above the bay door to illuminate the area inside. The air was warm and had the odor of rat urine and insecticide.

There were half a dozen folding tables set up, end-to-end. Metal shelves covered one of the walls. The shelves were at least ten feet high. Nothing was stored on the racks. I spotted a painter's aluminum ladder in one corner. I entered a larger part of the facility that I assumed was used as a shipping warehouse. There was no inventory. No bottles of pills. No cardboard containers, packages, or packing materials. Nothing to indicate drugs moved from here to places like Charlie Brown's porch.

I walked through the rest of the building. There were four offices. No furniture in them or recent signs of human habitation. I saw rat feces. There was one restroom. I lifted the toilet seat, a roach was floating on its back in the water, swimming in a circle, doing the backstroke. I flushed the toilet before trying the sink faucet. It coughed brown water for a few seconds before running clear.

The place hadn't been cleaned in a long time. Dead insects. Cobwebs. Dust and grunge. After spending a few minutes inside, anyone with allergies would probably feel like their sinuses were being attacked. I thought back to that day in the Tiki Bar with Nick when the bikers took a corner table, leaving after a news flash came on the widescreen TV.

I recalled what Nick had told me on the phone after he spoke with the dockmaster. *He overheard one biker calling the big guy Tank. I guess he's the leader.*

Was this small warehouse used to pack and distribute drugs by a guy with the street name Tank and other members of the Iron Fist? If so, Tank, like Elvis, had left the building. But would he come back, and would he bring his band of merry men with him?

I left and used the lockpicks to relock the deadbolt. I could hear motorcycles in the distance. The rumble of Harleys in mass was pretty much the Daytona Beach anthem. Lots of baritone notes. I jogged to my Jeep, drove the block back to the building, parked nearby, and waited.

The engines grew louder, probably still a couple of blocks away. Just maybe I'd get lucky and see them come to the building like bees returning to the hive. Was the man called Tank the queen bee, calling most, if not all the shots in Florida, or was he middle-management in the world of biker gang hierarchy? Was he taking orders from senior members of the club in Texas or elsewhere?

Less than thirty seconds later, four men on Harleys roared down the street, passing where I was parked. I looked at their backs. They were members of the Outlaws motorcycle gang. On the back of each man's leather jacket was a red-eyed skull with crossbones below it. Pistons were the crossbones. The sound of their motors reverberated off buildings on both sides of the street. They moved on, the engine noise soon becoming faint. I didn't know if the Outlaws had a presence in an area that I assumed was Iron Fist territory or whether the bikers were just passing through on their way to someplace else.

I stared at the front of the building and then called Dave, telling him what I found and added, "The only things with a presence in there are roaches and rats. Can you run a county property check on the building? See who owns it? If the Iron Fist own it, I'd bet the deed is registered under a shell company. Maybe you can find out if it's leased."

"I'm in front of my computer now. I'll do some research and get back with you."

"Are you in need of a task a little more challenging?"

"Now that you mentioned it, yes."

"These biker clubs have clubhouses. Not like the kind you'd find overlooking the eighteenth hole at a country club golf course. But I'm sure the Iron Fist clubhouse has its own unique view. If you can track down the location of their clubhouse, text the address to me."

"First place I'll check will be police reports. Where are you going next?"

"Into a bar called Snookers."

***

Byron Lopez wasn't preprepared for the image attachment on the email message. In his twenty-year career with the DEA, he'd seen a lot of things that caused his sleep to be punctuated with grisly images. This one would be a reoccurring ghost for the rest of his life.

He read the text. *Did you tell Salazar to hang in there? How long do you expect he can hang on? The DEA made the decision to go public with our discussions. Bad decision. I extended hospitality to Salazar as we communicated with you. The hospitably has ended, and the discomfort is just beginning. It is on you. I may eventually release him. That is on the condition you do not try to find him. Salazar, however, will never be the same man. If I get an indication that you are searching for Salazar, I will make an example out of what's left of him.*

Lopez opened the attachment. What he saw caused a chemical reaction in his body. He felt the urge to vomit. He looked at the photo of Tony Salazar suspended in the air by a rope around his neck. He was looking directly into the camera, eyes bulging, reflecting pain and horror from a tightened hangman's noose. His hands gripped the rope, muscles in his forearms knotted, his jugular vein undulating, like a small snake trying to crawl under the skin at the side of his neck. Lopez looked at the blood on one side of Tony's mouth.

He stood from behind his desk as if he'd been punched hard in the stomach. His legs felt weak. Lopez stepped over to a window and looked to the street below him, people going about their daily lives. Commerce flowing in the heart of Mexico City. Somewhere in Durango, it was other business as usual, too. The business of illegal drugs and human trafficking—the business of human suffering.

Lopez sat back behind his desk, sending the picture of Tony to DEA Administrator Christina Bowman. Lopez picked up his desk phone and placed a call to DEA headquarters. When Bowman came on the line, he said, "We have a reaction from Diego Navarro after he found out we'd gone public with the kidnapping."

"Reaction? I'm almost afraid to ask what kind of reaction. Tell me, what'd he say?"

"I'd rather show you. Are you at your desk?"

"Yes."

"I just copied you on the email Navarro just sent to me."

"Hold on, Byron. Let me open it." She was quiet for half a minute before coming back on the line. "Oh, dear God."

"He warned the DEA not to go public. Psychopaths, such as Navarro, have a gang of like-minded people around them. You can't intimidate them, especially in a public forum where we make them out to be another ISIS."

"That's what they are. You know that."

"What I know is that they'll do what they promised … decapitate Tony and put his head on the spire of a church in Mexico. Navarro, as delusional as he is, believes the court of public opinion in Mexico is in favor of what he does."

"I don't understand that."

"Call it the Latin male hubris or machismo, but Navarro and other drug lords think that they have the *right* to make demands of the American government. One reason is our presence here. The other is because they believe the U.S. isn't trying too hard to combat illegal drugs due to reasons these guys discuss in rooms filled with cigar smoke next to rooms where they pay people to count and bind the cash that they're raking in."

"We can't have this photo of Tony getting online or in the media."

"Then we need to go find him. Navarro may choose to release this picture or other photos the cartel has taken of Tony to paint whatever illusion they want. The reality gut check is that Tony Salazar doesn't have much time left."

SIXTY-FOUR

Brittany Harmon was brushing her teeth when she heard the knock. It was light. Under the sound of running water from the sink, she wasn't sure she heard it. Then it came again. Knocking at her apartment door. A soft knock, as though the person was apologetic for the interruption. Brittany left her bathroom, walking up to her front door. She looked through the peephole.

Nothing.

She moved over to one of the front windows in the small living room, looking through an opening in the drapes to the outside entryway. Although she couldn't see anyone, she did spot a cardboard box next to her welcome mat. It looked like the boxes she received in the past from Amazon. The smiling arrow on the side. She had ordered a book from Amazon, but delivery wasn't expected until tomorrow.

Maybe the package was early, she thought. She went to another window to see if there might be a delivery truck in the parking lot. There was a pickup truck and a trailer filled with lawn maintenance equipment. Two brown-skinned men getting out of the truck, sprinklers rotating on one section of the apartment property.

Curiosity got the best of Brittany. She unlocked the deadbolt, removed the brass chain from its lock, and opened the door. Barefoot, she stepped outside, her bathrobe tied at her waist. When she leaned down to pick up the box, Charlie Brown came from around the corner. He carried a long knife, using one arm to push her inside.

"Don't scream! Do it, and I'll cut your throat." He entered, slamming the door behind him. "You surprised to see me, bitch? Even a guy like me is offered bail."

"How did you know where I live?"

"Not hard, you're linked to a dead guy. All I had to do was ask around and say I wanted to express my condolences."

"What do you want?" She clutched the robe near her breasts, backing up against the alcove counter between the room and the kitchen.

"What I want is for you to get amnesia?"

She stared at him, not sure how to answer.

"You know how I made bail?"

She shook her head.

He grinned. "Because some very powerful, rich, dangerous people wanted me out. I told 'em I wouldn't cop a plea, so everything is cool. Everything but you, Brittany."

"What do you mean?"

"If you go to court and testify against me, tell them I provided the fentanyl to your dead boyfriend, that could be a problem. They'll want to know where I got the stuff, and that lets out the snakes."

She said nothing, Brown came closer—into her space. She could smell the weed on his breath. He trapped her in a corner. He held the knife in his right hand, using his left to touch her robe. "Please, don't."

"Or you'll do what?" He jerked the robe open, displaying her breasts, his eyes, taking them in, lips wet, a smile on the edge of his mouth. "Your hair's damp. Looks like you just got out of the shower. I bet you taste even better than you smell."

"What do you want?"

"Like I said, for you to come down with a bad case of amnesia. Maybe it'll be early dementia, whatever. The point is, we, that includes some of the most dangerous people you'll ever meet, don't want you to testify. Just go away, and we'll do the same. If not, these guys will stand in line to rape you. When the last man is done, they'll kill you … slowly. I'm just the messenger. You understand what the hell I'm tellin' you?"

"Yes. Who are you talking about? What men?"

"Dudes who had to sell their souls to the devil to get in the club. They're the one percent soldiers, and they make most biker gangs look like boy scouts. You hear me?"

"Yes."

"One last thing … don't think of calling your buddy, Sean O'Brien. He won't be around long enough to do a damn thing." Brown touched the tip of the knife to her neck. "Less than an inch below my knife is your larynx. We cut through that, and you'll never testify about anything. You won't be able to cry either. The tears will flow, but the crying will be like a kitten that's learning to say meow."

He walked out the front door, stopping to pick up the box before tossing it in the back of his van and driving away.

Through a gap in the drapes, Brittany watched him leave. She wiped the tears from her eyes, sucking in her breath, afraid to cry—afraid to hear her own sobs.

SIXTY-FIVE

If the dark walls could talk, Snookers was one of those bars that had stories to tell. Upon entering, I was met with the dank smell of sour beer and fresh popcorn. I waited a moment for my eyes to adjust to the lower light before heading to the bar. The place had its own Cheers vibe. Not a bar where everyone knew your name, but rather one that appealed to people who wore billed hats and worked with their hands. Plumbers. Electricians. Pipefitters. Brick masons. A working-class joint that looked like it had been there since the 1950s. This *was* your daddy's local bar.

There were about a dozen round tables scattered in the main room. Three pool tables were in an adjacent area, both rooms accessible through a wide-open archway. I counted four people shooting pool. All men and all with the look of blue-collar workers. Paint-stained pants. No leather jackets or biker club insignias. There were nine people sitting at the tables, most nursing cans of beer and nibbling fat pretzels. From a jukebox, Charlie Daniels belted out *The Devil Went Down to Georgia.*

Five people sat at the bar. It was a wooden bar that probably served as an altar of sorts for decades. The bar rail was a place to rest heavy forearms as some customers bowed their spinning heads. The dark wood looked like it came from the pews of an old church. Worn.

Four men wearing T-shirts and jeans sat on stools. At the elbowed section of the bar was a middle-aged woman with dark eyes, staring at the neon Budweiser sign behind the liquor bottles. Most of the customers sat on stools to the right side of the bar. I took a seat more toward the left. Close enough to overhear conversations.

The bartender was a woman in her late fifties. Hair dyed black so many times it began to take on the purple sheen of a ripe plum. She wore a low-cut shirt, skin between her cleavage like leather from exposure to the hot Florida sun. She flashed a cheery smile, but the knowingness in her eyes spoke of hard times through the years.

"What can I get you, handsome?" she asked, using a small, white towel to wipe a beer ring off the bar next to where I sat.

"According to one of your signs back there, you have Yuengling."

"We have it, and we darn sure sell it. American beer, and some of the best on the planet."

"Okay."

"Can or bottle."

"Bottle."

"Gotcha."

I was glad I didn't order a Dos Equis. She opened the stainless-steel cooler behind her and got out a Yuengling in the bottle, opening it, setting the bottle on a Snookers' coaster in front of me. She cocked her head, hands on her wide hips, as if she'd seen me somewhere. "I'm Brenda." She extended her damp hand. I shook it.

"I'm Sean. Nice to meet you, Brenda."

"Likewise. Haven't seen you in here before. I'd remember. What brings you to Snookers?"

"The beer and the service. Beer is cold and the service is warm."

Brenda smiled. Thirty years ago, I had no doubt she was a knockout. She still had high cheekbones and sensual eyes that looked turquoise in the dim light. I sipped the beer.

"Get you a menu? Beef sliders are good. So are the wings. Skip the celery and blue cheese."

"Thanks for the suggestion and the advice. The beer is fine for now. Snookers has a good feel to it. An established neighborhood bar. When I traveled to New York City, I always preferred the classic bars. One was called O'Connor's. Irish place that's been there since 1905."

"Snookers has been here in the same location since 1941. GIs coming home from the war used to hang out here. Not much has changed in all these years. We don't sell craft beers. Only the traditional stuff, a few imports, and lots of whiskey."

"How long have you worked here?"

"This time … goin' on seven years. Before that, it was three years."

"I bet you've seen a lot of changes in the area during that time."

She set a wire basket in front of me. It was lined with wax paper and piled high with pretzels. "I have seen a lot of changes. I'd love to say most of it was good, but I'm afraid our country isn't doing as well as it should. It makes good business in a bar, but bad business when you go to buy gas for your car. Hey, that sort of rhymes." She smiled.

"I'm thinking about switching to a motorcycle. Better gas mileage."

A guy at the end of the bar said, "Brenda, how 'bout another Miller?"

"How about that, Dale? Comin' up." Reaching back into the stainless-steel fridge, she pulled out a can of Miller, popped the top, and set it in front of the guy called Dale. The woman sitting alone asked for a refill of rum and Coke. After serving the drink, Brenda made her way back toward me. "Sean, are you from New York?"

"No, I've just visited there often through the years. I live in Florida, out toward DeLand."

"That's a great area."

"I'm always looking for opportunities in real estate. I think this part of Daytona Beach is in the line of growth. Do you know if the building across the street might be for sale?"

She glanced out the window toward the building. "I haven't seen any for sale signs on the window in a long time. It was for sale, maybe three or four years ago."

"It looks vacant."

"I don't think anyone works outta there on a frequent or regular basis. I've seen some bikers come and go. They're always at the back of the building. I park in the lot next to it. One time they were having a barbecue in their parking lot. That's been about a year or so."

"I wonder if they own the building."

"From what I hear, they lease it. One of the bikers came in here for a couple of beers. He told me the club leases the place. Who the hell knows why they use it? I didn't ask, and he didn't say. It's too big for a clubhouse. Maybe they keep some of their bikes in there. Work on them and what not."

I sipped my beer. The music from the jukebox changed to a song by the Marshall Tucker Band, *Can't You See?* I looked across the bar at Brenda. "You mentioned a motorcycle club ... which club?"

"They're called the Iron Fist. Don't know much about them, but from what I hear, they're not dudes you'd wanna cross."

I nodded. "No doubt. How long have they leased the place? Maybe their lease is expiring, and the owner might want to sell."

"Could be." She pursed her full lips. "As far as neighbors go, they're pretty quiet over there."

"And only one walked across the street to have a cold one here at Snookers, right?"

"At least on my watch. I work during the day mostly."

"If they don't come over here to have a few cold ones, I wonder where they go?"

"The biker told me they hang out a lot at a couple of dive bars. One's the Whistler off South Beach Road. The other is called Midnight Rider. It's further out of the city. I've never been there, but that place has a bad rep. If I had a daughter, I'd never let her go there."

My phone buzzed with an incoming text from Dave. *The owner of the building is listed as a corporation. Marathon Movers, Inc. Their papers list an address as a PO box in Orlando. Call me.*

SIXTY-SIX

Clubhouse. The word felt absurd referring to a biker gang hangout. In my Jeep, I called Dave. "Read your text. Any names connected to Marathon Movers or was there just a PO box?"

"The only name I could find was Simon Hogan, listed as president. No other details on the incorporation papers. So, I dug deeper, of course. Looked for other properties owned by Hogan or Marathon Movers corporation."

"Any luck?"

"Luck made through due diligence. Odd how that often works." Dave chuckled. "There is another property listed under the Marathon's moniker. I'll text you the address. I looked at it through satellite and street level maps. From what I could see through the razor-wire fence, it appears to be the clubhouse for the Iron Fist. I came to that conclusion after cross-referencing the address with Daytona Beach PD records going back the last three years. There was a police raid two years ago. Three members of the club were arrested for assault and battery stemming from a bar fight a day earlier. Two men were put in the hospital after the fight. One lost an eye. Simon Hogan was arrested as were two other members of the club."

"What were the victims' names?"

"William Kidd and Jack Dunn."

"Does it say which one lost an eye"

"Indeed, it does. William Kidd."

"Do the police records indicate whether the case went to trial?"

"No, but I also matched the timeline with the news media records. It appears that the people injured refused to press charges. This comes even after a week in the hospital suffering compound fractures and one man blinded in his left eye. The story in the local newspaper said the guy who lost one eye, Kidd, now wears a black patch." Dave grunted.

"From what you're telling me, it appears that Simon Hogan, assuming it's a real name, owns property and leases it back to the biker club—a club in which he's a member."

"Perchance the Iron Fist pays Hogan's mortgage on that building … or did. Both properties show no lien holders, the deeds in Hogan's name or rather that of Marathon Movers, Inc. Where are you now, Sean?"

"In Daytona. Just left a bar called Snookers. In the police reports and news story you read … what was the name of the bar where the fight occurred?"

"The watering hole is called Midnight Rider. Why?"

"That's where I'm heading."

"Ahh, serendipitous possibly or something more definitive? How'd you know it's a joint frequented by the Iron Fist?"

"By doing the due diligence that you mentioned. Got the name from a bartender, a woman who works in Snookers. The bar is across the street from the building."

"Well, it is always a good sign when the two of us can come to the same conclusions from opposite ends of the investigative spectrum."

"We're a team, Dave. I couldn't do it without you."

"And, if it weren't for you and your escapades as a PI, I'd only be doing crossword puzzles in my retirement years. Oh, one other thing that I started to mention earlier."

"What is it?"

"The guy, Simon Hogan. The police report indicates that his alias or biker name is Tank. It's tough to take down a tank."

"Not with a rocket launcher."

***

Midnight Rider looked like it could have been in Dodge City in 1880. It was an Old West-style saloon. Low-slung. One story. Two steps leading up to a wide wooden deck in the front. Cinderblock painted dark gray, tattered wood, brick, and tin. The words, *Midnight Rider Bar,* were hand painted in red across a façade above porch entrance. The tin gable atop the entrance was rusted brown and supported by six timbers, giving the building the look of a place where spurs would clatter across the deck leading to the swinging double batwing doors. A red brick chimney puffed white smoke.

I parked my Jeep in the shade of a tall cottonwood tree next to the gravel lot, away from the motorcycles. At least two-dozen were lined up like bullets in a 9mm magazine, the row of chrome glinting in the hot sun. They all were Harley-Davidsons. My phone buzzed. Brittany Harmon's name popped on the screen ID.

"Hi, Brittany, how are—"

"He was here! He came to my apartment and—"

"Whoa, take a deep breath. Who came to your apartment?"

"That guy, Charlie Brown. He's out of jail on bond. He had a knife and held it to my throat. He said if I went to court and testified against him, they'd cut out my larynx so I could never talk again."

"Who's they?"

"He called them men who'd sold their souls to the devil to get into the club. He said they're the one percenter soldiers, and they make most biker gangs look like boy scouts. And he said they'd line up to gang rape me."

I could hear her trying not to cry, the muffled sobs, turning her face away from the phone. "Brittany, listen closely to me, okay?"

"Yes."

"When we get off the phone, call the police. Ask to speak with Detective Winston Porter. Tell him what you told me. When someone makes bail in a felony, and then they go off and pull a deadly weapon on another person, they can lose bond privileges. After you speak with Detective Porter, call Andy's parents and tell them what you told me. Okay?"

"Okay."

"Call me if you don't hear from Detective Porter."

"Okay. Bye." She clicked off.

I reached into the console, lifting my Glock, ratcheting a round in the chamber. I picked up a second magazine. Between the two, I had thirty rounds. If I needed them, that should be enough. Maybe.

SIXTY-SEVEN

I could hear Brittany's voice in my head as I locked my Jeep. *He said they'd line up to gang rape me.* I wedged the pistol under my belt in the small of my back. Shirt untucked. The wind blew the white chimney smoke across the lot and over the skinny pine trees. I could detect the slight burnt smell of cooking meat. Somewhere below the brick chimney, pork or beef barbecue simmered on a grill inside the Midnight Rider.

I headed across the lot toward the entrance, the crush of flattened beer bottle tops under my boat shoes, a few beer cans flattened and faded in the sunlight. Four bikers stood on the plank-wood deck that was about two feet above the ground, three steps leading up to the deck. A biker leaned up against one of the support timbers. One sat on a thick fence rail bolted to all the beams. The other two stood, sipping beer from cans. Watching me.

I walked up the steps as two men on Harleys pulled into the lot, one guy doing a circle across the gravel and bottle tops, dust, and smoke drifting to the porch. On the deck, I could hear music coming from inside, Stevie Ray Vaughn singing *Crossfire*. I made eye contact with the bikers and said, "Barbecue smells great."

The man leaning up against the timber removed a chewed toothpick from the corner of his mouth. "Figured you for a vegan."

"Then you figured wrong."

He said nothing, spitting into the brown bushes below the deck. I walked by them, pushing open the double salon doors like I was stepping into the past—into an Old West saloon in Deadwood or Tombstone. But the cowboys here rode steel horses and had leather on their backs, not on saddles.

I walked into a drone of loud conversations, high-pitched laugher from a woman at one of the tables, and the smell of burning weed, spilled whiskey, testosterone, and barbecue. Lynyrd Skynyrd's song, *Simple Man,* now starting from the jukebox in the corner. I felt the collective stare of bikers who seemed more curious about me than anything else.

Maybe it was because I wasn't wearing a leather or denim jacket.

The bar was on the left, past a dozen tables. It was at least sixty feet long, with a brass rail at its base supporting biker boots. Along the bar were a couple dozen stools, nine people sitting. Behind the bottles of liquor was a smoky glass mirror mounted to the roughhewn wall.

I glanced around the large room. At least thirty people, about a third of them women. Busch NASCAR and Budweiser stock car signs hung on one wall. Displayed on the other walls were various posters of women in bikinis leaning up against some of the cars. The lone standout was a framed poster of Jimi Hendrix playing a guitar at Woodstock, a sweatband the color of a tangerine around his head.

There were three billiard tables at the far end of the rambling room. Bikers shooting pool on all three tables. I watched them for a few seconds, trying to match body size and mannerisms to a guy who calls himself Tank. But there were a lot of big guys. Lots of beer bellies. Plenty of ink and fur on exposed chests and arms in jackets and T-shirts with the sleeves cut off.

At the bar, I pulled out a stool and took a seat. From that angle, I could watch most of the room from the reflection in the wide mirror. Two women worked behind the bar, mixing drinks, and serving beer in cans and bottles. A plastic bobble-head statuette of Dale Earnhardt stood next to a bottle of Jack Daniels. The bar top, made from oak the color of dark honey, was pockmarked from cigarette burns, a frowning smiley face carved into the wood.

"Hi, I'm Kat. What can I get you?" asked a buxom woman with jade green eyes wearing a low-cut denim shirt and snug short shorts. She wore a Midnight Rider billed cap, her blonde ponytail threaded through the hole in the back of the hat. Her cheeks were flushed from keeping up with drink orders."

"Hi, Kat. Do you have Modelo?"

"Can or bottle?"

"Whichever one is closest for you. I can see you're busy."

"That's for sure." She reached in a tub of ice cubes, fishing out a Modelo. She opened the bottle, setting it on a cork coaster with the words *Midnight Rider Saloon* typed in a half-circle, a smiling crescent moon at the center. "Wanna run a tab?"

"I'll pay as I go."

"Okay. It's four dollars."

I gave her a ten-dollar bill. "Keep the change."

Kat smiled. "Thanks." She nodded and left, setting two plastic mugs under two draft spouts, pulling the handles at the same time, and wiping her hands on a towel. I looked into the mirror to catch some of the action in the room and back at the pool tables. The first thing I noticed was the lack of "colors" or motorcycle club patches on the backs of the bikers. Maybe the saloon was a neutral zone. I sipped the beer and scanned faces in the mirror, people sitting at the bar and to my left and right.

Something caught my eye.

To the left of the bar, a man sat alone at a table near three open side doors, the large alcove giving a clear view of the cypress trees around a small pond just off the property, the water a dark olive color with a chemical green slime on the surface. What caught my eye was the black patch the man wore over his left eye. I thought of what Dave said. *One man was blinded in his left eye.*

SIXTY-EIGHT

Maybe I was in the wrong biker bar. Dave said the guy who lost his eye in the fight was William Kidd. If the fight was three years ago, as Dave mentioned, did it mean that all was forgiven or that the man called Tank no longer frequented the Midnight Rider? The guy with the eye patch sipped from a can of Miller beer. From where I sat, he looked to be in his late forties. Shaved head. A gold hoop earring in one ear. He wore a black T-shirt and jeans.

Kat worked her way back up the bar to where I sat. "Can I get you something to eat? Racks of ribs are comin' off the grill."

"Maybe a little later."

"Sounds good."

"Kat, although I really like motorcycles, I'm not much of a biker."

"I could hardly tell." She laughed.

"I don't see many colors, or the motorcycle club patches on the backs of jackets in here. Why's that?"

"After Bike Week three years ago, management of a lot of the bars—places bikers liked to hang out, asked that they don't wear their colors if they come in any of the bars. Midnight Rider was one of them. But not everybody follows the rules."

"That's 'cause rules are made to be broken if you're a real biker," said a man sitting two barstools down from me, his hair the color of tarnished silver. Weedy eyebrows that looked like frost had settled on them. "Tats tell the story. Most dudes know who's who."

I looked over at the guy, nodding. I glanced at the tattoos on his bare left arm. One on the forearm was a human skull with angel wings on either side. In the center of his upper arm was a tat of a closed fist, the initials I-F below it. My plans were quickly changing. It's a lot easier to be invited to a party than it is to crash one.

Kat pulled a handle, filling a mug of draft beer, placing it on a server's tray. She looked at me and the guy on the stool. "You're right, Digger. Some people know who's who, and it's cool until you mix booze and colors. Almost always you're gonna get some dudes talking shit, and then one thing leads to another."

"There are a lot of good fellas that ride." The man took a long pull from his bottle, knuckles thick and scarred.

"And there are some really bad ones, too," she said, pouring a double shot of whiskey in a glass and setting it in front of another customer at the bar. She walked away, taking more orders, the music from the jukebox changing to Brent Cobb singing *Let the Rain Come Down*.

I looked toward the mirror, locking eyes with the guy two stools down from me. I turned to face him as his eyes shifted from the mirror to me. I nodded. "We're both drinking Modelo. I'm ready for another. How about you? I'm buying."

He had guarded, blue eyes that harbored a look of desolation as if he watched a ship on the horizon sail away with his final dream of hope. He finished the last swallow of beer in his bottle and took a deep breath. "Much obliged."

I signaled to Kat and ordered two more bottles of beer. She smiled, and I looked back at the man. His face was sprouting ashen whiskers, tiny blood vessels, like threads just under the craggy skin of both cheeks. He scratched at a bleeding scab on the forehead of a human skull tattoo on his left arm. Above the skull were the words *Harley-Davidson*.

Kat set the Modelo bottles in front of us and moved down the bar to take another order. The guy on the stool picked up the fresh beer and made a mock toast. "Here's to Mexican beer and señoritas." We sipped from the bottles. He set the beer down on the bar and cut his eyes over to me. "Name's Digger. What do you go by?"

"Shooter."

"Thanks for the beer, Shooter."

"You're welcome. How'd you get the name Digger?"

"Dug coal in Kentucky. Then I moved over to diggin' graves."

"You make a living as a grave digger, or did you have another motive?"

He grinned, sipping the beer. "I like the way you think ... like I was buryin' dudes I killed. I worked for a company that owned three cemeteries. We stayed busy most days. When I wasn't workin' as a grave digger, I put in irrigation systems, still diggin'. Black dirt always under my fingernails. My real name's Al Rowe. How 'bout you?"

"Military mostly. Overseas. Middle East. Afghanistan."

"Marines?"

"Army. Delta Force."

He cocked his head and looked at me, snorting. "Is that how you got the name Shooter?"

"Yes—it stuck from my military days."

"You see a lot of action over there?"

"Saw enough."

"Bet you did. I don't blame you for not wantin' to talk about that stuff. I've met a lot of dudes with PTSD and whatnot."

"And it's the *whatnot* that you gotta watch out for."

"I dig it. Digger digs it." He chuckled, taking a pull off the bottle. "Don't know about you, but I'm lookin' for baseball season to start. I go to a few spring training games in Florida."

"What's your favorite team?"

"I've always been a Braves fan. We didn't have pro teams in Kentucky, but we sure have the Louisville Slugger."

"My son's friend, a University of Florida student, was being scouted by the majors."

"Did he choose a team?"

"No, he had to put that on hold."

"Tell him not to wait too long. Strike while the iron's hot."

Something in the mirror caught my eye. The man was someone I recognized. He was one of the bikers that had been standing outside on the front deck when I arrived, the one who made the vegan comment. He was walking around tables and heading toward me.

SIXTY-NINE

The phrase, *play it by ear,* came to mind as I looked at the diamond stud earring in his left ear. Right at the base of that ear, should I need to, was an excellent spot to land a hard blow if he used his right fist to hit me. He came up and stood next to my stool. Leaning both forearms on the bar rail. The music from the jukebox changed to Shinedown singing *45.* I could feel the presence of my Glock against my back. Unless his pals showed up, I wouldn't need the pistol.

He smelled of stale smoke—weed and cigarettes, his denim clothes sour with old sweat. He made no effort to get the attention of the two bartenders. He looked over his beefy left shoulder at me and said, "You're sittin' on my stool."

"You have one right next to you."

"But it's not mine."

"Neither is the one I'm sitting on. I'm saving it for somebody."

"Who's that somebody?"

"A friend."

"You're not in a gay bar, buttercup."

"And my friend's not gay. He's … well he's hard to identify. But he knows who he is."

"Maybe he's wearing a pink bandana and matching boots. Get your ass off my stool."

I said nothing.

He shook his head, lopsided grin, like an idiot who thought he was smarter than everyone in the room. He looked down the bar. A couple of amused bikers watching him. I glanced at Kat's face twenty feet away. I could tell she knew the man and sensed that he wasn't in my space to sell me a timeshare unit on Daytona Beach.

266

The guy splayed his hands on the bar, tats on the back of both hands and fingers. He looked at our reflections in the mirror. "Last chance vegan breath. Get off my stool or you won't sleep so good tonight."

I stood. He pursed his wet lips and leaned back, standing straight. He had to look up at me, like a man straddling a motorcycle at a traffic light watching for the green light. I wasn't going to give him the chance to see the green light. "Move," he growled.

"Remember that friend I told you about?"

He grinned, looked down at his scuffed black boots, lifting his eyes up to me. "Yeah, looks like he's a no-show."

"Oh, you're wrong about that. He's here."

He sneered. "You mean the fella on the barstool behind me? His day in the sun done come and gone. It's just you and me, buttercup."

"That's right. That friend is me. He's one of my multiple personalities. He's the guy I go to when I need to channel my psychopath."

He ran his tongue on the inside of his right cheek. "You got a mental problem, or what?"

"It's more of the *or what* … because my friend is the guy I had to become when I shoved a ball-point pen into the eye of a Taliban leader. I'd been held prisoner of war in one of their qal'ahs or mud houses. I had to bite into his neck to keep him from screaming."

He grinned. I could tell by his body language he was about to throw a fist. I remembered that he had been holding a beer can in his right hand when I arrived. The first swing would probably come from his right.

And it did.

He reared back. As he tried to deliver, I lifted my left arm, deflecting his blow, grabbing his right wrist. Taking a step with my left foot, my right fist landing a hard blow behind his ear. I pulled his left arm, using my right leg like a low fence post, jerking him backwards over my leg, bringing him hard to the wooden floor. He was out cold.

The guy on the barstool grinned and said, "Damn, man! That was a three-second fight."

I nodded. "Didn't want my beer to get warm."

"No shit." He looked over at Kat and said, "Have one of your bouncers carry sleepin' beauty outta here."

"Already on it, Digger. Blake and Karl are coming now."

I looked at the mirror, spotted two burly guys weaving their way around the tables, most of the customers staring at me, talking in lower tones. Not sure what to make of a brawny biker sprawled on his back under the barstools.

When the bouncers arrived, Kat said, "The dude on the floor started it. Kept sayin' to—"

She looked at me, and I said, "Shooter."

"Right. The guy was hassling Shooter here before taking a swing at him."

"That's the way I saw it," said Digger. "Shooter was mindin' his business 'til this fella comes over and starts a fight, throwin' the first lick."

Both bouncers, sculpted muscle—gym rat bodies, wore Midnight Rider black T-shirts depicting a biker on a Harley with raised handlebars riding toward a crescent moon. "That's good enough for us," said one of them. He looked at his partner. "Blake, you wanna take the dude's feet, and I'll get his shoulders?"

"Sure." The men lifted the biker, carrying him toward the side entrance, doors open, the guy with the eye patch leaning back in his chair, amused. They took the sleeping biker outside, setting him on the deck and talking with a couple of his friends. I was hoping the bouncers told them to take him home before he woke up and decided to come back with a knife or gun. It happens.

Digger shook his shaggy head. "Gotta tell you … I've seen a lot of barfights. Been in too many to count. Don't recall ever seein' a man hit the floor so fast. What the hell was that— some combo of boxin' and judo?"

"Stuff you had to learn where I went."

"Are you a cop?"

"No."

"Would you tell me if you were?"

"What do you think?"

"I'm not sure what the hell to think, to be damn frank with you. I do know you're the kind of guy—strong, tough, and smart … that we're lookin' for."

"Who's we?"

"You ever think about joining a motorcycle club? Lots of military vets, especially Army and Marines, are in clubs across the nation."

"After the service, I became more of a lone ranger than a joiner."

"That's cool. But I'm not talkin' about some chicken shit club like the sons of Shriners or something like that."

"What are you talking about … Hells Angels?"

"Shit no. They went Hollywood years ago. Sold their asses to corporate America, at least partially. I'm talking about the number one club in five states—the Iron Fist."

"You belong?"

Digger pointed to the tat of the clenched fist on his left upper arm. "I wear my colors right here."

"Seems smart considering the Florida heat and humidity. Wearing leather, even the designer sleeveless kind, might cause a heat rash. And that would require baby powder."

"Man, you got a wicked sense of humor."

"How long have you been a member in the club?"

"It's goin' on four years now. I'm the oldest guy in the local chapter. I sometimes think they keep me around 'cause they like to hear stories about the good old bad days. Some of the fellas look at me as sort of a father figure. Most never had much of an old man at home when they were kids." Digger took another pull from the bottle, his cheeks shiny.

"Are any other members of the Iron Fist here today?"

"Not that I've seen. Some of the guys really like this bar. Others hang out at the Whistler or the strip clubs."

"Speaking of clubs, does the Iron Fist have a clubhouse in the area?"

"Yeah. It's down on Mulberry Street. That's where you'd come to meet with some of the senior members. I'd be your sponsor. We're not a bunch of bad asses. We just like to keep to ourselves. Our chapters do charity work for those communities where they're located. If you managed to get in, and lots of dudes don't make the cut, you'd be a member for life."

"That could be a long-term commitment."

"Depends on the way you look at things, I suppose."

I sipped my beer, glancing at the mirror before looking back at him. "Tell you what, Digger, let me sleep on it. Since I don't own a motorcycle, it'd be expensive for me to join."

"We can find you a used one in good shape."

"I'll consider it. I do appreciate the offer. How can I get in touch with you?"

"Lemme write my number down. Kat, can I borrow a pen?"

"Sure." She reached across the bar, handing a pen to him.

He picked up a dry napkin and slowly wrote his name and number. When finished, he slid the napkin over to me. "There you go. Like I said, you may never get in, and you may not be interested. But seeing how you handled that dude in a matter of seconds, I think you'd fit in damn good with the Iron Fist. Gimme your number."

I wrote it on a second bar napkin and gave it to him. He put it in his pocket. "Hey, Kat. You pour a whiskey for ol' Whiskey?"

"Sure." She filled a shot glass with Jack Daniels. Digger knocked it back and got up slowly from the wooden barstool, as if his lower back was stiff.

"Who's Whiskey?" I asked.

"My dog. Been with me for fourteen years. He up and died last week. Appreciate the beers." He started for the door, turning back to me. "Ever'thing I told you is between us. We cool."

"Yeah, we're cool."

SEVENTY

Clint Ward wasn't a man who turned to meditation for stress relief. He believed that the best way to deal with anxiety was to address the source of the problem. He stood on his patio at the back of his home, on the phone, waiting for Detective Winston Porter to answer the call. Clint inhaled deeply through his nose, releasing the air out of his mouth. He held the phone to his ear, clenching and releasing the muscles in his other hand to ease the tension.

Detective Porter picked up. "Mr. Ward, the receptionist said your call was urgent."

"Yes, it is. Brittany Harmon told my wife and I what happened to her. Charlie Brown forced his way into her apartment and held a knife to her throat. I strongly urge you to offer Brittany police protection around the clock."

"We'll find Charlie Brown and pick him up. In the meantime, we do have a police cruiser parked in front of Miss Harmon's apartment."

"Are officers in the car or is it just parked there?"

"We're conducting surveillance twenty-four-seven."

"We've already lost my son and another eight college kids are dead over in Panama City Beach. How many more deaths of young people will it take to see that this guy Brown, and his drug suppliers, are guilty of mass murder?"

"Mr. Ward, we are vigorously pursuing the investigation. We hope to prove that Brown is tied to some bigger fish, so to speak. These are the guys we'd like to arrest and convict. I understand your frustration. But the last thing I want to do is go to court with a case that doesn't hold water. Please let us do our job. I'll speak with you later." He clicked off.

Clint watched two squirrels playing tag, running around the base of a live oak. Slate gray clouds were gathering in the distance, the wind shifting from the northeast, windchimes tinkling. He could see streaks of rain falling beyond the horizon line.

He went inside where his wife Lauren was sitting in the family room, the TV on, the monotone rambling of a cable news anchorman. Lauren was working a crossword puzzle, paying little attention to the newscast. Clint walked through the room and did a double-take, stopping. He stared in disbelief at the screen.

The anchor man said, "The whereabouts or fate of U.S. Drug Enforcement Agent Anthony Salazar is unknown at this time. In a news conference earlier, a spokesperson for the Department of Justice said the DEA and the White House will not negotiate with members of the drug cartel that abducted Salazar from the house he rented in Mexico. Diana Price has more on this breaking story."

The image on screen cut to a mountainous, arid terrain. A reporter's voice-over narration began. "Down there is just some of the inhospitable land where it is believed that the feared Durango cartel has some of its hideaways. The FBI and DEA believe that, somewhere in that rugged terrain, the cartel is holding DEA agent Anthony Salazar hostage after they abducted him."

The video cut to exteriors of Salazar's house in Mexico. "The town of Durango is where Anthony Salazar was living as an undercover federal agent. He was in Mexico, like dozens of other DEA agents, to assist the Mexican government in efforts to curb the flow of drugs moving north across the border and into the United States. And it was here, according to a neighbor, where armed men abducted Salazar in his driveway as he walked to his car."

The video cut to an older man on camera who spoke Spanish. An interpreter's voice said, "It happened very fast. I saw two men come from the sides of his house. They held guns on the man and made him get in a van, and they drove away."

The reporter's narrative continued over video of the town, people walking, small motorcycles and cars whizzing through the streets. "The question is, where did they drive to … where did they take Anthony Salazar from the house he rented? The Durango cartel is operated by Diego Navarro, the eldest of two sons who assumed control of the cartel after their father, Sergio Navarro, was convicted of drug running and human trafficking and placed in a U.S. prison."

The video cut to a photo of Salazar wearing a sports coat and red and blue tie. "The DOJ is said to be in communications with Diego Navarro, trying hard to get Salazar released unharmed. When asked why Salazar was abducted, a DEA spokesperson had this to say."

The image cut to a woman in front of the Department of Justice building in Washington, D.C. "Diego Navarro has a vendetta. And he has complete disregard for human life. He is holding Anthony Salazar hostage and using him as a pawn. Navarro wants to negotiate, seeking the release of his father who is serving a life sentence in a federal prison in Florence, Colorado."

"Does Navarro want anything else?" asked a reporter in the crowd.

"The president has made it very clear that this nation does not and will not negotiate with terrorists. The Durango cartel, and others like them in Mexico, fit that definition."

The video cut to the reporter standing next to a flowing river, a breeze blowing her dark brown hair. "Behind me is the Rio Grande River. Across it is Mexico. The distance from here to the heart of the Mexican state of Durango is approximately 600 miles. That's how far a special mission would have to travel from the U.S. into the mountainous state of Durango for a rescue attempt. Currently, there is no word on whether any rescue plans are in the making. Reporting live from the southern border between the U.S. and Mexico, this is Diana Price. Now back to you in the studio."

Clint stared at the TV screen, his thoughts racing. Lauren looked up from her chair, setting the crossword puzzle on the coffee table. "Clint, what's wrong? You look like someone punched you in the stomach."

He turned around slowly to face his wife. "I know I don't talk a lot about what I did in the military in the Middle East and Afghanistan."

"No, you don't. I respect that. I know what you went through is difficult to relive. I'm glad you sought treatment for your PTSD years ago."

"Doesn't mean the nightmares ever went away."

"I know. I hear you talk in your sleep sometimes."

"I think about those who didn't make it back. Not because we left them behind. But rather because they were killed. There were two people who received the worst treatment by the Taliban. One was the man on the screen in that news story. Tony Salazar almost didn't get out."

273

"You said two. Who was the second?"

"Sean O'Brien. He got the worst as a prisoner of war for twenty-seven days before he could break out. Sean was our Delta Force squad leader. And the man who was just abducted by a Mexican drug cartel, Tony Salazar, was the second in command. After his military service, he took a job with the DEA as an agent. Sean, and I don't know why, went back for a final tour of duty. It's that one he won't talk about ... even to me."

"I didn't know."

"Very few people do. Probably not even Wynona."

"I don't know if Sean has heard the news about Tony, but when I tell him, he'll take it very hard. Let's hope our government can get Tony out of that hell hole."

"What happens if they can't?"

"Knowing Sean like I do ... he'd probably go in there by himself."

"That would be suicide for an American Delta Force veteran to take on a Mexican drug cartel."

SEVENTY-ONE

I smiled as I thought about Digger's invitation for me to be considered a member of the Iron Fist motorcycle club. I didn't know whether I'd pass their leader's scratch and sniff test, but it might be a good way to get me in front of a man called Tank. That was one option. The guy wearing the black eye patch and sitting alone might lead me to a second option.

I stood from the stool, Kat approaching behind the bar. "You haven't finished your beer," she said with a wide smile.

"Just heading to the restroom. Where is it?"

"For guys, it's to the left, past the pool tables."

Walking in that direction, I'd go right past the table where the man with the eye patch was sipping his beer. "Thanks, Kat. Back in a minute. Would you watch my stool for me?"

"Are you kidding? After what you did, I don't think any dude in this bar would try to take your seat. On second thought, I wouldn't put it past a few idiots to get drunk and place wagers. It's part of the alpha male biker psyche." She stared at me with a coy expression. "You sure don't come across as an alpha male."

"Really?"

"Yes. You seem like a gentleman. Just a guy minding his own business, chatting it up with ol' Digger 'til some dude wants to get in your face." She paused. "But, maybe just behind your nice face is something else."

"What you see is what you get—sometimes. Who's the fella over there with the eye patch? He looks familiar."

"His name's Billy, but most call him Cap'n Kidd 'cause he looks like a pirate. His formal name is William Kidd. He lost the eye in a nasty fight between bikers. That was when I first started working here, about three years ago. I heard they buried the hatchet, and today, they keep out of each other's way. At least for the most part."

"Interesting name—from the outlaw to the pirate. Who'd he fight?"

She stepped closer, glancing around. "Some dudes from the Iron Fist."

"Digger's motorcycle club."

"Digger's sort of like their mascot, the old man who talks people off the edge when they wanna start doing stuff that'll get them a prison sentence. The guy that Billy fought was Tank. He's the main man in the local chapter of the Iron Fist. I heard he reports to guys in the club somewhere in Texas."

A man wearing a black tank top and cut-off jean shorts walked up. "Hey, Kat, lemme have a cold Bud."

He looked at my stool and then glanced up at me, clearing his throat. I left and walked around the bar, toward the restroom. As I got closer to the guy with the eye patch, I looked at him, nodding. He returned the gesture like I had passed a test. He said, "Nice job in putting Tennessee down."

"Is that his name, Tennessee?"

"It's what he goes by. He's from Tennessee, some little hillbilly town back in the mountains. He's always talkin' about how much better Tennessee is than Florida."

"If that's the case, why doesn't he go back there?"

He laughed, looking up at me with the one good eye, his bald head shiny as a cue ball. "Maye he'll crawl on back there after you kicked his ass in less time than they give a cowboy to ride the bull in a rodeo … eight seconds. And you did it in front of a few dozen people."

"I didn't start it."

"But you sure as hell finished it. Where'd you learn to fight that way?"

"Here and there. Military mostly. I need to take a leak. I can join you for a beer. I'm sort of done with sitting over there on a stool."

"Sure, man. C'mon back."

"Are you staying with Bud, or you want something else?"

"A cold Corona would be good."

"Two of them would be better."

I walked across the bar floor over peanut shells and spilled beer, maneuvering my way around a couple of bar tables, toward the pool tables and restroom. Bikers chalked their cue sticks, or looked up from a shot, watching me. I wasn't going to the men's room alone. My close friend, Glock, was right behind me. He had one eye, too. A straight shooter.

And he had my back.

SEVENTY-TWO

In the next ten minutes, I would need everything I learned as a detective when I was questioning suspects. If I could gain his confidence, the guy with the eye patch had a story to tell. But did he have a score to settle? When I returned, I came back with two Coronas, a slice of lime in each bottle. I sat on the opposite side of the table, handing him a beer. He took it, pushing the lime into the bottle.

"Cheers. They call me Cap'n Kidd."

"I'm Shooter. Cheers, Cap."

He took a long pull. After he finished, I could see a small spot of red blood vessels in the corner of his eye. It had the shape of a tiny starfish. Probably an infection. "How long have you gone by the name, Captain Kidd?"

"Since I had to wear this patch. About three years. Before that, they called me Billy the Kidd … took some ribbing over that. Cap'n Kidd better suits my Scottish heritage. In the late 1600s, Cap'n William Kidd was a Scottish pirate who sailed the Caribbean. Where'd you learn those defensive moves? It looked like a form of judo I've never seen."

"It's called Krav Maga. It's taught at one place in Israel. The basic premise is not to just throw your opponent to the ground. It's to make sure he doesn't get off the ground."

"No shit. Were you in Israel?"

"Yeah."

"Military?"

"Army. How about you?"

"I joined the National Guard for two years. Never got outta Georgia. Now I could never re-enlist with one eye … my right eye."

"That's all you need looking through a sniper's scope."

"Damn straight. Were you a sniper or did you get that name shootin' whiskey shots?"

Sean laughed. "Definitely could put down a few shots in my younger days, but the name's a holdover from my sniper days in the military."

"I hear ya. I don't drink like I used to either—need to keep my wits about me. What was your marksmanship rank?"

"Expert. I once knew a fella who lost an eye as a boy. He was on a fishing trip with his dad. They were in a small boat in the center of a big lake. The kid caught a fish, a bass. He got it up to the boat, and when his dad leaned over to net the fish, the metal hoop on the net hit the bass under its mouth. The fish spit out the lure. The backlash was like a whip. One of the treble hooks lodged in the boy's eye." I sipped my beer, wondering if he'd share his story.

He nodded. "My situation wasn't like that. I had two good eyes all my life 'til me and a buddy got into a bar fight. It was right here at the Midnight Rider."

"What happened?"

"Two members of the Iron Fist jumped us. We were holding our own 'til two more of their guys came over and got into it. Then it was like we were bein' attacked by a pack of wolves. We got beat so bad, it caused both of us to spend a week in the hospital. My pal had two broken legs. I lost my eye because one dude held me in a headlock while the other used his dirty thumb to gouge my eye. Bastard tried to pop it out of the socket. Almost did." Kidd sipped his beer, looking into space, his thoughts distant and dark as his unseeing eye.

"How did you patch things up after those severe injuries?"

"You don't, man. You just keep your distance and lay low."

"Three years is a long time to lay low."

"Maybe. What they did to us crossed the line. I don't mind a barfight, but you don't have two men hold a guy down to take his eye out. When you do that, you block him from doin' the kind of work a man like me does."

"What's that?"

"Driving a truck for one thing. I used to be a long-haul driver. The truckin' company won't give me my job back. None of the others will hire me. I work part-time putting up drywall and slingin' a hammer on construction sites. I'll never be on the road drivin' a truck again because of the Iron Fist assholes."

I watched his anger build, his good eye misting as he sipped his beer. I decided to go for it—to take the risks. "Was Tank one of the guys who put you in the hospital?"

His single eye opened wider. "He sure as hell was. It was his dirty thumb. How do you know his name?"

"Because I'm hunting him."

"You're what? Huntin' him? Like a bounty hunter?"

"I'm not a bounty hunter. There's nothing in it for me except seeing people go to jail who sell fentanyl to kids, knowing one tablet can kill a sixteen-year-old in less than thirty minutes."

"Are you a narc?"

"No." I reached in my shirt pocket, pulled out the picture of Andy, and slid it across the table to him. "That's Andy Ward." I told him the story and added, "It was supposed to have been oxy. Some of it was. The rest was fentanyl. He died before he could dial 911. He was the son of one of my best friends, a guy I served overseas with in Afghanistan."

Kidd shook his head, taking a deep breath. He looked over my shoulder and back toward the pool tables. "How'd you track it to the Iron Fist and Tank?"

"Because one of his drug dealers in Gainesville admitted the biker gang is his supplier. Andy wasn't the only college kid killed. Eight more over in Panama City Beach bought from the same dealer, and they all died."

"Yeah, I heard about that. Sad, man. Damn sad. I feel for their families."

"Do you feel bad enough to help me get to Tank?"

"Hell, yeah. What do you need to know?"

"The older guy at the bar, Digger, you know him?"

"Yeah. He's an old biker who drives a beater pickup truck and tends bar at the Iron Fist clubhouse. Digger's a straight shooter. One of the few good guys over there. There are some more. Guys like Drywall and Axle. But that's about it. Rest of 'em would cut your throat if Tank said do it."

"After he saw me put that guy, Tennessee, on the floor, Digger said I might make a good recruit for the Iron Fist. He wants to sponsor me.

Suggested I call him, and he'll set up a time for me to meet the gang at their clubhouse. But I don't like being in small spaces … places I'm not familiar with, and vastly outnumbered by suspicious big men with shady attitudes."

"No shit."

"If you were going to have a little chat with Tank, how would you do it?"

"I don't know, man. He comes in here sometimes. I think he hangs out at the Whistler downtown more than out here. He rides a distinct Harley. Only a few people got one."

"What is it?"

"The thirtieth anniversary edition of the original Fat Boy. The bike is candy apple red and fast as hell."

"Where does Tank live?"

"Don't know." He sipped his beer, the music changing to a Tony Joe White song, *Out of the Rain.* "I know a guy who would be able to point you to Tank's house. And he might have a damn good reason to do it. His road name's Axle. Real name is Robert Holloway. Axle has an axe to grind against Tank and his minions. I hear that Tank had 'em cut Axle's cheek to the jawbone. That leaves a scar that's like a brand on a cow. Everybody knows. Way I heard it is the scar wasn't enough, and Tank ordered them to toss Axle into the river. Gator bait. Said he was a snitch. Somehow, he survived. He's layin' low."

"Do you know where he is now?"

Kidd sipped his beer, the one eye watching a fly on the table. "Yeah, I know. He's been movin' around. Last I heard, he's shacking with a stripper, his ex-wife. They have a kid together, so I guess it's in her best interest to keep him alive if he's paying child support."

"Do you have his phone number?"

"No."

"The ex-wife's trailer is off Bear Island Road down a dead-end dirt street called Mill Pond. Trailer is at the end of the road, on the left. The mailbox has a robin painted on both sides. His ex's name is Robin. Last time I was out there, I played a game of horseshoes with Axle and drank Jack from the bottle. If he's there, his bike won't be parked in front. He keeps it in a shed out back."

"Thanks." I stood to leave.

"If he is out there, be damn careful. I guarantee he'll be locked and loaded. A guy like Axle, considering what he's been through, will shoot first and ask questions later. But you gotta be alive to answer those questions. You can tell him we talked. Not sure how he'll take that. As for me, well, it's hard to sleep with one eye open anymore."

SEVENTY-THREE

I was just about as close to the county line as you could get. Mill Pond Road was a squiggly gravel and dirt road that snaked its way through tall pines in a remote and rural section on the edge of the Volusia County line. I drove slowly down it, trying to keep the dust from rising behind my Jeep. I passed a dark pond on my right that was full of green lily pads the width of large pizzas and lined with moss-draped cypress trees.

I could see a few trailers set back in the woods. Most of the mailboxes were rusted, metal mouths flopping open like a dog's tongue on a hot summer day. The road was a little less than a mile long. As I came to the end, I spotted the last mailbox on the left, a hand-painted robin on the side facing me.

The dirt driveway meandered about eighty feet from the road to the trailer. Even through the pines, I could tell the trailer was not new, faded vanilla paint turned amber, gray tree sap on one side of the roof. There was a wooden deck partially covered from the sun by a bleached out blue canvas awning. The end of the dead-end road was a circle large enough to make a complete turn. To the right of some tall pines was a small spur road, more like a trail, just wide enough for my Jeep. I pulled in there, threading my way through brush and honeysuckle vines that looked like spaghetti with green leaves.

I put my Glock under my belt and shirt, locked the Jeep, and headed through the woods toward the trailer. Captain Kidd said he didn't have Axle's number. Was he telling the truth, or if he wasn't, did he call Axle and tell him I was coming? If so, did he tell him it might be in his best interest to talk with me?

I doubted all the above.

Within seconds, I was on the property. The yard was solid pine straw, Brazilian pepper plants growing like wild shrubs. As I got closer, I could see that there were no vehicles in the driveway. There was a small pink bike. I hoped that the child was in school and not at home. I stayed behind the brush as much as possible as I made my way to the back of the trailer. A rusted dryer, the lid open, and an antique John Deere tractor, rear ties flat, sat among knee-high weeds.

To the left of a small outbuilding or shed, was a plowed garden. Red tomatoes hung heavy from the vines. Corn stalks moving in the breeze. There was a row of carrots and a partial row of pumpkins, all rotting like deflated basketballs. I moved further to my right toward the opening of a doorless garage. A motorcycle was parked inside.

I heard the smack of a screen door closing, a man stepping onto the wooden back deck. He was shoeless, dressed in torn jeans and a white tank shirt. Even from where I stood, from behind two pine trees fifty feet away, I could see the scar on his check. And I could see the small pistol under his belt. He moved down a half dozen rickety steps to the yard, walking through a dirt path to the garden.

He stood with his back to me, standing to the far left of the garden, urinating in a large pile of sawdust that looked like an African ant mound. I pushed the audio record button on my phone, reached for my Glock, and approached him silently, his back still facing me. "There's a pistol aimed between your shoulder blades." He flinched. Between his legs, I could see the urine stream abruptly stop.

He slowly raised his hands without me telling him to do so. "Tank send you?"

His voice was calm, like a man who'd looked down the barrel of a gun more than once.

"Don't move, Axle."

"How do I know you really got a gun?"

I aimed at one of the deflated pumpkins, pulling the trigger. The round blew a hole the size of my fist out of the pumpkin. I glanced at the trailer. No one at the windows. "Keep your hands in the air." I walked up to him, using my left hand to take the pistol out of his belt. I stepped back ten feet. "Turn around."

He complied, slowly turning around. His hands still in the air even though I had his gun. He looked at me with curiosity and hate. Often a deadly combo. "Who are you?"

"Tank didn't send me, but I'd like for you to point me to him."

"You the law? Where's your badge?"

"Don't have one."

"When did cops come up and pull on a man for no reason?"

"I'm not the law. Like the Iron Fist, I don't have a lot of boundaries. Captain Kidd sends his regards. He thought what I offered might appeal to you."

His lower jaw hardened, the pink scar looking wet in the sunlight. "What do you mean?"

I dropped his gun in the weeds before putting the Glock under my belt. "My name's Sean O'Brien." I walked toward him, stopping about six feet away, taking Andy's picture from my pocket, turning it to him. "His name was Andy Ward. He was a college athlete, scouted by the majors until he took a single oxy for pain in his shoulder. The fentanyl in the pill killed him. The pills came from the Iron Fist. Andy was the only son of a man I served with in Afghanistan. That's why I want Tank." I put the picture back in my pocket.

He took a deep breath, removing an unfiltered cigarette from behind his ear, twisting one end into a corner of his mouth, lighting it with a silver Zippo, and taking a deep drag. Seconds later, he released white smoke, like a cotton ball floating from the mouth of a goldfish. "You may have slipped up on me, but you don't stand a chance against Tank. He almost always has club members with him."

"The word *almost* is all I need. Looks like he did a number on your face—like what he did to Captain Kidd's eye. Tank likes to leave his mark on men. Makes you less of a man. Considering what he did to you, I'd bet you'd like to reverse the roles."

He blew smoke from his nostrils, glanced at the pumpkin with the wide hole, and touched his finger to the scar on his face. "Yeah, I'd like to see Tank go down with one right between his eyes."

"I'm not a hit man. But I can help send him to prison for life, where he'll never again be able to take a leak in the open air like you just did. Where is he?"

"Mostly, he's at the clubhouse."

"Is that where you'd go to speak with him?"

"Shit, they'd nail me to the walls. He keeps a coffin in there to remind members what's in store if anybody is workin' with the law. That's the sacred rule nobody breaks—being a snitch to the cops or FBI."

"I'm not any of them. You said he's at the clubhouse mostly. Where is he other times?"

"He hangs out at a strip joint called the Fox Hole. He lives in an old farmhouse out in the sticks past a sod farm. You go toward Cody's Corner on County Road 304 'til you hit Bunnell Road. Go left for a couple of miles. You'll take a right on Farm Lane. His house is about a quarter mile down on the left. There's an old red barn on the property. The only one like it for miles. He keeps a big pit bull there."

"Does the Iron Fist make the oxy laced with fentanyl, or does it come from somewhere else?"

"There's a lab at the clubhouse. They can make just about anything they want. But biz got so good with fentanyl, the club cut a deal with a Mexican cartel to be the supplier. The drugs come across the border, are taken to stash houses, and then shipped to the states where the Fist has local chapters."

"Which Mexican cartel?"

"Durango. Tank used to run with one of the Fist clubs in San Antonio. He speaks perfect Spanish, and he helped cut the deal with the Mexicans. Fentanyl changed the game. Mexicans call it *el dragón blanco* ... the white dragon."

"So, he knows the players in the Durango cartel?"

"Hell, yeah, he does. He can call 'em on the satellite phone. He's been down there, in Durango. I heard that Tank's got a shit load of money stashed all over. Most in offshore banks." He looked around the property, then toward a swing set in a side yard that had been mowed. "I hope you nail Tank because he deserves prison time or worse."

"If you enter a federal witness protection program—new name, new life, new place to call home, would you be willing to testify against Tank and the others?"

"If you're FBI, I need to see your badge?"

"I'm not an agent, but I can work with them and prosecutors to help you start a new life."

"It ain't just about me. I got a daughter. I don't want my little girl being raised by my ex-wife only. She's a good mother, but she makes some dumbshit decisions. I'm always tryin' to keep the boat afloat. It ain't easy."

"I understand."

"Tell you what I can do, I can be an extra set of eyes and ears for you. Let you know his whereabouts when I know. I still got a couple of good friends in the club. They keep me posted. Are you interested in what that asshole put me through?"

"I'm listening."

He told me what happened in the clubhouse, his escape from the river, and his hiding. When Axle ended, he crossed his arms and asked, "How would I reach you?"

I was about to take another risk, but considering his state of mind and circumstances, the fresh scar, the late-night baptism with alligators, maybe he was speaking the truth. If not, it was as close to a facsimile of the truth that evil could pretend to be. He'd crossed the line between good and evil so many times, he could no longer recognize the line. The life Axle lived wasn't as much about good and evil as it was about truth and lies. He used one—lies, from habit, and the other—truth, to excuse the lies. The seed was an endless cycle.

I pulled out one of my cards. "Here's my number. You can call or text me."

He took it, read my name and number. "Sean O'Brien. Okay."

"Just remember one thing, Axle … Robert Holloway. I found you once, and I can again, no matter where you hide. If you attempt to set me up or double cross me, I'll come back. And, when I do, I'll make Tank's action seem like a Boy Scout jamboree."

I turned and walked away, picked up his pistol, wiped off my prints, and set it on the back deck as Axle watched me vanish into the woods.

SEVENTY-FOUR

There wasn't a sign out front of the Iron Fist clubhouse, but there was no mistaking the message: *Keep Out.* The high razor-wire fence around the property spoke volumes. I drove my Jeep slowly by, looking through the fence and the scraggly brown viburnum to the parking lot and the building. In the past, the clubhouse could have been a parts house. Maybe a place that once sold auto parts or was a warehouse.

It was two stories, burglar bars around all the windows, ground and second floor. The white paint on the cinderblock was faded to the tint of graveyard bones. There were at least a dozen motorcycles in the lot. None of them fit the model of the candy apple red classic "Fat Boy." I assumed Tank wasn't inside the clubhouse planning the gang's next move. I could drive by the other bar, the Whistler, or the strip club, the Fox Hole, to see if his motorcycle was parked outside.

But I'd rather not have innocent people around when I confronted him.

I circled the block, studying the buildings around and across the street from the clubhouse. I looked for Plan A and Plan B height advantages, should I need to use a high rooftop to surveil the clubhouse—Plan A, or to look down through a riflescope—Plan B. Maybe it would not come to either of those choices.

My hope was to find Tank away from the clubhouse and deal with him one-on-one. I wanted to trap or entice him into admitting the Iron Fist's complicity in the distribution of fentanyl, specifically linked to Charlie Brown and the sales that resulted in the deaths of Andy Ward and the other eight college kids.

If I could get evidence of the Iron Fist's involvement, along with testimony from Charlie Brown and maybe Axle, the police would have a solid case to convict Tank and his sycophants, sending them off to prison. That would be the scenario I'd like to deliver to Clint and Lauren.

But would real justice prevail?

Perhaps. It would depend on how the cogs in the justice system turned. Prosecutors would have to deliver a strong, evidence-filled case. Jurors would have to be tamper proof, or at least not intimidated by possible retaliation from a motorcycle gang that, like a lynch mob, was only tough in a group. You don't prune evil from a group by cutting back the overhanging branches. You take out the tap root.

As I circled the block, my phone buzzed. Clint Ward calling. I pulled into a street parking spot across from the Iron Fist clubhouse and answered the call. "Have you seen the news?" Clint asked.

I never liked conversations that started with a question like that. The *news* rarely was good news or even accurate news. And I could tell by the tone of Clint's voice that something bad happened. "No, I haven't been in a position to catch the news, online or on TV."

"When was the last time you communicated with Tony Salazar?"

"Maybe eight months ago. We spoke by phone at Christmas. His home is still in San Diego, and Tony's working with the DEA. What's going on, Clint?"

"Tony was working undercover in Mexico. He was abducted in front of his rental house down there by members of a drug cartel. He's being held hostage."

"Why? Which cartel?"

"Durango. You told Lauren and I earlier that the pusher, Charlie Brown, said the Iron Fist motorcycle gang is distributing for the Durango cartel."

"Yeah, they are."

Clint sighed. "According to the news, the new drug lord is Diego Navarro. He has a younger brother named Angel. Both brothers are Sergio Navarro's sons, who is serving a life sentence inside a federal supermax prison in Colorado. Diego Navarro is demanding his father's release. If not, Diego says Tony will be decapitated."

I said nothing.

My thoughts flashed back to Afghanistan, when I was held captive in a Taliban compound, hands tied behind my back, fastened to a thick beam. The warlord entered, squatting in front of me, setting down a wicker basket. He wore a loose shirt, baggy pants, and a white turban. His brown face leathery, ratty beard, a deadness in his black eyes. I heard a fly buzzing in the basket.

"Major O'Brien," he said, staring at me. *"Sometimes, here in the mountains, we have a difficult time acquiring soccer balls. So, until such time as we get a new supply, the heads of your men will have to do."* He removed the top to the wicker basket, reaching inside, lifting out a decapitated head by the hair. *"As I understand it, this person was your Sergeant Roger Fuller. Next up will be Lieutenant Anthony Salazar. You will be the last one we slaughter."*

"Sean, are you there?" Clint asked.

"Yes. Just thinking." I took a deep breath, staring at the Iron Fist clubhouse.

"The president, of course, is saying he won't negotiate with Navarro. The DOJ apparently is more in a standby situation than a proactive movement. The DEA, taking its orders from the DOJ, is silent. I made a call to Tony's office in San Diego and explained that I had served with him on three Delta Force missions in Afghanistan and Syria. I asked for an update, and they told me there was nothing they could or would share. So, I called Tony's wife, Nicole, and we spoke for a while. She and the kids are devastated, of course. Nicole has no idea what the DEA is doing to get Tony out of there alive. They're keeping her in the dark, too."

"I have a friend who lives on a trawler at Ponce Marina. Ex-CIA. As a consultant, he still maintains contacts. He's connected, to some extent, with the DEA. Wynona has connections back to her former workplace, the FBI. Between the two, maybe we can get an idea as to what's really going on to get Tony out of there."

"Sounds good. To be frank with you, if the drug lords in the Durango cartel were the ones responsible for shipping the fentanyl that killed Andy, I'd like to see our military go in there and annihilate the Navarro's and everyone associated with them. Where are you now?"

"Sitting in my Jeep, watching the Iron Fist clubhouse."

"Are you by yourself?"

"Yes."

"Let me help you, Sean."

"You came to my home and asked me to help you bring Andy's killer or killers to justice because the cops weren't doing much anymore. I'm doing that, Clint. Charlie Brown is a low-level grunt. He didn't mix and press the chemicals that went into the oxy. Others did. I'll take the investigation as far as I can, handing what evidence I have over to the police, DEA, or FBI. Stay with Lauren. She needs you right now."

A change in the clubhouse parking lot caught my eye. Someone came out of the front door. I recognized him. "Clint, I gotta go."

"Be damn careful." He clicked off.

Digger stood in the lot, pulled a pack of cigarettes from his shirt pocket, and lit one, blowing smoke into the air. Seconds later, three bikers on Harleys pulled up at the fenced entrance gate. One motorcycle was blue. One black. The other was red—candy apple red. I could tell it was the Fat Boy model. And I knew the big guy straddling it was Tank. Wrap-around dark glasses. Body wide and solid with muscle. A black bandana on his head.

They all wore the Iron Fist colors on the backs of sleeveless leather jackets. Black T-shirts under the leather. Lots of ink on arms. Disheveled beards. The gate opened slowly, the bikers cranking their engines, as if a louder noise would make the gate open faster. When it was clear, the three bikers pulled into the lot as the gate closed behind them.

The guy on the Fat Boy took the open parking space closest to the front door. Even in a motorcycle club, upper management has its privileges. I watched him get off the Harley, walking with a swagger. He was at least a head taller than the rest of the bikers. He walked over to Digger, joining him for a smoke. The two other men entered the clubhouse.

A few minutes later, Digger followed Tank into the building. Maybe Digger was going to pitch me to become a member of the Iron Fist. I had his phone number. I'd wait awhile and give him a call. Perhaps he could set up a meeting between Tank and me. I'd suggest it happen somewhere away from the clubhouse. Around a pool table would be good.

I'd like to sink the eight ball as he stood behind it.

SEVENTY-FIVE

Digger waited to make the pitch until he and Tank were inside the clubhouse. As they headed across the main room to the bar, Digger said, "Lemme get you a beer, Tank. Got something I wanna run by you."

"All right." Tank made his way to the bar, a dozen members of the club sipping beer from cans and drinking liquor from red Solo cups. Some shot pool in one corner or played the two pinball machines. Others lounged on the furniture. Two paddle fans moved the hazy air around the room, beer signs glowing through the smoke like neon lighthouses in the mist.

"Make it quick, Digger. I got to head to the back offices for a conference call."

"No problem." He pulled two cans of Miller from the cooler behind the bar, popping the tops and handing one to Tank. "I was at Midnight Rider, just sittin' at the bar, mindin' my business, and I saw something I haven't seen in a long time."

"What was it?"

"This guy, tall and strong, looked like somebody you'd see leading a platoon of men into battle. Anyway, he was sitting at the bar a couple of stools down from me, and a guy called Tennessee started some shit. You know the routine: a big guy walks up and says, you're sittin' on my stool; get up and get lost. But, when the guy on the stool stood, he was a helluva lot taller than Tennessee."

Tank nodded, taking a pull from his beer. "This gonna take long, Digger?"

"No. Tennessee reared back with that big right fist of his. Before he could deliver the blow, the guy standing next to his stool took Tennessee down in two moves. He was knocked out cold and on the floor. The

292

whole thing happened in about three seconds. What made it really stand out is the guy who took him down didn't even break a sweat, and I doubt his heartbeat went up a notch. He's one of the coolest cats I've seen in a long, damn time. I don't usually go about recruiting dudes for you to consider as club members. I told him I'd talk with you to maybe set up a meeting. See where it might go from there."

"What's the guy's name, Quick Draw McGraw?"

"Goes by Shooter."

"Sniper or alcoholic."

"Sniper. Retired military. You wanna meet him?"

"What's his real name?"

"Didn't ask. Everyone we know goes by some weird street name."

"What if he's a cop?"

"Not this guy. He's not the type to follow police protocol. Dude has got the loner vibe."

"Axle looked the same way."

"I still think Axle was set up. He doesn't have the skills to be an undercover cop."

"Dog saw him coming out of a coffee shop with an agent."

"But we never found out if he was meeting the guy inside the shop, or if they just came out at the same time. Also, Axle was facing a court date on those charges of aggravated assault and battery from getting into a fight with a roadie after the Seger concert. Maybe it had something to do with that. The so-called agent could have been a detective workin' that assault case."

Tank finished his beer, crushing the can in one hand. "Because I respect you Digger and your ability to read most people, I'll meet with the dude. We'll frisk him for a wire and do a background check. If he's got the chops, we might see if he's got the grit to become a member. Nothing's real until it is. Set it up."

"Unless I really pegged this guy wrong, you won't be disappointed."

Tank threw the smashed beer can into the open aluminum trash can behind the bar. It hit the trash can hard, the reverberating sound like a bowling ball striking the pins.

SEVENTY-SIX

The sun was a molten tangerine color in a cloud-streaked western sky when I pulled my Jeep under the live oak near my river cabin. Wynona's car was there. I'd spoken with her on the phone, stopping at the grocery store to pick up some things she needed. As I walked to the back of the house toward the screened porch, I could hear Max's welcome bark before I could see her. When I rounded the corner, she was standing behind the screen door, head cocked, listening to the sounds my shoes made in the gravel and oyster shell driveway.

"Well, hello, Max."

She turned in a circle, Wynona opening the porch door, Max scampering down the steps and jumping to my knees. Holding the bag of groceries in one hand, I used the other to scoop her up, getting an instant lick on my cheek.

"Hi, Daddy!" said Angela, sticking her head around Wynona's hip.

"Hello. I really like the welcoming. You'd think I'd been gone a couple of days, but it's only been since early this morning since I saw you all."

"Well, all us females are glad you're home. Did you find the roasted chicken? Hope they weren't sold out."

"Yes. It's in the bag. Max already knows it's in there." I set her on the grass.

Wynona came down the steps and reached for the groceries. "You want to push Angela on the swing while I set the dinner on the back table? She's been talking about you pushing her on the swing if you got home before dark."

"I can do that. Come on, Angela. Let's see if you can watch the sun setting from the high spot on the swing,"

She grinned. "Okay."

I set her in the center of the wooden swing seat and pushed, Max sniffing the grass, a few fireflies getting a head start on the night. "What'd you do today?" I asked.

"School stuff. Mama showed me how to do some numbers. And we read books."

"Did both of you read, or did Mom read for you?"

"We both read. One book was about a cat that climbed a tree and was scared to come down. A boy who lived with the cat climbed the tree to help bring her down. The cat was a girl. It crawled out on a limb so the boy couldn't reach it. The boy climbed down and told his mama. She called the firemen to help. They put up a ladder to bring the cat down. The fireman, Mama said, was the fire chief, and he told the boy he was brave to climb the tree … and one day, when he grows up, he might want to be a fireman, too."

"That sounds like a good story. The boy was doing what he could to rescue his cat. That shows he was brave."

"Like you, Daddy?"

"Sometimes. But, sometimes I'm scared, too. I just tell myself that there really is nothing to be afraid of because my mind is more powerful than fear."

Angela said nothing for a moment, the wind from the motion of the swing blowing her hair front to back and then back to front. "You were brave to save me and the other children on that big boat."

"I was more afraid for you and the other children than I was for myself. That helped me find the courage to get you out of there. Do you understand?"

"Yes." She stared at the setting sun through the branches of the Cyprus tree near the river. The reflection of cherry-red clouds drifted across the water's dark surface.

After I pushed her on the swing, we walked down to the dock, Max in the lead. Angela watched a firefly rise from the lawn, hovering a few inches over the yard, its light falling on the blades of grass. The firefly landed at the top of a dock post, its light pulsating. We stood next to the post, the firefly's glow trapped in Angela's eyes.

"Daddy, why do fireflies make light?"

"Scientists think it is one of the ways the insects talk to each other without really talking. Fireflies use their lights to find each other in the dark."

"Does that mean they're never lost?"

"I believe so."

"I never want to be lost either."

"You won't."

"The light's so pretty."

"Their light isn't like the kind in our house—the light bulb. Fireflies have a chemical reaction inside their bodies to make the light you see shining from their tummies. It's a cold light. Never gets hot like a light bulb."

"Can I touch it?"

"Sure. Just put your hand next to the firefly and see if it'll climb on a finger."

"Will it bite?"

"No."

She slowly placed her small hand on the top of the post, a half-inch away from the firefly. Its light flashed as the insect crawled onto the palm of Angela's hand. "It tickles!"

Max cocked her head and made a slight bark.

Angela stared at the firefly in the center of her hand, watching in amazement as the soft light illuminated her palm, the radiance like a yellow flame glowing in her eyes. A few seconds later, the firefly opened its wings and flew from her hand, circling Angela's head before flying toward the red trumpeter flowers, their dark green vines growing over the wooden seawall.

The firefly rose higher in the sky, its yellow light standing out in a galaxy of white stars, twinkling like specks of ice, their light cold and mysterious.

SEVENTY-SEVEN

Even with Wynona's background as an FBI agent, I didn't know whether she would fully understand my deep, internal motivation to not stop in my investigation of Andy's murder. He died a slow, horrible death. As did the other kids in Panama City Beach. It was the aberrant indifference or disregarded value of another person's life that made it my obligation to do something.

Two hours later, we'd eaten dinner, did dishes, and read Angela a bedtime story. She barely made it to the end when her eyes closed, and her breathing became steady. Wynona kissed her on the forehead and joined Max and me on the porch. The night air was balmy with the hint of honeysuckle blossoms, and the stars were white and cold on a black setting, the latter holding the secrets of the universe.

As we sipped wine, I told Wynona what I'd experienced in the last twelve hours, sharing with her my brush with the Iron Fist and my possible invitation to meet the club leader, Tank. But I spent more time telling her about what happened to my friend Tony Salazar in Mexico. I added, "Tony was fearless in Afghanistan. Not that we didn't acknowledge our mortality, we just didn't dwell on it because that would interfere with the immediate need to survive the war."

"I've only heard you mention him once. That was right before you called him at Christmas."

"It's not that I don't think about Tony, Clint, or any of the guys who made it out of there alive. Too many didn't. I was the squad leader. I took the death of any of my men hard and personally. After enduring what we went through, none of us were ever the same again. That doesn't mean we came back fighting dragons and wresting the ghosts of PTSD out of our night sweats."

"What does it mean? And, if you don't want to talk about it, I understand. I'll leave it in the past as you try to do."

"When I say that we were never the same again after those war experiences, what I mean is that worldly fears no longer influence us. What we survived was, and always will be, much greater than any assault on the senses. You don't hold resentments, because to do so would become part of the trivial. The aftermath of war—intense combat gives the survivors a hard-earned perspective on life. The human weight of fear is no longer a burden because it is not there anymore. You don't dwell on the mundane. Speaking with self-centered people in shallow conversations numbs your mind. The voices in your head are your private sentinels."

"I think all of that, as brutal and life changing as it was, made you an excellent detective after you left the military. And today, it continues to make you a private investigator who isn't afraid to look in places where evil lies in wait." She sipped her wine. "Tony, like you, Sean, is a survivor. I think that somehow, he can stay mentally strong until the DEA rescues him from the cartel."

"That's assuming they're doing it. Without negotiations of any kind, it can force actions and decisions that can't be walked back. That's on both sides, the cartel and the DEA or DOJ. Do they storm the castle, and if so, will Tony be in the crossfire, or will they let the biased news media write and broadcast supposition in lieu of facts? The results could be the same."

"I know." Her voice was soft.

"In the Army, Tony used to talk about serving and protecting others. Not in some foreign country, but at home in America. He came up on the streets of hard knocks. Through it all, Tony was a stand-up guy. A man with a strong sense of right and wrong where the line isn't crossed or compromised. He used to say, if you did that, you only double-crossed your integrity."

Wynona set her wine glass down, Max on a mat between our wicker chairs, the distant call of a whippoorwill in the cypress trees. "Clint originally came to our home asking if you'd help with a stagnant police investigation into his son's death. Clint never knew a Mexican drug cartel was making and shipping the drugs, or that the pills that killed Andy were supplied to Florida dealers by the Iron Fist. Now we learn that the

Jennifer

Durango cartel is holding hostage a DEA agent who was one of your former Delta Force team members. In terms of crime, it's a small world. Unfortunately, so much of the illegal drug trade connected to the dark side is also linked to the illusive dark web."

"Perhaps this is one for the good guys—Dave is connected, too. He has a friend in a high-level position with the DEA. Maybe Dave can get an insight into what they're doing about getting Tony out of there. I know that you don't have the connections within the FBI you once had, but do you know someone there who may have a contact inside the DOJ? Someone who can say what kind of proactive offensive they're conducting to save Tony's life?"

Wynona looked toward the river, the moon just rising above the cypress tree line. "I know one person at a senior level who might help. Whatever he tells me will be brief and not in a text message or email. Just a phone call."

"That works."

"When we go to bed tonight, I will pray for Tony and his family."

"That works even better." I smiled, and we sipped our wine, the wind chimes just starting to tinkle. "Could be a storm coming."

"It feels like it. The temperature has dropped a bit. You told me that your strategy, or your hope, is to get the leader of Iron Fist, Tank, to say something that would incriminate him or the biker club. That's going to take some finesse and tact unless you're considering other options. And if you are, you should take reinforcements."

"Clint wants to help me, but considering his and Lauren's loss of their son, I don't think that would be wise. Clint might take needless chances that could put him in the morgue."

"Maybe you could check in with your old friend Dan Grant with the Volusia County Sheriff's Department. He could have an angle—intel, on the Iron Fist that you aren't aware of, something that you could use."

"I will. In an ideal situation, I would give Dan some leads, real evidence, that he could use to bust the Iron Fist with a task force set up between his office and the Daytona Beach PD. They could work with Gainesville and Panama City PDs."

"And then you could exit the investigation, and I could set a wedding date." She smiled, reaching over and touching my hand.

"That's the goal. If I can get Tank in a neutral environment, maybe I can leverage what I know about his involvement to entice him to do what Charlie Brown did."

"And that was to point a finger at the real wizard behind the curtain. In this case, it would be the Durango cartel and Diego Navarro. When you peel the onion back to that layer, will the DEA or DOJ try to make arrests in another country—in this case, Mexico?"

"Don't know. I do know that Tony must be brought out of there soon. We don't know how much time Navarro will give him. In my squad, we didn't leave a man behind in Afghanistan or Syria. Mexico is no different."

She finished her wine, a splinter of heat lightning marbling the clouds above the national forest, a breeze jostling the wind chimes. Wynona stood. "I'm a little tired. Teaching and working in my store are causing me to use parts of my brain that don't want to be disturbed. Are you coming to bed?"

"In a little while. I'll walk Max and be back there soon."

She leaned down and kissed me softly on the lips. "Don't wait too long. I still have some energy." She smiled, playfully squeezing my hand, and left.

I thought about what Wynona had gone through since she was shot, resulting in the death of our child. When Wynona came home from the hospital, I would hear her get out of bed late at night, enter the bathroom, and close the door. Although the light coming from the threshold was dim, her sobs spoke volumes. Somber and primal cries from the pain of losing a child, not because of natural causes, but from evil. The agony was a combination of sorrow and rage so great it echoed with the shared cries of women throughout the ages who have lost a child. It was more than a cut to the heart; it was the suffering of the soul because something precious was taken that would never return. And that kind of anguish only can be understood by those women who have experienced it.

I looked down at Max on her mat. "Come here, kiddo. Let's welcome the storm together. We'll hit the grass before the rain does. I lifted Max and held her in my lap. She looked at me with her big brown eyes, like she could read my mind. Maybe somewhere in her canine mind, she sensed something primitive inside me that I couldn't see. She licked my hand, curling up in my lap. I've often felt dogs possessed their own form of sixth sense, able to discern good and evil in people. Maybe good and evil have unique odors only dogs could detect.

Those odors were being carried by dark winds over the Mexican mountains and valleys like a sulfurous gas, blowing across the border on the backs of drug mules, paid coyotes, and hustlers. From the stash houses, the drugs moved like a poison through the veins of a nation. One of the main arteries was the Iron Fist. Their clubhouse may be surrounded by a razor wire fence, but that wouldn't stop a tornado.

"Let's take a short walk outside, Max. You can do your business, and after that, we'll hit the sack." I carried Max down the porch steps, setting her in the grass. She did her requisite exploring, turning half circles before she found the perfect place to pee. The balmy air carried the sweet scent of magnolia blossoms.

As the storm clouds were building in the distance, I watched a lone firefly hover above the orange trees, carrying its tiny nightlight into a dark world. I thought about my conversation with Angela earlier when I told her how fireflies communicated.

"Fireflies can find each other in the dark."

"Does that mean they're never lost?"

"I believe so."

"I never want to be lost either."

"You won't."

"The light's so pretty."

SEVENTY-EIGHT

Axle had a life-changing decision to make. To make it, he smoked weed, sitting on the bottom step leading up to the wooden deck at the back of his ex-wife's rural house. He took a long drag, holding the smoke deep in his lungs, thinking about his decision. As much as he craved revenge against Tank, Axle wanted his reputation restored.

He didn't think he could get vengeance and restore his reputation, too. "Gotta be one or the other," he muttered, releasing the cannabis smoke through his nostrils. He watched a black widow spider in a wood pile a few feet away. The spider's shiny exterior looked like wet coal in the morning sunlight. Axle could see the bright red hourglass shape on the underside of the spider's abdomen. He stared at the spider, taking another hit of weed.

After a few seconds, he whispered, "Hey ugly spider, I hear you kill and eat your mate after having sex. That's kinda like it is sometimes in the human world, too. Why do you think you got that name ... black widow? You got a nasty reputation." He held the joint in one hand and picked up a stick with the other, raising it over his head and bringing it down hard on the spider. He savagely attacked the spider and its web, striking a dozen times until the stick broke, spittle flying from his open mouth, strands of the sticky web clinging to the stick.

"Daddy, what are you doing?"

He looked up to the top step. His eight-year-old daughter was standing there with a lop-eared rabbit in her arms. A thin string of saliva dribbled from Axle's mouth onto his chin. "Killin' a spider." He dropped the remaining part of the stick onto the weeds and wiped his chin with the back of his hand.

"Is it poisonous?"

302

"It was. Dead now." He took a final drag of the weed, climbed the steps, and blew the smoke into the rabbit's face.

"No, Daddy! Thumper hates that."

The screen door opened, and a woman stepped onto the deck. Her eyes were puffy from lack of sleep. She was a bottle blonde. Bed hair like an angry porcupine, a tress stuck to her left cheek. Short shorts. A tattoo on her hip visible through the hole in the jean fabric. No bra under a tight T-shirt, the words *The Fox Hole,* on the front, an image of a smiling female fox, batting long eyelashes.

The woman stared at Axle. "I told you not to blow weed smoke into the bunny's face. That's bullshit stuff, Axle. You sit out here and get stoned, then get violent."

"I didn't hurt the damn rabbit. When I was a kid, we used to hunt 'em. Good eatin' and better than deer meat."

The girl stared at her father through wounded eyes. She backed away, holding the rabbit tighter. Her mother looked at her. "Get in the house, Kristi." The child said nothing, opening the screen door, vanishing inside. "Axle, pack your shit and get outta here."

"C'mon, Robin. It was nothing. No reason to get your panties in a wad. You want me to roll you one?"

"No! I want you to roll your ass outta here. I'm taking a risk—you hanging out here, considering all the crap that's happened between you and the Iron Fist. Last night in the club, one of the girls, after she did a lap dance for a biker, told her that Tank put a hit out on you."

"That's bullshit! I would know. Drywall would tell me. The Fist doesn't bring in outsiders to put out hits. They do stuff internal. I'm gonna call Tank."

"And say what? Beg to get back with the Fist?"

"No. I met a dude who's got a hard on to screw Tank into a six-foot hole in the ground. Tank believed that garbage about me, thinking I was a police plant. The guy I met is gunning for Tank because some of the drugs the Fist sold killed his friend's son."

"Where'd you meet this person?"

"He came here. Walked out of the woods quietly, like an Indian or some kinda ghost and he—"

"Go! Just go! If this ghost man can find you here, so can others. I won't have you around Kristi anymore. It's too dangerous. Go or I'm calling the cops, or maybe I'll call Tank."

"Kiss my ass, Robin." He turned and headed toward the shed. As he walked by the vegetable garden, he glanced at the pumpkin with the large hole in it. Inside the shed, he started to crank his Harley but paused as his ex-wife went back inside the trailer, locking the door. Axle made a call to the only real friend he had left in the world. "Drywall, it's me. Are you in the clubhouse?"

"Yeah. Why?"

"Level with me, okay? Did Tank put out a hit on me, giving it to the members or even the guys who retired?"

"No. At least I haven't heard that. And I ought to know."

"That's what I thought. I got some information to share with him to prove I'm not some kinda snitch or cop who's infiltrated the club. I wanna tell Tank about some real trouble brewing."

"What kind of trouble?"

"A big guy. Tall as Tank but not as wide. He's like a soldier on a mission. The dude's blaming the Fist and Tank for the drug overdose death of his best friend's son."

"We'll chew him up and spit him out if he comes around here."

"Listen to me, Drywall. There is somethin' about this dude … he comes across like a guy who can see inside your mind. I know it sounds weird. It's like he's on a mission and ain't nobody gonna stop him 'til he's got his hands around Tank's neck."

"What's this man's name?"

"That's one of the things I need to tell Tank."

"When you wanna meet with him?"

"Today. I don't think he can afford to wait."

"Let me talk to him. He's back in the office. Maybe the smoke between y'all has cleared since he originally fingered you to be workin' with the FBI."

Axle sat on the back of his motorcycle, his thoughts slowing from the THC in his bloodstream. "Drywall. We hung thousands of feet of sheetrock together. You taught me a skill when nobody else would give me the time of day. We're like brothers. All I want is to restore my reputation and gain a little respect back. I can do that with the information I need to share with Tank. If he doesn't listen to me … I got a feelin' he's about to be hit hard upside the head by a baseball bat."

"You think this guy you're talking about is a cop, FBI maybe?"

"Hell no. I think he's a hired gun, and he's got Tank in his sights."

"I'll talk to him. Don't come here 'til I call you."

SEVENTY-NINE

A thin luster of morning dew was on the planks when I walked down L-dock to meet with Dave Collins. Two white pelicans sailed above the marina water, which looked slate gray under an overcast sky. I looked across the bay—the Halifax River, and I could see a slight chop building as a crab fishing boat chugged its way toward Ponce Inlet, a smudge of smoke trailing from its exhaust pipes. The air was laced with the smell of salt and creosote. Seagulls flew above the sailboat masts, smiling, as only gulls can, greeting a new day.

I came closer to Dave's trawler, *Gibraltar* and Nick's boat, *St. Michael*. Nick stood near the transom, a mug of coffee in one brown fist. Two gulls circled twenty feet above his head. He looked up at me and grinned. "Mornin' Sean. These gulls are like stray dogs that won't go away. Always lookin' for a handout. They think I'm gonna clean some fish, and they come flyin' around me like bats outta hell."

"I got used to thinking that seagulls were your pets. I have Max, and you have a whole flock."

"Max doesn't poop on your cockpit."

"Not since she was a puppy."

"You can't train gulls. They'll laugh back at you." He grinned, sipping black coffee. "Wanna cup? It's all Greek. None better on this side of Mykonos."

"I'm supposed to meet Dave about now."

He shrugged his thick shoulders. "Okay. I'll bring over a bag of fresh ground beans and we'll make a pot in *Gibraltar's* galley. Dave loves this stuff."

***

Ten minutes later, we were sitting at the round table on Dave's trawler, sipping black coffee and eating Greek pastries laced with honey. Before driving to Ponce Marina, I had gone online to read every news report I could on the abduction of Tony Salazar and on the history of the Durango cartel. I had a good idea of how it happened. What I didn't know was whether Tony was still alive.

I brought Dave and Nick up to speed with most of what I'd experienced recently and added, "Clint Ward and I spent three years with Tony and others in our squad trying hard not to be captured by the Taliban or ISIS."

Nick said, "And now, all these years later, Tony's abducted by Mexicans or at least a Mexican drug cartel."

Dave set his coffee cup on a cork coaster and leaned back from the table. "There is a dramatic and sad irony to this. Tony survives multiple tours of duty in some of the world's most dangerous places, works out of the DEA's San Diego office in relative safety, and then heads back into a foreign country where he's abducted by a Mexican drug cartel. There are dozens of DEA agents working undercover in Mexico. Why Tony? Why did the cartel choose him?"

I leaned in closer, the sound of a metal halyard clanking against a sailboat mast. "My guess would be that someone, one of the assets that Tony recruited, had somehow breached or was discovered by the cartel. That's only a guess. When Tony comes out of that hell hole, I'll ask him."

Dave nodded. "When you began this investigation, it was about Andy Ward and finding the human scum who sold him the fentanyl. That would have been good 'ol Charlie Brown. Brown's plea bargain would help to indict members of the Iron Fist. And, digging deeper into culpability, members of the Durango cartel should be held accountable, too. I suppose that part of the crime—the people who made the pills with fentanyl, is almost untouchable considering the amount of corruption within the Mexican government, police, and military."

Nick grunted. "Maybe the DEA can go in there and storm the place, rescuing Tony. They'd need to leave so much damage that other drug cartels would think twice before capturing a DEA agent ever again."

Dave nodded. "The challenge with storming the fortress is that Tony Salazar would most likely die in the process. These Mexican drug cartels have their own paramilitary forces. Because they rake in billions of dollars, they can afford the best in terms of guns and men. Their arsenal and firepower would make many nations pale by comparison. The irony, in this perpetual *war on drugs,* is that most of those guns, 50-caliber armor-piercing weapons and others, were made here in the U.S. What are your thoughts, Sean?"

"I think Tony's life is in the hands of career politicians who are more interested in appearing on cable news, faking sincerity, and fundraising, than in doing anything substantial—like saving one of their own. They're all quick to tell us about the problems without offering or committing to real solutions. A few cabinet members, for instance, traveled down to the southern border, did photo-ops, talked in vague soundbites, then went back to Washington and ignored the problem they created."

Dave chuckled. "You're too subtle. How do you really feel?"

"I feel like Tony's life is on the line, and he's about to be another political football. If, or when, the DOJ fumbles this one, Tony will be dead."

"What the hell can you do?" Nick asked, a crumb from the Greek pastry at the corner of his thick moustache.

"I don't know." I eyed Dave. "You mentioned that you have a friend in the DEA. Can you contact him to see if he'll, off the record, give you an assessment of what the DEA or the DOJ is doing for Tony?"

"I'll make the call, and I'll do it while you're here."

My phone buzzed on the table. I looked at the screen, recognizing the area code and the number. It was from the Gainesville PD. I answered and Detective Winston Porter said, "O'Brien, since you're working as a PI for the Ward family, thought you might want to know what went down last night."

I instantly thought of Brittany Harmon. "What happened?"

"We found Charlie Brown. Or to be more precise, we found his body. A cemetery worker found it propped up at the base of an oak tree. Throat was slit. But the killer or killers weren't content with that. They cut out his tongue. It was probably meant to be a message—*don't be a snitch.* Maybe it's the Iron Fist. But right now, we don't have witnesses or evidence beyond the body. Whoever killed Brown left him on display, sitting next to an oak tree like he was watching over the graveyard. Talk later." He clicked off.

EIGHTY

One mile from the Iron Fist clubhouse, Axle decided to make what he liked to call a *pit stop*. He pulled his Harley into a gas station parking lot, entered the men's room, and locked the door. He opened a plastic baggie, pouring two lines of cocaine on the counter next to the sink. He rolled up a dollar bill, inserting it into his right nostril, pressing one finger to the left side of his nose, black dirt under the nail. He snorted the cocaine. Then he reversed the process, staring bleary-eyed into the mirror. "Just look Tank in the eye and tell it like it is," he mumbled.

A few minutes later, he was at the closed gate in front of the Iron Fist clubhouse. He put his Harley in neutral, revving the engine once, looking directly into the surveillance camera mounted on a steel post to the left. The gate began to open, the gears in the motor squeaking. Axle drove onto the lot, parking in a spot next to the candy apple red Fat Boy.

The door opened, and Drywall came outside. He was in his early fifties, beard the color of butter, deep-set eyes that were like emeralds catching the sunlight through an opening in a cave. He pulled out a pack of cigarettes from his shirt pocket. "Wanna smoke?"

Axle took it. "Thanks."

Drywall screwed an unfiltered cigarette into the corner of his mouth and lit it, passing the lighter to Axle who did the same. Drywall blew smoke from his nostrils and coughed. "Like I said on the phone, Tank's interested in hearing what you gotta say. He told me the clubhouse would be a neutral ground, meaning he won't screw with you. Least not here. Depending on what you tell him, maybe never."

"Fair 'nough." Axle took a deep drag from the cigarette, the effects of the cocaine kicking up his adrenaline. Even in the face of a threat like Tank and an army of Iron Fist members, he felt invincible. "Let's do this."

They dropped their cigarettes on the pavement and crushed the remains under their black riding boots. The men walked inside the building. About a dozen club members were there. "What's up, Axle," said a wiry biker walking over to the bar. "Digger, you got any Coors in the cooler."

Digger nodded. "Yep. Not much demand for that most days. We got six cases in the back room." He pulled a can of Coors from the cooler, popped the top, and set it on the bar. He eyed Axle and Drywall. "Good to see you, Ax. Wanna drink? I'd wager you could use one."

"Hold it 'til after I talk with Tank. Then I'll buy you a drink, Digger." He faked a smile.

"Sounds good. What about you, Drywall?"

"Think I'll shoot a game of pool while Axle sets the record straight with Tank." He looked at Axle and gestured with his head. "Go on back there. He's waiting for you."

Axle headed to a side door about thirty feet beyond the bar. He had to walk by the casket next to a wall filled with Iron Fist colors and badges. He entered the private area and moved down the hall to the last door on the right. He knocked. The door opened, and a tall biker with a Mohawk haircut and a ship's anchor tattooed on the side of his neck under the left earlobe stood there. "What's goin' on Axle?"

"Same ol' same ol'."

Tank stood up from behind his solid wood desk, a water stain marking its glass top. "Better not be the same ol' same ol' shit. Damn, the scar is healing up good. That's better than any tat you'll ever get, Axle. You oughta be singing my praises. Drywall tells me you got news I can use. Information that will take the noose off your skinny neck."

"That's right. And I wanted to bring it directly to you, Tank. No middleman gettin' shit screwed up. I wanna tell it to you just like I heard it and find a piece of common ground we both can stand on, man. That's all."

Tank looked at the man with the Mohawk. "Search him."

Axle stepped inside the office and lifted his arms. Mohawk man patted Axle down, opened his long sleeve shirt, and lifted his T-shirt. "Turn around, dog breath." Axle complied as the biker continued the search.

Mohawk looked over to Tank. "He's clean."

"All right, Axle. Whatcha you got?"

Another biker, a guy called Bulldog, because of his round face, double chin, and wide-set eyes, sat in a metal folding chair. He stared at Axle like a cat might gaze at a fledgling bird beyond the window.

Axle cleared his throat. "This guy I'm gonna tell you about came out of nowhere and approached me in the backyard of my ol lady's house. I got no idea how he found me. Anyway, here's the deal. He's a big guy. No fat. All muscle. Looks like he spent time in the military. He shoots well."

"Did he try to pop you?" Tank asked.

"No, he slipped up on me when I was taking a piss in the yard. He shot a pumpkin ten feet away from me."

"A pumpkin? Sounds like a bad ass to me." His men snickered.

"Hear me out. He held a gun on me. The dude might be a hit man. Said he was there 'cause the only son of his best friend died from a fentanyl overdose. He said he served in the military in Afghanistan with his friend. The dead dude was Andy Ward, a college student in Gainesville. This guy is blaming the kid's death on the Fist and you, Tank."

Tank grinned. "That would be a hard case to prove. Last we heard, the ol' boy who used to distribute for us up in Gainesville and the Florida Panhandle, the college towns, had an unfortunate accident. Looks like he fell on his sword. Cut himself real bad. Maybe somebody rolled him, took his money, and decided to carve him up."

Axle took a deep breath, making a dry swallow. "This guy was pumping me for information about you. Told him I didn't know shit, and he could go on and shoot me. He wanted me to tell him about you. I told the peckerhead there wasn't nothin' to tell except for the fact that, if he kept on, Tank would skin him alive. After that, whatever was left would be dropped into a barrel of acid."

"Bet you scared him."

"Hell, yeah. He backed off. Before he left, the guy gave me his card and said it would be in my best interest to call him if I saw you or if I heard anything about you."

"That sounds federal to me. Maybe he's FBI."

"He had no badge and showed no ID. Plus, he pulled on me. That pumpkin coulda been my head." Axle reached in his shirt pocket and took out the card. He set it on Tank's desk and took a small step backward.

Tank picked up the card, reading the name. "Sean O'Brien." He took a deep breath, setting the card down, clenching both fists, looking into space.

"You know this dude?" Axle asked.

"No, but I will. I'm gonna pinch his head off like I'd do a beetle."

"I know you can take care of yourself, but if I was gonna jump him, I'd have somebody to watch my back."

"Sounds like he put the fear of God in you."

Axle shook his head. "I've come across a lot of dudes who acted like bad asses. Most of them were anything but that. This guy, though ... this O'Brien, he doesn't puff his chest out and talk shit. There's something in his eye that is cold and calculating, like he'd cut your heart out and shove it in your dying mouth if you messed with him. I guess that's why his friend brought him in to help find out who killed his boy."

Tank slammed his palm down on the desk. His jawline was like concrete, eyes filled with a mix of anger and reprisal. "Enough! Nobody *killed* his boy. Nobody forced him to take the pills. He killed himself. Must have been suicide." He looked over at the biker in the chair. "Bulldog, go fetch me Digger. Bring that old man's bony ass back here. We got something to settle."

EIGHTY-ONE

My call went to a place I didn't want it to go. Straight to Brittany Harmon's voicemail. I waited for the prompt. "Brittany, it's Sean O'Brien. I don't know whether you heard, but the police found Charlie Brown's body. He'd been murdered. Please call me when you get this message." I clicked off and looked across the table at Dave and Nick.

"This isn't looking good," Dave said, getting up to refill his cup with black coffee.

Nick blew out a breath. "Sean, you think this guy's killer is comin' for Brittany?"

"I don't know. That would depend on whether Brown told the killer or killers about his meeting with Brittany and the fact that she taped their conversation. If he was killed by the Iron Fist, they'd only come for her if they thought Brittany could implicate them in Brown's fentanyl distribution and sales. But the Iron Fist wasn't brought up in the conversation between Brown and Brittany—only Andy's death and the fact that Brown sold the fentanyl to Andy, making Brown culpable."

Dave nodded. "But a weasel like Charlie Brown never accepts responsibility. They always blame someone else for their actions. Regardless of whatever plea deal he was making with police and prosecutors, dead men can't testify. A biker gang, like the Iron Fist, can keep doing what they do if there are dead victims and no witness to show up in court. Combine that with no evidence pointing to their responsibility, even though they're pushing pills mixed with a drug that's a hundred times more lethal than heroin, resulting in a form of genocide."

Nick wrapped one of his large hands over the top of his blue mug, like he wanted to break it in his palm. "Thugs like that are cut from the same kind of evil gene that created the Nazi death camps where millions of innocent people were gassed to death."

Dave looked from *Gibraltar's* open-air salon to a sixty-foot Hatteras leaving its berth on M-dock. "Sean, do you think you will hear from Axle?"

"I think every time he stares in a mirror, he'll be motivated. But I believe his fear … fear for himself and his daughter, will keep him from testifying. Will he take a chance and call me with more intel? Maybe. That might depend on whether his resentment against Tank builds or scars over like those slashes on his face."

"Based on your conversations in the Midnight Rider bar with Digger, and to some extent—Captain Kidd, do you think you'll be invited into the Iron Fist clubhouse to have a beer with Tank?"

"I don't know."

"If the invitation is extended, would you go?"

"I'd try to have that beer away from their clubhouse. Playing the part of the reluctant recruit, makes them want you more. It's like a football coach trying to get a player he saw score an impossible touchdown."

Nick grinned. "And for you, that touchdown you scored was puttin' the big fella on his butt inside the Midnight Rider."

"It's interesting how a word-of-mouth story sometimes becomes a bigger snowball the more it's told. With Digger and the other bar patrons who saw it, I hope Tank hears that I single-handedly fought off a rival biker gang. I'm more valuable then."

Dave stared at the surface of his coffee before eyeing me. "What are the odds that Axle would let the Iron Fist know you showed up with an offer that he refused? He might use that as leverage to get back into Tank's good graces."

"There's nothing good about Tank, and he has no graces. I thought about those odds when I walked up to Axle behind that trailer he's sharing with his ex and their daughter. I wanted to gauge the anger he had for Tank before I went further. It was like the hundreds of interrogations I conducted working homicide, playing one culprit off the other. Rats eat their own. I think Axle, clean and sober, wouldn't contact his former biker gang. But, if he's using cocaine or some stimulant in a pill, or if he finds false courage in his bong pipe, he may reach out to them. Probably through a club member who Axle believes will share a confidence."

Nick shook his head. "I know you don't go to the casinos in Florida to gamble, Sean, but you're takin' a helluva gamble to penetrate this biker gang. Now, you have a family."

"Everything I do is to get justice for Andy and for those eight other college kids. To bring some closure to Clint, Lauren, and the other families. The more I focus on these deaths, I'm seeing a wider problem and a greater reach into a darker spectrum. It not only includes biker gangs and the Mexican drug lords, but also China for shipping the chemicals into Mexico to make fentanyl. The devastation caused really bothers me."

Dave nodded. "When you look at 107,000 deaths from fentanyl in America last year and almost as many the year before, you ask three things. The first is why is this happening? Second, who's allowing it? And third, what can be done to stop it?"

I said nothing.

Dave picked up his phone. "I'm calling my DEA contact. You might want to remain here, Sean, just in case he has questions or says something that could lead to another road."

EIGHTY-TWO

Inside the Iron Fist clubhouse, Tank was coming unglued. He stood behind his desk, which looked more like a butcher's table under a piece of glass, glaring at Axle and Digger. "This shit doesn't happen in my chapter," he said, nostrils flaring, face red with fury.

Digger lifted his hands, palms up. "Like I said, Tank, I didn't know. All I know is what I saw. Figured the guy had what it takes to be a member of the Fist. Then I told you about him."

"This was after you told him about us. I'll never know all the things you said to him after knocking back booze at the Midnight Rider. Digger, I trusted your judgment. You tell me about some tough guy who you think could be a club member. I agree to meet him. A little later, Axle calls Drywall and tells him he has information I need to hear." He cut his eyes over to Axle. "And what this pissant tells me is a guy called Sean O'Brien, who sounds just like the guy you met, walks up like an Indian outta the woods while Axle's takin a leak and pulls on him."

Axle shook his head. "I had no idea that Digger had met with the guy earlier. Had I known—"

"You'd have done what?" bellowed Tank.

Digger folded his arms, a sore bleeding on his forearm next to a tat of a Harley-Davidson logo. "Lemme clear something up, Tank. I didn't meet with O'Brien or Shooter or anyone else. I was just sittin' on a barstool when the guy came up, sat, and ordered a beer. He musta pissed off Tennessee in the parkin' lot because Tennessee came inside like a pit bull, cocking his leg on what he called his barstool. Shooter looked at Tennessee like he was a fly. He hit Tennessee so hard and fast, I barely saw it, and I was sitting right by them. After that, Shooter and I struck up a conversation. So, there was no planned meeting. And anyway, how do we know we're talking about the same dude?"

"I don't give a rat's ass how you met him," Tank shouted. "He gave you a phone number—give it to me." Tank grabbed the napkin from Digger and picked up O'Brien's card. "Same damn phone number. You were played, Digger. Figures 'cause you're too damn old and senile to know the difference anymore. You're out of the club." Tank pulled out a knife and set it in the center of his desk, glancing across the room to Mohawk and Bulldog. "Mo, take this knife and cut the colors off Digger's back. Bulldog, take Axle out back. You and Bear slap some sense into him for showing his face on TV."

Digger took off his leather jacket, throwing it onto one of the metal folding chairs. "In more than forty years of riding, after being in three clubs, I was gonna retire out of the Fist and take my grandson on some fishin' trips. Never has anyone cut my colors off. You won't be the first, Tank." He turned around and walked out of the office and down the hall.

"You want me to go get him?" asked Bulldog.

Tank shook his head. "Let the old fart go. It's a damn shame he gets connived by this O'Brien and invites him over here to sing kumbaya."

Tank stared hard at Axle as Bulldog and Mohawk came up beside him. "I'm gonna make this real clear to you Axle. I appreciate you coming to me with the shit about O'Brien. But he never should have found you. After you get your ass kicked around, you get on your bike, fill the tank up with gas, and ride 'til it's almost empty, and do it again. Get the hell out of Florida."

"Tank, I was trying to do the right thing by the club. I contacted you soon as this guy came to my ex's trailer. That's not my fault. I just wanted to help and get back in the club."

"That ain't gonna happen. Listen to me. If we find you hanging out in the four-county area, we'll take you into the glades. We got a spot down there called the prayin' tree. It's a big ol' cypress tree in about three feet of black swamp water. As the sun goes down, we tie bad boys like you to the tree and leave 'em there. In twenty to thirty minutes, the gators come in and start with your legs. They grab a hold and break one off like you'd snatch a drumstick. Next, they'll chew off your balls, workin' their way up to your guts. What the gators leave behind, and it ain't much, the turtles and bugs eat up like a smorgasbord. That's where we're gonna take this O'Brien fella when we find him. Deep into the glades to the prayin' tree."

Axle stood straight, his heart racing. "What if I reach out to O'Brien. Set up a meeting. You guys can jump him and carry the dude down to the glades."

"You'd screw up a wet dream." Tank cut his eyes over to Mohawk. "Go down the hall and get Trucker."

"Okay."

He left. Tank said nothing, staring at Axle, admiring the scar on his face. In less than a minute, Trucker entered the office, Mohawk following. Tank slid a business card to the edge of his desk. "Guy's name is Sean O'Brien. Find out everything you can about him, from the time in his mama's womb up 'til today. I wanna know his background, probably military, and I wanna know if he's got a family. Especially a pretty lil' wife."

EIGHTY-THREE

I was impressed because Dave got a call back within fifteen minutes of leaving a message for an assistant administrator in the DEA. After thirty seconds of small talk, Dave got down to business. "Dale, I wanted to let you know that I'm sitting on my boat with a close friend. His name is Sean O'Brien. He's former Delta Force—Middle East and Afghanistan. Worked in law enforcement after that. One of Sean's former Delta Force squad members is Tony Salazar."

Dave paused, listening to the man on the phone and then said, "Yes. Correct." Dave told him about Clint Ward's military background, also mentioning the death of Andy. "So, Dale, you can see the extreme interest that both Sean and Clint have in the situation with Tony Salazar. These former soldiers are the embodiment, the true essence, of a band of brothers. They left no one behind in the mountains of Afghanistan or the deserts of Syria. They want to make sure that the same energy and commitment is being made to extract Salazar out of Mexico."

Dave listened, nodding. "Yes. I understand. However, as you know, Tony Salazar is becoming a political pawn. If the Durango cartel kills him, don't count on the Mexican government sending their miliary into cartel territory to do anything. Under the current conditions between Washington and Mexico City, it won't happen." Dave paused. "Okay. Can I put you on speakerphone so you can tell Sean yourself?"

He nodded and pressed a button on his phone.

"Dale, you're on speakerphone. Sean O'Brien, say hello to my old friend, Dale Lovell. Dale worked in the CIA before accepting a position at the DEA."

"Dale, thanks for talking with me." Nick got up and poured another mug of coffee.

"Sean, first let me say thank you for your service. I'm sure what you, Tony, Clint, and the others did in Delta Force over there was heroic, to put it mildly. As I mentioned to Dave, the DEA, through the oversight of the DOJ, is taking a very aggressive stance in getting Tony out of there. Problem is … we're not sure where Diego Navarro is holding Tony. The Durango cartel has dozens of small farms and the equivalent of stash houses under their control. Hell, they have small towns under their control. None of the native Mexicans are talking because there is absolutely no trust among them. The cartel is known for decapitating their enemies, putting the heads on spikes, and grotesquely displaying them like something out of medieval England."

"I understand. You said the DEA is taking a very aggressive stance in getting Tony out. What do you mean by that?"

"Our team in Mexico City, working through channels in Washington, is in contact with Navarro, reminding him that it is in his best interest to release Tony or there will be consequences."

"The threat of unspecified *consequences* doesn't scare a gang of like-minded psychopaths. Swift and severe action does. Since the president won't overtly negotiate with terrorists and drug cartels, can the DOJ or the DEA get a message to Diego Navarro? You can tell him that the U.S. government will not send in a clandestine hit squad, men who *will* find their way to Navarro, if Tony is released unharmed. They can take him to some remote part of the Durango state border to release him. At that point, we'll call it a draw, each party going their separate ways. At the same time, meaning now, we covertly send in a Special Ops hit squad to get Tony out of there. Navarro is like a high-strung horse, an animal that will spook easily. When he does, he'll start shooting people in the head. Tony will be first."

There was an eight second pause. "I appreciate your suggestions, Sean. I'll pass them on to people with a higher pay grade than me. Hopefully, they'll listen and send in a Special Ops team. I agree with you. Thank you. Guys, I need to get to a meeting. I'll stay in touch. Talk soon. Dave." He clicked off.

Nick sat back at the table with a fresh mug of coffee. "I wouldn't bet on the horse that fella is riding."

I looked over at Dave. "What did Dale do in the CIA before he joined the DEA?"

"For the most part, he was an intel analyst. Let's give him the benefit of the doubt. Dale can be persuasive. After listening to you, I hope he kicks it up a notch and convinces admin to pull together a Special Ops force, whether it's Army or a Seal Team, guys who can go in there like they are penetrating enemy lines undetected and get the job done."

I said nothing, thinking about serving overseas with Tony, remembering what a patriot he was … and is. My phone buzzed on the table. Wynona calling. I answered, and she said, "I spoke with my old friend Ed Lambert in the FBI's Washington office. He said the Bureau isn't involved in the Tony Salazar case because the DOJ or the White House is keeping it in the purview of the DEA. It's their baby … one that I hope they don't throw out with the bathwater as this thing becomes a political football."

"Did he offer any suggestions?"

"No. He said that the last time one of the Mexican drug cartels abducted a DEA agent it had a horrible ending. He added that, with fentanyl bought and sold on smart phones, it's emboldened the cartels, making the DEA's job very difficult. Where are you now?"

"With Dave and Nick on *Gibraltar*. Dave's contact in the DEA said they're taking an aggressive stance on getting Tony out of there alive. That aggressive stance means that the DEA's office in Mexico City is juggling balls in the air."

"Do they know where Tony is being held?"

"No."

"The White House should send an Army in there."

"You just gave me an idea."

"Well, I'm glad my phone call wasn't all bad news."

"It wasn't. I'll call you back as soon as I can."

"Okay."

I clicked off and looked up at Dave. "How connected are you to the Pentagon?"

***

Tank stood next to a large computer monitor in one of the rooms that the Iron Fist used to sell drugs online and within their distribution network. All financial transactions were completed through multiple routers on the dark web. The man called Trucker looked up from his keyboard and screen. He blinked like a gnat was flying in front of his face.

"Tank, here's the deal on this guy O'Brien. Not a helluva lot online. He has no social media presence at all. There are references to his military service in a couple of Miami Herald news stories back when O'Brien was a homicide detective down there. Part of the story indicated he had the best arrest and conviction record in the police department history. Information from a story in a local Daytona Beach newspaper points out that O'Brien helped Volusia County cops solve a serial murder case known as the Mermaid Killer."

"I remember something about that. So, O'Brien helped the cops catch this guy."

"No, he helped them find the dude. But, when the cops got there, the so-called Mermaid Killer was dead. The news story doesn't say that O'Brien killed him in self-defense. There is a Jeep Wrangler and a 38-foot boat, a Bayliner registered in his name. Boat is listed as *Jupiter*. But there is no address. Only a P.O. box. If he owns a house, his name's not on record in the three-county area. He could own a house under another name, or the deed might be listed under some corporate name. The dude keeps a low profile. Remember that guy who went by the name Barnacle?"

"Yeah. Didn't he work in a marina?"

"He works in a lot of 'em. He's a freelancer. He does boat cleaning. He'll SCUBA dive around the hull of a yacht and use tools to knock of any growth, stuff like barnacles. I got in touch with him. He said he worked on a boat called *Jupiter* in Ponce Marina. Said O'Brien hired him. He told me that O'Brien called his boat an antique and said that was fine 'cause his fiancée owns an antique shop in DeLand."

EIGHTY-FOUR

I thought about the human psychology of revenge and how those dark roots have spread into global conflict. Sometimes war. The Defense Department has shied away from the war on drugs because there is no territory to be conquered and no money to be made for the military industrial complex. Maybe there was one general with the Pentagon who might have a different agenda. A bone to pick.

I looked across the table at Nick and Dave. "Before Andy Ward was killed from fentanyl, before the eight college kids died the same way, some cadets out of West Point were on spring break in Fort Lauderdale. News stories indicate a half dozen of them were treated for acute fentanyl poisoning. Three were put on ventilators. Two suffered brain damage."

Dave nodded. "I read about that."

"You think the fentanyl came from the same source … the Iron Fist?" Nick asked.

"Maybe, since Florida is one of their states. What matters even more is that the deadly pills were made in Mexico and sold to distributors like the Iron Fist. I read that a four-star general serving in the Pentagon is the father of one of those cadets who suffered brain damage. Maybe the general could pull some strings and put together a small but powerful team. No more than six men, mercenaries, consultants, and former Special Ops. What matters is that they're warriors, guys who know how to successfully conduct extraction missions."

Nick grinned. "Sean, what you're suggesting sounds like something out of a Hollywood movie."

"The best movies are adapted from real life."

Dave removed his bifocals and used a paper napkin to clean them. "Your suggestion, without the authorization from the president, could result in the four-star general being stripped of his rank, tenure, pension, job, and maybe even face a military tribunal. Although I like the idea because this general would have a strong incentive to destroy those who severely hurt his son. Revenge is hardwired into many people."

Nick nodded. "It sure as hell gives the general a reason to hit back hard. The man's son is messed up for life. If I had a child, and if someone poisoned him or her—left the kid like a vegetable, I'd be a scorched earth kind of dad. Revenge would be sweet."

Dave folded his arms across his chest. "Sometimes. But the question remains, once the vengeance is carried out, the actual retaliation, what are the long-term effects of that revenge?"

Nick shrugged. "None, probably."

Dave glanced at me. "Sean, you might disagree, but there are psychological side-effects stemming from acts of revenge. Researchers who study this sort of thing have discovered that, instead of bringing closure, satiating the anger, the ghost of revenge remains because it prolongs the memory—the foulness of the original offense."

I said nothing.

Dave looked across the marina, gulls snickering, props from a 50-foot Bertram yacht churning the water. "When I was with the CIA, we certainly leveraged vengeance to play adversaries against one another. But the long-term effects were not unlike watching the mafia self-destruct. One hit leads to another, and the settlement of scores—real and manufactured, is endless. The wounds aren't allowed to heal."

Nick nodded. "It's everywhere. People are no longer tolerant when it comes to differences of opinion."

Dave eyed me. "I have no doubt that a U.S. Army general, a man used to battle, would enjoy revenge against those who caused his son to have brain damage. But sanctioning a half dozen men to take on the Durango cartel appears to be beyond the scope of personal vengeance."

Nick leaned forward, his thick eyebrows arched, eyes playful. "Sean, do you think six men would be all it'd take?"

"If it's the right men, yes."

"Sign me up. I'll go. Maybe we approach them by sea. I can get us there."

Dave chuckled. "You'd have to go through the Panama Canal and up the Pacific side. Durango is closer to the Pacific than the Gulf of Mexico. Sean, would you be one of the six?"

"Yes."

324

"That might result in a suicide mission for some, if not all, of the team. How would you approach Wynona with something like that?"

"First, I wouldn't label it a suicide mission. It would be a clandestine extraction. The element of surprise is crucial. Once we have the coordinates as to where they're holding Tony, we plan the approach. Could be that the best assault would be late at night when most of Navarro's guys are asleep or drunk."

Nick placed his wide hands on the table, palms down. "Do like my ancient Greek ancestors did when fightin' the Spartans in the battle of Troy. The Spartans thought the giant horse was a gift from the goddess Athena. Once inside the gates, at night, the Greek soldiers slipped out of the horse, and the rest is history."

Dave smiled. "It's most likely mythology, not history, but your point is well taken. Sean, the Mexican state of Durango is huge. Unless the DEA down there has solid intel, a team of six men could crisscross the state for days and not find one sign of Tony."

"Maybe that's where the general could enter the scene."

"In what respect?"

"Without committing a Special Ops team, he might have access to satellite and infrared imagery that could point to an area where Tony may be held captive."

"Indeed. For that matter, the CIA and NSA could have that, if it exists. I can make some calls on your behalf. See what stones I might uncover."

"Thanks, Dave."

"In the meantime, what are you going to do about the Iron Fist, considering what happened to Charlie Brown? Where does the investigation go?"

"To law enforcement. That's if I can find something for them to enforce. Although the police suspect criminal activities are going on in biker gangs, they'll need something far beyond probable cause to move. Witnesses, like Axle, even Digger, should he have a change of attitude, are hesitant to say anything because they fear retaliation. It leaves the pool of witnesses rather shallow—or empty."

My phone buzzed. I recognized the number. It was the number that Digger had written on the bar napkin. "Speaking of Digger. He's calling."

I answered.

EIGHTY-FIVE

There was a three second pause. I could hear a boat horn in the distance, the shadow of two pelicans soaring over *Gibraltar's* cockpit. "O'Brien! You're an asshole. You lied to me. When we were havin' a beer in the Midnight Rider, I asked you if you were a cop. You looked me dead in the eye and said *no.* I trusted you."

I mentally noted he said my last name. "I'm not a cop."

"Then I go back to the Iron Fist clubhouse and pitch you as a possible new member. Tank was on the fence but ready to meet you. Then comes in an ex-club member, Axle, who tells Tank you're hunting for him. Axle said you came up behind him in his ex-wife's backyard, pulled your gun, and pumped him for information about the Iron Fist and Tank. I know you're an FBI agent and—"

"Stop! Just wait a minute, Digger. I told you the truth. I'm not a cop or an FBI agent. What I am is someone doing a favor for a man who fought the Taliban with me. His son died from fentanyl—a one-pill-kill. The drug was sold by the Iron Fist to a dealer, who then sold it to Andy Ward. That was his name. Twenty-one-years old. In the bar, I told you about him being scouted by the majors. What I didn't tell you was that his life was cut short because he took one pill for pain. The pill was supposed to have been oxy—not fentanyl."

"How do you know the pills came from the Iron Fist?"

"Because the dealer admitted it. The same dealer who sold the same Iron Fist poison to eight other colleges kids who died from taking it … the same dealer who was murdered."

There was a long pause. I could hear him breathing, a slight rasp coming from his throat. "I had nothin' to do with that. Sure, I know the club runs drugs. They all do. I go there three times a week to tend bar and shoot the shit. At least I used to go there. Tank stripped me of my colors in front of the others and kicked my ass out of the club. In my sixty-five years on earth, I've never felt the kinda shame that dude put on me. He took my dignity away."

"Want it back?"

"Yeah. Only problem with that is I'd get killed in the process."

"No, you won't. Digger, you impressed me as a stand-up guy, a man who stands up for victims. You joined biker clubs because you enjoy the camaraderie. Not because you want to poison kids."

He snorted. "That's the God's truth. There are good people and bad people. A lot of good bikers and a bunch of bad ones. In all my years riding, I did more of the better than bad."

"And now you can continue that streak and get your dignity back."

"How?"

"If Tank and the others complicit in distributing the lethal fentanyl are arrested, you can testify. Help send them to a place where they can make license plates but not fentanyl. As a member of the club, you didn't sign up for mass murder. And that's what it is." Before he could answer, I asked, "Where's Axle?"

"Don't know. Last I heard is Tank told him to leave the state or they'd take him down to a spot in the glades they call the prayin' tree. Tank likes to feed people alive to gators."

"If I can find Axle, and if he agrees to testify to stop this rampant abuse of fentanyl, would you be part of *that* club?"

"If the law can come up with something that will really stick to Tank, yes. But, if they have some half-ass charges that'll allow a slick lawyer to get Tank's ass out on bail for weeks pending charges, hell no. When he's arrested, the charges gotta be strong and at a level he won't make bond. If he's given bail, he'll skip. Probably go down to Mexico."

"Is that because he gets his fentanyl from the Durango cartel?"

Another long pause. "How'd you know that?"

"I've been tracking Tank and others like him. Are you tight with Axle?"

"I used to spend time with him at the bar in the Fist clubhouse. Axle's father walked out on the family when the kid was just five. The old man left his wife and three children. Axle's mother caved under the pressure of tryin' to raise those kids. She got into drugs. Prostitution. Pretty much numbed her brain down to a point where it never came back. The kids were separated and farmed out in the foster system. Axle had a rough life. Some of it he won't talk about."

"Does Axle use drugs?"

"Sometimes. I think all his life, he's been searching, wanting to belong to something. That's what got me into biker clubs. The camaraderie … the fellowship of guys who had to step up to step outta the crap they were usually born into."

"Can you reach Axle and have him call me?"

"I can try. I know he's pissed, having gone through what Tank did. But will he be willing to stand up in court and testify against Tank and some of the rest? I guess that'll depend on how good you are at wrapping this up."

I said nothing, watching a 42-foot catamaran drop its sails and motor into the marina.

"Tell you what I'll do, O'Brien. I'll reach out to Axle. See where his head's at right now."

"Thanks."

"I got a good friend who is the ride manager at a carnival setting up at the fairgrounds. The carnival will be here for a week. If Axle needs to get out of town and still make some side money, I can ask my pal if he'll take Axle on to work some of the rides. That way, Axle could travel, earn some money, and not be looking over his shoulder all the time. If you need him to testify, I just call my buddy to see what town they're in at the time."

"Sounds good."

"Before I let you go, lemme say this. Tank's gonna go full bore to find you. He doesn't play in a world with boundaries. He'll take you down and your family. You got a dog?"

"Yes."

"He'll kill the dog. Probably just before he shoots you and your wife if you're married. He'll kill kids without batting an eye. Be damn careful. You just walked in a cave full of rattlesnakes, and the sun's setting. So, you got no way to know where you're stepping to find your way out of there." He clicked off.

I set my phone on the table. Neither Dave nor Nick spoke.

EIGHTY-SIX

Axle stared at a man he knew but no longer recognized. He looked at his reflection in the mirror of a gas station restroom, holding cool wet paper towels to his face and forehead. Two of the Iron Fist club members had taken turns hitting him while two more held his arms. A flap of skin was torn above his left eye, and the area around the eye was plum-colored and swollen, pressing the eye shut. His lower lip was split, and dried blood caked his right nostril. And the scarring X, which had been healing, was bright red, covered in welts, and circled in bruises.

He ran cold water in the sink, bent down, and used both hands to splash the stream onto his face and head, the water coming off his skin like rusted iron swirling down the drain. He spit blood into the sink, using the water to wash out his mouth.

After he finished, Axle walked back outside, squinting, like a bat caught in the harsh reality of morning sunlight. He stood next to his Harley, slowly getting on it, pain in his right leg. As he was about to start the motor, his phone vibrated. He looked at the screen through his good eye, recognizing the number. He answered. "What's up, Digger?"

"You okay? Drywall told me they took you behind the clubhouse, and Tank unleashed the dogs. You need to get to a hospital?"

"I got no broken bones. I do have some knots on my head. My face has looked better. Still got all my teeth. A couple are loose, though."

"What did Tank tell you before the fight?"

"Wasn't no fight. Four on one. At least I'm alive. Tank said, if they find me in the area, it'll be a one-way trip down to the prayin' tree in the glades."

"Come out to my hunting camp in the Ocala National Forest. Don't many people know where it is. I'll bring some antiseptic, bandages, whatnot … and meet you there. You remember how to get to it?"

"Yeah. We shot tin cans, plinkin' with a .22 long rifle there last year."

"I got something I wanna run by you. The Fist used to be your average motorcycle club. Doing what most clubs do to pay the rent. And then along came fentanyl. Tank was transferred from Texas to build up the club's distribution in Florida, and people—mostly kids, started dyin' like flies. Getting stoned on weed is one thing, snorting coke is another, but sellin' killer pills to sixteen-year-old kids crosses the line."

"There's not a damn thing that we can do about it. As much as I'd like to nail Tank to a cross, he covers his tracks well. Between the bribes and the payoffs, he's got people bought."

"Not everybody. I know you met the dude, Sean O'Brien. He might—"

"Whoa! Wait a minute, Digger. Tank's a mean and heartless bastard, but this O'Brien is one crazy freak. He's not right in the head. I can see it in his eyes, like he wants to stare death in its ugly face. That ain't right by no stretch of the imagination."

"Listen to me, Axle. If you do, you might live to be an old man like me. I know you've had a rough life. None of that is your fault. People, like Tank, think they can use you and then throw you out like snot on a tissue when they're done with you. O'Brien has the balls to cut Tank back a few notches and stop the killin' of kids. He's askin' us to partner with him to help put an end to the deaths of kids."

"I don't know. It's not just Tank, it's the whole damn club that's in five states."

"All it takes is someone to stand up to 'em, get some hard-time prison convictions, and you'll see the Iron Fist and others back away from sellin' poison pills. I'll see you at the hunting cabin in an hour."

"Okay. Just one thing. Tank's pulling out everything he can on O'Brien. It's only a matter of time before he hits O'Brien or messes with his family, if a man like that even has a family."

***

Wynona came from a back room of her antique shop, *Moments in Time,* to the front area, Angela and Max following her. The shop was filled with antique furniture, ornate framed paintings, lamps, glassware, vintage magazines, vinyl records, globes, and relics from the Civil War era. Late afternoon sunlight streamed through the windows on the western side of the two-story building.

Wynona approached the counter where her assistant, Sandy Stewart, was putting a price tag on a crystal perfume bottle made in 1890. Sandy, in her early thirties, wore her auburn hair in a pixie cut, a pearl earring on each side of her oval face. Wynona smiled as she stepped behind the counter. "Thanks, Sandy, for holding down the fort again today."

"How'd the homeschooling go?"

"Good. Angela's reading comprehension is improving every day. Her grammar skills, punctuation, phonics, and math are ahead of her grade level."

Sandy glanced down at Angela. "What's your favorite part of school?"

"I love art because I like to draw and paint things. I have a whole bunch of different colored pencils and used them to draw a picture of Max. Mama's going to put it on our 'frigerator."

"Great idea. Can I see it?"

Angela nodded, walking quickly back to the office, and returning with a picture of Max. "See—does it look like her?"

Sandy smiled, glancing from Max to the drawing. "It sure does. That's a beautiful picture."

"Thank you." Angela grinned.

Wynona looked at her watch. "I can handle it until closing. Why don't you take off and beat the rush hour here in DeLand?" Wynona smiled, glancing through the front windows to Mainstreet in downtown. There was one pickup truck at the intersection, the driver waiting for the light to change.

"Okay. But one day there really will be a rush hour in our lovely little town. It's just a matter of time before people up north discover it."

"I think you're right."

Sandy picked up her purse from a bench behind the counter, heading toward the front door. As she opened the door, she turned back. "See you three tomorrow."

"Bye," Angela said, Wynona waving, and Max trotting toward the door.

Angela looked at a porcelain antique of a colorful parrot and glanced up at Wynona. "Mama, can I go back in the room and draw another picture?"

"Of course, you can. What are you going to draw?"

Angela pointed at the porcelain parrot. "That bird."

Wynona smiled. "That's a parrot. The antique is very old. I'll carry it back there for you and set it up near your desk."

"Okay."

Wynona lifted the parrot, its mustard yellow claws wrapped around a porcelain branch that was made to look like a limb that had grown from the base. They went back to the office, Wynona arranging the parrot, so it was eye-level for Angela. "Okay, sweetie. Here's a piece of art paper and your colored pencils. You can sit in your little chair and draw a masterpiece."

"Thanks." Angela grinned.

"Just don't lift the bird. I'll carry it back when you're done."

"Okay, Mom. I won't."

There was the loud rumble of multiple motorcycles in front of the shop. "What's that, Mama? Sounds like thunder."

Seconds later the chimes jingled at the front door. Max barked. Wynona looked at her daughter. "I think a customer is in the store. Stay here, okay?"

"Okay."

EIGHTY-SEVEN

When Wynona saw who'd walked into her shop, she made a beeline to get behind the counter. Three bikers—beer bellies, fur, beards, and tats, moving through the store, their eyes roaming over the antiques as if they were watching lights blinking from a pinball machine. Max stood on the wooden floor a few feet from the glass counter. She barked a second time.

Wynona called her. "Come here, Max. You know you're not supposed to bark at customers." Max trotted behind the counter, pausing once to look over her shoulder at the closest biker. Wynona smiled. "Please excuse my dog. Her bark is really a greeting."

The man looked over to Wynona with dead eyes. No effort to make conversation. He wore a reddish goatee. Pockmarked face. A tattoo of a hawk in flight on the side of his neck. Stained sweatband across his forehead. The other two bikers made their way through the shop, floorboards creaking, wide shoulders brushing against some of the fragile relics.

Wynona unlocked a drawer, looked at the 9mm Beretta in a holster that Sean had mounted behind the board at the front of the drawer. "If there is anything I can help you gentlemen with, please let me know. Are you looking for something in particular?"

The biker with the hawk tattoo was closest to her. "You got a lot of old shit in here."

Wynona smiled. "That's why it's called an antique store."

"Some of this stuff looks like it came outta my grandma's house."

"Maybe one day she can come in to visit."

"Only if granny can crawl out of her moldy grave." He snorted. His friends laughing.

One of them said, "Hawk, you ought not to be talkin' about your granny like that."

One biker, looking like a Norseman—dirty blonde hair and a Viking beard to match—came closer to Wynona. His deep blue eyes caught the afternoon sunlight through the windows, like the flames of a butane torch. He stopped in front of a suit of armor display, one of the knight's metal hands wrapped around the grip of a long sword.

"What's hap'nen, fella? Are you standing guard, watching over this place?" He reached out, touching the sword. "Blade is dull. Be hard to whack off a head on the first try." He wrapped his hand around the sword's grip, pulling.

Wynona said, "Please, don't try to take out the sword. It's not made to be removed from the suit of armor."

The biker grinned. "Suit of armor. Isn't that a fancy name for a tin man? Looks to me like his joints are a little rusted. He wouldn't be much help." All three bikers came closer to the counter, the men about fifteen feet away. Wynona's hand was near the gun.

"Mama, the green pencil tip broke," said Angela, coming out of the back room. "I can't find the sharpener." She walked about halfway from the room to the front of the store, stopping. All three of the bikers turning toward her.

Wynona reached for the Beretta, her hand on the grip.

Angela looked like a little girl who'd just walked into a land of giants. She stared up at the bikers, her face curious and fearful. Wynona said, "Angela, go back to the office. I'll sharpen your pencil as soon as I'm finished with the customers."

Angela nodded, bit her bottom lip, and ran back to the room. The three men turned to Wynona. The one with the blonde Viking beard took another step closer. "You got a pretty little girl. I like that name … Angela. It sort of rolls off the tongue. Be a shame if anything were to happen to her. Same thing with that lil' dog of yours. I could take that knight's sword, skewer that wiener dog, and roast it over a hardwood fire. Bet the dog would taste like chicken."

Wynona gripped the Beretta firmer. "What do you want?"

The man with the hawk tattoo grinned. "You, mama, for a starter. We had no idea walking in a shop that sells old things, we'd find a young child and a fine-lookin' woman. You got that hot exotic look. Like an Indian princess. Where's your man?"

"Who are you talking about?"

"Like you got no idea. Sean O'Brien. Where's that piece of human shit hiding?"

"I assure you … he's not hiding. And I can assure you that you'll never see him coming. Even in broad daylight. Get out of my store."

Viking said, "Maybe I'll just come around the counter and suck on your pretty neck—like a vampire." He grinned. Incisors sharp as fangs. "When O'Brien sees you, he'll see my mark on his woman. The next one, if he keeps comin', will be between your legs. Then we'll have our way with the kid. Hawk likes 'em tight." He took another step.

Wynona pulled the Beretta, holding it with both hands, feet parted—shooting stance, like she'd done often in the FBI. "Take another step closer, and I'll put a round between your eyes. Get out of my store."

"Whoa, mama. Chances are you'll miss. Even if you do manage a kill shot, my two horny hombres will be on your nice, round ass like white on rice. They'll take turns with you in that backroom while the kid watches. Your man's got no idea who he's messin' with."

"Come closer, and you die on the spot. I'll drop the others before they can blink twice. Want me to prove it? Take another step. By the way, you've been on camera the whole time you three have been in my store. High resolution video evidence is better than eyewitnesses because the camera never blinks or forgets."

The man lifted his hands in a mock surrender. "We broke no laws, hot mama. Just three customers talking about antiques. You're feisty. Bet you'd be like a filly in the sack … the kinda woman we could ride all night. Especially with a little chemical in your blood."

Wynona aimed the Beretta at his heart. "Get out!"

"We'll leave. But we'll be back if O'Brien makes another move. If he approaches any member or ex-members of the Iron Fist, their ol' ladies, or if he so much as drives by our clubhouse, we got cameras, too. C'mon, fellas. Let's leave before she gets a can of oil and lubes up the tin man to start swingin' his sword at us."

Laughing, they walked out the front door, straddled their Harleys, and revved the engines so loud the front windows shook. Wynona grabbed a pad of paper and a pen, looking through the windows, writing down the tag numbers before the bikers left.

"Mama, can I come out?" Angela asked from the open door of the back room.

EIGHTY-EIGHT

Nick got a look in his eye that I rarely see in him. The lively energy was quickly replaced with the gaze of deep trouble. After I shared with him and Dave what Digger told me, Nick popped the top off a bottle of Corona and sat on one of the three stools in front of Dave's small bar on *Gibraltar*. From the speakers in the background, John Coltrane's jazz tune, *Equinox,* played.

Nick looked at me. "I know I recently brought up you pulling those bikers off me some years back at the Tiki. But, with you dealing with bikers now, I've been thinking about it. I want to return the favor. I'll help you deal with these guys. Call it karma and payback."

"The circumstances are much different now. I appreciate the offer, but I can't accept it."

He shook his head. "You're gonna need somebody, Sean. Why not me?"

"I think that local law enforcement will shake my hand off if I can find the evidence they'll need to win in court. The Iron Fist ended up in my sights because they're a big part of the cause and effect of fentanyl deaths. If something could be done to take down the Florida chapter, sales of this drug would plummet. Maybe save lives."

Dave nodded. "Indeed. But for how long? It would be just a matter of time before the bikers were replaced with another group. The Durango cartel would have an influence on that."

My phone buzzed. The call from Digger came quicker than I expected. Maybe it was good news. I answered, and he said, "O'Brien, I got Axle with me. We're in the sticks in an old huntin' cabin I have on the edge of the national forest. Anyway, Tank's boys put a hurtin' on him. I got Axle patched up. He'll stay out here for a couple of days. He's agreeing to work the carnival circuit. Here's the deal. We'll both go toe-to-toe in court if the real cops can file charges that could send Tank to prison for the rest of his sorry ass life."

"Excellent. Tell Axle that I hope he feels better soon. I thank you both for agreeing to do this. I know it's not easy, considering the circumstances. We'll stay in touch."

"All right. Game on." He clicked off.

Dave cleared his throat. "That sounded positive."

"Digger and Axle are both going to testify if I can find enough hard evidence to turn over to law enforcement for police to file charges."

"Maybe it's time you called your old contact in the sheriff's office, Detective Dan Grant."

Nick used one thumb to wipe away the condensation from the bottle. "I remember that guy. You helped him nail the Mermaid Killer, right? And wasn't the detective shot and down?"

I nodded. "Yes."

"This guy, of all the cops on the planet, ought to trust you, Sean, to deliver the goods. You won't come to him with some half-baked evidence."

Dave stood from the table, pouring a glass of cabernet. "Care for a drink, Sean?"

"No thanks."

"Let's examine what you have, don't have, and hope to get. You managed to enter a warehouse controlled by the Iron Fist. But you could find no physical evidence that the place was used for storing and shipping drugs. That doesn't mean it always has been that way, just not the day you popped inside. You've lost Charlie Brown, but his voice lives on digitally. That can be powerful played back in court before a jury."

"I'll need more than the ghost of Charlie Brown in court."

"You're right. Even though you have two ex-bikers, guys humiliated by Tank and the rest, who will testify that the biker gang is selling fentanyl, without physical evidence or Tank admitting it, a slick defense lawyer will say that Axle and Digger are seeking retaliation from having been tossed out of the club. Maybe their testimony will be so compelling, so heartfelt, that a jury will believe it. But a dose of physical evidence will help."

"I have a plan that might work."

My phone buzzed again. This time the call was coming from Wynona. I answered and she said, "Sean, three members of the Iron Fist came by the shop today. They were here to intimidate me."

"Did they touch you or Angela."

"No, but if their eyes could physically touch me, then I feel like I've been raped. Angela is okay. She was a little mystified or maybe even traumatized by their presence and language."

"Tell me everything they did and said."

"They may have done or said more had I not pulled my Beretta on them." Wynona gave me the details. Listening to her, I fought back my rising anger. She added, "It's no longer safe here. I must do homeschooling with Angela somewhere else. Maybe at home. I can shut the business down temporarily."

"If they found you at your business, they'll find us at our home."

"Where can we go?"

"Let's stay on the boat or at a hotel until this thing is over. Or could you visit your mother on the reservation as an option?"

"Of course. She'd love to spend more time with Angela. But I'm not the type of woman who flees. Maybe I don't walk into danger like you, but I don't run from it. I stand my ground."

"Now we're standing ground with a young child. That's the difference. Well, okay, Angela does love the boat, and we have protective friends here. She looks at Nick as a crazy, fun uncle and Dave as a grandpa. So, here's what we can do. I'll log in and access the shop's video of those three guys. You and Angela can leave the shop, and I'll meet you at the house. You get some clothes, whatever you need, and come to the marina. I'll try to come back here with you. If not, Nick and Dave will help you carry anything you bring and escort you to the boat."

"Nick and Dave? Where will you be?"

"I want to meet with the guy I told you about, Digger. He'll be able to ID the three men and give me an insight as to where to find them."

"Sean, I don't have to tell you the number of years I spent with the Bureau and then as a detective for the tribe. I've come across lots of scumbags in my time. These three would rank in the top ten most heinous people I've met. Not only did they smell of weed, but they also stank of evil. You can surveil them if you need to, but don't approach them if they're together. Please, don't let your love for me and Angela influence you to the point of making bad decisions."

"I'll see you at home in forty minutes. Be careful. They may be tailing you, and it wouldn't be on motorcycles. If you notice anyone following you, call me and head directly to the marina."

EIGHTY-NINE

On my way to our river cabin, I called Detective Dan Grant's cell phone. He'd been with the sheriff's office for over twenty years. He was African American and one of the best detectives I have ever known. Perceptive and with the tenacity of a bulldog. He answered and said, "Sean O'Brien, how the hell are you? No wait, before you answer, I know something's going down because you only call me when the shit's hitting the fan."

"Hi, Dan. Don't ever let anyone accuse you of being subtle."

"Just tell it like it is … like I see it. Those two things usually match. What's up?"

"What do you know about the Iron Fist?"

"Whoa, that's like asking me what I know about evil angels. For the most part, guys who get into biker gangs, like the Iron Fist, are at the crossroads with the devil. I'd bet that most of them cut the deal, sell their soul, and ride their Harleys through the gates of fire. The Iron Fist are suspected to be involved in everything from strong-arm racketeering, gun running, human trafficking, drug sales, and probably murder."

"Why are they still standing?"

"I used the word *suspected.* Their society is so closed, it's very difficult to prove crime when victims are scared to testify. Most of the evidence is circumstantial, not the stuff a prosecutor can use to nail the coffin shut. Why do you ask? Are you investigating some member of that nefarious biker club?"

"Yeah, the whole damn club with a special emphasis on a guy who goes by the name Tank."

"I know the name. But more than that, I know his reputation. He's the equivalent of a mafia boss, into acquisitions and enforcement. Runs a tight ship behind the razor wire of their clubhouse. Before he became the leader of the local pack, he served five years for extortion. Since then, he's been untouchable because he delegates everything. The Iron Fist has a lot of members in the southern states where they have chapters. Here in Daytona Beach, club members would rather face jail time than testify against Tank and the others in the gang."

"Not all of the members or in this case, ex-members."

"What do you mean?"

I told Dan about Andy Ward and the circumstances leading up to my interest in the Iron Fist, including Axle and Digger's commitment to testify under the right conditions. I added, "When Tank sent three of his goons into Wynona's shop in DeLand, he crossed the line."

I heard Dan blow out a breath. "Sean, you have earned our mutual respect over the last few years. I wish I could convince you to join the department and hang up your PI shingle. But I know that's smoke in the wind. As your friend, I advise you not to push in the direction of the Iron Fist. To take them down requires weeks, maybe months, of surveillance. Physical proof of a crime that can be traced back to them, and witnesses willing to take the stand in court and testify against these criminals. Usually, they fall on their own swords. Greed, infighting, and mistrust among club members thins out the herd. They eat their own. You saw that with this guy Axle. He's lucky to be alive."

"But more are willing to join the pack."

"Such is the nature of the criminal mind. Like the Iron Fist, it knows no boundaries."

"Dan, what would you do if members of a biker gang threatened your wife and child?"

"File a report. Put something on record in case it escalates."

"It will escalate. It always does because that's the nature of evil. Relentless, like a growing cancer until somebody cuts it out."

"Sean, don't put yourself in the middle of a pack of wolves."

"When you face a pack of wolves, you bring your shotgun."

"I'll forget you said that." He sighed. "You get into a pinch, call me. I'll send in the reinforcements."

"What I need is for you to get a warrant to search the Iron Fist clubhouse."

"I've got a judge who would probably sign that order. What you've given me might be enough to do it. Send me over what evidence you got. I'll try for an early morning raid."

"I will as soon as we hang up. But let's work in sync. I think I know how to get as many of the Iron Fist members as possible into one parking lot. After your search, you'll probably be ready to make arrests. The parking lot of the Midnight Rider seems like a good place. Get your SWAT team ready."

NINETY

A little while later, I had made a crucial decision that I hoped would play out well within the next twenty-four hours. I decided to find the three bikers or at least two of the three and have a brief discussion with them. Very brief. And there was no better time than tonight. Tank sent them to send a message to me. I would respond but deliver more than a message. Action spoke more succinctly than words.

Maybe the three amigos would be lifting a few beers, toasting the way they had frightened a little girl and her mother. The way to make it happen would be to secure Digger's help. I needed him to ID the men and hopefully tell me where I might find them.

I stood in the cockpit of *Jupiter*, my 38-foot Bayliner, ready to make a phone call. Wynona and Angela were in the boat's salon finishing some grilled red fish that Nick had caught and cooked. I lifted my left pant leg, strapping a small holster above my ankle. Inside the holster was a Smith & Wesson M&P 9.

Twilight was enveloping the marina in a sepia tone of a colorless world. Wynona came into the cockpit, her skin soft and flawless in the diffused light. She stood there for a moment, silhouettes of two pelicans sailing over the marina toward a mauve-streaked western sky. Wynona started to say something but changed her mind and went back inside. Max trotted out, pausing to look up at the first few stars making an appearance in the dark sky over the Atlantic.

I made the call to Digger. "Didn't expect to hear from you so soon, O'Brien."

"Things change quickly in the world of good and evil."

"That's the truth. It's constant."

"Digger, I need you to take a look at a short video and tell me who's in it."

"What makes you think I'd know?"

"Because they're all members of the Iron Fist. They came into my fiancée's antique shop today." I told him what happened and added, "I want to find them tonight. Maybe they're out celebrating their victory over a little girl and her mom. I'll text the video to you."

"All right. Soon as I get it, I'll have a look. I know ever'body in the club. So does Axle. He might know more about their social lives than I do. But, between the two of us, we ought to put the pieces together. Send it." He clicked off.

In less than thirty seconds, I sent the video. I stood in the cockpit, the marina water flat and dark as a crow's feather, the smell of burning charcoal and grilled steak in the evening air. I looked over L dock at *Gibraltar*, facing the opposite side from Nick's boat. Both Dave and Nick would be watching *Jupiter* closely. I didn't think more of Tank's troops would come here, considering they'd made their first intrusion earlier today. They drew a line in the sand. One that I wanted to cross tonight.

I reached down to pick up Max, holding her above *Jupiter's* gunwale so she could begin her neighborhood watch patrol by scouting the marina. She loved going up to the flybridge, giving her a doxie perch on top of the world. She watched the single light from Ponce Lighthouse, the beam scanning the Atlantic all the way to the curvature of the earth.

"Max, you keep your ears up and eyes on the lookout for strangers, okay? Be the great watchdog that you are for Wynona and Angela. We humans just don't have your radar." She looked up at me, tilting her head forward as if she was nodding. I believe she was.

The phone in my pocket buzzed. I set Max down and answered Digger's call. He said, "I showed that video to Axle. We know their road names and their real names. More importantly, Axle said he knows where they'd probably be on a Friday night after messin' with your family."

"What do you have?"

"One guy is called Hawk. Real name is Eddie Logan. The guy with the blonde beard and Viking look is Magnus. The name his parents gave him is Neil Singleton. The last dude's road name's Rooster. Real name's Larry Lambert."

"Who's second in command in the Florida Iron Fist? The guy under Tank in hierarchy."

"That'd be Randy Bates, or Blade as we know him. He's got the biggest collection of switchblades I've ever seen. I'd call it an obsession."

"Any idea where Hawk, Magnus, and Rooster might be tonight?"

"Axle told me that, out of the fifty or so Fist club members, these three guys are tight. They hunt and fish together. And they most often drink together. He said one of their favorite hangouts is a dive bar called Bonito Jack's. It's off Seabreeze Avenue. Right next to a strip joint called the Black Garter. Who you takin' with you."

"Nobody."

"That might not work out so good."

"Okay, because you asked. Three friends ... Smith, Wesson, and a guy who always has my back ... Glock. Thanks, Digger." I clicked off as Wynona and Angela were walking from the salon to the cockpit.

"Daddy, can you help me find the Big Dipper?" Angela asked.

I glanced at the night sky. "Now that the clouds have moved far offshore, let's see if we can find the big ol' dipper." I lifted her into my arms and pointed to the sky. "First, we find the North Star. There it is. See it?"

"Yes. It's bright."

"Okay. If we trace an imaginary line down from the North Star, you'll see the Big Dipper's handle, and then you can see the whole dipper." I used my hand to guide her.

"I see it, Daddy. Can I wish upon that star?"

"Of course."

"I wish I could go fishing again with you and Mama ... and Max."

Wynona smiled, looking in the northeast direction. "I see it, too. In the Seminole language, it's called the Lone Star ... meaning the star that does not move."

Seconds later, a fiery meteor carved its way against the blackness. I pointed as the fireball faded in the eastern sky. "That star moves."

"Wow!" Angela said, her face mesmerized. "What is that?"

I looked at Wynona. "Why don't you tell her?"

"Okay. It's a shooting star. Some people call those things comets or meteors."

"What are they?"

"It's really a big piece of a rock that is flying through space, and when it comes close to our earth, it hits the atmosphere—the air we breathe. And that causes it to ignite, to light up with those sparks you saw because it's moving so fast."

Angela seemed satisfied with the answer. "Can it do it again?"

Wynona smiled. "When it catches fire, it can burn out. But there are lots of meteors flying through space. Sometimes they get close to earth. Many other times they don't. It's always fun to see one. Take Max back inside. You can watch one TV show before it's time for a shower and bed."

"Okay. Come on, Max."

When they went into the salon, Wynona asked, "Did Digger ID those men?"

"Yes."

"What are your plans?"

"To hand all of this over to the Volusia County Sheriff's Department. I'm working with Detective Dan Brown. He's getting a warrant to search the Iron Fist clubhouse. But right now, the police wouldn't do much about three bikers entering an antique shop and intimidating a mother and her small child. But what they said and did, and what they might say and do, could lead to criminal activity. I'm going to follow that path and see where it leads. If I must, I'll blaze a trail."

Wynona leaned in and hugged me tight, like she didn't want to let me go.

***

Fifteen minutes later, I drove north near the Atlantic along Highway A1A, thinking about holding Angela in my arms and looking at the North Star. *I see it, Daddy. Can I wish upon that star?*

NINETY-ONE

Tony Salazar looked through one of the open vents on the roof of the horse stables, the stars bright in the night sky. He thought his arms were going to pop out of their sockets. The ropes around his fists were tied high over a horizontal support beam in the stables, pulled taut, making him, again, stand on the balls of his feet. The skin around his wrists was chaffed and torn in spots, blood oozing into the fibers of the ropes.

He stared into the heavens and remembered something his grandmother used to tell him about stars. *The light you see from the stars, Antonio, has come from very far away. Some of the stars may no longer live, but their light continues moving through the dark. Never forget, there is a light inside your heart that will see you through dark times.*

Tony thought about his wife, Nicole, and his children—Lucas and little Eva. *When are you coming home, Daddy?* His eyes welled, staring at the stars.

The main door to the stables opened, overhead lights on, Diego Navarro entering with two other men. As they approached, the horses sensed the evil that had come in with the night wind. There were nervous snorts and movement from the animals in their stalls, ears erect, eyes wide in the soft light.

Navarro walked up to Tony and grinned. He looked at the taut ropes, the bloodied wrists, the muscles on Tony's back knotted, cramping from fatigue, trying to balance for hours on the balls of his bare feet. Navarro spit into Tony's face, the saliva dripping down his forehead and over one eye.

In Spanish, Navarro said, "Isn't it a bad feeling not to be able to use your hands to wipe my spit from your eyes? Soon, the pain will be so great that you will ask for the rope around your neck rather than your wrists. Every man has his breaking point. And I can tell that you are getting close to yours. Do you not deny this?"

Tony looked at Navarro and said nothing. A stallion in a stall closest to them whinnied, kicking the back of the wooden wall.

Navarro walked in a small circle around Tony and stopped to stare at the bleeding slashes on Tony's bare back. Navarro looked amused. "The cuts on your back are getting infected. I think some of the barn flies have laid eggs inside your skin. We made it easy for them to gain access to your body where the maggots will feast. What's left is your soul, and that will be mine because I collect them for my protector, Santa Muerte." There was a private luminosity in his cold eyes, like a dim light through a keyhole.

Tony stared at him. "You're sick. Your father will rot in prison. You will, too."

Navarro came back around, standing two feet away from Tony. "That is a fantasy you are having as your body starts to shut down, going into the dying process. I have seen it many times. After a while, you will be crying and begging your mother to come save you. But there is nobody. The DEA has written you off. Your own government has turned its red, white, and blue back on you. There is no one to help you. So, what is left?" He looked over at his two men, a wicked smile forming across his wet lips.

"What is left, Tony Salazar, is what I decide to do with you … or what I decide to do with what's left of your body. What I know is what my father taught me. Raise the bar high and set examples for others to follow. The bar is raised. Our family is making more money than all the other cartels. Why?"

"Because you are crooks," Tony mumbled.

"We run our operation like the business it is. We have partnered with your country because your borders are open. It's unbelievable. Crazy. We take drugs over day and night. Millions of dollars every week. In the old days, my papa had to find ingenious ways to smuggle across the border. Now, not so much. So, what does that tell you about your value to the DEA? You're down here with the rest of the sweaty Mexicans, and the gringos in DC don't give a shit."

Navarro lifted his eyes up to Tony's fists. "Your hands are turning blue. As they become useless and wither from a lack of circulation, perhaps they will be the first things we cut off."

NINETY-TWO

Bonito Jack's was a crossbreed of architecture. It looked like an old barn expanded to resemble a large bait shack. The gabled roof was made from corrugated tin, corroded in sections. The rustic front deck was supported by five timbers. The words *Live Bait Sold Here* were spelled out in a glowing red neon sign on an exterior wall. Beer signs hung inside the windows like holiday ornaments.

In the cool turquoise colors of the Caribbean Sea, the *Bonito Jack's* sign was glowing from an eave above the overhang, as if it had been propped up and bolted to a rain gutter. I could see taut guy wires supporting the sign. There were nine motorcycles, two pickup trucks, and three cars in the small parking lot. I pulled my Jeep in, tires rolling across gravel and bottle tops. Tall bamboo grew thick to the far left and right of the parking area.

I parked as far away as I could in the lot away from the motorcycles, near strands of bamboo. I looked at the piece of paper that Wynona had given me, the license plate numbers of the motorcycles on the paper. My driver's side window was open, the sounds of the bamboo creaking as the wind caused the stalks to rub against one another.

I could hear music and loud talking coming from the bar. It was near midnight. I assumed that, if the three bikers were in there, they'd have had alcohol, slowing their reaction times. It was something I was counting on, just like the Mossberg 590 combat shotgun wedged between my seat and the console. The gun had a twenty-inch barrel and was loaded with seven shells of double-aught buckshot. Between my Glock and the S&W in my ankle holster, I might not need the shotgun. But the backup was there.

I opened the app on my phone and played back the video from when the bikers entered Wynona's shop. I had grabbed screenshots of each man's face, staring at them for about ten seconds apiece. Then I watched the video again, studying the mannerisms, looking at whether they used their right or left hands in the shop. I tried to learn as much about my prey as possible before I set the traps.

I knew it would be to my disadvantage to start something with them inside the bar. Too many people. Too many potential witnesses or victims, depending on how things went down. I had to get them outside and not draw a crowd while doing it. I picked up a metal baseball bat from the back seat, locked my Jeep and headed toward the parked motorcycles. As I got closer, I scanned the eaves and porch area for cameras. I spotted one at the far upper corner of the overhang. I figured with my height and the extended reach of the bat, I could connect with the camera.

I walked with my bat to the right, away from the camera lens. In seconds, I was on the wooden deck. I moved under the overhang to just beyond where the camera was mounted. The music from inside the bar was loud, too loud for anyone to hear what I was about to do. I climbed up on one of the handrails that ran to the support timbers. I grabbed the eave, leaned back, and from behind the camera, I used the bat as leverage to push the camera lens toward the midnight sky.

No damage. Just a celestial view of the stars while a small vignette of hell on earth was about to happen. I lowered myself back to the porch, walked down three steps, and hid the bat behind a shrub in need of trimming. I had memorized the license plate numbers, walking behind the nine motorcycles. Seven were Harleys. One Triumph and an Indian Scout. I spotted the three motorcycles I was looking for parked in a row together.

A man and a woman came out of the bar door, the woman laughing at something the man said. I watched them walk down the steps, both people tipsy. He wore ripped jeans and a T-shirt. She was dressed in white shorts and a tank top, cleavage displayed under the neon lights. "Glad this isn't a big lot. I can't remember where I put the truck," said the man, his words thick.

"It's over there," the woman pointed to a pickup truck across the lot.

I waited for them to have their backs to me as they shuffled across the gravel lot. I pulled out my tactical knife from a sheath under my shirt, slashing the front tires of all three motorcycles in seconds. I put the knife back and walked inside Bonito Jack's.

In less than ten seconds, I spotted the men I was hunting.

NINETY-THREE

Walking into Bonito Jack's was like walking into a large crab trap with barnacles and crustaceans. The nautical theme went from corner to corner. The bar was to the left after entering the door. Behind the bar were two large fish mounted almost face-to-face. The fish on the left was a bonito. The one on the right was a yellow jack.

A man and woman slow danced on a scuffed, wooden floor. The woman, stringy beach blonde hair, wore a sundress and flip-flops. The man was in jeans and cowboy boots. The bar smelled of weed and beer. Music from the Wurlitzer jukebox was Bob Seger singing, *No Man's Land.*

The three men I was hunting were at a corner table to the far right of the bar. They sat with their backs to the wall, facing the entrance, a pitcher of amber beer in the center of the table. Mugs half filled. Most of the customers appeared to be bikers. Lots of leather and denim. Gold chains under chest hair. The mix was more men than women. They moved around under the soft light like silhouettes in a neon rain.

I scanned the faces without locking eyes. I assumed that most of the people, or at least the men, were carrying either a knife or a gun under their leather. Some probably carried both. I walked around two tables on my way to the bar. The tables were belly deep in bikers and their women. For the most part, everyone seemed to be having a good time in a close environment that carried the odor of testosterone, weed and cigarette smoke, stale perfume, and the hair-trigger risk of a shootout at any time.

I walked to the bar, glad to see it too had a mirror behind the array of liquor bottles. Maybe the mirror motif was a leftover from the saloon days of the Wild West when a cowboy could sip a glass of whiskey while keeping an eye on the patrons behind his back. Not only did I recognize the three bikers in the far corner, but it also was easy to spot a man who could see with just one eye. Captain Kidd sat at the bar's elbow, sipping from a can of Yuengling beer.

The music on the jukebox changed to the Allman Brothers, *Midnight Rider*. I approached Captain Kidd and said, "Seems odd to hear *Midnight Rider* in Bonito Jacks. The last place we had a drink, it could have been that bar's theme song. Maybe a Buffett tune would set the mood in here."

He looked up at me with his one eye, reddened and puffy. He grinned. "What's up, hoss? You making the rounds to some of the best dive bars in Daytona Beach?"

"Yeah, I'm thinking of starting a travel blog – best of the worst dive bars in the South. What do you think?"

"Damn good idea. When a dive bar is the worst, it really makes it the best. Go figure. What brings you into this place on a Friday night. You lookin' to hook up with a biker babe? You current on your shots?" He smiled and took a pull from the beer can.

"I came here because the business that was started against me when I last saw you has escalated. It now has moved to threatening my family."

"Damn. What's goin' on?"

"The same guy who took your eye out is threatening to take out my fiancée and our daughter."

"Man, you must have pissed in Tank's chicken soup."

"Something like that."

"I guess you found Axle. The way I heard it is Tank had a couple of his big dudes turn Axle's head into a cauliflower. At the same time, Tank kicked Digger outta the club. Word gets around fast. And now, you better have eyes in the back of your head."

I glanced up at the mirror behind the bar. The three men at the far table were still there, a blonde server in tight jeans and a low-cut T-shirt brought another pitcher of beer to their table. I glanced over to Kidd. "There are three members of the Iron Fist sitting not far from the two pool tables at the back of the room. Do you know them?"

Kidd glanced up and into the mirror, his single eye squinting. Then he turned around in his barstool to look in the direction I mentioned. "Yeah, I know 'em. Not well. Just enough to know they ride with the Iron Fist. Why?"

"All three of their Harleys have flats. Front tires. Looks like some lowlife slashed the tires. I noticed that the restrooms are in that area.

Maybe on your way to pee, you might want to mention to the fellas that when you walked by the motorcycles coming in, you saw the damage."

He looked at me, a gleam in his one eye, red and blue neon light floating in the black of his iris. He grinned. "Hell, yeah, I can do that. I guess you'll be somewhere outside."

"You guessed right. Thanks for your help."

"It's the least I can do to help you take Tank down a few notches. I hope you can take him all the way down."

"If you think of anything else that might be useful, call me." I slid a card in front of him. Kidd glanced down, read it, and discretely put it in his wallet.

He slithered off the wooden stool, standing straight. "Good luck, O'Brien." He sauntered around the tables, heading for the three men in the back.

I went outside and waited.

NINETY-FOUR

Diversion. It was one of the stealth tactics I learned serving in the Delta Force. It's easy to divert the average person's attention, providing the greater advantage in a surprise attack. When people hear a gunshot, they look in the direction of the sound. That's not always where the shooter will be found. I knew that when the three bikers came out of Bonito Jack's, they'd beat a path to their motorcycles and assess the damage before looking around to find the source.

When they ran out the door, they'd jump down the steps and move to the right where their motorcycles were parked. I stood in the shadows to the left of the porch, my steel bat still perched where I'd left it—next to a bush, halfway between me and the motorcycles.

Bonito Jack's front door opened, the three bikers hustling over the porch, running down the steps and over to their Harleys. As they cursed, swearing vengeance to an unseen enemy, I picked up my bat, walking to within fifteen feet of their backs.

"Don't you hate when that happens?"

The men whirled around, a mixture of fury and disbelief on their shiny faces. Three ducks in a row. Their eyes were wide and angry—the look of bulls staring at a matador's red cape. The alcohol causing their heads to bob left to right like three dogs watching cats scamper in a sand lot.

"You did this?" bellowed the man I knew was Hawk.

"You catch on quick. Don't mean to ruffle your feathers, Hawk."

He started to charge me. His pal to the right, the guy with the blonde Viking beard and haystack hair to match, held his hand up. "Wait a sec, Hawk." Viking looked at me, his head angling as if it were hard to think. "Hey, shit for brains, how do you know his name?"

"The same way I know your name, Magnus, and your biker bud Rooster. I do my research. But you three opened the book for me. I know your real names, your rap sheets, and the jobs you failed at before becoming full-time parasites. You opened that book when you entered the antique shop. The woman you threatened is my fiancée. The little girl you scared is our daughter. My name's Sean O'Brien. Any questions?"

"How 'bout a statement," Rooster said. "We'll go back to that antique store, lock the door, and take turns with your woman. Magnus will go last 'cause he's hung like a mule. It'll take the fun away from me and Hawk. Will that ruffle your feathers, O'Brien?"

I said nothing.

"Don't forget the kid," said Hawk. "She'll be a sweet dessert."

I knew Hawk was the only lefty in the group. He reached under his sleeveless leather jacket. I saw the wink of the chrome pistol in the neon light. I charged. A steel bat doesn't have the knockdown power of wood. But it has twice the control. I brought the bat down across his left arm, snapping the bones. He winced in pain as I swung the bat into his right knee, crushing it. He fell.

One down. Two to go.

Magnus pulled a knife from his belt. The blade was at least six inches long, serrated on one side. He charged, swiping the air in front of my face. I dropped the bat, grabbing his right arm and twisting it hard behind his back. I pulled his hand up between the shoulder blades, tendons and bones snapping like guitar strings cut in half. As he went down, I brought my right knee up hard and into his nose, shattering the nostrils and bridge. Blood gushed down the front of his shirt.

I picked up the bat. "Here you go Rooster." I threw it to him. The second his hands reached for the bat, he was open. The instant he pulled the bat back over his shoulder, he was defenseless. I stepped up, driving my right fist into his lower left jaw. I felt his jaw pop, breaking it, his eyes rolling back. He slowly dropped to his knees, holding the bat like a kid too short to make the little league team.

I grabbed him by his denim jacket. "Before you go night-night, when you wake up in the hospital tomorrow, deliver this message to Tank. Tell him I'm coming. He's next. And there is nothing he can do about it."

Rooster looked at me through glassy eyes. He mumbled, "Huh?"

I hit him hard in the mouth, knocking out upper and lower teeth. As he went down, I said, "It's going to be hard for you to crow now, Rooster."

I picked up my bat and started for the Jeep. I glanced up and at the front door of Bonito Jack's. Captain Kidd stood there with a can of beer in his hand, grinning, his black eyepatch visible in the blue neon like a pirate at the entrance of a Spanish galleon under the moonlight. He raised the can in a toast.

I nodded, got in my Jeep, and left.

***

Forty-five minutes later, I was back at Ponce Marina, walking down L-dock, where a late-night dew had painted a brushstroke of wet luster across the wooden planks. Mist rose from the marina water, giving the bats an ethereal look as they chased moths in the glow of the dock lamps. The rubber marine bumpers groaned as the rising tide pushed the boats closer to the dock posts. Other than that, all was quiet.

I boarded *Jupiter* as lightly as possible. I undressed in the dark of our master berth, Wynona sleeping on the right side of the bed, Max sitting up, part of the sheet hugging her head like a babushka. Soft moonlight came through one porthole window, the AC on, the cabin cool. I petted Max, whispering, "Hi, kiddo, you go back to sleep." I got into bed beside Wynona and lay there, knuckles sore, the events of the past few hours swirling in my mind.

Wynona touched my forearm, her hand warm in the cool cabin. "Thank God that you're back safe. My prayers came true."

I wanted to tell her to keep praying because I wasn't done. The heavy lifting was now facing me. I leaned over and kissed her softly on the lips, then rested my head back on the pillow. I would have to rise before the sun tomorrow to do what I hoped would bring down Tank and the Iron Fist. I knew how and where he was vulnerable. To get to the point, I would be on the road less traveled.

NINETY-FIVE

I considered attacking before dawn. In wars throughout the centuries, the early dawn approach is a good strategy because often you have just enough light to see your enemy while they're still asleep or barely awake, wiping the sleep from their eyes. If I used this approach with Tank, it would give me an advantage and might give Detective Dan Grant the opportunity to serve a search warrant to the Iron Fist clubhouse with less conflict.

I drove away from Ponce Marina two hours before sunrise. Wynona and Angela were still asleep when I left. Max, watching me through half-closed, dark brown eyes, somehow knew to remain in bed—that what I was going to do required me to go it alone. She was right.

Half an hour later, I pulled into a Waffle House parking lot, went inside, and bought two large black coffees. As I drove toward Tank's residence, the smell of coffee filled my Jeep. I remembered what Axle told me after I shot a hole through the pumpkin. *You'll take a right on Farm Lane. His house is about a quarter mile down on the left. There's an old red barn on the property. Only one like it for miles. He keeps a big pit bull there.*

When I came within three miles of Tank's house, I pulled over to the shoulder of the road. The land was remote and rural, a mixture of tall pines and live oaks. Much of it cross-fenced. The only visible industry was sod farms, citrus, and cattle. It was still dark, morning sun like a smoldering match behind mauve clouds in the eastern sky. I used my thumbs to write a text to Detective Dan Grant. *I'm heading to Simon Hogan's house—AKA Tank. Are you moving forward with the search warrant?*

I sipped the black coffee and waited for a response. I didn't have to wait long. He wrote: *Yes. Call me.*

I made the call. He answered and said, "I'm heading out the door. Judge signed it. I have a team in place."

"The clubhouse is basically a warehouse for illegal drugs. Sometimes they use another building Tank owns across town."

"Let's hope we hit the mother lode today."

"Tank is going to call a meeting, and he's going to have it at the Midnight Rider bar. It's a big place. Lots of refreshments and often likeminded customers who won't interfere."

"Why would he do that?"

"Because it'll be in his best interest. It'll be at noon. Could be up to fifty members of the Iron Fist there. You'll have time to have your men staked out and ready to make arrests. I don't have to tell you to bring a lot of firepower. You may need it."

"Let's hope we find the evidence this morning to support this. We'll have the teams ready. Between the sheriff's office and Daytona PD, we'll have it covered. I hope we have enough room in the county jail."

"Dan, your raid should give you the physical evidence you need. That, in addition to testimony from Axle, whose real name is Robert Holloway, and Digger, whose name is Al Rowe, along with how the Iron Fist's drugs killed nine college students in Florida, you can shut down the biker gang's operation in the state."

"Let's hope. Gotta go. Let me know whether the noon thing really will happen."

"Thanks, Dan." I clicked off, sipped the coffee, and drove the last three miles to Tank's house. The sun was a pink and yellow sliver on the eastern skyline when I spotted the red barn. It sat in a field behind a large brick house with black shutters. At least two hundred feet from the road, the home was surrounded by lush landscaping, and it had a long driveway that formed a circle in front.

I drove slowly by the property, looking for signs of light in the house. It was dark. I spotted something moving like a shadow next to a sidewalk that ran from the garage area up to the front porch. A large dog was on a chain, lifting its hind leg to urinate on a sycamore tree. I could see a Porsche Cayenne SUV parked in the circle. Next to it, and closer to the black front door, was a Harley-Davidson. It was made and sold on the thirtieth anniversary of the Fat Boy model.

And it was candy apple red.

NINETY-SIX

I sat in my Jeep a few hundred yards past Tank's house, studying a digital image—an aerial map of the property. There was a small dirt road that wove its way through a citrus grove and came within a hundred yards of his land. I drove that way, soon finding the road, which was more of a wide trail. I followed it for a half mile. The scent of oranges and tangerines in the morning air floated through my open window.

I stopped at a barbed-wire fence that separated the property. From there, I parked near a long row of orange trees. I could see the roof of Tank's house on the adjacent land and hear the caw of crows in the pines bordering the south parcel. I tore a five-inch piece of black painter's tape from a roll I'd packed, sticking the tape to my sleeve. I got out, put the Sig in my ankle holster, and the Glock under my belt. I crossed the fence and approached the house.

Within two minutes, I was in the backyard, moving past the right side of the house, checking for security cameras. I couldn't see any. Didn't mean they weren't there. I came around the side of the house near the garage and crossed the driveway. The dog's back was to me. I calculated that the length of the chain was about thirty feet. I made a soft whistle.

The dog lifted its ears. It stood, turning in my direction. I waved. The pit bull uttered a low growl and then did what I expected. It charged me, barking and snarling, the dog's lips curled back, white teeth snapping. I disappeared back the way I'd come, circling the house, and approaching from the opposite direction of the barking dog. I stood about twenty feet from the front door, peering through the limbs of a short magnolia tree.

In less than a minute, the front door opened. The man known as Tank stepped out and onto the concrete porch. He was barefooted, shirtless, and wearing blue jeans. In his right hand, he carried a .44 magnum revolver. A

360

big gun for a big man. From where I stood, I knew he was a couple of inches taller than me and at least fifty pounds heavier. His tattooed arms were thick with muscle. Chest like a bull. The tattoo on his back was of a man in a hood, face dark, wings on the hooded guy's shoulders.

"What's goin on, Bear? Something wake you?"

The dog turned toward him, before staring at the last place the animal had seen me vanish. Tank stood there, looking around his front yard, sprinklers on, the soft morning light breaking through the pine trees to the east side of the property. He walked a few feet over to his Harley, eyeing it.

I quietly lifted the piece of tape from my left sleeve, coming around the magnolia tree, staying close to the brick wall near the front porch. I saw the Ring doorbell and pressed the tape over the glass lens before pressing the audio record button on the phone in my front pocket.

Three seconds later, I was ten feet behind Tank. "Move and I'll blow your head off. Drop the gun."

He stood there, holding the .44 magnum in his hand. The pit bull turned, charging. It came close before the chain ended, the dog snarling, canine teeth biting the air. "Drop the gun! Last chance, Tank."

"How do I know you're armed?"

"You don't. Life's a gamble. But do you really want to play those cards?"

He said nothing. Two seconds later, I shot a hole through the gas tank on the Fat Boy. The pit bull stopped barking, gasoline pouring from both sides. I reached in my pocket, took out a zippo lighter, igniting it, tossing the lighter into the pool of gas. The Harley went up in a ball of flames, the dog whining.

Tank ducked and whirled around to face me. I had the drop on him. He knew it. My Glock pointed at his chest. "Settle down! I put a round through that tank, and I'll do the same with you, Tank. I'm here because you invited me."

He lowered the gun, staring at me through flat eyes. The glare was like a glint of moonlight off dark water at the bottom of a well, something seething in the back of his eyes, embers stoked from the fires of hell. He spoke in a gravelly voice, like he'd chewed glass. "I don't know who you are, fella, but I do know that this will be the day you die." He held the pistol down by his thigh.

NINETY-SEVEN

As I held my gun on Tank, I didn't want to be shot in the back. I would make a bluff, something that didn't require a yes or no answer, and I'd look for the subtle tells of a lie. "I've been watching your house, Tank. It's what cops and PIs often do. I saw you take the woman inside. You want to tell her to come out? She'll be safer that way?"

"What woman? Do you mean my gal pal inside there who'll put a round in the back of your head? Nah, I'll let her stay inside and pop you through the window."

The body language and change in speech pattern told me he was lying. He stared at me, his left fist clenching, then stretching his fingers straight. His revolver was still in his right hand, muzzle pointed toward the ground.

"As I said, you invited me here. The moment your goons walked into my fiancée's store and threatened her, and my daughter, was the day you crossed the line with me."

"So, you're the asshole Sean O'Brien."

"And you're the serial killer, Simon Hogan, or Tank for short. You killed nine young people in Florida alone in the last couple of months. Put some in the hospital. Turned healthy college kids into human vegetables."

"That's bullshit!"

He ducked, pointing the .44 at me. I put a round into his thigh. He managed to squeeze off a shot, the round whizzed by my right ear. I shot him in his right shoulder. The gun fell from his hand. He charged me like an NFL linebacker, knocking me to the ground. He was on top of me, blood running down his chest. His hands were around my throat. Squeezing with everything he had. I slammed the pistol grip into his forehead. The blow caused him to loosen his grip. He grabbed my right wrist, pulling my arm down, trying to turn the muzzle toward my face.

I used my left hand and arm to push back, the barrel now directly under Tank's chin, his eyes wild. He hit me on the left side of my head, the blow was like I'd been hammered with a wooden mallet. My ear rang, eardrum hurting. I drove my right elbow into his mouth, splitting lips, gums, and teeth. The blow stunned him long enough for me to roll way, the pit bull snapping at my feet.

I stood and looked down at Tank, blood spurting from the gunshot wound in his thigh. He stared up at me with dull eyes, trying to hold one hand to his leg. "You're losing blood from your femoral artery. It wouldn't take long before you bleed out. Bad way to tank, Tank. Your heart pumps until there's nothing left to pump. Just hot air. And you can't live on that."

"I need an ambulance! Call 911!"

"In thirty minutes, you'll need a grave digger."

"What do you want?"

"The truth. I know that's a stretch for you. But I'd bet your life that you can manage it. Take the phone out of your back pocket. You're going to call Randy Bates or Blade as he's affectionately called."

He spit out blood. "And tell him what?"

"Tell him to send a group text to every active member of the Iron Fist. You'll be holding a meeting in the parking lot of the Midnight Rider at noon. Let's call it high noon. Do it! Put the call on speaker. If you don't want Blade to hear your last words on earth, make sure you don't screw the message up."

He held his bloody thigh with his right hand, sitting up, taking out his phone, and punching a number. A few seconds later, a groggy voice came on the line. "Hey, Tank. What's going on? You don't usually call in the morning unless—"

"Blade! Just shut up and listen. Send a group text to the members. Tell 'em I'm holding an important meeting in the parking lot of the Midnight Rider."

"When you wanna meet?"

Tank looked up at me and said, "Noon."

"Okay. Got it. You okay, man? Sounds like you got a helluva hangover or something."

"Everything's copacetic. Gotta go." He clicked off and set the phone on the grass, both hands now pressed against the wound, blood seeping through his fingers. He looked at me with disdain. "I did what you wanted. Call for an ambulance."

"You want to live … you answer a couple of questions. If you lie to me, I'll put another round through your other leg. What drugs are shipped from the Iron Fist clubhouse every week?"

"Oxy, Percocet, Vicodin, Xanax, Prozac, Adderall, and others."

"Would the others include fentanyl?"

"It sometimes comes in the batches. We don't mix the shit anymore."

"Which batches?"

"Oxy."

"Where do the pills come from?"

"Mexico." He coughed.

"Which cartel?"

"Durango. I need an ambulance. I'm gonna die! I'm sweating like a pig."

"As president of the Iron Fist, Daytona, what roll do you play in the distribution of fentanyl?"

"I make the orders through the Fist headquarters in Texas … San Antonio."

"How many counterfeit pills are you selling each month?"

"I don't have those figures. Business is good at spring break and tapers off some during the summer."

"Are your drug deals done online?"

"Some are. Others we supply to local dealers, and they work their own online sites."

"Can anybody with a smart phone buy your illegal drugs?"

"Pretty much. C'mon! I'm seriously injured. It's getttin' dark! I need an ambulance."

"Then you make the call." I picked up his phone, tapped 911, put it on speaker phone, and handed it back to Tank.

"911 what's your emergency?"

"I've been shot! I'm bleeding out!"

"What is your address, sir?"

"It's 1875 Farm Lane. West Volusia County not far from Cody's Corner."

"We'll dispatch an ambulance to that location."

When the call ended, I looked at Tank. "Take off your belt, set it on the grass, and turn over on your stomach." He did as I ordered. I wrapped the belt around his leg and tightened it, making a tourniquet. From the porch, I picked up a concrete planter with a dead flower inside, bringing the planter back to where Tank was lying on the ground. The pit bull paced in the shade, watching me.

"Turn over on your back." Tank slowly did so. I lifted his leg, setting it on the planter, elevating the leg above ground. I looked at the bullet hole. The bleeding had stopped. He held his left hand to the wound in his right shoulder.

I pulled Andy's photo from my shirt pocket, holding it for Tank to see. "His name was Andy Ward. He took one of your oxy pills for shoulder pain. The fentanyl in it killed him." Tank looked from the picture up to me, his eyes flat and cold.

I walked toward the center of the front yard, under an oak, out of earshot and called Detective Dan Grant. I told him what happened, and added, "I have his confession on a digital recording. I'm emailing it to you now."

"When he lawyers up, his pasty-faced lawyer will say the confession was obtained under duress."

"But, the fact is, Tank held a .44 magnum in his hand and pointed it toward my chest. It's called self-defense. In my book, when someone agrees to have a little chat, it's called a confession. Regardless, Dan, you can use it as leverage. How'd the search warrant raid go?"

"We found thousands of counterfeit pills in the Iron Fist's clubhouse after we delivered the search warrant. There was only one biker in the building. He was alone, hungover, asleep on a leather couch. We took pics and video, confiscated the drugs, and everything connected to them."

"Good. I hope all works just as well at noon today."

"Me, too. You can throttle back now, O'Brien."

***

After the ambulance left with Tank still alive, the unit was followed by two uniformed deputies who would arrest Tank when he was stabilized at the hospital. I filled the pit bull's bowl with water from an outside tap and set the bowl down for the dog. "There you go, Bear. Stay cool."

I used water from the faucet to remove the dried blood from my hands and right ear. The dog watched me as it sat under the shade of a magnolia tree. "It looks like you may need a new place to call home. I have a friend named Digger. He recently lost his dog. Whiskey died of old age. Maybe you two would be a good match: an old biker and a young pit bull."

NINETY-EIGHT

Even with the ringing in my ear, I could hear two things when I called Wynona. Relief and concern. I told her what happened and added, "My hope is that the high noon arrests of the members of the Iron Fist don't result in something like the legendary shootout at the O.K. Corral."

"I guess there will be three more arrests at the hospital—the three men who threatened Angela and me."

"Make that a total of four arrests. Tank is in the same hospital."

"Sean, I know you must be hurt. How bad are you hurt?"

"Except for the ringing in my ear and a few sore ribs, I'm okay."

"Come home. Let me take care of you. Are you heading back to the marina?"

"Should be there in half an hour."

"See you soon." She clicked off as another call was arriving.

I answered, and Dave said, "Well, part of my question is answered."

"What part?"

"Whether you were alive."

"I still have a pulse."

"Nick and I had breakfast with Angela and Wynona this morning. She told us what you were facing. I'm almost hesitant to ask: what was the outcome?"

I gave Dave a brief update.

He was quiet for a few seconds before responding. "Let's hope Detective Dan Grant can take the baton you've handed off to him and hit the finish line. I can only imagine that whatever happens in the parking lot of the Midnight Rider will go viral. You know that somebody will capture the takedown on their cell phone camera."

"Bring on the video. Prosecutors can use everything they can get."

"Speaking of video, in watching the national and cable newscasts, most of them are getting the story of Tony Salazar wrong. That's according to my sources in the CIA. If you watch the so-called news, you'd believe that the DOJ is working hard to secure the safe return of Salazar. Communications between the State Department and the Mexican government are at a stalemate."

"I'm not surprised."

"The presence of DEA agents in Mexico has been, and probably always will be, a bone of contention with the Mexican leadership and their military. I don't discount that this type of sentiment is bleeding over to the average Mexican citizen."

"And that comes regardless of whether the DEA agents down there can help the Mexican military and police curb the tidal wave of fentanyl—the tsunami of money. Is Tony still alive?"

"From the intel I'm getting, yes. He's been beaten. Not sure of the severity of his injuries. But right now, Tony is the physical brunt, the punching bag, of Navarro's anger and hatred for the DEA, its agents, and probably America. Although I would suspect that he's happy that so many Americans are buying the junk he's walking across the southern border."

As I drove, I pulled the photo of Andy from my shirt pocket and glanced at it for a second. "Dave, will you check if anyone's brought my idea of a covert rescue mission to General Frazier's attention in the Pentagon? After all, these are the people ultimately responsible for his son's vegetative state. If he wasn't interested before, maybe he will be now since there seems to be no activity going on to rescue Tony Salazar."

"I recognize that tone in your voice. What do you have in mind?"

"I'm going to call Clint to get his read on what I think can be done to swiftly bring Salazar out of the hell hole."

"You mentioned before that Frazier wouldn't have to commission a Special Ops team if he felt it was too risky for him, but instead, you would pull one together, right?"

"Yes. Clint is one of a half dozen former Delta Force members I've stayed in touch with over the years. One, whose name is Miguel Romero, speaks fluent Spanish. The others all have their talents, from marksmanship to creating and diffusing bombs to hostage negotiations and terrorist situations. Our government doesn't want to admit it, but

Delta Force members have been secretly used to rescue hostages all over the world. We took out that Colombian drug lord, Pablo Escobar. Few people know that."

"You said *we*, Sean. Were you part of that?"

"No."

"If General Frazier is interested in offering whatever assistance he could, in a covert kind of fashion, of course, what would you need?"

"If we can find out where Navarro is holding Tony, we could use access to a plane. All these guys went through HALO training—high altitude and low opening of parachutes. We could fly high above the area and drop through the sky at night. We'd freefall most of the way, opening our chutes a few hundred feet above ground. From there, we advance to the target. The challenge is having enough firepower to carry out the mission."

"I know you are restricted with the weight you can carry when you skydive. It'd be hard to carry a rocket launcher."

"Another option would be to make a terrestrial crossing. We could make a border crossing at El Paso, Texas, driving on Highway 45 from the border almost due south until we hit Durango. That way, if the general could get us across the border without the Mexicans inspecting our van or truck, we could carry plenty of firepower."

"That would take some persuading. It might be doable. Fort Bliss is right there. From the information I've gathered, the command at the base reports to General Frazier. The Army runs part of the Delta-2 division, or the Global Response Force. Fort Bliss has dozens of tanks and Bradley Fighting Vehicles. Too bad you and your team can't borrow one for this mission."

"I'd settle for a van with plenty of firepower inside it. We just need a way to cross the border with the weapons to do the job."

"That effort will probably result in payoffs to the Mexican border patrol to look the other way. Or, if they were in a cooperative spirit to really combat the fentanyl flood, they'd join you."

"If that was the case, there'd be no need for this mission."

Dave said nothing for a moment. "If you can't get guns across the border, maybe the DEA in Mexico City could meet your team somewhere and supply what you need."

"If we could work with someone in that agency down in Mexico and not have to go through Washington, that's a possibility. What we can't have is a situation where we arrive in Durango and the weapons, for some bureaucratic reason, aren't there. I don't want to face Diego Navarro using rocks and slingshots."

"Let me make some calls to see what I can find out. I'll also work on getting any information I can to help narrow down where Diego Navarro might be. Chances are, wherever Navarro is, Salazar is being held in close proximity."

NINETY-NINE

I entered the Ponce Marina parking lot, thinking about how the past was about to shape the future. I pulled my Jeep up to the shade cast by a half dozen royal palm trees in one corner of the lot and parked. As the engine ticked while cooling, I thought about some of the missions I'd shared with Tony Salazar in the Middle East and Afghanistan. One time, the day after a roadside IED bomb exploded, killing two U.S. soldiers and severely injuring three more in an RG-31 armored truck, Tony and I stood in the desert. We looked at a sunset bleeding red over the Safed Koh Mountains in the distance.

"That's where they're hiding," Tony said, lifting binoculars to his eyes.

I nodded. "They're only hidden because they haven't been found yet. I think it's time to find them."

He lowered the binoculars. "I second that, sir."

The sound of gulls chuckling above the parking lot brought me back to Ponce Marina. The ringing in my ear had subsided somewhat. My rib cage was sore. Knuckles on my right hand torn and bloody.

I took out a pen and paper from the console, jotting down ideas for a covert mission deep into Mexico. I could plan that—I could lead it. But planning how I would tell Wynona was not easy. I had no doubt that she would give it her blessing, but inside, she'd harbor fear for me.

When I left for Mexico, Wynona would try to mask the internal anxiety when she took walks with Angela and Max on the beach. But, as she strolled through the surf holding Angela's hand, Max chasing gulls, Wynona would look toward the vast horizon and wonder if I'd come home alive. She'd put on a brave face, but deep inside the fear would churn in her stomach.

From where I sat in my Jeep, I could hear music coming from the jukebox in the Tiki Bar, *Fields of Gold*, by Sting. I called Clint Ward and told him what had happened thus far in the day. When I finished, there was a long pause. "Sean, I never asked you to take on a biker gang, trying to hunt down those responsible for Andy's death. But I'm glad you did, and I'm thankful that you weren't hurt any worse than you were."

"A situation has been dropped into our laps. Those ultimately responsible for Andy's death are the guys who put fentanyl into the pills. And that's the Durango cartel, the same boy scouts who are holding Tony Salazar hostage in a global game of chess. Only problem is our country refuses to play. Tony's a pawn. We brought Tony out from behind enemy lines in Afghanization. We can do it again down in Mexico. If I put together a team of ex-Delta Force guys, people from our squad, would you go?"

"You don't even have to ask. I've stayed in pretty good shape, not like you, Sean, but I can chop a cord of wood and not be too sore in the morning. And, with a sniper rifle, I can still sight down on a bad guy from a thousand yards away."

"I want to see if we can get Miguel Romero, Preston Bell, and Jordan Mann."

"With you and me included, that'd be a helluva team."

"After I reach them, I'll call you back. We'd have to move on this fast. Unless someone intervenes, I don't think Tony has much time left. Since nobody is stepping up to the plate, that *someone* will have to be us."

"If I can do more to find Andy's killers and save Tony at the same time, hell yeah, I'm in. Let's roll!"

***

Twenty minutes later, I was with Wynona in *Jupiter's* salon. Angela and Max were playing on the dock in front of the boat. Wynona was dabbing antiseptic to the torn skin on my scalp just above the ear. "This really should have stitches," she said.

"I've had worse."

"And I've seen the scars. Maybe your dark hair will hide this one."
She cleaned the blood from my ripped knuckles and wrapped a bandage

around my sore ribs.

I glanced at my watch. "If all goes well, Dan Grant and the sheriff's department should be making arrests at the Midnight Rider right about now."

She nodded. "Let's hope gunshots aren't fired. And, after it's over, maybe the prosecutor's office will have enough to slap serious charges on the gang members. Out of forty-five to fifty bikers, I'd bet a few will turn state's evidence and cooperate in plea deals."

"I know of two who will. Maybe more are going to follow." I buttoned up my shirt and took the picture of Andy from the pocket, showing the photo to Wynona. "It started with Andy's death, and it's exploded from there. I don't know where this case will end, but I know my job isn't finished. Let's go up to the flybridge. I want to let you know what's at stake."

ONE HUNDRED

Having faced depths of evil that were so dark, so reprehensible, that I still dealt with them and the night sweats, I was convinced that the words *devil's seed* weren't just a term sometimes used. Evil, like good, is omnipresent. Good can exist on its own. But evil needs a victim. It is predatory, always looking for good to harm. Because of its stealth nature, it is better at hiding on the periphery of your senses.

I thought about that—considered what I might have to share with Wynona to have her grasp what I was facing. But it wasn't just me or Tony Salazar. It was another 100,000 young people who'd die like lab rats after ingesting fentanyl. A lot was at stake.

We climbed up the ladder and onto *Jupiter's* flybridge. Nick was using white chalk to draw a hopscotch diagram on the dock in front of *St. Michael*, Angela helping him, Max keeping the pelicans from coming too close. I opened all the windows, allowing a breeze from the Atlantic to blow through the open wheelhouse. I sat next to Wynona on the bench seat, her eyes filled with concern, as if she already knew what I wanted to tell her.

I set Andy's photo on the seat and looked up at her. "When I told Tank what his poison did to Andy, when I held up his picture, he looked at Andy's face with contempt. The Iron Fist buys directly from the Durango cartel, the same bunch of misfits who, as you know, are holding Tony Salazar. He was one of my team members in Afghanistan who was held prisoner by the Taliban. There were three of us ... Tony, Roger Fuller, and me. Roger was beheaded. Tony and I managed to make it out alive."

"I can't imagine what you and your men went through to survive."

"Tony will die soon in the hands of Diego Navarro unless someone stops him. The White House, DOJ, and even the DEA are sitting on their hands. It's not about a policy of never negotiating with terrorists … it's about saving a man's life who served our nation well in undeclared wars overseas. After that, he dedicated his life to fighting the war on drugs. And now Tony may become the second DEA agent murdered by a Mexican drug cartel."

"Are you planning to do something to bring Tony out of there?"

"Not just me, but other ex-Delta Force members who served with Tony. One speaks Spanish. He, and the others, are some of the best in the world at extractions—going into hostile situations unnoticed and bringing out the victim or victims alive."

"How many former members of your team would go?"

"Probably all of them, but that would be too many. With Clint and I, we'll ask three others. We could enter Mexico from El Paso and drive south into Durango."

"But you don't know where Diego Navarro is keeping Tony."

"No, but we'll find out. Dave is using his contacts to look at satellite images of the area, and to turn over rocks where Navarro is mostly likely to be."

"Have you already made up your mind that this is what you're going to do?"

"Wynona, I can't leave Tony down there to die at the hands of a psychotic drug lord … not after what we did to serve this county. We put it on the line in ways I won't talk about. But we did what we had to do with the mission we faced. It's no different now. Our government may not have Tony's back, but I do."

"When you were in the Delta Force, you didn't have a fiancée and a daughter. Now there is more at stake. As much as I want to see your friend, Tony, out of there alive, I fear for your life. You will be entering some place that is heavily guarded by armed men. With the cartel's money, I'm sure they own the latest security and trespassing detection devices."

I looked at her tenderly. "Wynona, Tony has a wife and two young children. If it were me in that situation, you'd be grateful if the team went for me."

Wynona's eyes misted, and she nodded her head. "How would you go through what are essentially machine gun nests to find Navarro and Tony?"

"The approach will depend on where they're holding him."

She took in her surroundings—looked at a hard blue sky over the Atlantic, the sun beating down on the boats in the marina, felt the breeze warm and seasoned with sea salt, and listened to Angela and Nick laughing. "Sean, maybe there is some grander purpose in what's unfolded in the past few weeks. When Clint came to our home, it was to jumpstart a cold case into the death of his son. That accelerated to a dealer connected to a dangerous motorcycle gang whose members are linked to one of the world's most brutal drug cartels. Maybe our universe, or our place in it, isn't so small after all. Perhaps these connections, the paths you're following, were destined. And you're not unlike a knight on horseback going into a distant land to find the white dragon of truth."

Sean smiled. "You must be spending a lot of time hanging out with that knight in your antique store. But interesting you mention a white dragon?"

"Why?"

"That's the street term for fentanyl."

Three gulls flew by the flybridge, squawking as they made a right turn, soaring above a dozen sailboat masts. Wynona watched the gulls disappear into the horizon over the Atlantic. "I didn't know that was the name of the drug. Since I've known you, all the cases you take are usually in Florida and occasionally in other states. But you've never gone into another country. And now, without the sanction of the government, you're talking about invading Mexico with a small band of ex-Delta Force fighters to take back one of their own. These cartels, on the other hand, eat their own. They live and die by the sword. Loyalty is what they preach, but they preach it from the pulpit of greed, meaning loyalty goes to the highest bidder. You will face a diabolical evil that you've never faced before."

"After Sherri's death, and before I met you, I met a teenage kid who I had never known existed. She was my niece. Her name is Courtney Burke. She came to the marina and told me about a chapter in my life, or at least that of my family, that I didn't know about. I'm telling you this story because it took me to Ireland, where the mother, I also never knew, was raped by a priest in the church she attended. She became pregnant and later gave birth to a boy." I paused and looked at the lighthouse in the distance.

"Was the priest your father?"

"No. He'd fathered someone I also had never met, a man who had raped Courtney in her early teen years. She was hunting for him."

"Why?"

"To kill him. His name was Dillon, and he was my brother."

"*Was* ... or is?"

"Was. It came down to this: could a priest rape and impregnate with what was essentially the devil's seed? I raise that question due to the consequences of his action and because of what Dillon chose to do throughout his life. I discovered things about him that would make the atrocities committed by the Taliban almost seem pale in comparison. I tracked Dillon through Ireland and eventually found him back in the States. Our meeting was somewhere beyond the bounds of the Garden of Eden and Gethsemane. It became a Cain and Abel battle. I killed my own brother before he could kill any more innocent people. When I looked into his eyes that final time, I saw traces of me and my mother. And I saw an aura—a stain, from a brutal priest who violently raped my mother on his altar table during a thunderstorm as my biological father was driving in the rain to pick her up. Because of repercussions from that single act, and concerns for my safety, my mother had the very difficult decision to let another family raise me. It broke her heart. I had a few days with my mother in South Carolina before her death. She told me everything."

"Sean, I'm so sorry." Wynona looked up at me, blinking back tears. She reached over Andy's photo and took my hand. "Do whatever it takes to save Tony and bring him back to his family. Your family will be here when you return."

I used my thumb to wipe a tear from her cheek and kissed her softly on the lips.

ONE HUNDRED ONE

Watching Dave in action, I could see how good he must have been within the CIA. For the next few hours, I spent time on *Gibraltar*, mostly in the salon figuring a tactical approach for the Mexican mission. Dave worked the phone and his computer, often both at the same time.

I had called three of my former Delta Force team members. Two of the three committed to the mission. The third man, Jordan Mann, had an upcoming surgery scheduled. That meant we would go with four guys—hoped that would be enough.

Dave disconnected from a call, tapped his computer keyboard for a few seconds before glancing up at me. "Take a look at the computer screen." He enlarged the screen, using his curser to point to areas in the satellite images. "This is a remote section known as the Santa Rita region. Allow me to zoom closer." Dave enlarged the image. "And this compound is one of the places where you might find Diego Navarro."

"Why there?"

"Because the CIA knows it is one of three homes he has. Three are in the state of Durango. One in Sinaloa, and one on the beach at Mazatlán. The one you see here is the largest and most secluded. It's a compound that consists of a main home. Very large. There are various types of barns, horse stables, and guest houses scattered on the property. Would Navarro take Tony there or to some more remote place? The cartel apparently owns many small farms and ranches. It's believed that some of the facilities are used to make counterfeit drugs."

"Somebody in the Santa Rita area probably knows what's going on there and whether Navarro is staying at the big hacienda."

"But would they risk their lives for bribe money? That would depend on how much money Navarro spreads in the area to buy silence and loyalty."

"Does your contact or contacts know anything unique about Navarro? For example, does he buy prostitutes? If so, where do they come from, and if he has a favorite mistress, would she talk? Does Navarro go into his preferred Catholic church to confess and ask for penance?"

Dave grunted. "I doubt you'd find a priest who'd share that, regardless of Navarro's criminal life. Not that Navarro sees value in religion. Wait a second, now that you prompted me, I read something in the notes that is interesting." He clicked on a file and scanned Diego Navarro's profile. "Okay, here it is. Seems that Navarro might have disdain for traditional Christian orthodoxy, but he does have an interest in something on the other end of the scale."

"What's that, Satanism?"

"It's called the religion of Santa Muerte. Otherwise known as Holy Death. The imagery of this dark deity resembles a female version of the grim reaper … a skeleton wearing a white robe or wedding dress, holding a scythe in one hand and a globe in the other. Maybe the lass is global. Nonetheless, it appears that Diego Navarro rebuilt a Santa Muerte temple or cathedral after a fire destroyed part of it. Does he frequent the place? Who knows? These notes do suggest that, in the dark world of Narcos drug lords, these greaseballs believe Santa Muerte will protect them if they pray to her and come bearing gifts. I hear she's fond of tequila and blood. Not necessarily in that order."

"Where is the church that Navarro rebuilt?"

Dave used his index finger to point on the screen. "Right about there. Moving from the dark side of drug lord allegiances to a light at the end of the tunnel—here's the deal. General Stan Frazier is pulling a few strings, probably all he can pull without the action being traceable back to his office in the Pentagon."

"What did he agree to do?"

"Officially, nothing. Off the record, he's arranged for ground transportation and weapons."

"What are the arrangements?"

"There will be a non-descript dark blue van waiting for you in a parking lot across the street from the Cassidy gate or the western entrance to Fort Bliss. The van will have a Texas license plate that is not registered to any real person or company. The van's been fitted with a larger gas tank, and it'll be filled. You'll have twenty gallons of additional fuel in a sealed canister. If, for some reason, you must leave the van in Mexico, do it."

"We'll need it to get out of there."

"Not if it's full of bullet holes or the tires are shot out. You might commandeer one of Navarro's vehicles, or we might have to arrange a flight from a crop-duster airstrip. Inside the van, you and your team will find four M4-Carbine rifles, a half dozen magazines for each rifle, plenty of ammo. There are four tactical, 12-gauge shotguns, fitted to hold seven shells each. Lots of double-aught buckshot. There will be four Barrett MRAD sniper's rifles. Included in the package are 9mm Berettas, knives with belt sheaths, night vision goggles, and scopes."

"How about communications?"

"There's GPS navigation in the van and on the watch that you'll strap to your wrist. You also will have a satellite phone. I will be your only contact, Sean. As far as General Frazier or the Army are concerned, you and your men do not exist. If you are captured, the U.S. government won't acknowledge who you are … or were."

"We won't be captured. We'd be killed, but I'm going to try my best to keep that from happening. How do we get that kind of arsenal through the Mexican border checkpoint?"

"You'll find a *FastPass* in the van's glove box. It's the kind of pass that commercial vehicle drivers use each day when traveling to and from Mexico. There's a specially designated traffic lane for that. You'll enter Mexico through the Paso Del Norte checkpoint. We're scheduling your entrance at close to seven a.m. on Thursday. That's right before the shift change and close to the morning rush hour. Let's hope the Mexicans on third shift are tired and want to go home."

"What if, for some reason, they decide to look inside the van?"

"Take plenty of crisp hundred-dollar bills and hope for the best."

"That's reassuring."

"You said Clint will be flying with you from Orlando to El Paso. How about the other two men? What's their logistics?"

"Miguel Romero lives in New Mexico. He's driving in from Las Cruces. Preston Bell is flying in from Billings, Montana."

Dave leaned back in his chair, took his bifocals off, and rubbed his bloodshot eyes. He looked up at me. "Sean, if you and your men manage to pull off this extraction, your strategy should be taught at West Point and other military schools. The unfortunate fact is that anonymity will have to prevail. The situation is far too political, unfortunately. But that's our world today. Men like you must reinvent yourselves and your tactical approach to do what needs to be done regardless of the politics."

"Anonymity is fine. It's never been about the glory."

ONE HUNDRED TWO

Nearing 6:00 p.m., I had packed, secured my passport, and was ready to catch a plane. Clint and I would be on the same flight. The last time we flew together was in a C-130 troop transport plane. And we were heading to Afghanistan from Syria. I walked from *Gibraltar's* salon to the cockpit where Nick stood near the transom, turning fish on a small grill, white smoke carrying the scent of lemon butter and garlic. Angela was near Nick, watching as he gave her cooking pointers, Max on the opposite side. Dave and Wynona were in the salon, talking.

"Daddy, the food's almost ready."

"Have you been helping Nick with the cooking?"

"Yep. He let me and Mama make the salad, too."

Nick sipped his beer, closing one eye to avoid the smoke. "Angela is my lil' helper. We inspire each other. Go tell Dave and your mama that the food's ready. I need for somebody to bring a platter to me."

"Okay." Angela went into the salon.

Nick turned a piece of fish, the juices and sauce sizzling off the hot mesquite coals. "Sean, are you sure you can't take me along with you to Mexico? Hell, I look Mexican. I can blend right in with the people."

"Not the people I have to face. You can't mix with evil. It's not in you, Nick. You'd be spotted in seconds."

He sipped his beer, grinning, eyes animated in the golden twilight. "Like Popeye, I yam want I yam. Let's eat!"

We all gathered under the trawler's overhang between the cockpit and the salon. Dave turned on the TV screen behind the bar. A news anchorman was on camera, the words *Breaking News*, at the bottom of the screen. Nick said, "Whoa, crank up the sound."

Dave adjusted the volume. The newscaster said, "Witnesses said it was like a scene from a movie when police and SWAT teams converged on the parking lot of the Midnight Rider bar in Daytona Beach at the noon hour. Channel Seven's Jennifer Miller has the story."

The video cut to a wide shot of the Midnight Rider parking lot, with bikers scrambling, reaching into their motorcycle saddlebags, and pulling out pistols and knives. Through a megaphone, a SWAT team member shouted, "Put the guns down and step to the middle of the lot. Now! You are surrounded." The image cut to SWAT snipers on the roof of the bar, and other police crouched behind the open doors of their vehicles, guns drawn. Seconds later, the bikers moved slowly, hands up, unharmed, to the center of the lot. "On your knees!" ordered the SWAT leader.

The reporter said, "What could have been a deadly shootout ended with cooler heads prevailing as dozens of police and SWAT officers had guns drawn on forty-seven members of the Iron Fist motorcycle club. Police converged to arrest as many members of the club as possible on charges of illegal fentanyl sales. The Iron Fist, according to Detective Dan Grant, controls the fentanyl market in Florida and four other southern states."

The video cut to an interview with Grant. "We found evidence of substantial fentanyl distribution from the Iron Fist clubhouse. In addition, we pulled computer records from the gang, and our IT specialists say the forensic evidence of drug sales is overwhelming. Illegal fentanyl distribution kills tens of thousands of Americans each year. Busts like this will go a long way in sending a message that it won't be tolerated in Florida."

The video cut to shots of handcuffed Iron Fist members loaded into sheriff's vans. "In addition to the arrests, thirty-five handguns and twenty knives were confiscated. No drugs were found on the men or their motorcycles. Police say the Iron Fist sells fentanyl online, and they also distribute to dealers in geographic regions of Florida, from the Panhandle to Key West. Officers aren't saying why so many members of the motorcycle club were in the bar parking lot at the noon hour. One former biker has his theory."

The image cut to a man who looked like he'd just come off a cattle drive. He wore a sweat-stained Stetson. Leathery face creased, steel gray beard. "Somehow, they got duped. Yup, that's my guess. It's like they were called here for a meeting or something, and when they all showed up, the law stepped out from behind the bushes and buildings. What a surprise."

The video changed to scenes of police loading the last half dozen bikers into a van before cutting to the reporter standing next to a sheriff's car, emergency lights flashing, bikers and customers from the bar in the background. "Detectives say the online fentanyl sales appear to be at least fifty percent of the club's net income. Those deadly purchases are available to anyone with a smart phone. Unfortunately, the slogan from the DEA, *one pill can kill*, seems to be ignored in what can be a dicey game of chance when buying illegal drugs like fentanyl online. Reporting from Daytona Beach, I'm Jennifer Miller. Now back to you in the studio."

Dave muted the sound. He looked over at me. "One group down … one more to go."

I said nothing.

ONE HUNDRED THREE

El Paso, Texas

In the dark of a sultry Texas morning, just outside the El Paso International Airport, I felt like I'd stepped through time. Clint and I met Miguel Romero and Preston Bell in the rideshare and taxi area. Both Miguel and Preston had stayed in good shape, and twenty years later, they were ready for what we all knew could be our final call of duty. Regardless of how it would play out, we were going without reservations. And, if we could bring Tony Salazar out alive, we'd return with few regrets.

Miguel, with his swarthy face, black hair, and wide smile, was still running marathons. Preston had the rugged look of a roughneck oil field worker. Dirty blonde hair, a square face, and piercing blue eyes that cut through a lot of life's mundane rhetoric. Preston saluted me and said, "Major O'Brien, Sergeant Bell reporting for duty, sir."

I smiled. "At ease."

Miguel chuckled. "You can take the soldier out of Delta Force, but you can never take Delta Force out of the soldier."

"That's the truth," Clint said, slapping Miguel on the back. "Good to see you guys. Thank you for coming."

Miguel said, "After Sean called and told us what happened to your son, and then what went down with Tony, I was packing."

I nodded. "Let's catch a cab. No Uber and the digital trail it'll leave behind. We're about to go far off the grid. From here, all cell phones are history. We use only the satellite phone in the van." I flagged a Taxi. The driver was dark-skinned, squatty, and sleepy-eyed. The van smelled of fried pork sausage. He turned down the mariachi music on his radio. I said, "We're heading to the Cassidy gate entrance to the base. Off Sheridan."

"I know the place," he nodded. "Get in."

It took us less than fifteen minutes to arrive. I spotted the lone van in a dark parking lot. I pointed. "Over there." When he let us out, I paid with cash as we unloaded our bags. I waited until the red taillights of his taxi vanished into the night before we approached the van.

Two men came from out of the shadows near a warehouse. "Good morning," said the taller of the two. They were dressed in civilian clothes. Military haircuts. They had the straight posture and the look of military police. "Which one of you fellas is Mr. O'Brien?"

"That'd be me."

"Can I see some ID?"

I opened my passport holding it up to him.

"Thank you, sir. Here are the keys to the van. Let us show you what's in the back."

We followed the two men to the rear of the van. Instinctively, my men and I stepped to one side, not directly behind closed doors. In this business, trust is earned. They opened the doors. Under the dome light, we could see the weapons and boxes of ammo. Everything neatly arranged and secured so none of the guns or rounds would slide around during turns.

The tall soldier said, "It's all yours. Don't know where you guys are going, but we wish you luck."

"Thanks."

Clint said, "We appreciate the delivery."

"No problem." The two men turned and walked toward the base, taking a left and vanishing on a side road. I looked at Miguel. "Since your Spanish is a tad better than any of us, you're our designated driver, at least through border checkpoints."

He grinned. "I accept the task, sir. Now, give me the damn keys."

I tossed the keys to him. We got in the van, Miguel driving, me in the front passenger seat. Clint and Preston in the back seat. We set the GPS navigator to get us to the bridge, Paso del Norte.

Ten minutes later, we were approaching the bridge. I glanced at my watch: 6:55. The traffic on both sides of the check points was getting heavy. A lot of commercial vehicles. Trucks of all sizes, exhaust billowing, drivers sipping coffee from paper cups. We followed the signs to the FastPass lane. There were three vehicles in front of us. One was a semi-truck, the other was a U-Haul truck, followed by a Ford Escape.

I watched the interaction between the Mexican border agents and the drivers. The agents were saying very little, waving drivers through. A few minutes later, we eased the van to the checkpoint. A Mexican agent, wearing military clothing, held his hand up, signaling for us to stop. We did, and Miguel lowered the driver's window. The agent came up to the van's door and, in Spanish said, "Passports please." We each had a passport on the console. Miguel picked them up, handed them to the agent, and replied in Spanish, "Good morning. Are you just starting your day or ending it?"

"I'm ending. Been here since eleven last night. What is the purpose of your trip into Mexico?"

"Business."

"What type of business?"

"We're scouting locations for a new Costco store."

The guard looked over at me. "Anyone else in the back of the van?"

Miguel shook his head. "No. Would you like for me to open it so you can inspect?"

As he started to answer, three more Mexican agents came out of the administration building. Each one held a paper cup of steaming coffee. They were chatting, ready to begin their workday. The agent near Miguel said, "That will not be necessary. As I'm sure you know, we have a Costco in Ciudad Juarez. Maybe you can build one in Chihuahua where my mother lives."

Miguel flashed his grin. "You never know."

The agent stepped aside, and we drove ahead, crossing the international bridge into Mexico as the sun rose in the east.

From the back seat, Preston chuckled, "Damn, Miguel. That took balls, asking him whether he wanted to inspect the van."

Clint said, "Let's hope that kind of luck continues."

Heading south on Highway 45, I said, "Somewhere between here and El Dorado, let's pull off the road into one of the remote desert areas and make sure the guns work before we get there."

Miguel nodded. "Sounds like the first order of business, but where is *there*? And where the hell is the cartel hiding Tony in Durango?"

"It's part of our job to find out." I gave them the last update on possible areas where Diego Navarro might be holding Tony. "The state of Durango is a big place, full of mountains and hills. Would Navarro hold Tony in the largest of the haciendas that the cartel owns? The main compound is more than a thousand acres, heavily guarded, no doubt. Would he be so arrogant and brazen that he'd keep Tony in that compound like one of the trophy horses Navarro owns?"

"He might," said Preston. "The reason could be because Navarro may think it'll be the last place the DEA would penetrate considering all the other properties scattered over the mountains. Or Navarro could be hedging his bets, playing the DEA, knowing they won't do much to avoid being blamed for Tony's death, should they conduct a raid."

I studied the digital map on the van's GPS screen, using my fingers to enlarge it, then zooming in on the state of Durango. "Our first stop will be a town called Ciudad Lerdo."

"Why there?" Miguel asked.

"Because there is an old cathedral there that seems to have a special place in Diego Navarro's dark heart. It's one of places across Mexico where the underworld goes to church. Not to worship God, but to cut deals with the devil. Maybe there's somebody who has seen Navarro, and who knows more about him than what he'd share with his mistress."

ONE HUNDRED FOUR

Ciudad Lerdo, Mexico

The first thing that caught my eye driving into Ciudad Lerdo was a tall and ornate clock tower in the center of town. It was Mexico's version of London's Big Ben. The city itself was a dusty postcard from the past. Old Mexico. Aging buildings built a century ago and maintained in good condition. A half dozen church spires rose in the sky above everything else.

We drove past Victoria Park in the center of the city, the park with its large bandstand at the end of a concrete path lined with leafy trees. Tamale stands and food vendors thick as the pigeons strutting on the sidewalk. People moved about with a slow rhythm in the heat of the late afternoon sun.

Miguel drove through the light traffic, his eyes scanning the buildings. "This place is full of cathedrals. According to the map, the one we want is about a half mile from where we are right now."

"Let's hope the priest is home," Preston said from the back seat.

Clint chuckled. "Priest? I doubt the Catholic church would have anything to do with a religion that centers on an alleged goddess called Holy Death."

Miguel shook his head. "If my grandma were alive, as a devoted Catholic, she'd have a lot to say about a religion that implies you can get away with murder and still go to heaven."

"That crap sounds like something drug traffickers would buy into," Preston said.

Miguel chuckled. "Funny thing down here in Mexico ... most everyone is raised within some structures of the Catholic church. So, the future Narcos scum, as little boys, were exposed to the Bible and its teachings. But, as they grow up and violate just about every sacred tenet in the Bible, they look for some other way to seek divine protection, because they believe in the power of prayer but feel they're beyond it. And along comes something called Santa Muerte."

"What do you think, Sean?" asked Preston.

"I think that if you could reason with idol worshipers, there'd be no idol worshipers."

"Yep. Couldn't have said it better myself."

A few minutes later, we took a side road toward the Cathedral de la Santísima, passing buildings made from cornerstones of Mexican adobe. Street vendors sold fresh produce—tomatoes, shucked corn, avocados, potatoes, and fruit. People walked or moved around on bikes and mopeds. Miguel took one hand from the steering wheel and pointed. "That looks like the place. And, according to our GPS, we've reached our destination."

"Not yet," I said.

We parked across the street from the Cathedral de la Santísima, the building cast in shade from palm and cedar trees. Miguel looked over at me. "What's the plan, Major?"

"You are center in the immediate plan because of your language skills. Let's go inside and see what we can see. I'd like to find the person who runs the place and ask him or her about a parishioner of interest." I turned to Clint and Preston. "Why don't you guys stretch your legs while Miguel and I see what's behind the altar?"

"Sounds good," Clint said.

Miguel and I walked down the concrete path, through the deep shade, toward the front entrance. The cathedral was made from what appeared to be coquina stone, beige-colored, and old as fossils. The wooden front door looked like a side entrance to a castle—dark redwood with large black hinges. The door opened, and a woman appeared. She wore black clothing as if she was in mourning. The skin on her face was wrinkled from age and poverty, and her eyes were small and dark. She looked at me for a moment as if she recognized or had been waiting for me.

I nodded. "Buenas tardes, señora."

"La catedral esta vacia." She clutched her shawl with one hand, fingers crooked, scurrying by us, disappearing down the path.

Miguel looked over at me. "She doesn't come across as a drug trafficker."

"What did she say?"

"She said the cathedral is empty."

"I bet."

"If we find some sort of priest in there, what do you want me to ask him?"

"Don't ask anything. Just say that we were sent here by Diego Navarro. Let's see if there is recognition of the name in the other person's face. If not, we can drop a donation in the plate and ask additional questions to search for truth."

"I'm not so good at spotting deception in people."

"Just follow my lead."

"That's why we're here."

I opened the door to the sound of creaking hinges and the smell of burning incense.

The dim hallway was cool and smelled of cemetery stone. We followed the scent and the passageway for about eighty feet, past two closed doors. There was no light coming from the base of the thresholds. The corridor opened to a large room. We walked inside what appeared to be a sanctuary. Shadows from flickering candles danced in glass vases along the walls. There were four wooden pews.

"Check that out," Miguel said, pointing to a figure behind what I assumed was an altar, a long table with a white cloth over it, candles burning on opposite sides. "So, that's the patron saint of criminals … our lady of holy death."

"And from here, I can tell that it's a real human skeleton." The skeleton wore what looked like a white wedding dress. In its left hand was a wooden scythe with a shiny metal blade at one end. In the other hand was a globe. I assumed that, under the dress, someone, maybe a carpenter, had rigged the skeleton's arm so it could support the weight of the plastic globe.

Miguel grinned. "Yeah, she's not my type. A little too skinny. That takes on a whole new meaning when you say you need to put some meat on the bones. Looks like she's all dressed up and ready to go to the vampire ball."

"The question I have is where did the skeleton come from? Did someone dig it out of a grave? Or was the person killed and left in the Mexican dessert for a sun bake and vulture feast?"

We walked to the altar and looked at the money—coins and bills on a large bronze plate. Directly in front of the skeleton were chocolates, flowers, apples, and three small bottles of tequila. There was a clear glass canning jar. Even in the moving shadows from the candles, I could tell that the liquid inside the jar was blood. It was maybe a day or two old, but it was blood.

Miguel looked at it. "I mentioned vampire ball as a joke, but I'd bet the dark red stuff in that jar is blood … probably human." He studied the skeleton and the things left on the table.

"Bienvenida a la catedral de la Santa Muerte."

We turned around to see a woman standing there in a long red robe with a shawl over her shoulders. She wore hoop earrings and a white headband across her forehead with what looked like a small ruby in the center. Her eyes were deep set, like black marbles, suspicious. She shifted her gaze from Miguel to me.

"Thank you for the welcome," I said. "Do you speak English?"

"Some … but not very well. I am high priestess Adriana Garza."

"Your English is better than my Spanish." I smiled. She did not. "I'm Sean. This is Miguel. We were sent here by our friend."

"Excellent. Who is your friend? Perhaps I know the person."

"Diego Navarro."

The woman's eyes opened a little wider. She looked at the altar table and made a dry swallow. "I am sorry, señor. I do not know that name. We have so many parishioners, and the church is growing. It is most difficult for me to remember everyone."

"Why are you not telling the truth?"

She stared into space, candlelight moving like flames in her eyes.

I took a step closer to her. "I can smell his presence."

She looked at me with disdain and said nothing.

"Want to know why I can smell it, high priestess? Because, like death, evil has an odor. Diego Navarro left it here. Maybe this will help your memory." I pulled a wad of bills from my pocket, peeling off a half dozen hundred-dollar bills. "Where is Navarro?"

She stared at the money, stepping closer. "He comes here one day a month. Usually, it is the first Monday of the month."

"That's not for another two weeks. Where is he right *now*? This stays between us. No one will ever know."

The woman shifted her eyes from me to the skeleton. "La Santa Muerte knows. I will take your money as a donation. But it is time for you to leave."

"I won't donate money to a religion that tells people they can murder and still go to heaven under the guidance of a horror prop in a bad dress. I will, though, give you the money if you tell me where I can find Navarro."

She shook her head. "It is time for you to leave. If you refuse, I will place a curse on both of you."

"What you don't seem to know, high priestess, is this place is already cursed."

ONE HUNDRED FIVE

On our way back to the van, someone moved behind a red cedar tree. The old woman we saw when we first entered the building came from around the cedar like she was part of the tree. She looked at me and then at Miguel before saying, "Sé por qué estás aquí."

Miguel glanced at me. "She said she knows why we are here."

"Ask her how she knows that and why she thinks we're here."

He asked the questions. The old woman nodded. In Spanish, she said, "It is because you seek Diego Navarro. He is not a good man." Miguel translated.

I looked at the old woman. "I agree. Can you tell us where we might find Navarro? He is holding our friend captive and threatening to kill him."

Miguel interpreted and waited for her response. When she finished, he turned to me. "She said her nephew used to work for Navarro but no longer does. Her nephew's friend still works for Navarro. And he told her nephew that they are holding an American at a place known as the casa de las montañas. It means the house in the mountains. She said it is about seventy-five kilometers northeast from here."

"Meaning it is the big ranch hacienda." I pulled some money from my pocket and placed the bills in the old woman's gnarled hand. I could feel her bones and swollen knuckles. I thought about the skeleton's hand around the scythe. "Gracias, señora."

She smiled and nodded, looking at the money and then up at me. Even with very few teeth left, she had a beautiful smile.

***

The full moon would be our guiding light. As we neared a quarter of a mile from Diego Navarro's hacienda in the mountains, I spotted a small clearing on the side of the road. "Miguel, pull over there." I removed my iPad from the console. In seconds, I had the satellite images on the screen. I held the tablet so everyone could see. "Okay, it's time to take a closer look at what's around the bend."

"It's great to see the layout," Miguel said. "It'd be even better if we knew how many men we're facing and where they are."

"I'm calling Dave Collins in just a minute." I pointed to the images on screen. "Here is the big house. Heavily guarded, no doubt. I don't think they'd hold Tony inside the house. But there are three more smaller buildings that appear to be guest houses. There's a barn and what looks like horse stables. I'd bet the stables can accommodate at least two dozen or more horses. If you were Diego Navarro, where would you hold an American DEA agent hostage?"

The men studied the images. Clint said, "In the barn or stables. Either building gives Navarro and his men more room to beat and interrogate Tony."

Preston said, "Maybe we can check the barn first. If Tony's not there, we look in the stables. Hell, we'll go through every damn building on the property 'til we find him."

I nodded. "Agreed. It would be ideal to slip in there, inspect the barn and stables, find Tony alive, and leave quietly. But I don't think that will be the situation. That's why I'm getting Dave Collins on the satellite phone. I gave you all a brief bio on Dave. Suffice to say, after thirty years as a CIA officer in the field, and still called upon occasionally as a consultant, he knows his way around hostage situations. Dave has some pretty sophisticated communications equipment on his boat, courtesy of the CIA."

I called Dave. He answered and said, "It's about time I heard from you. Where the hell is your team?"

"I'm putting you on speaker so all four of us can hear. Checking with the digital maps, looks like we're close to Diego Navarro's ranch in the mountains. According to what we've learned, Navarro is holding an American hostage there. Last time I checked, Tony Salazar was the only American DEA agent being held hostage in Mexico. Not sure where he's being confined on a thousand-acre spread, but I believe Tony's in there. We just need to go in and bring him out alive."

Dave grunted. "Okay. Give me a minute to pull up what I can from the satellite feeds." We could hear Dave tapping his keyboard. After half a minute, he said, "From what I can see, in a live feed, there are a lot of lights on around the property. Let me zoom in for a closer look."

From the backseat, Clint said, "Wish we had this kind of technology when we were looking for the Taliban in the Afghan mountains."

"Amen," said Preston.

Dave cleared his throat. "From the bird I'm on in space, I can see the main house, outbuildings, a barn, and a stable. More importantly, I can see seven vehicles. Two in front of the stables and five in a circular drive at the main house. With thermal mapping, I can see people. I will assume I'm looking at sentries standing at various guard posts. At the entrance to the compound, there are half a dozen sentries standing guard. Two are near the front gate. Two more are about a hundred yards up the driveway. Two more, another hundred or so yards."

"Can you see other access driveways?" I asked. "I am assuming that Tony, if he's breathing, will not be in good enough shape to hoof it out of there to our van on the side of the road. We need to drive up there for a more reachable option and for munitions reinforcement."

"Hold a second … yes. It looks like there is at least one ancillary drive. It's on the east side of the main entrance. There appears to be a gate, without a doubt, locked. That drive goes through woods, a pasture, and comes up to the rear of the stables. That'll be your best bet for an entrance route. For your exit, you'll have to play it by ear."

"Good enough. Dave, we'll call you back when we take down that remote gate." After I clicked off, I looked at the faces of my men. "Let's get the guns ready. It's time we're locked and loaded."

***

Tony Salazar hung by his wrists, hallucinating in and out of consciousness. His bloody body burned with fever and infection. Even through the agony, he managed to stand on the balls of his feet, flexing his hands and fingers enough to allow some blood to circulate through his dying flesh.

He stared at the full moon through the roof skylight. He thought about his wife Nicole, and their children, Eva and Lucas. "Got to hold on," he whispered through the dried blood on his lips. "Got to believe." He coughed, spitting out fresh blood. "If this is my last prayer, God, take care of my family."

ONE HUNDRED SIX

The gate was made from galvanized steel. Too strong to ram it with the van and risk damage. A thick chain locked the gate. Preston examined it and said, "We could easily shoot through it, but that might alert someone. Among the ammo cases, the guys at the base gave us bolt cutters. I'll get them."

Under the moonlight, Preston cut off the lock, opened the barrier, and waited for the van to clear. After closing the gate, he threaded the chain back into place to make it appear the entrance was still locked. "It's showtime," Miguel said, behind the wheel. "I can drive under the moonlight. I'll keep the van's lights off.

I called Dave again. "We're on that spur road, heading to the main house and stables."

"Got it. From where I am, it looks like there are at least six men outside the buildings in the area you're moving toward. There are guards at each end of the house. One in the back and two in the front area. It looks like they're on a large veranda. I can't tell if they're guards or members of the Navarro family. The barn looks to be about fifty yards to the left of the stables. I don't see any sentries posted at the barn."

"Which tells me that Tony is most likely in the stables, if he's still here and alive."

"That would be my deduction."

"Okay, Dave. At this point, I'm going to clip the sat phone to my belt, and we'll keep quiet. If you hear shots, you'll know bullets are flying."

"All right. I'll have your backs as much as possible from outer space. Good luck, gentlemen."

The spur road was little more than a one-lane dirt path. More like a cattle trail. We drove with the windows down through woods thick with pines. A half mile later, we came to cleared land. I could see moonlight reflecting off a lake. The cattle were bedded down under some of the oaks, the warm air carrying the smell of manure and fish.

Clint and Preston leaned forward, all of us watching the GPS image on the van's screen. I pointed at the screen. "We're about three hundred yards from the compound. The barn is on the far right. There looks to be a grove of trees to the left of the stables, about a hundred feet from the rear of the building. Let's park there. We'll approach the stables from the back side. If there's no rear door, we'll go through the front door. I'd bet that as soon as we round the front of the building, under all those lights, there will be guards, guns, and surveillance cameras."

Clint said, "Let's hope a back door is an option."

We parked and got out. Clint and I were carrying 12-gauge shotguns. Preston chose an M4-Carbine. Miguel picked up one of the sniper rifles. All of us were packing two 9mm pistols each and plenty of ammo. I had the satellite phone on my belt. Dave could hear everything.

Preston looked at Miguel and said, "Hey, bro, don't forget the van keys. We'll probably need them real soon."

"You think?"

"Let's go," I said, leading the way.

In seconds, we were at the rear of the stables. I could see where a back door was at one time. It had been removed, new boards put up, the white paint not quite matching the rest of the large exterior. "Hand signals from here on out," I whispered. "Miguel, you and Preston go to the left of the building. Clint and I will take the right side. We'll work our way around. Although there are only four of us, we have the surprise factor on our side. At least for the first few minutes. That's when we must eliminate as many hostiles as possible."

Clint and I moved stealth-like through the shadows, the whinny of a horse coming from inside the stables. A tall windmill was silhouetted in the moonlight, its blades turning in the breeze. When we got to the edge of the building, I could see two guards standing about fifty feet in front of the entrance. They were talking and smoking cigarettes with their backs to us. There were two pickup trucks and a Cadillac Escalade in the drive.

I looked to the other side of the stables, signaling to Preston and Miguel that Clint and I would take out the guards. We snuck up behind them. One man dropped a cigarette butt, smashing it under his boot. They heard us approaching and whirled around, reaching for the guns in their holsters. I brought the butt of the shotgun down on the center of one man's forehead. He fell out cold.

Clint used his right fist, hitting the second guard on the jaw. The blow caused the man to drop to his knees. At that point, Clint brought the butt of the shotgun down hard in the center of the man's head, cracking his skull.

The big house was Mediterranean style—a two story with a white stucco exterior, lots of exposed beams, wrought iron terraces, and a red terracotta tile roof. There was movement on the veranda. I signaled Preston. He nodded, approaching, and standing behind the Cadillac. In seconds, he fired two shots, dropping two more guards. He took cover behind the trucks.

At the sound of gunshots, two more men came running from the left side of the house. They fired at us, bullets whizzing by and glass shattering. Clint stood from behind the bed of a pickup truck, firing. "Cover me!" I shouted, running toward the right side of the house. More guards appeared, two coming from the front entrance and two from around the right side of the home. They saw me.

I zigzagged in the shadows as their rounds tore through the landscape. I fired back with my double-aught buckshot. In the moonlight, I hit two men in their chests. More guards fired rounds through the pickup trucks, some bullets ricocheting off the concrete driveway.

Two more men came from the left section of the house, automatic rifles blazing in the night. The rounds blew out the remaining truck and car windows. Preston and Miguel returned the fire. I saw Preston get hit. The round brought him to his knees, dropping his rifle. I signaled for Clint and Miguel to cover me.

Immediately, Clint cut loose with five quick blasts from his 12-gauge, the rounds knocking off tree limbs, exploding brick, causing Navarro's men to take shelter as I moved closer. Miguel followed me, firing rounds with his rifle. Two men came from opposite directions, rifles like machine-gun fire. I aimed my shotgun, the buckshot blowing through one guard's chest. Miguel used his rifle to take out the other man. We crouched behind an ornate brick wall in the shadows of tall canary palms. An eerie silence. No movement, only the smell of gun smoke and blood.

400

I looked back at Clint, giving him hand signals that we were advancing toward the house. He ducked and ran through the lush tropical landscape, keeping low, heading to the right side of the house. I looked at Miguel. "Go take care of Preston. He was hit. Make sure he doesn't bleed out."

"Yes, sir."

I stayed in the deep shadows, stepping over bodies, the driveway slick with pools of blood. As I got closer to the porte-cochere on the left side of the house, where two cars were parked, a Bentley SUV and a white Land Rover, I could hear shouting in the house, one man giving orders to others.

The side door opened, and four men stepped outside. Three carried automatic rifles. One, Diego Navarro, held a pistol. I recognized him. I stayed behind a palm tree as they approached the Bentley. Then I stepped out and said, "You're not going anywhere." I had a dead aim at Navarro's chest. "Keep your guns pointed down, and you might walk out of here."

His men paused, not sure whether to risk their boss's life. They knew I'd kill him before they could raise their guns. Navarro looked at me, his eyes like a cobra, unblinking. His mind focused on me as prey. He flashed a wicked smile. In perfect English, he said, "There are four of us against you. You will not win this fight. When I kill you, I win."

"But you'll die before me."

"You cannot kill me. I'm protected by a powerful force … the same force that helped me build an empire. My spirit can't die."

"But is your spirit strong enough to survive the ghosts of your past? That's the question you need to ask yourself, Navarro. Where is Tony Salazar?"

"Dead. As you are about to be."

I held a steady aim at his chest as I lifted the photo of Andy from my pocket. "His name was Andy Ward. You killed him with one of your fentanyl pills. His father is standing right behind you."

ONE HUNDRED SEVEN

I faced four guns. It was one of those moments where I could hear my heartbeat off the walls of my skull. I was standing on a tightrope amid life and death with no safety net, balancing between earth and a fall into eternity at one misstep. My sense of clarity was so heightened that everything around me moved in slow motion. I could detect the slightest movement. Hear bats flying in the dark. Smell fear. I saw Clint out of the periphery of my vision, but I kept my eyes on Navarro. And I held my aim at the center of his chest.

Navarro smiled. "There is nobody behind us."

"Do you really want to take that chance?"

"We've got four guns. As far as the guy in the photo, he got what he deserved."

Clint fired a round going through the back of a bodyguard's head, coming out the front of the skull. At the same second, I shot Navarro in the chest. A bodyguard got off a round, the bullet grazing my left arm. I shot him, and Clint killed the last man. In four seconds, four bodies were sprawled on the concrete next to the Bentley.

I signaled Clint. "Let's check the stables. Navarro said Tony's dead. If that's true, and if his body's in there, we're taking it back to his family."

Clint and I ran down the driveway toward the decorative brick and wrought iron wall where Miguel was elevating Preston's upper arm. Miguel said, "I think the round severed his brachial artery."

I nodded. "Glad you got a tourniquet on it and stopped the bleeding." We helped Preston to his feet. "How are you feeling?"

"A little lightheaded, sir. But it could have been worse."

"You two stay here in the dark and out of the line of fire just in case anyone shows up. Clint and I will go to the stables. If we're lucky, we'll find Tony. And if we're really lucky, he'll be alive. Watch our backs."

"Yes, sir."

Clint and I wound our way back to the stables as a cloud covered the moonlight. We opened the front door and saw something that hit me in the gut like a baseball bat. Tony was suspended by two ropes over a beam near the ceiling. Taut ropes wrapped around his wrists, his arms looking as if his shoulders had been yanked from their sockets. We ran to him, Clint to his left, me to his right.

I pulled my knife from the sheath. "He's alive. Hold him up while I cut the ropes." Clint held Tony as I quickly cut through the ropes, Tony's arms dropping to his sides. Limp. He opened his swollen eyes, staring at me, disbelieving. He whispered, "Is that really you, Major O'Brien, or have I died?"

"You're alive. It's me, Clint Ward, Miguel Romero, and Preston Bell. We're taking you home, soldier."

Tony's eyes watered, spilling tears down his cheeks. "I'm ready to go, sir."

I put Tony's arm over my shoulder. Clint did the same with Tony's other arm. I said, "If you can use your legs, try to walk. We're not going to let you fall. Not now. Not ever. We have a van nearby."

As we walked Tony toward the open door, Dave came on the satellite phone's speaker. "Sean, you and your men need to get out of there. The guards at the front gate and along the perimeter are heading your way. You only have a few minutes."

"Got it!"

At the stable door, we could see headlights in the tree line a half mile away. I looked at Clint. There's no time to get Tony and Preston safely into the van." I looked to my left. "Let's put them in this empty stall." We gently laid Tony in the stall and hustled back to get Preston, Miguel following and covering us. After we placed Preston in the stall, I looked at Clint and Miguel. "I'm taking one of the sniper rifles and climbing the windmill. It'll give me a clear shot at the main driveway and parking area."

"What do you want me and Miguel to do?" Clint asked.

"You stand to the left of the barn. Miguel, you go to the right of the stables. I'll take out as many as I can from the windmill. You guys keep them from entering the stables."

"Okay."

I sprinted to the windmill as the headlights came closer. I climbed the wooden ladder up the side of the tall windmill, the blade turning in the night breeze. When I got to a spot just below the props, I braced the rifle's stock on one of the windmill's support timbers. I guessed that I was sixty feet above the ground. From that perspective, I could cover most of the front property. I couldn't see Clint or Miguel from where I stood, armed, and waiting, but I knew we were about to put up one hell of a firefight.

Three vehicles arrived, dust billowing behind them. Two pickup trucks and one Ford Expedition. They parked in the shadows, the men staying in the safety of their vehicles for a minute. The moon was still behind a cloud when I heard the doors open and the men get out, ratcheting their shotguns. There were eight men. They spread out, guns ready, zigzagging toward the house and stables. Faces hard. As they got closer to the stables, I knew my team was seconds away from a shootout.

The clouds parted and moonlight flooded the land. The men cast long shadows as they crept closer. I had a bead on the man farthest from me. I squeezed the trigger. The round exploded the man's head, a wisp of pink mist in the pale moonlight. Before his body could hit the ground, I shot a second man in the head. The remaining men looked toward the windmill and started shooting, bullets tearing through the metal blades and timbers. One round tore into the flesh on my left shoulder.

Clint and Miguel opened fire on the men still standing. I shot one in the neck. In eight seconds, eight men lay dead or dying in the parking area. I scrambled down the ladder, blood soaking my shirt as I ran toward the stables. Clint and Miguel followed me inside. "Let's get Tony and Preston in the van. This battle is won for now."

Clint looked at me, nodding. He saw the blood on my shoulder. "Sean, you're hurt."

"The round grazed me. Let's get Tony and Preston medical help. And then we're out of here. Every man is going home."

Miguel smiled. "We did it, sir."

Clint gave me a salute, his eyes welling, shiny in the moonlight. "Let's go home."

ONE HUNDRED EIGHT

Two months later, I stood on my river dock at sunrise, thinking about our upcoming wedding that afternoon and reflecting on the consequences of recent events. When you travel through the dim keyhole to the dark underworld and swim across the black waters of the River Styx, you are never the same. For better or worse, it changes you. You grasp the curse of Achilles, feeling the soft spot of personal exposure deep within your pores.

Even though you might dial down the voices in your head, you know your armor is conditional, and the vulnerability of your heart is much greater than the flesh on your heel. Your soul stands in the middle of the bridge called revelation, where you can never unsee the darkness you saw or undo your deeds of choice.

You become less burdened by mundane conversations, like the white noise you learn to tune out. Petty things are like gnats in your face, so you walk through them and move on. For me, this wisdom has come from surviving the killing fields and from climbing that hallowed mountain, finally grasping that the dim light at the edge of the universe held a secret and a promise.

I thought about Tony Salazar. He was out of Mexico and back working in the DEA's office in San Diego. His injuries had healed, but the scars would remain for life. He told me that what he'd experienced would make him do his job even better than he had before he was abducted. And he told me he would make it to my wedding.

The mainstream news media reported very little about what happened in Durango. Maybe it was because they didn't know the facts or didn't care to seek them. Any witnesses that were in Navarro's house, such as his wife, and any injured men who survived, would talk about how four Americans took on a platoon of heavily armed Mexican drug dealers and won.

Although we'd covered our tracks well, the CIA and DEA knew what happened. However, the official statement from the DOJ indicated that Tony Salazar was found on the side of a remote road in Durango, severely injured but alive. And that Diego Navarro, and many of his followers, were killed by a rival drug cartel.

"It's not unusual in volatile situations like that," said a balding, bespeckled DOJ spokesman, standing next to the president in the White House rose garden during a news briefing.

Tank—Simon Hogan, was facing a life sentence in prison for knowingly selling deadly drugs—fentanyl, that directly caused at least nine deaths in the state of Florida. A dozen of his men were facing similar charges. They were all held in jail with no bond due to a potential flight risk. The rest of the gang members were plea bargaining for lighter sentences by turning state's witness. Digger and Axle were to be the prosecution team's star witnesses, with a guarantee of being taken into the witness protection program as soon as the trial concluded.

I turned and walked down the dock. The next sight I wanted to see would be Wynona coming down the aisle in the church where we would be married in six hours.

ONE HUNDRED NINE

It is simply called the Chapel by the Sea. The small wooden building, painted white, was built in 1905 and made from oak and cedar. It has a steeple with an iron cross at the top. The old church, which is near the Ponce Lighthouse, has somehow withstood time and hurricanes. The sound of breakers rolling on the beach, gave the grounds a sense of tranquility.

To get to the front door, you parked in a gravel lot and walked on a crushed shell path for about a hundred feet through lush, tropical gardens filled with birdsong, bromeliads, hibiscus, ferns, angel trumpets, and date palms. Butterflies darted in and out of the flowers, following the beckoning of floral scents.

Stepping inside the church was like stepping into a period of old Florida. A simpler time. There were seven stained-glass windows, most depicting biblical scenes of Jesus meeting with his followers. There were twelve wooden pews. I stood at the front, the altar table behind me. The pastor, dressed in a white robe, was a slender man with kind eyes. He watched people enter the church. In ten minutes, the pews were filled, some people having to stand at the back.

Wynona's mother, wearing a dark blue dress, sat in the front row. Her skin was the color of sunlight through a glass of tea. Long silver hair, braided. A lovely face with high cheekbones and astute eyes. To her left were four members of her family, and three rows behind sat close friends from the Seminole tribe.

Dave sat to her right and wore a sportscoat, dress shirt, and tan slacks. Nick compromised and left his swim trunks on the boat. He wore a white polo shirt and pressed jeans. Boat shoes. No socks. I'd never seen him so formally dressed.

Also in the front pews were Clint and Lauren, Brittany Harmon, Miguel, Preston, and Tony and Nicole. Many of the employees from the marina and Tiki Bar, including Flo, were there. And a few of Wynona's friends from the FBI were in attendance.

In one corner was an upright piano. The pianist was a middle-aged woman with rhinestones embedded in the frame of her glasses. Sitting at a small table behind the piano was one of the servers from the Tiki Bar. His hair shaggy. Round, shiny face. He had a portable music player connected via Bluetooth to a Bose speaker about the size of my fist. The music from that speaker, *Fields of Gold*, by Eva Cassidy, filled the church with remarkable fidelity.

An usher at the door cued the man with the music player. He nodded as the song ended and started another one by the same singer, *Somewhere Over the Rainbow*.

Angela, wearing a pink and navy floral dress, came inside the front door. She paused at the beginning of the aisle, took a deep breath, smiled, and started walking. She carried a small bouquet of pink and white flowers. Everyone was smiling as she came closer to the altar. When Angela got beyond the front pew, she paused, looking up at me. I could see the colors of the stained-glass in her wide eyes, smiling, dimples popping. On her head was a circle of flowers—daises—a perfect daisy chain. I smiled and winked at her.

Dave motioned for Angela to sit in the space between him and Nick. She sat in the pew, the flowers on her lap, her shiny shoes not touching the floor. I couldn't have been prouder. The music from the player faded, and the usher at the door cued the pianist. She nodded, adjusted her glasses, and began playing the bridal chorus—the wedding march song.

Wynona stepped through the wash of afternoon sunlight at the front of the church like an angel who'd walked in from somewhere celestial. She took my breath away. She looked beautiful in her white wedding dress, her black hair up, face flawless, and smile so radiant that I felt everything in the world paled in comparison. She was an easy woman to love. Because Wynona's father had died years ago, she wanted to be walked down the aisle by her childhood friend, Joe Billie. Joe, now a close friend of mine as well, would present Wynona to me.

I was honored.

Joe was almost my height, with black and silver hair pulled back in a ponytail. His relaxed face was the color of a walnut. He wore a denim shirt, a dark blue sports coat, pressed jeans, and boots. He smiled at Wynona as she took his arm, and they began walking down the aisle toward me.

A minute later, Wynona and I were facing each other. It felt like my heart skipped a beat. The minister stood in front of us, the congregation watching. After his opening remarks, his voice booming in the old church, he said, "Marriage is more than a promise. It is a sacred vow as seen in the eyes of the Lord. We do not enter this holy covenant lightly or with conditional understanding. It has deep significance and is as relevant today as any time in history. Perhaps, even more so now."

He paused, read a verse from the Bible, and then looked at us. "I understand that you both have written some special words you would like to say to one another. But, before we get to that, let's set the mood with the vows. Sean, you are first. Please repeat after me. In the name of God, I, Sean O'Brien, take you, Wynona Osceola, to be my wife, to have and to hold from this day forward."

I said, "In the name of God, I, Sean O'Brien, take you, Wynona Osceola, to be my wife, to have and to hold from this day forward."

The minister continued. "For better or worse, for richer or poorer, in sickness and in health … to love and cherish, until parted by death." I looked into Wynona's eyes and said, "For better or worse, for richer or poorer, in sickness, and in health, to love, and cherish, until parted by death."

The minister started to repeat the vows to Wynona. She smiled at him and asked, "May I say the words, Reverend Jordan?"

"Absolutely." He smiled.

Wynona looked deep into my eyes. "In the name of God, I, Wynona Osceola, take you, Sean O'Brien, to be my husband, to have, and to hold, from this day forward … for better or worse, for richer or poorer, in sickness and in health … to love and cherish, until parted by death. Also, I will be there for you always. You are my best friend, my confidante, my playmate, and probably the greatest challenge I've ever known. And I mean that in a good way." There was a laugh from the audience.

"Sean, you amaze me. Not only because of the man that you are, but mostly because, through you, I know the power of love. You are the love of my life, the man I share my heart and deep secrets with. You have made me happier than I ever thought possible, and you have helped make me a better person. I am truly blessed to be part of your life … now our life. And I will never take you for granted. I promise to love you through eternity." Her eyes welled. Someone in the pews sniffled.

I smiled. "Wynona, I see my vows as more than a promise. They are privileges because of you. So often, in all you do, who you are, your beauty inside and out, you take my breath away. Thank you for loving me as I am, challenges and all." I smiled. "Thank you for taking me into your heart and loving me the way you do. I make an oath to walk by your side and to love and encourage you in all that you want to do. I will always listen to you and love you with my soul. I will stand on a mountaintop, holding your hand, welcoming the promise of each new day with you." I looked in the pews. "Nick, do you still have the rings?"

"Maybe. Lemme check my pockets." People laughed. He stood, stepped up to us, taking one gold ring from a small velvet pouch. He gave it to me and did the same with Wynona before sitting back down.

I looked into Wynona's eyes. "I give you this ring as a symbol of my vows and of giving you my heart. Forever. The ring has no beginning or end. It does have a center when I put it on your finger." She extended her left hand, and I placed the ring on her finger.

She looked at it for a moment, lifting her eyes up to me. "Sean, I give you this ring as a symbol of my vows and of my deep love for you. As it encircles your finger, I hope it will remind you that you are always surrounded by my love." She put the ring on my finger, and we looked at the minister.

He cleared his throat. "Sean and Wynona, before God, and by the authority vested in me by the state of Florida, I now proclaim you as husband and wife. Sean, you may kiss the bride." I leaned in and softly kissed Wynona's lips, touching her face with my hand. The audience applauded, and the portable music machine began playing *You'll Accompany Me* by Bob Seger.

I held Wynona's hand as we walked down the two steps from the altar area. "Come here, sweetheart," I said to Angela. I took her hand,

and the three of us strolled down the aisle to the music and sound of applause. As the church emptied, we greeted our guests outside. Dave, Nick, and Flo approached, followed by Wynona's mother, Aiyana, and Joe Billie. Nick looked at us, eyes playful. "I bet, for a second, you guys thought I left the rings behind." He grinned.

Wynona said, "If you had, I would have had Flo ban you from the Tiki Bar for life."

Flo laughed and said, "I sure as heck would have enforced it."

Nick shook his head. "Ouch, that's hard. Or a hard time. Okay, speaking of less hard things, I'm heading to the reception. The *Hard* Rock Hotel on North Atlantic Beach, right?"

Dave said, "I know the way, Nick. More importantly, I'll know the way back to the marina after the reception." We laughed. He looked down at Angela. "You were magnificent in there today. Your dress and flowers are so pretty."

"Thank you."

"I especially like the crown of flowers on your head. They are lovely, just like you."

Angela looked at Wynona's mother. "My grandmother made it for me. We picked flowers by the river, and Grandma tied the ends together. It's not a ring like Daddy and Mama have on their fingers. It's a ring for my head."

"Che-me-hok-te," Aiyana said, nodding and placing her hand on Angela's shoulder.

"Grandma said you're a pretty girl." Angela beamed. Wynona added, "To the Seminole, daisies symbolize purity and eternal love. And when we look at you, Angela, that's what we see and feel."

I picked Angela up. "Okay, we have a reception to attend. I get to dance with two princesses. One I'm holding now … the other I'll soon be holding and swaying to the music."

The End